T0354339

How It Worked Out Between Them

by

Fred Weekes

iUniverse, Inc.
New York   Bloomington

How It Worked Out Between Them

iUniverse books may be ordered through booksellers or by contacting:

iUniverse
1663 Liberty Drive
Bloomington, IN 47403
www.iuniverse.com
1-800-Authors (1-800-288-4677)

ISBN: 978-1-4401-3999-4 (pbk)
ISBN: 978-1-4401-4000-6 (ebk)

Printed in the United States of America

iUniverse rev. date: 6/1/09

Why read romance? Perhaps because it's one of the most common activities on earth. We have memories of holding a loved one in our arms or being held in the arms of that special person. Our recollections are generated by the activities that come our way during a lifetime. Think of this: sitting next to that special person on the beach when the sun is setting and it's cool enough to wear a sweater. The setting is calm. You're sharing a drink. Or you are dancing a slow number toward the end of the evening with someone you never suspected would make you feel so good. Or you find that it's pleasurable and a simple matter to discuss most anything. That other person is informative and amusing. You've found a mate.

We started at the age of ten. They were different. At first it was an awakening. Then it became desire. That grew into appreciation. Finally came commitment, that building a life together. The whole business is so important to each of us that we devote half our waking hours to thinking over what romance has meant to us. There's no denying, it's central to our lives.

Table of Contents

THE WILD WEST

THE WILD WEST
PART I

After the Civil War Jed worked his way west. In '63 he'd ridden in Custer's brigade at Gettysburg. It was part of Kilpatrick's division. He rode against J.E.B. Stuart in '64 down in the Wilderness campaign, and then in '65 he was with Little Phil Sheridan at Appomattox. Jed liked it that Little Phil carried a silver whiskey flask. It meant that his men could carry one too.

In the War Jed carried a seven-shot repeating carbine made by the Sharps Company. He had it with him on the campaigns and he used it when he was dismounted. He preferred his Colts while in the saddle. But he had to load these revolvers with powder and ball, and when he had fired all the rounds he had to find a tree to hide behind to reload or fight dismounted from a distance, shooting his carbine.

When they broke up the Army after the war, Jed could have stayed in but he'd had enough bad food. He got rid of all the pieces of his uniform. They marked him as a Yankee. He moved to central Texas where the cattle drives started. They headed for Kansas and the railroad that took the animals east. The town they headed for was Dodge City but they called it Dodge, and they were right to do so because there was no city. It was a long hot ride there and plenty dangerous going through Oklahoma, still Indian Territory, where the Comanches liked to capture white men and make them slaves. They learned plenty about slavery from what had been going on in the South. There were Cherokees around these parts as well and they were nicer people than the Comanches.

Jed did the cattle drives for about a decade. He liked to spend the winters in Chicago, which he did every year. The cold there made up for the hot on the plains. He would put away his guns and rough life and concentrate on women, or even one woman, read his books, and pick up a little work. As for reading, he liked action thrillers for fiction and the memoirs of the Civil War generals who knew a good thing when they saw it. That is, they made plenty of money with their books. He was glad in '69 when Grant made president. He was a West Pointer, class of '43, and it was good to see a tough fighter make it. Jed was saddened in '70 when Robert Lee died. He was another West Pointer, class of '29, who just fought on the wrong side. Jed thought he was the best of the lot and could have ended the war in one year if he'd worn a blue suit. Lincoln offered him the job, everybody knew that, but Lee turned it down. He could have made president easy and lived in the big house at no rent if he'd been Union commander in place of Grant.

Time was going by. Jed was 17 at Gettysburg. He was 33 this year, 1879. Custer, his old commanding officer, had bought the farm up in Montana at the Little BigHorn, cut down by Crazy Horse and Sitting Bull and their band of warriors. Jed had always told himself that he would settle down with a wife on a nice spread with a creek running through and have some kids. He'd better start now.

It was the spring of '79 and Jed, just reacting, went to Dallas from Chicago. You could do that by train now. He bought a horse there that he called Red because he called all his horses Red. Less to remember. He rode a bit north of Dallas to the Harris ranch where he knew Harris would be getting ready for the season. Harris didn't have a first name, or leastwise if he had one Jed never heard it. Jed's last name was Loomis but he never used it because it sounded girl-like.

Jed found Harris working in the barn. They shook hands and started talking about the season coming up. Jed said he wanted to settle in California and he ought to get started. "How much money do you have left after your winter in Chicago?" "About twenty dollars in silver," Jed answered. He wasn't talking about what he'd saved and stashed away in his bank vault over these past winters.

"I suppose you came to ride with us to Dodge like you've done in past years. I pay good, you know that, and you head west from there. And I'll buy your horse and saddle from you. You'll be loaded up."

"That's mighty good of you," Jed said.

"And besides, you need to get the rust out after taking it easy in Chicago. I bet you haven't shot much since last fall, and you haven't ridden either."

"No argument there," Jed said.

"You know those trains are plenty dangerous between Indians and the train robbers that ride along."

"I've heard tell," Jed said.

"Sometimes Indians ride alongside the train and shoot at the passengers. They think it's sport. Trouble for them is they ride at the same speed as the train so they're sitting ducks. Ain't even target practice for a man like you."

"How about the train robbers?" Jed asked.

"I hear they get on somewhere and work the train before the next station. They jump with their loot when the train's going slow up a steep grade. They ain't too smart as a breed because they don't have horses for a getaway. Lot of them end up swinging from a tree by nightfall."

"I don't like the sounds of it," Jed said.

"Take the front seat in the front car. Change the seat around so you're looking back to where you come from. They ride in the cars just like passengers and get up and make the rounds with gun in hand. You don't want anyone at your back."

"Gotcha," Jed said.

So Jed signed on for another cattle drive with Harris and three other men he knew from past drives. Between them they had five repeating rifles and eight Colts. Three of them carried two revolvers and the other two men carried just one. David, a one-gun fellow, told Jed that he used to carry two but one day it was time to draw and he pulled the trigger before he got the gun out of the holster and he ruined his left boot. "When you ruin one boot it's like ruining both," David said.

Jed thought it would be an easy drive because the Indians and cattle rustlers had slowed down lots. And besides, no one wanted to argue with a fifteen-shot repeater of the new type. Jed had bought himself a Winchester repeating rifle that held fifteen cartridges. As for revolvers, he owned two Colt 45s each carrying six cartridges. No more of that loading powder and ball like they used to do in the Civil War.

When they got to Dodge, Harris sold the cattle at the stockyard, paid off everybody, and bought Jed's horse, just like he said he would. Jed had plenty of the silver dollars minted at Carson City, all new ones.

Harris had advice to give to Jed besides gunplay on the railroad. He asked, "How far you going?" Jed said, "Don't know. There's plenty of good land in the foothills of the Sierra Nevada."

Harris thought that over for a bit. Then he said, "Listen. Go all the way to the end of the line at Oakland. Take the ferry to San Francisco. You have to see that city before you settle up in the hills."

"Beautiful, is that it?"

"Has everything for a man like you. Women, hotels, restaurants, and plenty of action. People are organizing things like bringing in a new gold mine and such like."

"I have my heart set on getting going as a family man, but I'll think about San Francisco."

The idea of going to the real city of the west, better than Denver, caught Jed off guard. It excited him. He knew he was taking the train back to Chicago to see Vivian again and get all his things and maybe even her. Now that he was heading to San Francisco he had to buy some decent clothes. He just let Harris assume that he was headed west. No use telling people where you would be if they didn't need to know. Chicago first, then San Francisco.

PART 2

Jed had written Vivian right away when he reached Dodge City. If his letter caught the first train to Chicago then in all likelihood she would receive it before he arrived. To let the letter gain a little time, he holed up in a good hotel, drank his fill, and ate a big steak. He had to get to Wichita, Topeka, Kansas City, and St. Louis, then finally Chicago. He might get off the train one night partly to break the routine and partly to get to Chicago on Wednesday afternoon.

He had kept his room in the boarding house because his gear and his books were there. The owner, a pleasant woman named Agnes, charged him almost the same whether he occupied the room or not. When he was off for a few months, she charged Jed a dollar a month less because she didn't have to heat water for his bath Thursday nights.

The rooming house had three floors and you got hot water on Tuesday, Thursday and Saturday, depending on the floor you lived on. Vivian and Jed were second floor folks so they had a hot bath Thursday evenings.

Vivian was a girl with an eye out for men. She sure was anything but pretty, but Jed thought her body was perfect. Her face looked like an animal had stepped on it. Each room had a stove to heat the place in the evening. Vivian would cook a vegetable and meat stew and Jed would fetch some beer. This was always on Thursday nights when they cleaned up. Jed didn't understand how she knew not to have babies. He wondered if there was something special about Thursday nights.

Jed liked the arrangement and if he could have slept with Vivian every night, he would have. His way to get close to her was to propose marriage, but Vivian got it right away that it was a question with two parts. Would she marry him, and would they move to California? Vivian had a two-part answer. Yes for part one, and for part two, no, I'm staying in Chicago. They could not reach agreement on these questions so they spent three seasons on Thursday night loving. Jed didn't know whether Vivian was waiting for him to relax his terms and conditions, or whether the arrangement met many of her needs but not all. He knew that he had come to the end of the road. He wanted that spread in the California foothills with a stream running through it. Maybe he could find 160 acres to homestead and get some mules and horses.

Vivian worked in one of these new stores that Chicago was getting that sold everything. She sold clothes to women. Jed planned to go there to get his new outfits for San Francisco. Because she worked in this type of store she didn't need that bath very badly on Thursday evenings. Jed, on the other hand, when he came back off the trail, worked in a stable around horses. If the weather was good he could let the cold water run over him at the stable but in the winter he had to wait for the hot bath.

Vivian was nice to him. He couldn't complain. There must be other men in her life because she was normal and wanted the ring on her finger and to move into a home of her own. Jed guessed that if she weren't so homely she could have had the pick of the crop when she finished schooling and moved to Chicago. That was four years ago. Jed had theories. One, that she went to bed with the boss, the big boss in fact, and hoped that he would abandon his family. Another was that she would find a man here and there for an evening of going out. There didn't seem to be any steady fellow. He didn't like himself for his theories, but then, he couldn't account for the fact that she made certain that he was kept in place, always available to marry her, but not quite willing to do it. It seemed to Jed that she was on the lookout for a better match and would take it if it came along.

Sometimes they would go out to dinner at a restaurant after the bath and before turning in. She liked undressing in front of him, slowly, with just one candle for light, talking all the while. It drove him crazy. That's why he could swear that she had a beautiful body.

One night, a month after he got back, she changed her tune and asked him how much he knew about California. He said that when you came down from the mountains it didn't snow and San Francisco had everything Chicago did, only different, because it was a port on the Pacific. After a short discussion in which Jed told her all he knew, reciting what Harris had told him, she said, "Do you want to get married here or in California?"

Jed was unprepared. He realized later that he should have jumped at the chance of marrying right then. But he said, "If we get married in California you can determine whether you like the place before taking the plunge." Other than that, he didn't understand her. He thought she loved him and wanted to marry him. What difference did it make whether they married in Chicago or California? She had been good to him. They took two weeks to arrange their affairs and pack their things. Vivian quit her job and they told Agnes that they were on their way west to start a new life.

Agnes said to Vivian, "You know, it's the same old life, a different cast of characters, and some new places to look at, but other than that it's pretty much the same thing." When Vivian repeated this to Jed, he said, "That wise old owl may be right. But you can get oysters on ice at the Palace Hotel."

When they packed, Jed placed his two revolvers in a small case. Most men recognized the arrangement and Jed wanted it that way. If he was carrying two revolvers, fully loaded, the adversaries may as well know about it. No use hiding the evidence. They could draw on him and he would have no way to defend himself, but given any warning, they were in trouble. He placed his 15-shot repeating rifle in a suitcase the right length and traveled with it. His big suitcase, holding his books and his new clothes traveled in the freight car. Vivian also had a big suitcase filled with clothes. Their two suitcases would stay at the depot in Oakland until Vivian and Jed had lodgings and he went to fetch them.

She wanted to know how long the trip took. Jed said, "About a week. First we get to Omaha on the old part of the road. Then we get on the new part to Promontory Point in Utah, then on to Sacramento and Oakland." "I can't sit up that long," Vivian said. "We'll get Pullman tickets so we can eat when we want to and sleep at night. No sitting up and no carrying lunch baskets." She wanted to know how much. Jed said, "Well, it's about $100 from Chicago to Oakland but I guess it's twice that much traveling by Pullman."

Jed thought that once on the train they would talk about the wedding and what they would do afterwards. He assumed that they were engaged. On the first leg of the trip, Chicago to Omaha, they did make some plans. Jed wanted to know what Vivian had to see of California in order to decide whether to go ahead and marry. On the question she said, "Well, Jed, you don't have a job so I'm going to see what there is to do so I have income."

Jed answered that when they married he would be responsible for her as the husband and she wouldn't have to worry about money and all that.

"It sounds good," Vivian answered but the way she said it Jed knew she didn't believe a word of it. She went on, "You spend the money you have on a farm, or a spread as you call it, and it takes a year to bring in a cash crop. Maybe longer. I don't think you know the first thing about farming."

"Well, I'll learn fast. I was brought up on one," Jed said.

Past Omaha, when they were on the new part of the track laid in 1868 and 1869, Vivian spent time taking in the scenery. She remarked how beautiful it was. They got off the train at most of the stops, eating a fast meal in the twenty-five minutes allotted to get a change from the meals served in their Pullman car.

Jed tried to bring up the matter of the marriage. He asked, "Should we have a church wedding or go to City Hall?" "Let's decide when we get there," she said. There was no Thursday evening activity on the train. Jed thought he could wait until they were in a hotel in San Francisco. Anyway, Vivian didn't encourage him.

They read on the train, and held their talking to a minimum. The final conversation of any significance had to do with her wedding dress. "Do you want a fancy one, all white with lace?" "That would be appropriate," she said. Then Jed added, "It's a damned shame about wedding dresses. You wear them once, never wear them again, and then put them in a trunk to get yellow. Hardly seems worth it."

When she didn't answer, Jed realized for the first time that a wedding dress was a testament to an important event for a woman and for the man just a pretty thing that showed up once, only to vanish. He thought he was through bringing up important matters for the time being.

Jed went over what Harris had told him about Indians and train robbers. He doubted that these things would take place on the main line. This was for spur lines running through unpopulated places.

As they moved west, he kept an eye out for developments. He didn't know what to look for, exactly. It could be two men riding in the car with them. Jed didn't think anything would take place until they were in the mountains, if then. Nothing had happened in the Rockies. But when they were in the station in Reno, Jed noticed four men in two pairs boarding the train. They were carrying small bags so couldn't be going very far. As they left Reno and headed up the Sierra, Jed put himself on alert. They had made the stop at Truckee and were headed for Donner Summit when Jed saw the shadows of two men on the roof of their car. He said to Vivian. "Sit on the opposite side." He opened the case and pulled out the revolvers. The men, as they came down off the roof, had to open the door to the car from right to left. When the legs of the first man appeared, Jed cocked his revolvers. When the first man landed on the platform, the man pulled out his gun. When the man opened the door, there would be a speech. The man would say for everyone to stay still and that no one would get hurt, and that they were only interested in jewelry and cash. The man was holding open the small suitcase that Jed had seen on the station platform. The man pushed open the door with his body. Before he could say the first word of his speech, Jed shot him in the heart four feet away. He dropped dead immediately, propping the door open. His compatriot, who was now on the platform, reached for the rungs of the ladder so that he could climb back to the roof. All stretched out that way, Jed shot him in the middle of the chest. He fell to the platform and then onto the tracks.

Jed thought that the other train robbers had heard the gun play and might move forward to see what it was all about. Or they might conclude that they had lost the game and it was time to leave the train. He didn't know. He took his case off the overhead rack and got out the 15-shot repeater. He opened the windows on both sides. He said to Vivian, "They'll jump off one side or the other. You take the right side. More than likely they'll jump when the train slows for a grade."

"Are you going to shoot them?" Vivian asked.

"Yes, I'll try to get as many as I can," Jed answered.

They jumped from the left side of the train, the side facing the inside curve so that the passengers could see the robbers as they made their way into the trees. The two men were carrying their small suitcases holding wallets, rings, purses, jewelry and cash. Jed got off his first shot and the lead man dropped in his tracks. The second one turned toward the train. "How stupid," Jed thought. He aimed and shot again and this man fell to his knees then flat on his face. Jed looked at his watch. It was 4:40. "We want to report the time at the next stop, at Donner Summit," he told Vivian.

"You're a cold-blooded killer," Vivian said.

"You get me wrong. If someone wants to take something away from me that belongs properly to me, they have to kill me for it."

"So I see," she said. It was obvious to Jed that most everything between them had changed.

THE WILD WEST
PART 3

The holdup of the passengers had taken place between the stops at Truckee and Donner Summit. At Donner Summit several events took place.

An employee of the railroad came aboard to talk to Jed. He could not have been high up in the organization because Donner Summit was such a small community. He thanked Jed for protecting the passengers. He determined that besides the dead man in the car where they were sitting there would be his compatriot along the tracks and two men near the woods. There would be two small cases near these men that contained the valuables.

The passengers assembled on the platform and this same employee asked for a volunteer among the passengers leaving the train in Sacramento and another volunteer from among those passengers going on to Oakland. The trainman told the volunteers that they could help get the valuables back to the rightful owners. There was no shortage of volunteers as many of the passengers had lost everything.

The employee said he would organize a posse right away to go back to where the bodies were, bury them, and to return with the valuables they found. The railroad employee said he was keeping the meeting short because the train had to stay on schedule.

By the time the train came into Sacramento Jed had stowed his 15-shot repeater into its case and put the case back up on the overhead rack. The two revolvers were put away. Vivian said to Jed, "Well, most everyone is happy you settle scores right away."

"Most everyone leaves out who?" Jed asked.

"It leaves me out, Jed. You played judge, jury and executioner one after the other without so much as a how do you do."

"I've been around those types of men. You see lots of them in the West. They take what they want. The word of what I did will spread along the railroad towns and it will be calm for a while."

Vivian, Jed and the other passengers made it to Oakland on time. They walked from the train depot to the ferry. They could look across the Bay, seven or eight miles, and see the buildings on the hills that made up San Francisco. The ferry they boarded had paddle wheels on the sides and made it across the Bay in about thirty minutes. They walked off the ferry to waiting carriages. Jed said to the driver of the carriage, "Can you take us to a medium priced hotel close by?"

Jed and Vivian hadn't brought up the matter anytime on the train ride so Jed didn't know what to expect when they made it to a hotel on Montgomery Street. The driver got out and said, "Why don't you wait just a minute and I'll go in and see if they have a room." Vivian leaned forward and said to the man, "Rooms." She emphasized the s at the end of the word. The man said, "Yes, ma'am."

They sat together in the carriage in silence. Jed knew right away that it was as good as over, if not over completely. Vivian had been cold on the trip, and then turned ice cold after the shootings. He might squeeze out one more Thursday evening but now that seemed unlikely. A porter took their bags up to the second floor. Their rooms were a few doors from one another. When the porter had gone downstairs, Jed went to Vivian's room. He looked in and said, "Well, you can see the Bay." "What's your view?" she asked. "I can see the street," he answered. Then Jed said, "I'm going to walk around and look at the town. I'll meet you downstairs in the lobby at six, if that's all right with you. We can go to dinner." It was late afternoon.

Jed walked around looking at stores and hotels. He had a drink in one of the bars on Post Street. He decided to have it out with Vivian over dinner. They would be in a public place so there wouldn't be any shouting.

The clerk at the desk told them about a restaurant close by on Bush Street. You had to like fish, the clerk added. Jed and Vivian looked at one another and acknowledged in a few words that there was risk in eating fish on the basis that neither had eaten fish more than a few times. Once in the restaurant, Jed waited until they had ordered and said to Vivian, "What do you think? Shall we put all the cards on the table?" He didn't have to go beyond that.

Vivian played with her knife and fork then looked up and said, "I thought I wanted to marry you starting three years ago. The only thing that got in the way was that I didn't love you enough. I always knew that."

"Lots of men and women just start off with what they have and hope for the best," Jed said.

"I was hoping for the real thing," Vivian said.

"Knowing what you know, why did you decide to come to California and marry me out here?"

"I thought it might work. Nothing was happening in Chicago."

"Are you going back to Chicago?"

"No use. I'll find work here and start over. They tell me it doesn't snow in the winter and there's no wind from the Arctic." Jed said, "I told you that in Chicago."

They arranged to go their separate ways during the day and have dinner together. Vivian spent the days looking for work. It only took a week to locate the same job she had held in the store in Chicago. She could start right away and that made her look for a room in a boarding house not far from the store.

Jed hired a carriage to take her things to her new home. He went with her so that she didn't have to lift anything heavy. He took her ticket from her and made certain that the box of clothes in the depot in Oakland was delivered to her new address. "They're winter clothes," Vivian told him. "I don't know if I'll need them again."

On their last day in the hotel together, Vivian had said to Jed, "I need you as a friend. I want to know where you are when you find work." They talked about the restaurant where they might have dinner together. There were two where they had eaten that they liked. Vivian placed her hand on Jed's shoulder and stroked his cheek for a moment. "I know how to say farewell to a good friend," she said. Jed knew to go to the desk and arrange for a hot bath before dinner.

Jed didn't feel the pressure to get work the way Vivian did. He'd started with more money than she had and the management of the railroad had given him money in appreciation. Part of the citation read, "Your prompt action helped preserve our reputation for safe travel across the continent." The gift amounted to about two weeks' expenses in San Francisco at the rate he was spending his savings.

He was being caught up in the charm of the city. The idea of living far away on a farm was losing a little appeal each day. One Sunday he and Vivian had taken the horse- drawn trolley to Golden Gate Park and spent the afternoon looking at the plantings. They had an early meal in one of several restaurants that had sprung up.

On one of his walks up Bush Street he passed a store that sold stationery and books, and perhaps other items. From the street he could see a woman sitting at a desk working on a ledger. Her desk was not at the window but a little way back. She lifted her head and nodded. He touched the rim of his hat and nodded back. From this little distance he could see that she wore her brown hair short and seemed to be pretty. He couldn't discern any more than that. He registered exactly where on Bush Street he was and knew that he could come back when he and Vivian were done. He expected that it wouldn't be long.

It was about a week later that he was on Bush Street with the intention of entering the store. He hoped that the pretty brunette would be there. His legitimate question had to do with used books written by Civil War generals. It was almost too easy, Jed thought. From the sidewalk he could see that she was working at the desk. He entered, and although he could see that there was a clerk on the floor he went straight to the lady at the desk. Again they exchanged smiles. Perhaps she remembered him. Before he could get into his discourse he noticed that her left arm was anchored across her waist and that her left hand arched back as though the entire assembly, arm and hand, was frozen into this position.

He got to his question right away and the woman, rather than sending him to the clerk, got up from her desk and said, "Let me show you what we have." She walked with difficulty. Jed saw that her feet pointed in. Her gait was cramped. Jed didn't know the source of this condition but assumed that she had had it from birth. He had no name for it. It occurred to Jed that the woman had gotten up on purpose so that there would be no question in his mind about her condition. He thought as well that she, having lived with cramped limbs all her life, had passed beyond embarrassment.

Jed did buy a book, finishing the transaction through the clerk. On the way out he returned to the brunette's desk and said, "Mighty nice store, ma'am. My name's Jed Loomis."

"I'm Blanche Hill, Mr. Loomis. I hope you'll come again."

"You can count on it," he said.

Back on Bush Street, with his book under his arm, Jed wondered why he could be so attracted to this crippled woman. The first reason that came to him was that as a single man he could direct his attention toward her. Jed knew he was being egotistical when he guessed that she would welcome it. Then he thought it natural to be sympathetic toward someone who had been dealt a bad hand at cards.

THE WILD WEST
PART 4

Without Vivian to occupy his thoughts and time, Jed lost most of his direction. He had not been serious about finding work and he knew the reason: that if he stayed in the city the only thing he could do was work around a stable or with wagons. He hoped that this part of his life was over, but he had nothing else to turn to. Buying land and raising animals was an alternative, but Vivian had been right: he knew nothing about farming and ranching. He thought about sheriff's work. There was no question that he could handle guns but he knew that most times sheriffs were elected, that they took care of an entire county, ran the jails, hired deputies, found money to pay them, and all that government business besides. Again he had no experience in that line of work and he suspected it would bore him.

Jed could see the ships coming and going in and out of the port. There was activity around the docks. Perhaps he could find work there. The Army was busy at Angel Island. Even though headquarters were kept in St. Louis, the Army shipped men and materiel in through Angel

Island to run the summer campaigns against the Plains Indians. But he had no enthusiasm for anything that had come to his mind. He needed a woman in his life, a woman to marry and start a family with, a woman to replace Vivian. He missed the sharing they had done, even as it ran down to nothing at the end.

Blanche Hill was never far from his thoughts. He guessed she would welcome his presence in her life. He guessed also that she spent a fair amount of time alone at home after work. He didn't know whether she had family in the city, or had friends, or attended services at her church, if indeed she had one. He surely didn't have one. He'd have to find out. It would cost him another book.

He walked to the store one afternoon and when he arrived he went straight to her. He removed his hat and said, "Nice to see you, Miss Hill. How are you?"

"I'm fine, Mr. Loomis. Glad you're back."

They chatted a bit and then Jed said, "I'm looking for an action book this time."

"Let's go look," Blanche said. They found a book that interested Jed, stories from Arizona, and how the territory was being settled. That included stories about the Navajo, Zuni and Apache. On the way out Jed asked Blanche, "How does someone get to know you outside the store?"

"It's simple, really. You come to my home Saturday afternoon at six after I've closed the store and we'll have tea or coffee and something to eat."

"That's hospitable, Miss Blanche," Jed said.

She wrote her address on a slip of paper. He was familiar enough with the layout of the streets that he knew he could walk there from his hotel in half an hour. They set it for Saturday next.

On walking back to his hotel Jed thought he would discuss work with Blanche. She knew more about the city than he did and he might as well wait from this Wednesday to the following Saturday to get her opinion. He admitted to himself that he was counting on her just a bit to help him set up his life in San Francisco.

It was a day in the fall of 1879, a clear and brisk day on which to walk from his hotel to the address Blanche had given him. These last three days he had read his book and finished it. There were stories of gunplay in various parts of Arizona. The author portrayed the territory as lawless, a place where desperadoes settled matters violently with their six-shooters. Some of the men were familiar, such as Billy the Kid, and others were new to him. The idea that there was a town named Tombstone and a cemetery named Boot Hill appealed to him in the sense that among outlaws the worst of them were being killed along with those not quite so bad. In the end all of them met that fate. That's the way the author wrote about it. For his next book he thought he might go back to the history of the Civil War. Maybe Blanche would have an idea for him.

He arrived at her address. It consisted of a house divided in two. There were two front doors on the porch. Jed looked at his pocket watch. It was five after six. He knocked on the left door. He could hear Blanche making her way slowly in the halting way she moved. When she opened the door he noticed right away that she was wearing a colorful long dress and had a black choker around her neck. It was made of velvet, perhaps two inches wide, and tied up into a bow in the back. He knew she could not have tied it.

There was welcome written all over her face. She led him into the parlor. When they were seated in their own chairs around a small table, a woman appeared from the kitchen. Jed guessed she had been born in Ireland and her voice backed him up. "Miss Blanche, you said you would ask the gentleman if he wanted tea or coffee."

"Which will it be?" Blanche asked Jed.

"Thanks for the choice," he answered. "I'd prefer the coffee if that's all right."

Blanche volunteered that she had let her clerk close the store and that she had come home the usual way in a horse and buggy. The same driver took her in both directions just about every day. Jed could hear the boiling water being poured and in a few minutes the woman came in with a tray holding sandwiches and cakes, followed by another tray with cups, saucers, and the pot of coffee.

"Thank you, Denise," Blanche said. Jed realized that Blanche would find out all she could about him at this first sitting, as though they would never see one another again. She wanted to know where he had been born (Michigan), how long he had stayed in school (through his fourteenth year), how he got involved in the Civil War when so young, about the battles, and how he decided to move to Dallas after the War and get into the cattle business, as she put it.

Jed did manage to get in a few questions of his own. She had been born in the city in 1854, making her twenty-five years old. "I'm not a forty-niner, though my parents are," she had said. Her father was the captain of a whaler that sailed out of New Bedford. By 1842 he had tired of that life. He brought his wife along on a trip around the Horn. When he made San Francisco he sold his vessel, which went right away into coastal trade, mostly bringing logs down from Oregon. Her father started up in the shipping business inside the Bay. He owned the ferry that brought them from Oakland and he engaged in commerce up to Sacramento and to the small ports scattered around inside the Bay. His three children, two boys besides Blanche, were born in San Francisco.

Jed could see that she was rooted in this community and sustained by her family. He wanted to know how her close relatives dealt with her condition. They could have pushed her out into the world to make do as best she could, or they could have kept her close and guarded her against the bumps that would come along. He knew they could do a great deal but they couldn't find a man for her. That she would have to accomplish on her own.

Jed couldn't bring himself to be as direct as Blanche had just been with him, so he started at the edge, or so he thought. "Tell me about the store. Did the owner hire you because of your knowledge of books or because you could keep records?"

"Neither," Blanche answered. "I'm the owner."

It took a while for Jed to absorb the news. He knew women ran rooming houses and that some women took in boarders but he had never heard of a woman who owned a business. He went mute.

Blanche said, "My father knew my interests. He purchased the building and gave me the money to lay in inventory and pay wages, the clerk's and mine, for six months. He said he didn't want the money back and gave the reason that my two brothers are in the shipping business with him."

They were both silent. Jed reached for another cake. He wanted to say the obvious, that her parents must have concluded that there was no chance that Blanche would marry and have a family so they set her up early to be independent. But Jed knew you couldn't tell the future what to do so he said, "Don't tell me your father owns this house, too." Blanche answered, "He does, and he charges me a little rent to occupy this half."

"I'd certainly like to meet your family sometime," Jed announced. He knew it was too soon on this first visit to say that but he was at a loss for words.

Blanche answered, "I think you'd like them. Very direct people, just as you are. Both my brothers are married and have children. The children don't know what to make of their Aunt Blanche."

It was the first reference Blanche had made to what the children must have thought of as somebody different from other people. Jed thought for a moment and decided against mining that vein. He would leave it for another time. He went off on a different tack. "Do you have any ideas on the kind of work that I might find here?"

"All I know about you, Mr. Loomis, is that you like books and read a lot. You might enjoy working in the city library."

"What do you suppose they'd have me do?"

"The first job people are assigned is to restock books. People bring them back and they have to be returned to their places on the shelves. It's the lowest paying job, but that's where you start."

"You'd lose a customer," Jed said.

"Yes, but I've made a friend."

Jed indicated that he would enjoy coming the following Saturday if that was all right with her.

It didn't surprise Jed that he met Vivian on the street late one afternoon after the store where she worked had closed. He felt that sensation in the chest as she walked toward him. He gave her face a glance and went right past her clothes to her body that he knew so well. You don't get everything, he acknowledged. With Blanche he got a pretty face and a body in trouble. With Vivian, it was the other way around. He went to what he had heard other men say, that you loved them at night so it didn't make any difference what they looked like. It was the body that counted.

She had recognized him and she kept a smile on her face. In the time it took them to come together he thought how Blanche was uncomplicated and sweet to him. He thought she liked him for what he was but wasn't certain what that might be. He knew he was polite to people. Vivian, on the other hand, was complicated. She worked around him and made him dance to her tune. He couldn't say it to himself any clearer than that.

When they were face to face, Vivian kissed him on the cheek and asked him how he was and whether he had found work. When he said that he was thinking about working in the library, she said, "Jed, you don't know anything about farming and now you talk about working in a library and you don't know anything about books."

"I can read, so it shouldn't be very difficult." He saw one of the differences between the two women right there. Blanche would never expose a weakness in him.

Vivian asked, "Do you suppose we should have a meal together and catch up with the news?" To Jed the question meant that she had not found a man yet. When he answered, "It may not be such a good idea right now," he knew Vivian would interpret his answer to mean that he had found a woman and didn't want to step out on her.

Vivian said right away, "Who is she? Tell me."

Jed answered, "A nice lady but too soon to go into details." They talked about Vivian's work and how much she was enjoying San Francisco and soon enough they parted ways.

Jed turned around and stood there watching Vivian move away. She might have been saying that they could pick up where they left off. It wasn't too late. His sense of it was that Blanche said what was on her mind. Vivian, on the other hand, talked in a way to make him, Jed, do the things that would help her out in some way. She held the reins. She rode around on him using a light whip. He knew she used her lovely body to get her way.

He had not known Blanche long. He wondered, as he turned and started to walk away, whether she too would use her body to get him to do what she wanted him to do. They were women, after all.

THE WILD WEST

PART 6

Jed knew he could not lie down on his bed in the hotel room and read all day, nor could he pass the time by walking to places in the city that he hadn't visited. He had asked Blanche about work. She had suggested the library. He couldn't go back to her store nor could he show up on the Saturday following at her home without making an attempt at the library.

It was located downtown and he determined easily enough how to walk there. For no particular reason he said to himself that he would appear at two o'clock on Tuesday. He dressed in one of his new outfits, selecting a gray-white-black string tie to wear with one of his new white shirts. When he arrived, he thought it best not to pause. He went up the few stairs, pushed open the door and walked straight to a desk with a lady sitting behind it. Jed said, "Miss Blanche Hill sent me." His mouth went dry. He felt like a schoolboy standing there with his hat in both hands.

"I don't happen to know any Miss Blanche Hill. What was her reason for sending you?"

Jed relaxed a bit. The lady was not about to bite his head off. In fact, Jed thought there was kindness in her voice.

"Miss Blanche Hill owns the book and stationery store on Bush Street. She sent me to talk to you about work."

"The person you want to talk to about work is Mr. Hernandez. I'll take you back to his office."

They walked to the other end of the building and paused at a door. The lady knocked and waited to hear a voice from inside. She opened the door. Mr. Hernandez looked up. The lady said, "This gentleman came in looking for work. A Miss Blanche Hill sent him."

Mr. Hernandez stood up, came around the desk and took Jed's hand. He said, "I know Blanche Hill and her family. How did you meet her?"

Jed told Mr. Hernandez about going to Blanche's store and buying two books, but he left out the part about being invited to her house. He'd tell him if he had to.

"Sit down and tell me your name," Mr. Hernandez said. When Jed gave him his name, Mr. Hernandez turned his head around quickly to look out the window and perhaps do some thinking. In that moment Jed sized up Mr. Hernandez. There was no Spanish accent, yet he was old enough to have been born here before 1846 when California changed hands. He could have been from an old Mexican family that had married into a recently-arrived Anglo family. The gentleman's hair was half gray, his body was getting nicely rounded, and he must have been in his early fifties.

Mr. Hernandez turned and said, "You might be the Jed Loomis of the train robbery."

"Yes, I am, sir."

"There was a half-column in the paper three or four weeks ago. There was mention of a woman traveling with you."

"Yes, that's right. We were intending to get married here but she changed her mind, found work and took new lodgings."

"What might you like to do here at the library, Mr. Loomis?"

"Miss Hill said to start at the bottom by putting books back on their shelves. She said that's where you started."

"Well, in fact, Mr. Loomis, you start by cleaning the building and emptying the waste baskets. But we have a man who has been doing that for a few years. I know he only reads the simplest words. He's happy with his job."

They were silent for a moment, and then Mr. Hernandez went back to the incident on the train. "Did you hear anything more from the state or the sheriff's office?"

"No, sir. I didn't hear from anyone but the railroad. They sent me a citation and a reward for providing safety to their passengers."

Mr. Hernandez thought it over for a minute and said, "I guess the railroad went to the Supervisors in Alpine Country and asked them to forget all about investigations and suchlike because you really did them a good turn."

"It was automatic with me," Jed said.

"Where are the guns now?" Mr. Hernandez asked.

"I have them under lock and key in my hotel room."

"As long as people know you have guns and have killed with them, they'll put you in a special category. You won't be thought of as completely civilized."

"I suppose I'm not," Jed said.

Mr. Hernandez ignored this last remark and went back to resolving his main point. "Take a ride on the ferry to Oakland and back. On the trip break down the two revolvers and throw all the parts into the Bay. As far as the repeater is concerned, sell it at a gun store. It's probably useful for hunting game in the hills. When you've done that, come back and tell me and you'll find work here." He paused, and then said, "Let me be clear. Those are conditions for employment in this library."

It seemed to Jed that Blanche and Mr. Hernandez had worked out this plan. Locate work for Jed. Have Mr. Hernandez offer work under conditions. Change Jed's way of life.

Mr. Hernandez stood up and put out his hand. Jed thanked him. When he had taken a step toward the door, Mr. Hernandez said, "Miss Blanche. She's so pretty. It's strange that God doesn't hand out blessings evenly, somehow."

Jed turned and asked, "How do you know her, may I ask, sir?"

"We attend services together. That's a mighty fine family."

Jed knew he had plenty to think about. It was his first lesson in running a civilized society. Miss Blanche needed a husband. Jed needed work. Mr. Hernandez probably needed an employee. Mr. Hernandez and Blanche must have worked together in the background. Jed was being prepared for Blanche and for life in San Francisco. Clean him up a bit. If he started attending services and meeting families then he needed to be cleaned up. That's what occurred to him. Jed thought some more: that the event with the guns on the train in the Sierra would never disappear. The only way he could lessen the impact over the years was to change his life, and to do that he had to get rid of his three guns and everybody had to know it. Jed knew he had done right on the train, but he could understand that not everybody would see it his way.

It was Tuesday afternoon. On Wednesday he thought about taking the ferry ride to Oakland to dispose of is revolvers. He hesitated on the basis that they had cost him a good sum of money. Mr. Hernandez might not know just how much. On Thursday he sold the repeating rifle and the two revolvers at a gun store and made certain that he received a sales slip. On Friday he returned to the library and told Mr. Hernandez what he had done and gave his reason. Mr. Hernandez said, "Well, all right, but those revolvers are not out of circulation. That was my intention, to make certain that they left San Francisco." Neither said anything for a moment.

He was hired to start on Monday. Mr. Hernandez turned him over to Mrs. Edwards at the desk, who described his duties to him. Jed was prepared for Blanche on Saturday.

Blanche wore the same dress as the previous Saturday but the velvet choker was missing. Jed guessed that Blanche had not hired the servant girl this time. Blanche went right away to that point by leading Jed into the kitchen. She asked him to help bring the food into the parlor and pour hot water into the coffee maker.

Jed brought up the two meetings with Mr. Hernandez, the sale of his guns and the new job that started on Monday. Jed surmised that Blanche knew most of the story, but if she did she didn't let on. She did say to Jed that he had done the right thing. There were choices in life. She went on, "It's still the Wild West up in the Sierra, not all the time, but now and again. Down here in the city we want to get rid of lawlessness. You made a good choice."

They talked about the library, his working hours, and his duties. Jed mentioned that he would move out of his hotel and find a place near the library that provided room and board. "I'm not that big and don't eat much," he said. "But I like a room with a view of the Bay. I want to see the ships come and go."

They talked about the store and particularly how she determined the titles to purchase from the publishers back east. Even though he hadn't worked his first day at the library, Jed was letting it come over him that books were his life.

When it came time to go, Jed thanked Blanche for the sandwiches and coffee. They moved toward the front door. Once there Blanche took his hand and stopped walking. This is a woman who wants to be kissed, Jed knew. He held her lightly in his arms. There was enough light that he could see details in her face. She was looking at his mouth, as though she might miss it. Her mouth was open just a bit. He leaned over and kissed first the lower lip then the upper one, then her entire mouth. He let his tongue run against her teeth. When he pulled away, she said, "Oh, Jed." He then kissed her on the neck and moved up to her ear and across the face to the other side where he ended up on her neck. To this she said, "That's nice." Jed would learn that those two expressions were the ones that Blanche used when she wished to express her pleasure.

He put his hand on the back of her head, buried it in the soft brown hair and kissed her again. When he released her she kept her good arm around his neck and said, "Jed, you're the first man to kiss me."

He believed her and thought that she had made up for the lack of practice in kissing by talking to one of her sisters-in-law or maybe reading up on the matter. There might be a book with something like that in it.

Work imposed its regular schedule. Jed turned up five and a half days a week at the library. He returned books back to their proper place on the shelves and in that way came to know how the library's collection was divided. There were many topics, each allocated its area in the building.

Jed would see Mr. Hernandez on a daily basis. They would exchange greetings. One day in his third week, Mr. Hernandez asked Jed about his favorite topic. When Jed answered, "History," Mr. Hernandez said, "I'm not surprised. Most everybody says that, although literature ranks high with the ladies." Before Jed could say anything, Mr. Hernandez went on. "Try to understand the collection in the history section. You realize that we buy new books on a regular basis. We have to know our readers' tastes and match that against new purchases." As they broke away, Mr. Hernandez said, "Someday I want you to understand the entire collection." Jed said, "Yes, Sir." He thought Mr. Hernandez said that to all the employees, but he knew he couldn't ask around because he didn't want it to get back to Mr. Hernandez that he was questioning his word.

Jed discussed the events at the library with Blanche. He knew she purchased new books for her store. They discussed how she decided on titles. They spent time in her store going over the types of books and how they were arranged. She told him that she sold more Bibles and dictionaries than anything else.

Jed started seeing Blanche in the middle of the week. He would pick her up at the end of the working day and they would walk to a restaurant in the area. On one occasion Blanche brought evening clothes. She changed into them at the store. Jed had to button up the back of her dress. They went to the theater and ate afterwards. It was the first time that Blanche had been seen by some of her acquaintances with a man other than family. She was pleased that none of them came over to her during intermission to say a few words so that she did not have to explain Jed to them.

Having kissed that first time at the doorway, they never missed repeating. They went from kissing at the door to sitting next to one another on the sofa in the parlor and kissing leisurely. Jed would let his hands wander over her body and she never stopped him. Usually she would say, "That's so nice, Jed." He knew the boundaries and stayed within them.

On Jed's initiative, the matter of meeting the family came up. Blanche's solution covered plenty of ground. She suggested that he come to her house on Sunday at 10:30. One of her brothers and his wife came by for them. They would attend services together where he would meet the other brother, his wife and Blanche's parents. After services, the entire family would repair to her parents' house for lunch.

"Are you baptized?" Blanche asked.

"Yes, Methodist, I think,"

"The rule in the Catholic Church is that you must be baptized Catholic to take communion."

Jed didn't say anything. Blanche got by the impasse by telling Jed that he would be surrounded by Catholics and it would work out.

"When we go to the rail, I'll take your arm and you just do what everybody else does."

He was welcomed graciously by all the members of the family. Jed guessed that this was the first time that Blanche had appeared with a man, at least with a man that she had got on her own. He could hear her tell the members of the family to be on their best behavior and not to bring up the killings in the Sierra.

Jed managed to stand, sit, and kneel at the proper moments. He noticed that Blanche did not kneel. She leaned forward and placed her arms on the pew in front of her. This was the first time in memory that Jed had been to church. The mass was in Latin and he understood nothing of it, so he was doubly pleased when the priest gave his sermon in English. He told the story of Jonah and the whale. Jed had heard the expression but had not understood its significance. The priest started out by saying that the story was an allegory. Jed didn't know the meaning of the word. He told himself that he would remember it and look it up in one of the dictionaries in the library. The priest said that the story made the point that with God there is always a second chance.

The story, as best Jed could piece it together, went like this. North of Israel there lived Assyrians, vicious people. They lived where Turks live now. Their capital was Nineveh. The year was around 800 BC. They were responsible for the disappearance of the ten tribes living north of Jerusalem. God ordered Jonah to go from Israel, where he lived, to Nineveh and tell the Assyrians that they should change their ways. Jonah knew that he would be put to death if he dared to go there. His solution was to head in the opposite direction. He bought passage on a trading ship that was on its way from a port in Israel to one in Spain. A little time out of port, a storm welled up, terrifying the sailors on the ship.

Jonah went below and fell asleep. The sailors prayed to their Gods and hoped that the storm would abate. When the storm did not slack off, the sailors went below, brought Jonah back on deck, and asked him to pray to his God. This Jonah did but when the storm kept up, Jonah realized that God was angry with him for having failed to go to Nineveh. He offered himself as a sacrifice. Knowing that suicide was a violation of the law, he asked the sailors to thrown him overboard. This they did, and the storm lost its violence promptly.

Jonah sank to the bottom of the sea. He became entangled in seaweed. At the moment he was about to drown, a large fish swallowed him. The priest interrupted the telling of the tale to emphasize that the large fish was God's providing Jonah with a second chance. Jed noticed that the priest said large fish and not whale. There might not be whales in the Mediterranean Sea, Jed guessed. Jonah survived three days inside the large fish, which swam back to the shores of Israel. Jonah was deposited on the beach near where he had started his journey. He walked to Nineveh and he preached to the people, asking them to mend their ways. They did this and the king followed suit.

Jed listened mostly but took time to react as well. Why wasn't Jonah required to engage in mortal combat with the king? And why did the populace listen to Jonah, a man from enemy territory traveling alone on foot? They could have cut him into small pieces and fed him to the dogs.

The priest summed up this way. Jonah had failed to get to Nineveh on his first try, but he succeeded because he had tried a second time. Jed thought that the sermon was aimed straight at him. Blanche was a second chance, having come right after Vivian. The job was a second chance at working at something other than around horses in a stable. There was plenty to think about.

Lunch was a hospitable affair. The men of the family, Blanche's father and her two brothers, treated him as an equal. Because gunfights were off limits, they talked about cattle drives, the trip across the country on the railroad, and his work at the library. Jed countered with questions about transportation on the Bay, but he was outnumbered three to one. They asked three times as many questions as he did. The two wives made certain that their three children spent time sitting near Blanche and talking with her to the extent that they could. It was obvious to Blanche that the children were more interested in playing on the floor with their toys and with one another.

The same brother and wife who fetched them returned them to Blanche's house. It was late afternoon. Blanche and Jed drank tea and when Jed made motions about going home Blanche took his hand. Jed could tell that she had been rehearsing the words when she said slowly and with hesitation, but without any embarrassment that he could detect, "Jed, will you come upstairs and lie on the bed with me?"

"That's so different from what we've been doing," he said.

"I know it is. I'm tired of being left out of the pleasures that so many other women enjoy. Can we have one rule?"

"Yes. What would that be?"

"No baby. I can't do that. It would ruin my life."

"We can do whatever you wish, Blanche."

They moved upstairs slowly. She held the banister. Jed realized that going up and down stairs was an effort for her. When they were in the bedroom Blanche said, "I'm leaving on my bottom layer."

They undressed part way. Blanche did not open the bed. She lay down on it and pulled a thin blanket over her. When Jed settled in beside her she said, "I want to feel your hands on my body, Jed." He knew that to mean that he should caress her and give her pleasure. He took his time. Blanche said, "Oh, Jed," several times. When he had succeeded, she said, "That was so nice."

He pulled her into his arms and said, "Blanche, I need you in my life.

You make it complete." She didn't say anything for a moment, and then answered, "You're just right for me. I know you are." They kissed and held on to one another quite a while, and then Jed, without saying anything, took Blanche's crippled hand in both of his and worked it back and forth gently. He straightened her fingers then let them go. He worked his way up her arm to her shoulder. He wanted to measure how stiff she was. He thought that if he massaged the arm and hand every day and made her exercise, then some of the strength and flexibility would return.

He dressed and they went downstairs so that she could lock up after him. He said, "I hope the neighbors aren't looking at this moment." She said, "It's wonderful being a full woman with a fine man like you."

On the walk home, he went over the sermon and how it meshed with his life. Blanche had provided a new life, or, as the priest said, a second chance. He started thinking about when they might marry. There it was. It came to him on the walk home that Blanche had used her body to bring out his interest in her. Jed put the best face on it. First, he thought that she had never had a man's hands on her body and wanted the sensation. Second, that she wanted him to know that she was like other women in her enthusiasm for a man, and she knew what men and women together were all about.

As he walked, he tried to figure the difference between Blanche and Vivian. He thought that if he found the difference it wouldn't be much. Maybe Blanche gave herself without condition and with Vivian you paid a price. But that wasn't it exactly. Maybe life with Blanche would be more interesting than life with Vivian. Blanche and he had books in their lives while he and Vivian were two people brought together by chance, finding themselves on the same floor in their boarding house in Chicago. If he had married Vivian, Jed guessed, they would have started life together with little in common.

THE WILD WEST

PART 8

The priest, Father Sebastian, baptized Jed into the Catholic Church. He gave Jed a few instructions and asked him to learn the *Pater Noster* in Latin and English. Father Sebastian gave Jed an English translation of the mass along with the original in Latin. "An intelligent man such as you won't have any trouble mastering this material," the priest said. Jed grasped that flattery was at work once again.

Blanche and Jed were married in January 1880, after the Christmas season died down. She walked slowly up the aisle on her father's arm. As he watched her, Jed realized that he had grown accustomed to her infirmity. He never referred to her as being crippled. He had heard Mr. Hernandez describe Blanche's condition as an infirmity and if that word suited Mr. Hernandez then it suited him.

As Jed stood near the altar with Blanche's two brothers, he tried to imagine what the guests were thinking. Most of them would be saying to themselves that Blanche couldn't do any better because of her condition. None of the attractive bachelors of San Francisco had paid court. They might be thinking that the family was relieved that Blanche was taken at last. Her man was respectable but his prospects were poor. He only held a lowly job at the library. He was neither tall nor handsome. They might be thinking that Blanche had settled for this man because he would be the only man to come along. It would be her only chance. And a few might be thinking that this cowpoke, drifter, and gunman had taken Blanche because he knew the marriage gave him a position within a prosperous, well-known San Francisco family.

Blanche was approaching. Jed turned and offered her his arm. They moved forward toward the priest and the ceremony began. Blanche wore a white silk dress with little decoration. The veil had been worn by her mother. Jed went in and out of paying attention until his turn came to answer questions. Soon enough they were married. The priest said, "You may kiss the bride." With that Blanche removed the veil with her good arm. As they started down the aisle, Blanche paused to kiss her mother. One person started to clap. In a moment all in attendance were clapping. Jed just smiled. He looked at Blanche. She was smiling and a few tears were on her cheeks.

There was a reception held next door to the church and as the sun set Blanche and Jed were taken by carriage to their home. "This is the best day of my life, so far," Blanche said. Jed could only think to say, "For me too."

In the previous six weeks they had speculated on whether she could have children and if she could, would they be born with her condition. Once she asked, "I don't know what you will do with me if I can't have children." He had answered right away, "It's you I want, Blanche. But any children you have will be just fine. I know that."

She had told him once of a role that he would play in her life. "I don't want you to take the place of my father or my brothers, but I know you will protect me and our honor." Jed was mystified. He had never worried about his honor, or the honor of anyone else. He answered, "That goes without saying."

There were three children born in their first six years of marriage. The children were perfectly normal in their walking. Blanche's body loosened over time. She could hold a child with her bad arm and tend to other matters with the good one. She was able to shake off her shuffle and walk more normally than as a young woman.

Blanche never let go of her store. She advanced her clerk to greater responsibility and hired another junior person. Jed stayed at the library. After Mr. Hernandez retired he moved up two rungs, then in 1896 he became head of the library. He did not sense that his or Blanche's honor ever needed to be defended, although on one occasion word got back to him that an acquaintance had asked about "that little opportunist librarian and his slightly bent wife." Jed did not repeat the remark to Blanche but he did say to the bearer of the rumor that the man who made the comment would live only because he, Jed, no longer owned guns. He added, "If I still had my Colts I'd put twelve holes in him as he fell to the ground." Jed never knew whether his comment was conveyed to the acquaintance, but in any event nothing came of it.

Only their family and a few friends were able to see beyond Blanche's infirmity. The constant that others failed to notice was the deep love each felt for the other. It had been there from the beginning. They soon realized that each needed the other to get through life successfully.

Jed found Blanche all he wanted in a woman. She didn't have the beautiful body that Vivian had but she needed him and wanted him. She had an eagerness about being loved by him that he found compelling. He never sensed an urge for another woman. He knew she was clever enough to set it up that way. Jed developed a sense of the public's tastes for books, which he shared with Blanche. This information guided her in the titles of the books that she stocked at the store. Blanche taught Jed all she knew about business and accounting. The accounting part did not come naturally. His mind wandered when she explained the fine points.

The earthquake of 1906 did terrible damage to San Francisco. Jed, Blanche and the children escaped unharmed at first. On the second day after the quake Jed was walking home from the library when a cornice fell from a building and killed him instantly. He was buried in the cemetery associated with his church. His in-laws already occupied plots. He was interred next to them and space was left for Blanche next to him. His headstone gave his name and dates, 1846 – 1906. Blanche gave instructions that the words, "Devoted Husband," be added.

Blanche dressed in black. Six months after losing Jed, a friend and widower said to Blanche, "If you ever get over your grief, we might talk." She never remarried. She lived to the age of eighty-two and died in 1936.

JUNIOR YEAR ABROAD

JUNIOR YEAR ABROAD
PART I

Allison had both hands on the railing. She was looking west at the Palisades across the Hudson, aware of her friends standing next to her, but occupied with the significance of the moment. Her mother and father had left the ship right away when the "All ashore..." announcement came over the loud speakers. They stood on the dock for a while, her father waiving the white handkerchief he kept in his breast pocket. The gangways were removed and the lines securing the ship to the dock fell away. There were four blasts from the ship's steam whistle as the Queen Mary slipped stern first into the Hudson River. A tugboat helped turn the ship around, heading it south. She started her slow descent down the Hudson into the Atlantic. It was late June 1959. Allison felt she was away now, away for a year and a bit, on her first trip to Europe. She was twenty, had finished her sophomore year as a French major, and was pleased that her parents had encouraged her to take this junior year abroad. They may have guessed the fantasies that filled her mind most evenings as she fell asleep. They had to do with men, what it would be like to spend a night against a man's warm body, what it would feel like to have a man enter her body, and where would it be likely that these adventures would take place, and who would be the man, how would she choose him?

Sullying one's reputation, that's what you called it at home. Some of your friends might start to gossip. But on a different continent, that was another matter. The stories wouldn't cross the Atlantic, and anyway France was a more tolerant country than America. It was expected that young people paired off and embarked on life's great experiment. It was a natural activity, they said.

The Statue of Liberty faded. They were opposite Staten Island. Allison looked to her left. There were Kitty, Penny and Ann. They all wore low-heeled shoes, a dress and a lightweight coat. Their hair blew in all directions. They had met as freshmen in their all-girls college and started discussing spending their junior year abroad when they met sophomores who were also planning the trip and seniors who had completed it. The language majors and the European History majors tended to be candidates. Girls studying biology stayed home.

Allison's mother had surprised her a week before leaving. As Allison was sorting out clothes to take and starting to fill her first suitcase, her mother came into her bedroom, sat on the bed, and started talking about clothes. After a moment, she asked Allison. "Are you a virgin, darling?" The question was not out of the blue as Allison and her mother had engaged in all the conversations required to get a daughter through adolescence. "Yes, I am, Mother," she had answered.

"Well, in the coming year, you'll probably lose it. Away from home, with insistent young men, and a sexuality of your own, it will probably happen."

Her mother was silent for a moment. Allison continued folding blouses and filling the suitcase. Her mother started again. "Your father says that an erect penis has no conscience. You'll want to remember that.

Very few men worry that they might get you pregnant. Their primary goal is to get you in bed."

"I suppose women understand that, Mother."

"Yes, and I've got something for you."

Allison's mother left the room and returned in a moment with a small package. "Here are a dozen condoms. These should keep you from getting pregnant. You and I are going to examine one right now. If the man tries to put it on one way, it won't unroll and he might decide to forget it. The other way it rolls down the shaft and you're safe. There's no reason you can't put it on him and get it right."

In one of her suitcases Allison had the package, now containing eleven condoms. Her mother had told her that she could buy additional ones at a pharmacy. Her mother had concluded the conversation by telling Allison she was not suggesting that her daughter engage in an affair, but if she did she should avoid becoming pregnant, even if she had to remain in charge of some aspects. "Don't worry about spoiling the spontaneity of the moment," were her mother's final words on the matter.

It seemed to Allison and her three friends that life never returned to normal as long as they were at sea. Waiters hovered in the dining room, the orchestra played for their dancing pleasure, young men from several colleges on the East Coast were taking the grand tour, and a party atmosphere prevailed at most times. Allison and her friends did spend afternoons reading in their deck chairs. Allison made friends with several couples her parents' age. It dawned on Allison that so far her life had been led on top of the waves, insulated from rough times. She only knew people from her stratum. There was at least one layer above hers, perhaps two, and these people were traveling first class. One afternoon she was on a deck near the stern, watching the gray sea, sunning herself, when a lone female appeared above her on a space reserved for first class passengers. This woman was dressed as stylishly as one can be and stood alone and still for quite some time. The scene would not have made an impression on Allison had another person come along, either a man or a woman. But the woman remained in place, at least twenty minutes. Allison was close enough to her to notice that her face was solemn and sad. It impressed Allison that one could be rich and isolated and unhappy, all at the same time. She got from the experience that finding the people with whom to lead a life required patience and skill. So far that aspect of life had not been under her control. Soon enough, the choices would be hers. The experience stayed fresh in her mind for years. She had wondered many times how her life might have changed had she waved at the woman.

The ship pulled into Le Havre. The estuary of the Seine is wide and Allison noted how different the harbor was from New York's. Being right on the English Channel, breakwaters and sea walls had been built to form a port. New York was shielded from the sea so that docks perpendicular to Manhattan could accommodate the ocean liners. The docks in Le Havre must have been in repair because the ship did not tie up. Passengers walked down the gangway to a waiting barge and went ashore in this primitive fashion. There were busses for the short trip to the railroad station and a waiting train. The students were met in Paris and directed to their living quarters off Boulevard Montparnasse.

The young men whom Allison met on the ship were dispersing. Some were scheduled to spend the coming year in Paris and she saw a few of these from time to time. None of these men excited her. It was acceptable to see them occasionally but a large dose of anyone of them did not appear appetizing. She was hoping to meet French men.

Allison Connors came from Cleveland. Her father was the oldest son and was making a career in the family business. There was a plant in England that had been opened between the wars and it served as European headquarters. The talk around the house was that there would be additional plants, perhaps two or three, in other European countries.

Her father had come occasionally to England on business but never seen fit to bring the family and make a vacation of it. Allison's move to a college in New England was as close to Europe as she had come.

The purpose of this year in France, as Allison viewed it, was to broaden horizons in as many areas as possible. Of course, there would be mastery of a foreign language. She insisted that she would learn the political vocabulary so that she could read a French newspaper with ease. It disappointed her that she lived in a building filled with fellow students who spoke a great deal of English to one another. On the other hand, if she lived with only one student in the apartment of a French family, she would be cut off from many activities that her house organized, and the number of people whom she met would fall away.

Allison came to realize that there was an American look that she wore in common with her friends. She wanted the French look, the look carried by rich French women. She had an allowance and most of it would be spent on her wardrobe. The touristic horizon was a simple enough matter. She and her friends would circulate among the museums and walk the boulevards where the important monuments were. She and her friends could take day trips by train to view nearby points of interest.

She was baffled by the inaccessibility of French men. They were everywhere but how could you meet one with whom you could fall in love? On her walks she would see them singly or by twos or threes, and she would see an attractive couple in a café, particularly in an expensive café where high-class clientele would gather. Perhaps her year would go by and she would be denied the opportunity of having an affair with a French man of her class. Her mother had recounted a conversation between her and her father soon after they married. As her mother told it, she had asked her new husband why he had selected her of all the women available. He answered that there might have been fifty women who crossed his path over the years, each slightly different from the others, and that from among them he was looking for a particular combination of characteristics that he would not be able to put down on paper. He knew many of these qualities existed in his subconscious. Over time he lost interest in all women except Allison's mother. "It's a process of elimination, mostly automatic," he had said.

Allison fretted about the short time left to her before her year was over and the slow pace at which opportunities to meet attractive French men came her way. The junior year abroad would be a success in any event but without a love affair it might not provide her with those life-long memories.

Allison was realistic. Everything about her was adequate but nothing was outstanding. Her face and body would slow them down but she knew that to hold a man of consequence, she would be required to use the correct combination of brains and personality. For someone her age she had absorbed a great deal of literature and history. Politics followed. She found that these three topics converged. One led naturally to the others. She thought that the cornerstone of her personality was her pleasant quietness. She could listen with ease, and only take her turn talking when a new topic was called for, or the diverse opinions expressed needed consolidation. On the matter of sex, she knew you could always give it away. There was no shortage of men who would oblige her. They would take everything away and leave precious little, for a net loss. For Allison, the physical part of a relationship could only come when both parties were guided by a strong emotional attachment, one for the other.

By the time Jean Pierre Belmont de Villeneuve came into Allison's life, at Christmas time, her mastery of the language, though not complete, was adequate. She had absorbed the French habit of café life and taken on the French look with supplements to her wardrobe. She wore low-heeled shoes because there was a fair amount of walking in her daily life, and because she noticed that French men were slightly shorter than the American men she was accustomed to. Allison called Jean Pierre by both first names, as though they were one, which she had learned early on they are in France. It wouldn't do to call him either Jean or Pierre. They met as guests at a pre-Christmas party. Students had been invited and they gathered in a hall at the university and many of the foreign students attended. Jean Pierre was the guest of the professor in charge of the event. He and his family were part of the same social circle as the professor. The hall was decorated with a Christmas tree, dinner was served, and wine of medium quality flowed freely. It was the professor's idea that the evening would be successful if he could introduce young French people so that friendships might form. In the few remarks the host made as they sat down to dinner he said that attending classes had its place in visiting another country but it was the people you met and came to understand that produced lasting results.

Jean Pierre had come up to her not long after she arrived with her three friends. He asked whether she was Swedish, Canadian or American. The professor's guests had been primed to carry on conversations in French at the risk of insinuating that the foreigners hadn't mastered their language.

Allison answered that she was an American, as he would be able to tell as soon as she spoke a complete sentence. For the occasion she wore a dark green woolen skirt and a lighter green sweater with a V neck. She wore a scarf to cover the plunge to her bosom that the sweater provided. The scarf was yellow and green, made of silk, purchased as part of her refurbishment. He wore a dark suit and a conservative blue tie. It didn't surprise her that he worked at the branch of an American bank on the Place Vendôme.

They sat together at dinner and talked to other people as well as each other. Allison felt more mature than she ever had, as though Jean Pierre filled in the parts of her that were not complete. It seemed to her as the meal wore on that he was the missing piece, the partner in conversation who could grow in importance over time. He was not demanding in any way. He exuded calmness and consideration. At the end of the evening he went first to the professor and his wife to thank them, and then he discussed arrangements with Allison's friends on returning to their living quarters. These young women didn't want to intrude into Allison's territory and said that they would find their way home easily enough.

He took her hand when they were on the street and did not let go of it until they were at her door, except for the time spent in the Metro. He said he could not leave without knowing how to reach her. She thought he might kiss her after writing down her telephone number but he said how pleased he was to have met her and added that he would call her soon.

Before falling asleep Allison wondered what Jean Pierre thought of her. She hoped that her figure was right for him. She would be out of luck if he preferred the tall lanky build that could take on or lose ten pounds without the public knowing. But from the many women present he had singled her out. Allison thought of herself as well built and desirable but she worried that after having a child or two the inevitable weight would come at the expense of her appeal. Jean Pierre was compact, about two inches short of six feet, and probably good at one or more sports. He had the build and looks that she admired. She fell asleep imagining that he was at her side.

He enjoyed films and liked taking her to a restaurant for a leisurely dinner. On either Saturday or Sunday he would ask her to go walking with him, around the city, or in the Bois de Boulogne. His parents lived in a flat in the 16th while he had an apartment in the 6th arrondissement, to which she had not yet been invited. He indicated that his father was an attorney and that there was property from his mother's side in the region of Dijon, where grapes grew and wine was made. This was another universe for Allison about which she knew very little. She tried drinking wine with discernment but she knew that she could not distinguish between average and good wines.

Allison put together a party of twelve for her birthday in mid-February to which she invited Jean Pierre. He arrived with flowers and a small flask of perfume. She had already learned that it was the most expensive available. After unwrapping the present, she leaned over and kissed him lightly. They had crossed that bridge earlier.

March came and went and Jean Pierre had not invited Allison to his apartment. She thought that by now – they had known one another three months – he would have tried to get her alone. But she realized that he had not reached out, said how he felt, and hadn't indicated how the possibility of her going home in June or July would affect him. Perhaps he didn't want to expose himself or risk showing his hand only to be rejected. Allison couldn't think of anything that she might do to pry him open. She guessed he was spending ample time trying to think it through.

In mid-April he asked her to spend a weekend at the family's place south of Dijon. He told her it was his favorite time of the year, when all is green and new again. He said, "That's not an original idea, exactly, but with many others I enjoy the awakening. The birds are back in force. Perhaps they have spent the winter in Sicily." He said his parents would be there and were looking forward to meeting her.

She knew from those words that she had been discussed and that his parents wanted to know all they could about her and a weekend under the same roof would accomplish a great deal. She surmised that the invitation was as much from the parents as from Jean Pierre. He wouldn't invite her to the family seat on his own. In a reversal of roles, she wouldn't invite a new friend to her home without discussing it with her parents.

They took the train around noon on Friday for Dijon and were met at the station by a man whom Jean Pierre introduced as Monsieur Guillaume. Jean Pierre addressed him as Paul. Monsieur Guillaume called Jean Pierre by his first name.

They walked to a black Citröen, not the latest model whose front resembled a shark, but the model before that one, samples of which were found everywhere in France. The police used them, as did the president. They drove south toward Beaune, with vineyards on both sides of the road. He explained to her, not at length, that the land on the right, rising gently, produced better grapes than the land on the left, which was flat. Rain would run downhill and prevent the roots of the vines from absorbing too much water. On warm summer days, when the sun set, warm air would rise from the plain to be replaced by fresh air coming down to cool the grapes on the hills.

Allison remembered the words about the grapes but didn't have a logical place to store them. They were just sentences. She hoped that they would fit into a larger pattern someday. They drove through the town of Nuits St. Georges, which name didn't make sense to Allison, and soon after they turned off to the right and drove for what seemed to be a half-mile to the top of a slope and stopped on the circular driveway in front of a farm house. It was L-shaped, a two-story house made of stone, with blue shutters and a roof of slate.

When they were out of the car and Monsieur Guillaume had taken their two suitcases off the front seat, Jean Pierre's parents appeared. While the father was exchanging kisses on the cheek with his son, the mother embraced Allison, added an e to the end of her name, making it Allisone, and insisted that she be addressed as Claire and her husband as François. It wouldn't do to say de Villeneuve all weekend.

The sun was setting but there was still enough light that Allison could see the date 1732 carved into the keystone of the arch above the front door. Claire showed Allison around the downstairs. They sat on the terrace and had tea. "No food," Claire said, indicating that it was too close to dinner time. When they were finished, Claire told them to reappear in the living room at seven o'clock.

Jean Pierre led her upstairs to the L-shaped portion of the house. There were two bedrooms, baths, and a sitting room. Allison unpacked and dressed for dinner as Jean Pierre suggested they should. So this would be the room where it happened, Allison guessed. It interested her that he had taken no steps in Paris when he might have, but chose to be in bed with her at his home, as though by the act he would welcome her into the family. She thought the parents assumed that long since they had become lovers. They didn't know all there was to know about their son.

Allison put on a simple blue dress and wore a cashmere sweater over it, white with blue piping. At seven Jean Pierre knocked at her door, which she had left ajar. She asked him in. He wore a sport coat, dark trousers and a blue shirt and tie. Allison had seen that look in the windows of men's stores and admired it. She went over to him, kissed him and told him that it was all a dream. He kissed her back and said, "You're the dream."

François dressed as did his son. Claire wore a blue and white polka dot dress. Allison thought she might be fifty. She was vivacious while her husband displayed Jean Pierre's calm. They had aperitifs in the living room, the conversation turning inevitably to the war in Algeria. Claire said, "De Gaulle will end this madness. Colonies are a terrible burden. We were one hundred years in Indochina and were forced out." She praised Mendez-France for his negotiations that ended the Indochinese war. François moved the conversation to discussing New York. His parents had taken him there in the late 1920s to see the city and the Empire State building halfway through its construction. They made the crossing on the Ile de France, he recalled. It was his first of many trips to the United States, always on business. Allison asked him how they had fared during the war. He said that he had been mobilized and was stationed near Nice on the Italian border and when orders come to cease all hostilities he had purchased civilian clothes and made it back post haste to this spot where Claire and Jean Pierre were. "I did not give up Paris entirely," he said, "but I tended to the vineyards." He said that he knew Cleveland to be on Lake Erie but he had not been there. "You must invite me," he said to Allison.

Allison noticed that Claire served one warm dish only, a quiche that came out of the oven. The soup was cold. The salad had been made at the last minute. Cheese, bread and fruits came from the store. The wine was seven years old and came from the property. Jean Pierre praised it as a very fine Burgundy. Coffee was served in the living room but before Claire and Allison joined the men they moved the remains of the meal to the kitchen. "The dishes are for tomorrow," Claire said.

A clock sounded ten and François announced that his bed was waiting anxiously for him. He and Claire disappeared up a different set of stairs from the set used by Allison and Jean Pierre. The young set stayed in the living room for a few minutes. Then Jean Pierre stood up, took her hand, and said, "What a brilliant idea, going to bed." When they were at her door, true to form, he asked if he could join her in a few moments. "Of course," she said.

When he came into her room she was in bed with the lights off. The window was open, as were the shutters. Moonlight streamed in. She pulled back the covers for him and he slid into bed next to her. It was the first time she had felt the warmth of another body along side hers. He put an arm around her and kissed her, and started talking, whispering, really. "You might like to know that my mother thinks that you're terrific."

"How could that be? I haven't done anything."

"It's not what you do. It's who you are."

He was silent for a moment. She said, "Go on."

"What they see in you is an intelligent, accomplished woman who listens well – you're attentive – who makes the effort to understand the people around her, to contribute the right amount. You do very little to bring attention to yourself."

"That's so flattering. Your parents are wonderful just to have me here." He started caressing her and his conversation turned to how lovely she was and how fortunate he felt to be with her. Their night clothes came off and at first he placed her on top so that he could pass his hands over her shoulders and down her back to her waist. Then he was on top of her, keeping his weight on his elbows. In an instant it was done. She recalled that several friends had said that all your life you can remember that moment with your first lover and that your first lover maintains a special place in your heart. When they were side by side in each other's arms, she whispered, "I love you, Jean Pierre. Is it alright for me to say that?"

Of the few months that remained of Allison's stay in France, a goodly amount of time was spent in Jean Pierre's apartment. If there was any regularity it occurred on Sunday afternoons and evenings. On these occasions they acted as though they were newly-weds. He was affectionate in his considerate way and she felt herself mature as they established an easy camaraderie. He was always prepared to help Allison understand the colloquial expressions and the jargon found in newspapers. They conversed in French more than half the time. He proposed in late May, a month after the weekend at the vineyard. In a subsequent trip to celebrate their engagement, she met Claire's sister and husband, Marguerite and Clément. They lived in Dijon where he worked for an insurance company.

Allison dispatched the news to her family that she and Jean Pierre planned a marriage toward the end of summer and that she expected to take up permanent residence in Paris. She had written about Jean Pierre three times previously and described him in detail, particularly making the point that he worked for an American bank and spoke English well, albeit with an accent. The third letter was written after the first weekend at the vineyard and in it she explained Jean Pierre's family. This fourth letter, containing the important news, was not tentative. Allison told her parents what her future would consist of. She could not guess how her news would be received.

In the return mail, Allison received a letter from her mother, who laid out her plans. Her father had on his schedule a visit to the plant in England. They would fly to Paris to discuss events and meet Jean Pierre and, if possible, his parents. Allison noted a lack of any congratulations and as well, the absence of recriminations. The letter had a let's-see feel to it. She showed it to Jean Pierre. He read the letter and said, "I'll protect you through these difficult times." They both laughed.

Her parents had flown to Paris at Christmas, between the party at the university when Allison and Jean Pierre met, and her birthday party, the evening that Allison felt certain that something would develop between Jean Pierre and herself. Her parents had left her younger brother and sister with family and armed themselves with Christmas presents, all of them small and easy to pack. Her father purchased a tree on the street, perhaps four feet in height, which he decorated with cotton purchased at a pharmacy. It was a brief but warm occasion. Allison knew this second visit would be different. She expected her parents to apply pressure but she could not guess the form it would take. She knew them well enough to assume there would be no threats. The negotiations would be conducted with sweet reasonableness.

There were two lines of attack. The first was that Allison should complete her education. There would be untold benefits, they said, from obtaining a college degree at a well-respected institution. The second was that Allison and Jean Pierre had only known one another six months and as they were rooted in different cultures it would be wise to let marriage wait until the following summer, right after she graduated. As a lure, or as compensation, Jean Pierre was invited to spend any amount of time with them, particularly the two weeks around Christmas, and again in the spring, if he wished.

The parents met at the large flat on the Avenue Foch. They were extraordinarily civil to one another. Jean Pierre was an only child so there were no siblings in attendance, but Marguerite and Clément were brought in as distractions, or at least to prevent intensity from building up. Claire and François spoke fair English, as did Marguerite, but Allison's mother had to drag out her rusty French to talk to Clément.

In the end, Allison caved in. She couldn't bring herself to thwart her parents' wishes. She stayed in Paris until the last week of August, fell more deeply in love with Jean Pierre and became completely attached to the French culture and the French way of doing things. They decided that she would return to France in June of the following year to be married at the vineyard.

It did not work out that way. Allison was dismayed and more when Jean Pierre wrote that he would not travel at Christmas. He made no excuses, but broke the engagement. He did not say that he had met another person. He simply claimed that the trans-Atlantic nature of their relationship was too difficult to master.

Allison accepted that Jean Pierre's words were final. She would have to put him out of her mind. There were other men around. The colleges within less than a day's drive had hundreds of them in stock. She had only to identify one among many who would suit her needs. It turned out that he was Ned Bullard, from Connecticut and New York. She had met him at the end of her freshman year and stayed on the periphery of his life since then. Without Jean Pierre, she poured her affections into Ned. He responded and they were married in late summer. While there were no longer vineyards south of Dijon in her life, there was a summer home on Long Island Sound and housing, connections, clubs and college friends in New York City. These were the unspoken parts of the contract with Ned.

Allison's parents were silent on the rapid turn of events. Ned Bullard must have been what they were after. Having succeeded in keeping her in the Western Hemisphere they could not complain that she and Ned did not know each other well enough for marriage.

The Christmas after her marriage – this would be a year and four months after leaving Jean Pierre and France – Allison received a letter from Marguerite, addressed to her parents' home in Cleveland. The return address was Jean Pierre's apartment. It was a short letter crammed onto a Christmas card. There was news of the family and of Jean Pierre. She referred to him as JP, no doubt to save space. There was a woman in his life and Marguerite hinted something would come of it. Allison answered right away, giving her New York address, starting an annual exchange between the two of them. While her husband Ned knew a fair amount about finance, he knew no French. Even if he had, there would be no harm in his wife's catching up on the news of her old friends.

By the following year, Jean Pierre's wife had given birth to their first child, as had Allison. Two years went by before both had a second child, as though they were living synchronized lives. There were no more children for either. On her trips to Europe with her husband, Allison made no effort to see Marguerite, although they could have managed it. On the twenty-second Christmas, Marguerite announced that Jean Pierre and his wife had separated. Allison was forty-four and Jean Pierre must have been fifty or fifty-one. Claire and François were getting on and Jean Pierre was devoting more and more of his time running the vineyards. He had kept his apartment in Paris and Allison wondered whether he opened her Christmas card before Marguerite did. Allison thought that his involvement in the correspondence was unlikely. Jean Pierre and his wife lived in a different section of Paris than where his apartment was. Over the years, though, Allison guessed that it might have been Jean Pierre who suggested the contents of the Christmas card.

After the twenty-fifth Christmas, Allison wrote Marguerite saying that she and her husband would be in Paris in the month of May. A return note said that she would be happy to see Allison any time while she was in Paris.

In April Allison wrote giving the date that they would arrive. A return letter instructed her to telephone on arrival. Allison presumed that she would be telephoning the apartment, but she might be telephoning Marguerite in Dijon. She could not read the region of France into the phone number. On reaching Paris in the second week of May, she telephoned and Marguerite came on the line. She was at home in Dijon. They made arrangements to meet at Jean Pierre's apartment. Marguerite said that she hoped that Allison would come alone.

On the appointed morning, Allison told her husband that she was to meet Marguerite and that it would be an all-French session. She had to explain who Marguerite was and how she fitted into her year here as a student a quarter-century ago. Ned announced right away that he would ride an excursion boat on the Seine, one of the long ones, something he had wanted to do, and he knew the quay that they left from. Would she be back for the cocktail hour, he had asked.

Allison knew the subway to take, the stop where she would transfer, the stop to get off and the walk to the apartment. She wondered whether she would be met by Marguerite, or Jean Pierre, or both. She sensed as she pushed the button for the apartment one flight up that her life might change. A female voice came back: "*Oui?*" Allison said, "*C'est moi.*"

The buzzer sounded and the lock released. Allison walked up to find the door open. She and Marguerite embraced, Allison saying that Marguerite had grown to resemble her sister Claire. They chatted for only a moment when Marguerite said, "Jean Pierre is here." He came out of the bedroom and walked the few steps in the hall. He didn't say anything. They kissed briefly on the lips and stood looking at one another. "I would recognize you anywhere," he said, "but we have changed." Allison still hadn't said anything. Marguerite noted that the two lovers – she called them that – had a great deal to talk about. She pulled on a light coat, said goodbye and left.

Jean Pierre and Allison were standing in the middle of the living room, their arms around one another. "It's all my fault, really, it's all my fault," he said.

They started kissing. He kissed the same way he used to, she recalled. She had always liked his lips and the soft, sweet way he kissed her. "I think about you everyday," she said, breaking her silence. He smiled. "With me it's every evening." They sat close together on the sofa. He had an arm around her and was holding her tight. "Is your divorce final?" she asked. "Yes, three months ago. Remember that my wife and I had been separated a few years."

"What made you decide finally to divorce?" she asked.

"It was my wife. I was responsible for the separation but then my wife met a new man much to her liking," Jean Pierre said.

Allison remained quiet. Her eyebrows were arched up and Jean Pierre knew that she was asking for further details.

"What caused the separation, that's what you want to know," he said.

"Yes."

"People run out of love, you know, and why did we run out of love? We lost interest in one another, and why that? We had said everything and explored everything and we were empty."

"There are an infinite number of topics to talk about and explore."

"Yes, but you can't move beyond the limits of your partner. There are billions of topics, as you say, but we deal with finite minds."

"Were you dying of boredom?" Allison asked.

"Yes, and in the evenings I would ask myself what it would have been like to explore those topics with you," Jean Pierre said.

They paused for a minute then Allison asked, "Tell me the reasons why you decided against coming over that Christmas and broke the engagement."

"As I said, it was my fault entirely. But my parents were enormously persuasive. They didn't want their only child migrating to America."

"They might have had two more children, as my parents did."

"They ought to have thought of that much earlier. The inheritance laws may have played a part in this case. With one son there would be a very well-known vineyard in Burgundy owned by me. With three children, under our laws the estate would be divided three ways. I never explored it with them in detail."

"Do they remember the part they played in your life? I mean, do they ever bring up the matter?" Allison asked.

"No, they never bring it up, but my mother has it on her mind, perhaps on her conscience. Who knows if they have analyzed what they set in motion. If they talked about it they would have had to examine all the results."

Again they were silent. Then Jean Pierre asked, "How is your life, your marriage?"

"It's only one question, isn't it? My life and my marriage, one thing. I recall from my days here that a compliment you could pay a mediocre wine was to say that it was drinkable. Change the words around to describe my marriage."

"Are you running out of things to say to one another?" he asked.

"No, plenty of things to talk about, but they are not subjects of my choosing. I lead one life in my mind and another life out loud with my husband. He's a perfectly decent soul but after the birth of my second child I realized that I had made a mistake. Yet, I have those two children and they fill me with hope and a sense of accomplishment. And I love them, of course."

"Yes, my two children mean to me exactly what yours mean to you," Jean Pierre said.

JUNIOR YEAR ABROAD

PART 4

They stayed close together, both comfortable in each other's arms. Their conversation would slow to a stop as they searched for the next topic. After one such pause, she asked, almost blurted out, "What should we do next?"

"I'm so glad you asked. Why don't I propose to you again?"

"I'm married, Jean Pierre."

"It didn't sound like a permanent bond, one that couldn't be loosened."

Again a brief pause.

"Our four parents are alive. Do you think they will rise up again?" Allison asked.

"No, this time they will reflect on the havoc they caused." Then he asked, "If you do come, how soon will that be?"

"Propose to me and I'll come as soon as I can, but of course I'll still be married."

She kissed him as a way of accepting his proposal. Then she said,

"Don't take all the blame. My parents were using the same arguments as yours and I agreed with them at the crucial moment."

He moved from the sofa to the desk and wrote for a bit. He handed her a piece of paper with five addresses and telephone numbers: his bank in the Place Vendôme, his parents' in Paris, his parents' at the vineyard, his in Paris, and Marguerite's in Dijon. "Telephone me everywhere and I'll be at one of the numbers. I'll come fetch you, wherever you are."

She made it back to the hotel in time for cocktails. Ned described his afternoon and she hers, implying that she had been with Marguerite and that they had had tea at her place. They went to London for five days then flew home. Allison wavered and dreaded the scene she would create if she asked Ned for a divorce. On the plane she relived a Saturday spent years ago with Jean Pierre in Chartres. When he asked her to take the train there and spend the day, she said, "Kitty, Penny and Ann and I have been there, last month, in fact. Are you certain that I should make a second trip so soon?"

He said, "I'll have the pleasure of your company and perhaps I can show you things you missed before." It was as he said. He knew the history of the cathedral, that it had been built in a hurry, requiring only thirty years from start to finish, all done in the middle of the thirteenth century. Much of the work had been performed by men from the region who might give a half-year of labor for the greater glory of God.

Inside the cathedral they selected seats along the nave to watch sunlight pour through the large circular stained glass window. He had brought a basket containing lunch and when they were done with the interior they moved outdoors and he led her around to the back of the cathedral where there was no one. It was the first day of spring and they took off their coats and installed themselves on a bench. He looked up and told her that these were elm trees around them. He fell quiet and they listened to the breeze rustling through the leaves. He got up from the bench and walked farther away from the cathedral to survey buildings that were taking the place of farmland. He put his hands against a stone wall that marked the end of the cathedral property and Allison could see that he was taking in all within his view. She let him be and understood that he was experiencing the time and place. There were no events taking place that he might react to, or over which he might exercise a degree of control. The surroundings were leading him. When he returned and took his place on the bench she rearranged his hair. He didn't need the attention as the wind had only made minor alterations. He kissed her hand then reached for the basket and spread out the lunch he had brought. After a while, they walked to the center of town, not far, to a hotel called Le Grand Monarque. He felt that Henry IV had had some connection to the town. Perhaps he had been crowned in the cathedral and that this hotel was named in his honor. He admitted that his comments were speculative and should not be taken seriously. They had coffee and cake before walking to the train station. It was that afternoon that Allison caught an important glimpse of Jean Pierre's character. He sought the meaning buried beneath the obvious. He liked the land, life and living things, and nature and its cycles. There was simplicity about him and while he did not avoid complications presented to him by modern society, he preferred to be partners with the countryside, the land and people who lived off it. This last point she learned on her first weekend at the vineyard. He treated the families who worked on the place neither as equals nor inferiors. In his own direct way he made contact with each person, understanding their capabilities, interests and aspirations. His attention to the individual was the opposite of the control imposed on him by his parents in the matters surrounding him and Allison. She had seen several children come and take his hand when he would appear in their vicinity and walk with him to his destination.

Allison contrasted Jean Pierre's view of life with that of active people who engaged life and participated in shaping events. Her husband and his male friends were part of that group. She could not attach any right or wrong with either attitude but she preferred the introspective personality to the driven, achieving one. In the company of one or the other, she felt that there were greater rewards for her in reaching for simplicity, with more time available for an inner life and personal reflections.

While she understood why she liked, admired and loved Jean Pierre, she had only an inkling why Jean Pierre liked her. They were always in harmony and it was obvious to both that they found serenity when they were together. Other than that, she couldn't say.

On the flight from London to New York, as Ned put his head back and closed his eyes, Allison reviewed some of the stories she had heard of people who had spent their junior year abroad. Most women escaped untouched but two of her friends had had love matches that ended on a bad note for the same reason that hers had. In a joke to herself, she referred to it as parental guidance. Parents who were not doing very well leading their own lives were insisting that a child live according to their rules, guaranteeing disasters. A third person, an acquaintance from her parents' generation, had reacted violently to the news that her daughter planned to marry a Frenchman. Having lost the challenge, this mother disowned her daughter and never acknowledged the existence of two grandchildren, even though they, the wife, husband and two children came to America regularly to visit relatives.

Allison and Ned flew in on a weekday afternoon. The following morning he went to work. When he returned late that afternoon she asked him for a divorce.

"For Christ sake, Allison, get me a drink, will you?"

She did as he asked and fixed one for herself.

"Everyone's getting divorced. Whom did you meet in Paris that afternoon?"

"A fiancé from a couple of decades ago, from my year abroad."

"Has that been festering in you all along, all the time we've been married?"

"In varying degrees."

"Is he that much better than I am?"

"No, but different."

"How can I talk you out of this?"

"I don't think you can, Ned."

"Do you realize this means lawyers and dividing property and all that mess?"

"I don't want anything. You've been a perfectly decent husband, Ned, and we're not having any of that."

"When do you want to leave?"

"I have a reservation at a hotel near the airport. I want to talk at length with the children. I'll fly out tomorrow morning."

"If it doesn't work out, please don't come back here. I couldn't take it."

"Agreed, Ned."

He found his suit coat, a magazine, and keys and left without saying a word. Allison guessed he would go to a neighborhood restaurant and return when he knew she would have left. She took a taxi to JFK, having packed two medium suitcases. She telephoned her two children from the hotel and explained what had taken place years ago, before she was married to their father. Her son said that he didn't understand adults, not having been one very long. He promised to come to France early in the summer. Her daughter cried and said that there was more to love and marriage than she suspected. "I must meet him," the daughter said. Her last telephone call was to Jean Pierre, who was asleep in his apartment. It was three o'clock Friday morning in Paris. He wanted to know where he could meet her. She suggested that he should return to his apartment right after work and she would get from the airport to his place by taxi. Jean Pierre said he would track her flight by telephone to the airline.

He was standing on the sidewalk in front of his building when the taxi pulled up. He read the meter and paid the driver. There were but two suitcases. He remarked, "The Duchess of Windsor always travels with six or eight."

Allison, Jean Pierre and the two suitcases made it up the flight of stairs. "The last thing I did was to have a very stiff drink with my husband. I might have managed without it knowing I was coming to you."

"The drink filled you with courage. In your place, I might not have been able to face a husband of twenty-some years and say that you are off to another man."

"With luck, you and I still might have a longer marriage than the ones we've had," she said. She asked, "Are we off to the vineyard for the weekend?"

"Yes. I've called my parents. Monsieur Guillaume has retired. We will be met at the station in Dijon by Louis Fabre. The old Citröen is still on the place and Louis keeps it running."

"How will your parents react?"

"Starting ten years ago, my mother began asking about you. Then her sister Marguerite shared the correspondence. She's been following developments for quite a while. She told me that she would put flowers in our bedroom. Let's see if she puts a red rose on your pillow."

GORDON MCNAIR

GORDON MCNAIR

PART I

When the first symptom arrived, Gordon McNair wondered if it was part of the often-referred to mid-life crisis. The expression had joined the lexicon and mid-life crisis described to him the actions of men forty-five and over who left their wives, had affairs, or bought convertibles. He hadn't done any of these but was tempted. Gordon McNair was much like the other American men his age. He did not address the philosophical questions: what is life all about, why am I here, what is my purpose on earth? He did ask himself, however, am I getting my share of the benefits available, am I experiencing the thrills, am I enjoying the pleasures, and finally, am I sleeping with a variety of women?

Gordon could answer a partial YES to the first three but a resounding NO to the fourth. It wouldn't do to cheat on his wife. She had been phenomenally pleasing and generous to him in the important matters. The issue remained and it came down to this: is it necessary to sleep with several women besides his wife to feel that he had led a complete life?

Gordon calculated that the mid-life crisis did not come and go in a day. For him it had appeared at forty-five and he put the cause at boredom, not dissatisfaction with the life that he and his wife led together. He would become bored once in a while with his work. It was repetitive. He became bored with a few of his friends. He had known them too long. He thought he needed a new job and a new set of friends but recognized the impossibility of making those changes. Gordon could not understand why he thought sleeping with a variety of women would cure a mid-life crisis that had at its roots his work and a few of his friends.

As far as how long this feeling lasted, Gordon guessed that thirty years was about right. If the mid-life crisis insinuated itself into the average man's life at forty-five, then it would vanish at seventy-five. He might not live that long. He was already fifty-two. The peak of the sensation would probably come in the middle, when he was sixty. Those would be the dangerous years. He concluded that most men would have thirty years to experiment. He needn't be impetuous. Certainly he had to take care that his wife never found out. She deserved better. She had been devoted to him.

Gordon did not know whether women, his wife in particular, were subject to mid-life crises of their own. A few women philandered; he knew that. He guessed that on the whole they were more interested in maintaining the nest they had created than in flying around the neighborhood in search of thrills. He reasoned that if women were subject to mid-life crises the fact would be well-known, and men, husbands in particular, would not sense the need for extreme caution. After all, if both parties were sinning, the stigma associated with the act might tend to diminish.

Gordon McNair had fallen into the habit of walking for exercise Saturday mornings. About twenty people would gather at seven o'clock to circle the track of the local high school. The track was a standard quarter-mile, which Gordon could circle in five minutes. He walked twelve laps, or three miles, between seven and eight on Saturday mornings. A few of the walkers, incorrectly named, jogged half the time.

Most of the walkers had lived close by the high school twenty-five years or so. They knew one another well. Occasionally one family would move away to be replaced by another, then a walker would vanish while the new occupant of the house that sold might or might not hear about the activity and join up.

The walkers were not always the same individuals Saturday after Saturday. Most of the walkers were men. A few were wives. Gordon, a regular, was part of a small pack that carried on a continuous conversation. They discussed local, national and international politics. They volunteered movie reviews. They went over the books they had read and they repaired for coffee afterward to continue the discussions. By nine o'clock they had dispersed.

One Saturday morning a woman whom Gordon did not know passed him on the inside. As she went by he only caught the view from the rear. She wore a gray sweater and gray pants. These were not loose fitting sweats that were also called warm-ups. These were tight on her body and he could imagine what she looked like naked. Starting at the top he saw light-colored hair, either gray or blond or a mixture. The shoulders were wide and her back long. It was the long back that attracted him, and this was a new sensation. He had never experienced such a preference before and wondered how it had passed undetected all those years. He was fifty-two and had been in the grips of womankind since the age of fifteen or so. In the car en route for coffee with two other men, he asked, "Who was that tall number?" They told him that she was an administrator, maybe a nurse, maybe both, at the high school and they knew her from their days of attending PTA meetings. Gordon dropped the matter. He did not want to let on that he was captivated.

On Sunday afternoon, the next day, Gordon and his wife, Delia, drove a few miles to the home of a couple they knew. The daughter of this couple, Marguerite, had been married on the East Coast. She and her new husband were visiting for a few days so that all could see firsthand how well she had married.

The guests the age of Delia and Gordon knew one another and introductions were unnecessary. Among the guests were a few young people in the twenty-five to thirty range that Gordon and his wife did not know. Presumably they were friends of Marguerite, the new bride.

Gordon glanced around and spotted two tall young women who had the same body style as Saturday's jogger. It appeared to Gordon that one of these young women was married. She wore the requisite rings. Her husband stayed close, perhaps to cover shyness, perhaps to be introduced. The other woman could have been engaged to the young man who clung to her. The solitaire diamond so indicated. The engaged couple was seated for most of the afternoon in the garden. He kept an arm around the back of her chair, although Gordon did see that on occasion he had let his arm slip down around her shoulders.

The married woman wore a tight-fitting red shirt and brown trousers. There was a floral design on the red shirt. The unmarried woman wore a long sweater that went a distance below the waist. It appeared to be knit from thick wool. It must have been warm inside. She wore a skirt of light, silky material with a floral design as well. She wore red high heels, about three inches high. The effect was of two beautiful women that Gordon could not ignore. They were built the same -- tall, small breasts, long torsos, and slim legs.

The following Saturday, Gordon was able to confirm that the administrator in the gray warm-up suit had the same body as the two women at the garden party. She stood still in her crowd, chatting for a minute or so before her group set off. They were younger than Gordon and preferred jogging to walking.

Gordon's wife, Delia, was an Italian beauty. He knew he had married her for her looks but this didn't take away from her other charms. She had come one summer some time ago to stay with a family whose daughter had gone to Italy previously to stay with Delia's family. Gordon, at the time, was recently graduated from college and had become employed as an insurance salesman. As a man of action he knew that he might have Delia if he married her before her visa expired and she headed for home. Delia felt that marrying Gordon would be a romantic adventure. By comparison, she thought that her boyfriend in Naples was tiresome though persistent. Marriage to Gordon would solve everything. They were now on their twenty-ninth year of a good marriage. Their three children were comporting themselves correctly and advancing through the stages of life properly. Said differently, Gordon and Delia were blessed in many ways. There were no more pieces of good luck to be dropped into their lives as they had already received more than they could expect. They both looked at it that way.

Delia was short.

PART 2

Delia's father, Carlo Ascari, refrained from speaking about his early years in Naples, first under Mussolini, followed by the brief brush with the German Army, then during the American occupation from 1943 to 1945. Delia understood that her grandfather had paid an undisclosed amount of money to a functionary in the Italian military apparatus to keep his only son out of the army. Her father did not appear to be sickly at the time but a case was made that he had a weak heart and that his fragile physique would not withstand the hardships suffered by infantrymen. The certificate was obtained easily enough from a doctor known to the family and filed in the army's Naples offices.

Carlo Ascari finished his schooling and found work in the water district as a lowly keeper of records and plans. He did not venture out into the little nightlife there existed and avoided the friends of his parents. Many had sons who had been killed in North Africa or were now languishing as prisoners in Allied camps. His sole diversion, his reason for living, was Gabriella, a lovely flower whom he had met at school. They told one another that they would marry after the war. They had said these words in 1940. By 1944 they were prepared and anxious but both sets of parents advised them to wait longer. Their argument was that the white gown, the church bells and the minor festivity could only appear acceptable when the solders had gone home, taking their guns with them. They married in 1945. Carlo's heart recovered. He continued working for the city in the water works. Gabriella and Carlo found a modest apartment on a hill overlooking the harbor of Naples. They could see Capri in one direction and Mount Vesuvius in another. After the first son arrived, they moved into a large flat in the same building.

Carlo loved what the fates had sent him. Gabriella was pretty and had a delicious body. They had shown restraint in the final years of their courtship. When they were married, restrictions were abandoned. Carlo did not care for the few dark hairs on Gabriella's upper lip. He thought they marred her beauty. He did not make the connection between the superficial hair and her enormous lust for him. Perhaps this connection had not been made yet by medical science. Certainly Carlo did not know that the level of testosterone in a women's blood accounts for her libido. Gabriella had more than the usual amount coursing through her veins. Besides those few dark hairs on the upper lip, testosterone had given Gabriella her low-pitched voice and aggressive personality. Carlo had no reason to treat these traits as an ensemble. He held them separately. He became accustomed to the facial hair and no longer noticed it. He enjoyed the lower tones in her voice. She sounded secretive and conspiratorial at times. Her mildly aggressive personality brought out in him a desire for redress so that he learned to stand his ground, which he would not be inclined to do without her influence. Above all, his appreciation of her powerful sex drive overshadowed all his other feelings for her.

Gabriella was a master at controlling reproduction, with the result that they had but three children, two sons followed by Delia, who arrived in 1955. She grew up in a family in which dispute was not out of the ordinary. She and her brothers witnessed an occasional emotional flare-up lasting a day or two. The children accepted this behavior as normal. They also saw affectionate exchanges, heard romantic words and from time to time noticed erotic caressing. Delia brought her mother's personality intact into her marriage with Gordon. She did not, however, inherit the facial hair, with the result that it fell to Gordon to be the initiator. However she had enough testosterone to be a willing accomplice.

When Delia's brothers had left home to start their families, the father and mother, Carlo and Gabriella, entered into an exchange program in which an American girl would spend the better part of a year in their apartment in Naples, attending school, and learning the language. The guest student would be immersed in Italian as no one in the family spoke English. In exchange Delia would have a year in America. It hadn't dawned on her parents that she might not return.

Because Delia had finished her schooling by the time it came her turn to go abroad, she elected to devote a summer, but not longer. She came independently of any exchange program as she was no longer a student. It was 1977. Delia had learned a smattering of English from her guest, a girl named Shirley Moss. She was on her way to Florida, to the city of Daytona Beach, to spend four months with the Moss family.

Bikinis had been invented twenty years previously. Brigitte Bardot gave them her stamp of approval by sporting them on the beaches of the Riviera. They had become acceptable swimwear among young people anyplace where sand, sun and sea came together. Delia had her own collection of bikinis and wore them routinely, swimming and sunbathing on Daytona's sandy beach. She did not meet Gordon on the beach, but on the street in front of the house where she was staying. The McNair and Moss families lived on the same block. Although they were on the beach together soon after her arrival, it was not only the female form on display that attracted Gordon. After all, he had been in contact with female bodies since adolescence. Gordon found Delia to be a previously undiscovered element in his life, a European woman.

Delia thought that Gordon resembled the young men at home. In Italy, the Romeos and party boys might have different hobbies than their American equivalents but they treated women in the same fashion. In Naples, the young men clung together in small groups, working lightly at their jobs and chasing women with the sole purpose of taking them to bed. Conquests and failures along this line were important topics of conversation in any male crowd. Delia found that Gordon worked hard. He had finished at his university and began selling insurance for homes and cars. He spoke of having his own agency one day. He had a fair amount of explaining to do so that Delia understood his aspirations. His principal hobbies were fishing and playing softball. After two weeks in his company Delia concluded that although Gordon had studied commerce at the university and played sports in high school, he read neither newspapers nor books, and as a consequence knew absolutely nothing. It surprised her that his fine mind was empty. His two redeeming characteristics, she thought, were that he was kind and polite.

Gordon did not disappoint her on the romantic front. He started kissing her when moments presented themselves. He was eager to move ahead but Delia's respect for the Moss family held him at the water's edge. It wouldn't do that the Moss parents would be obliged to correct her conduct. Shirley, who was enjoying the summer before her final year in college, spent evenings together with Delia in such a way that ardent young men were kept at the appropriate distance. Delia never knew how Shirley might have spent the summer had she not arrived from Italy.

Delia, on finishing her schooling, had started at a bank. First she studied to be a teller, and then became one. It was part of her hiring agreement that she would have a summer off without pay for the purpose of mastering the English language. The manager to whom she reported thought that his branch could use her new skill when she returned. There were many Americans in Naples, some tourist, and the balance personnel from the American fleet for the Mediterranean, which used Naples as its homeport. There was ample correspondence in English to be deciphered.

Before the first month of her American experience had ended, Delia found that she and Gordon were running out of conversation. All the superficial and obvious things had been said. She decided to begin filling his empty mind. They started with the atlas in the living room of the Moss family. She made him find Naples on the map, then the islands of Sicily, Sardinia and Corsica. She explained to Gordon that Corsica was sold to France in 1768. One of her uncles had emigrated from Naples to France in the early years of the Mussolini era and became a French citizen. He chose to settle in Nice as many immigrants there spoke Italian. Delia made Gordon find Nice on the map. She told him that this region of France, which she had visited, was purchased from Italy in 1860, another date she knew. She explained the roles played by Victor Emanuel, Cavour and Garibaldi in the formation of the present-day Italy. She described the evolution of the Italian language, explaining the formative contributions of Dante, Boccaccio and Petrarch around the year 1300. The language had not changed greatly since these literary giants assembled it from the street Latin as it was spoken at the time.

Delia exhausted the information stored away in the mind of an above average student who had graduated from an Italian high school. To make her point about Dante, she had Gordon accompany her to the library where they sat in a reading room while she explained the *Divine Comedy* to him.

The part of Gordon's mind that could store valuable information came to life. He arranged all that Delia had told him in logical fashion.

There had never been such a person in his life. He wanted to break the barrier of the bikini in the worst way but was learning that there were restrictions to human interaction.

Elaine Manning was a native of Daytona Beach. She had never felt a need to move away because everything she wanted was at hand. After high school, she entered nursing school and on receiving her RN went to work at the local hospital.

The young male doctors in the hospital called her "The Body." There was competition for the title among other women on the staff but Elaine, it was agreed, deserved it most. She had been known as "The Body" since the age of sixteen when she developed into the best free-style swimmer at school. Several colleges in the region were prepared to grant her a scholarship but she decided that remaining in Daytona Beach was more to her liking. She enjoyed the ocean and the warm, comfortable life.

There had been men, starting in high school. Her two sisters, both older, took over her education. It was they who explained the workings of the female body and they who advised her on conduct with men. The idea, her sisters explained, was to keep the men at bay and allow them to approach ever so slowly. Both sisters were virgins when they married in their early twenties. After the sisters embarked on their new lives, it was left to Elaine to chart her own course. Her mother had not involved herself with giving Elaine advice.

Elaine's sisters had moved out of her life by the time she had reached the stage of being kissed and allowing men to touch her above the waist. The touching was done in an automobile, on a couch, or standing up, but never in the supine position. She knew the latter position would lead quickly to activity below the waist and she was not yet ready.

The activity that she had experienced so far was enjoyable and she wanted it to lead to the obvious conclusion. There were two conditions of her making. The first was safety and the second was that the men she selected could not overpower her emotionally. She needed average men for indoctrination, men who would not and could not attach themselves to her so strongly that they suggested marriage. She felt she needed to mature more completely before selecting a mate for life.

There was an ample supply of men to select from. They enjoyed sports, women, the company of men for drinking, and some were serious about their work. None were ready for marriage. Elaine allowed three of them to enter her life, each for about a year. From them she learned that they would take away anything she made available without the least thought of emotional entanglement. Inasmuch as she was in the playful and educational stage of her life, as she categorized it, she could find no reason why these men should turn serious. She did not want them to. She had selected men who would allow her to learn the sensation of being together as two people engaged in casual living on dates and outings. She outlawed weekends out of town and sleeping over in her apartment. When the first one of these three, a certain Carl, made his move, Elaine decided not to erect barriers. After a few times in bed with Carl, she concluded that the activity might be overrated, at least as he presented it. The second and third men were more sophisticated than Carl and this she determined on the basis that they introduced interesting variety to their lovemaking.

Three men over three years. Perhaps as many as one hundred occasions in bed. A firm grasp on what she liked. A deeply-held suspicion that marriage was no simple matter -- that if she were to marry she would fail. She had yet to feel the mystery of love.

At the age of twenty-five, a doctor from the hospital named Roy Brewster entered her life. He was a few years older than she. He found her irresistible. She found him acceptable. It was normal to marry at this age and Elaine was ready to accept his proposal if he offered it. Half the nurses married doctors, just as half the flight attendants married pilots. Elaine decided she wanted Roy Brewster. She felt she might fall in love with Roy, either before or after they were married. For Elaine, the time had come.

Roy Brewster was a family doctor at the hospital where they both worked. On their first evening out he made the point that his specialty was Family and Community Medicine. He wanted Elaine to know that the previous title of general practitioner had been supplanted. Elaine attached no significance to this distinction and said to Roy over dinner, "I know exactly what you do, title or no title."

"I wanted everything to be clear," he answered.

"You're not ashamed of what you do, are you?"

"No, of course not."

"Well, you sound sensitive."

Their first evening together consisted of defining positions. He told her that he had attended medical school in North Carolina and was not certain that accepting the offer made by the hospital was the best move for his career.

Elaine, annoyed at Roy's taking the time to explain his change in titles, wanted to deflate him but found no obvious way of doing it. But given time he might look better to her. He kissed her at the door of her apartment and told her that she was a beautiful woman and that he would telephone her soon. He did so two evenings later.

The courtship was brief and energetic. Elaine knew that Roy felt it was time to marry – he was twenty-nine – and she on her part could find no reason to delay. He was handsome, taller than she, and well paid. She knew exactly how much he earned.

They started sleeping together. It was the only time in their relationship that he slowed down and behaved in a sensitive fashion. He was a careful lover, satisfying his needs while making certain of hers. Roy proposed in bed. She had imagined that he would ask her to marry him when they were fully dressed rather than in this moment when she was vulnerable. How do you refuse a proposal when you are naked in bed, having just enjoyed a sexual encounter? Perhaps he had proposed to another woman while standing up and been refused. She accepted and he celebrated by engaging in sex with her again.

Five years of marriage persuaded Elaine, followed by her husband, that their life together had become pointless. At first there had been the diversion of sex, but the love to sustain it had never come, with the result that they lost the desire. There had been no children and they had made no effort to determine the reason. Both were pleased that they were childless when it became obvious that there was nothing of substance between them. They might have found a solution had either brought up the matter for discussion, but neither was interested. They did not seek counseling. Both knew that the marriage had failed, although they did not identify the reason.

During the fifth year of their marriage, Roy suggested that he take his two-week vacation alone so that he could explore alternatives in his career. They only discussed details to the extent that he wanted to change to another specialty, Internal Medicine, with a subspecialty in Cardiology.

When he returned he told her that he had found what he wanted in Miami and because there would be four years of training during which he would be at the hospital for long stretches, he suggested that they divorce. He told her that she might find a fulfilling relationship with another man. Elaine did not object. She asked him when he would be moving south. A divorce was started through the courts. She was surprised at how impersonal were the discussions that led to the dissolution.

After Roy left for Miami, Elaine moved to a smaller apartment and sold excess furniture. She began to rely on her family more than before. Mother, father, brother and sisters and the next generation were spread out nearby in Central Florida. She counted on one friend from high school days and on a few among the nurses at work. Most of her married friends drifted away. Elaine was not surprised that living alone did not differ appreciably from living with Roy. She had become accustomed to prolonged silences.

"What happened?" her mother asked her a few months after the separation.

"I realize now that there hasn't been much substance all along. How do you and Dad keep it going?"

Her mother explained that her husband was special and that she felt joy so often in his presence. Elaine told her mother that her father did not appear to be a special person. She went on by asking her mother to be more detailed.

"Your father cares about me, for one thing. I know by what he does that he's thinking about me when we are not together. Then he's a very sweet man, doing things around the house to please me without being asked. He's thoughtful."

Her mother was silent for a moment then she added, "There's no way you would know about this but he can't get enough of me nor me of him. He's very romantic." Elaine didn't want to enter into the details of her parents' life together so she fell silent. They were in the kitchen preparing Sunday lunch. After a while, her mother continued, "It's magic, dear. You do need plenty of luck."

Elaine thought over her mother's remarks while driving back to her apartment. She concluded that her parents' personalities blended, and that there was no set of traits that made for a good marriage. You couldn't find two people that fit a formula and expect that they would work it out together.

Elaine recognized that she and Roy had not shared interests. They talked about medicine, the cases they were involved with and the administration of the hospital. They gossiped about others they knew. Beyond that, neither had lifted their head to scan the horizon and find aspects of civilization that might interest them, a few topics that they could share. Elaine concluded that there must be life beyond nursing and having men look at her as she walked the corridors of the hospital in her crisp, white uniform. In her peripheral vision she could see that most men turned their heads as they passed by and she assumed that they would study the view, concentrating on her legs. She had two feelings about being the object of their attention. The first was that men were all the same in that they could not avoid studying her, if only for a moment. The second was that if this was to be the case, it might as well be she who had the noteworthy body. She could not reconcile her own empty life with the fact that there were quite a few dumpy, physically unattractive women working at the hospital who appeared to be happily married.

About a year after Roy moved to Miami, it occurred to Elaine that she might make a change also. Being a floor nurse was demanding work that she had mastered long since. It might be time to become a nurse at the local high school where she either administered simple medications or directed sick students to the appropriate physicians. The pay was comparable but the work carried less stress. The next level of responsibility was to become a Physician's Assistant in which she would act the part of a family doctor without the responsibility of prescribing drugs. She knew that three years of additional education and training were required to become a Physician's Assistant and was not certain that she could make the commitment.

Elaine might not have applied at the high school had it not been for a nurse at the hospital who suggested it to her. She would be thirty-one on her next birthday and it seemed to be the right moment to embark on a new career. She made the move.

After Roy left, men came around promptly. There were doctors and administrators at the hospital and an occasional person from her earlier years. The men wanted the same thing. One man explained that it was inconsistent for her to expect commitment before she made it possible for him to know what he was committing to. Elaine admitted that he had a sound argument but she pointed out that she was not looking for commitment just then. She turned him down because he was too slick.

On occasion she went to bed with one of her pursuers. There was loneliness to consider. She chose men who tended to be average in demeanor and about average in conversation and she knew that her purpose was to treat herself to a social life while avoiding the issue of marriage.

Elaine recognized finally that she had never experienced love. She told herself that she would know it when it came along. Roy had provided her with status and money but a year into marriage she was forced to conclude that their relationship was one of convenience, which could dissolve when confronted by the smallest challenge. Roy's desire, perhaps need, to change the path of his career had been enough to whisk him away. When he left, she had no objections. The world was not flat but the sensations she experienced in it had become so.

Two weeks previously, Gordon had noticed the tall woman in the tight warm-up suit. One week previously, they had stood about ten feet apart. Another walker stood between them. On this Saturday, as the two groups, the walkers and the joggers, were milling about getting ready to start at 7 a.m., Gordon found himself next to Elaine. He turned toward her and introduced himself. "I'm Gordon McNair." She gave her name then added, "I must know your wife from PTA. Haven't your children attended school here?"

"The two younger ones of three," Gordon said.

The conversation confirmed to Gordon what he already knew, that Elaine worked at the high school. It upset him slightly that Elaine knew his wife. He was not imagining an affair on the horizon but he enjoyed the sense of freedom that anonymity gave him.

"And how many laps do you run?" Gordon asked.

"We do about eight and it takes us thirty minutes. Then, as you've noticed, we walk and cool down for the balance of the hour."

Gordon smiled at her. "You and I may end up chatting during your second half."

With that Elaine and the others were off on their run. Gordon's walkers arranged themselves in the customary conversational groups and started. The runners passed the walkers a couple of times. When the runners had finished their laps and slowed to a walk, Elaine and Gordon were near one another. She asked, "What have you slowpokes been talking about?"

"We've gone over the big war and the current politics in Europe and we were discussing the times of the Revolution here and the writing of the Constitution."

"Where does all that brain power come from?"

"It's spread out among us. Don't you suppose much of it is filled with errors?"

"I would have no way of telling," Elaine said.

"Well, we read the papers and watch the news, so we start with those inaccuracies, then we add our own biases and stores of misinformation so I can't say that what we end up with is anywhere near the truth."

Elaine said nothing. She looked at him with his good posture and brown wavy hair. She didn't think he was as handsome as her former husband, but she recognized a self-effacing personality and an interest in the world that was absent in Roy. She wished that he would go on, but then, what would she say if he wanted her opinions? She thought to introduce a new, safe topic. "Do you follow Florida politics?"

He started with the outcome of the Florida vote in the year 2000 presidential contest and moved to actions of the supreme courts, both at the state and federal levels. He talked about the personalities involved and asked her whether she approved of how the vote went.

Elaine had learned long ago to get out of a tight corner by answering a question with a question of her own. "What happened to the secret ballot?"

"It's in good shape," Gordon said. "Just for not giving me your opinion, I won't tell you how I voted."

They discussed the important personalities that played a part in the aftermath of the vote. Elaine suggested that many actions were driven by the need to have a president to inaugurate on 20 January 2001.

They talked until the hour was up and as they dispersed to go their separate ways both said they looked forward to the following Saturday. Elaine wondered what they would talk about. She had enjoyed the conversation and found an ease and confidence in herself that she was not accustomed to. She guessed he made it easy for her to express her opinions.

On the way to coffee in the car with two of his friends, Gordon was asked what he and the tall number had discussed. Gordon went over the topics and one of his friends remarked, "She's a lovely looking woman, divorced, no children, perhaps on the prowl. So watch out!"

Gordon asked, "If I talk to her next week, what will you think?"

Gordon's friend didn't hesitate. "You'll be in trouble. It might be fun, though."

The three of them chuckled over what they imagined might take place in the future.

Elaine, once home, thought about the pleasure of talking freely and on equal terms with a man who was not in pursuit. She wondered, for the first time, if it were possible to change her life so that she might enjoy the sensation on a regular basis, not with Gordon, but with a different man.

Gordon went home to Delia and felt ashamed that he had exhibited an interest in another woman, particularly as his interest had sexual overtones.

On days that she ran, Elaine ate a midday meal and slept for an hour. She tried to work in a nap on Saturdays and Sundays. On Saturday afternoons she went to the public tennis courts where friends gathered at three o'clock. Elaine tended to play doubles and had settled on a partner who played the game about as well as she did. After tennis many of the players went to one of several eateries to sit outdoors and have supper. There were no men in her life at the moment. Elaine thought of it as a vacation from the inevitable emotional turmoil.

Gordon might or might not find Delia at home when he returned. She could be on errands or at the library. Because their three children had cousins in Italy, Delia had brought the language into their home. Gordon had been reluctant to learn to read, speak and write Italian but when the family started flying the Atlantic in the summer, he understood the wisdom of it. Their children were being raised with bilingual facility. Delia had worked hard to learn English, particularly the grammar, and did not tolerate errors in speech in her home. Gordon found out that his visits to his in-laws were progressively more fruitful as he learned his way around their language.

Gordon had understood long ago that while he had earned a degree from a respected university, it was Delia who was devoted to learning about civilizations and filling her mind with the ways of the world. She was the intellectual while he was the worker bee who earned the wherewithal to support a family. He loved her for the way she was. She would be off to Italy with one of their children in four weeks. He would follow ten days after with a second child. The third was in Spain for a year of studies. Gordon could not get it out of his mind that there would be a few days when he would be alone, the child who would accompany him still being in school, away from home.

Gordon and Elaine continued half-hour long conversations on their Saturday morning walks. Because he knew a fair amount about Italy, its history particularly, including the Roman days, it was easy for him to explore that topic. Elaine was familiar with a bit of the material and could contribute occasionally to the conversation. She had a curious mind and followed the discussion as it evolved week to week.

In the month leading up to Gordon's ten days without his family, Elaine felt her interest in Gordon grow from curiosity to admiration, perhaps tinged with envy. She did not admire him so much for what he was but for what he signaled to her -- that there were men, civilized, cultured men, who could hold her interest and bring hope that there might be one such man who would come her way and move into her life. Her life was full except for the void a man could fill. In the years that she and Roy had been divorced, she would speculate from time to time that her life had men passing through, but that none of them settled down for a life-long stay. When she thought about this aspect of life, she believed that not one of these men she had known intimately had the characteristics that could make it possible for him to be a permanent part of her life. So far, all her men had been provisional. However, she classified Gordon as a man who comes along rarely, who demonstrates that life-long unions are possible and preferable to the temporary liaisons she was accustomed to. Elaine was experiencing awakening and desire. She envied Delia and Gordon for what they had.

Gordon found pleasure in divulging to Elaine what he knew about Europe. He knew he was playing the part of teacher, and he knew as well that the role could only be played so long before redress is required. Elaine would have to find her own topic and divulge all she knew about it to an attentive Gordon. In any event, Gordon would have to leave off his role as educator. Gordon had learned this from Delia. He did not possess a reservoir of information that he could dispense to her. She understood the formula and moved slowly in the education of her husband. She was invaluable to him in conquering the Italian language but she left most of the chore to books, tapes and records. Her rewards to her husband for learning were frequent and perfumed.

Gordon could not get the long beautiful body out of his mind. One Saturday Elaine came to the track in a pair of white shorts, shorter than those she wore on the tennis court. She did have a perfect body. He had to concentrate to carry on his end of the conversation.

When the time came for Delia to fly to Italy, Gordon said to Elaine, quite simply, "I'll have to fend for myself for a week and some." Without skipping a beat, Elaine answered, "You must let me cook a meal for you."

GORDON MCNAIR

PART 5

Having extended the invitation, Elaine set a date and instructed Gordon to find her address in the telephone directory. They decided on six-thirty to seven. Elaine said that she would keep the meal simple. She thought a salad and a roasted chicken from the market would be about right.

The weather was warm and dry. A light breeze came in off the ocean. She dressed as she might for any activity: skirt, blouse and sandals. As she dressed she reflected on how Gordon had started a friendship limited to the track on Saturday mornings. She was certain that he was enamored of her body. Long since, she had recognized that a certain class of men wanted to see her nude, wanted to hold her, to feel her, to kiss her.

Of course she had discussed such men with other women who concluded that they, the women, were being used when men sweet-talked about being captivated yet were inattentive and drifted off once the love act had taken place. Elaine viewed the sexual attention as a normal response on the part of men who liked what they saw. She had told herself that the right man could come along but that his love-making would have little to do with how attractive she found him. If they were attracted to one another it would be for reasons of the mind.

Elaine had had a few very brief adventures with married men but she did not want a married man to break his vows and start life anew with her. Her theory was that these men wanted to see if she was as good in bed as they had imagined. When they discovered that she was a normal woman who could give them pleasure but not ecstasy, they would drift away satisfied in their exploration but uninterested in further pursuit.

Gordon was relieved that Elaine lived in a different part of town. There would be no chance that a friend would see him enter a supermarket to buy a bottle of wine and cut flowers. He knew Italian wines and bought his favorite. He was aware that what he was doing was insane, risking everything of value in his life.

Hers was a second floor apartment with a view of the beach. She let him in and they moved to the kitchen where she found a vase for the flowers. While the flowers and vase were still in her hands, he leaned over and kissed her on the cheek. She set the vase on the kitchen table and turned toward him. He put his arms around her and said, "I didn't know I had so much pent-up."

Elaine hadn't expected the moment to arrive so soon but as she recognized that certain events would be inevitable before the evening came to a close, she took Gordon's hand and led him into the bedroom. It seemed like the natural thing to do. He sat on the bed. The sun had set. Standing directly in front of him she removed her skirt and blouse and took a step toward him. He reached out for her and the thoughts, hopes and plans he had been harboring for a month began expressing themselves.

It was still twilight as they had entered the bedroom. An hour later, when she awoke, it was dark. She passed her hand over his face and hair. She said, "We've forgotten dinner." He held her and kissed her face and neck without saying anything. She released herself and said, "We were hungry a while ago."

He said, "We could make a life together, Elaine."

"I know we could, but it would be a hurricane sweeping through your life. I hate to think of the wreckage. You already have all there is to be had in life."

They dressed and placed the simple dinner on the table. Gordon opened the wine and announced that he needed to drink some presently. "So do I," she said. "Wine goes well after love," she added.

They had been talking lightly, mostly about the people at the track, giving their various impressions. When they had finished and were dividing the remains of the wine, Elaine said, "In a moment, we're returning to the bedroom. I want you to get your fill of me, get as much as you can, anyway you want, long, slow, complete. When you leave tonight, you leave with all the sensations I can bring out in you, and you will know me, the woman in me, as well as you ever will."

"I'll miss you all the more, Elaine."

"That's not been my experience. You've been interested in my body, certainly not my mind and personality, which I feel are average. My body seems to drive some men wild. I knew I would enjoy your hands exploring me, but I know that once you've done that, it's just about over. No man of quality has wanted to build a life with me." Elaine paused for a moment. Then she said, "I have a powerful sex drive, did you notice?." After another pause, she asked, "Did you know I've been married?"

"Yes, one of the men at the track knew that."

"Well, my husband walked away, but it was not a hardship for me. Someway, somehow, we had never connected intellectually, or spiritually, or however you say that."

"What are you trying to say?"

"That he walked away from my body and sex with me. He had it at his disposal for five years and availed himself less and less over time. Having a beautiful body has its rewards, but they seem to be temporary, even fleeting, if the two of you can't mix the real cement to make it stick."

"That's a beautiful analogy. Is it original with you?"

"Just this instant. To continue, if you and I were to try to make a life together, there's a good chance that our efforts would wind up where my husband and I did."

"And where was that?"

"In a divorce court."

"Do you think it would be that bleak for us?" Gordon asked.

"We're not starting out as equals. I might not catch up. To attract someone I want to keep, whom I will value, I have ten years of work ahead of me. I'm sure of that now."

Gordon said nothing. Elaine went on. "You leave here with all your needs for my body satisfied and your questions answered. There shouldn't be any longing, any leftover or pent-up desires. You're a married man and you're going back to your wife. This is a delightful evening for me. For you it should be confirmation that you can have a little of this and plenty of that but you can't have everything. You could end up with nothing."

"You're wise for your age, Elaine."

"I guess you have everything and want more. It's a slippery path."

"Will we chat on the track?" Gordon asked.

"Yes, no doubt as though nothing had happened."

"Of course a great deal has happened."

When they were on the bed and starting to undress one another, she said, "In this month or so, I've come to understand that it's not you I want, it's what you have as a person that I want. I've needed it all along and not known what it was. What do I have to do to attract and keep someone like you, someone who makes me feel the way I feel tonight?"

"It's marriage to the right man that you want. Is that what you're talking about?" Gordon asked.

"Yes. I suppose that's what I've wanted all along, starting soon after Roy and I split up. The right marriage is what I'm looking for."

Gordon sensed that Elaine was formulating her longings into words for the first time. They were lying on her bed with most of their clothes off and Gordon thought to himself how odd the situation was.

Elaine started talking again. "I have the sexual part figured out, obviously, and I can be affectionate, particularly when it's returned. And my character's OK. I don't have any great flaws that I can detect. It's the rest of it that I've never mastered, or even encountered. I believe it's the closeness that comes from exchanges at the intellectual level. I've sensed this closeness between us and that's why you're here tonight. I wanted to affirm that to you. I want to be a lover to a man with whom everything is right."

"You're a lovely woman, Elaine. You know what you're looking for. You attract a great number of men. It's just a matter of selecting the right one."

"It hasn't been that easy," Elaine said. They stopped talking and became interested in one another. After a great deal of exploring and activity, it had reached midnight. They were standing at the door. Elaine had slipped on a bathrobe. Gordon had his arms around her. "I know what I had with Roy," Elaine said. "We led two parallel lives in one house. So many seem to have that. I want two lives that converge."

"For someone they call 'The Body' you do your share of thinking," Gordon said.

GORDON MCNAIR

PART 6

The impression Gordon left on Elaine, the principal impression, was that he carried around a vast body of knowledge. He knew the Italian language, the history of Italy, portions of the history of Europe and the politics of the United States. Elaine realized that she did not know enough about any of these topics to judge how well Gordon was grounded. It was clear that he could talk easily when he ventured into these areas. The bonds between them, she concluded, were based on his interests and their combined willingness to talk and listen. Their conversations at the high school track had not consisted of the usual banal examinations of local people and matters. Gordon, Elaine decided, was interesting. She concluded also that she was less interesting than he was because she did not hold in her brain the results of twenty some years of reading about, reflecting on and sorting out related materials. Gordon had not said so but she guessed that his interest in the workings of the Congress came in part because he was aware of the part played in ancient Roman affairs by their Senate.

Elaine wondered about Gordon's wife, the pretty, dark-haired mother of three. Were her interests the same as her husband's? Did they share an interest at the core and branch out on their own? She had no way of knowing. In the week after Gordon came to dinner, in a moment of revelation, Elaine sensed that she should take seriously a notion that had been near the surface for a few years, that she should learn Spanish. This language was spoken by a quarter of Floridians, by her estimate, and the ability to speak Spanish, even the common phrases, would help when conversing with the parents whose youngsters came to her infirmary at school.

The Community College in Daytona Beach was a substantial affair. Elaine knew in general that it was a stopping-off place for students finishing high school and also an opportunity to resume learning for people long beyond their school years. It was a simple matter to enter the parking structure after work, at about 5:30, and find her way to the bookstore where catalogs were on sale.

Elaine asked for the whereabouts of the cafeteria. Once in line she thought that coffee and pie would suffice. She was eating dessert first. After paying, Elaine hoped to find a place along the wall where she might read the catalog in peace. She spotted a table for two, one place with an empty chair and the other seat part of a bench attached to the wall. She sat down, aware that there were people at the adjoining tables, a couple on the right and a middle-aged man to her left.

She expected that the middle-aged man would engage her in conversation. He had finished his meal and was reading a magazine and must have been observing her because when she had taken the last bite of pie he turned and asked. "Looking for a course to take?"

Elaine had noticed him on sitting down but now she went over his face and dress. His original brown hair was graying. He was clean-shaven and his eyebrows were trimmed. He did not wear glasses although he was holding a magazine. He wore a dress shirt open at the collar with a pen and pencil set in his breast pocket. He was tan on the surfaces that Elaine could see. She knew that many Floridians use the beach and that he might be a regular stroller, possibly a swimmer.

She answered his question. "I thought I would look into Spanish."

"May as well. We've become a province of Cuba and on our way to being the capital of South America."

"I hadn't heard that."

"Do you know any Spanish?"

"Ten words. I couldn't construct a sentence."

"You'll enjoy yourself, but to be honest, it's hard work."

"And what do you take here?"

"I like ancient history. I wish I could read the old pieces in the language they were written in. I'd love to know classical Greek and Latin, but I have to be satisfied with a phrase here and there."

"Sounds like an interesting hobby."

"Well, it is. The material doesn't change over the years. I have a pretty good book collection at home, all in English, of course."

They fell silent, but only for a moment. The man said, "I'm here Tuesdays and Thursdays at this hour. At this table, I might add."

"If I sign up for a class on those nights we might see each other again." Elaine stood up and added, "I'm Elaine Brewster."

The man, who had been studying her, said, "I'm Trevor Conby. With a name like Trevor you must know my lineage is English."

Elaine deposited her tray and walked to the parking structure with a catalog in hand. At home she examined the courses offered in Spanish and found one for beginners in the early evenings of Tuesday and Thursday. She had left Trevor Conby with no intention of coming to class two evenings per week but then there would be conversations with Trevor and the session lasted only fifteen weeks and if she was to learn Spanish she may as well be serious about it. A connection to Trevor could not have romantic overtones. She was conscious of the difference in their ages. It would be based on friendship only, a first for her.

Trevor was good to his word. When she entered the cafeteria on the first evening of classes she looked in his part of the room. He had placed the dishes in front of him and his tray on the other side of the table. He was holding a newspaper and this time was wearing reading glasses. He looked up as she approached. He smiled and said, "I see you've made a commitment."

"Yes, two nights a week, Spanish for beginners."

The conversation became personal. They found out that they lived four blocks apart and that both used the beach. On the issue of why they had not met, he said, "Say you played on Saturday and I played on Sunday at the same tennis club for thirty years; we might never see one another." They agreed that they should walk and swim some time. They did not exchange telephone numbers but did so on the following meeting.

Studying Spanish became an everyday affair. With two three-hour classes per week to prepare for, the five remaining days were filled with homework, unless she was going out. The teacher had recommended a book containing the conjugation of a few hundred verbs and a particular Spanish-English dictionary. Elaine enjoyed being a student. Gordon, on hearing the news from her on their Saturday mornings together, exchanged information on irregular verbs, which he thought were the most difficult aspects of learning a new language.

Trevor telephoned one Sunday afternoon to suggest a walk on the beach. He came to her address and they headed out together. She wore the same short white shorts that she had worn on the track once. Her purpose was manipulative. She wanted to see whether Trevor could be made to comment on her figure. He didn't take the bait.

Trevor wore khaki shorts and a white shirt with long sleeves, and a hat. His legs were thin and he had no stomach. Elaine supposed he had always carried the correct weight. When Elaine commented on how fit he appeared, he did allow that he was in good shape for an antique.

Elaine said, "You can't be an antique. You don't squeak when you move."

"Well, sixty-four years old, if you prefer. I've been blessed."

He went on to talk about his wife, telling Elaine that she had been taken from him two years previously. Then they discussed his marriage.

"How long were you married?"

"Thirty-seven years, four children."

"How would you sum it up?" Elaine asked. "I really want to know what contributed to its success."

"Well, you're right about success. Only a few stay married if it's a failure. I woke up one morning and she wasn't in bed. I went downstairs and found her in the living room where she'd been all night, reading *Gone with the Wind*. Must have been around 1975. It wasn't published that year, of course. She read the book at one sitting. She was impulsive that way and she liked most anything new. Any adventure. Loved to travel. She especially liked going to New York. Had her favorite hotel. We went to plays, museums, Carnegie Hall and the Metropolitan Opera, then Lincoln Center. We must have taken that trip once or twice a year. The radio was always tuned to the opera Saturday afternoons. I would call her a great lover of culture. Tremendous reader."

"How about on a more personal level?" Elaine interrupted.

"You mean around the house?"

"Yes. Between the two of you."

"My career was as a broker, stocks and bonds. I managed other people's money. I managed our investments but she took care of our money. Once it arrived in the house it was hers to spend. She saved up for those trips."

"On an even more personal level than that?" Elaine pressed Trevor.

"She was completely agnostic. Told me one day that she had severed all ties with the Almighty. She was convinced you are allowed one ride on the planet then it's the next person's turn. She had a light touch. I don't mean you had to hold your sides but when you were in her company there were few serious moments. Not interested in gossip. Had legions of friends. It's hypocritical but we had a service for her that filled the church. As a lover, sometimes wild with passion, other times more subdued, but we had some great moments."

"Go to the fundamentals, if you will," Elaine said.

"You sure bore in, Elaine. She was kind and thoughtful and kept a lovely home, with some help. I learned to cook in self-defense. Very often she'd meet me at the door with a glass of sherry. She'd know when the Dow had slipped. Wonder we didn't become alcoholics." Trevor stopped and as an afterthought he said, "Fundamental traits, you ask about. We were happy to be together."

At the end of the conversation they turned around and walked in the opposite direction on the beach. Trevor said, "By your line of questioning I would guess that you were asking for a formula that leads to a successful marriage. Is that about it?"

"Yes. Fair enough. My marriage failed. I want to try again but this time it has to work. You didn't lay out a formula for me."

"For the simple reason that there isn't one."

"There must be ingredients. A good marriage isn't an accident. Are you conscious of why it worked?" Elaine asked.

Trevor looked at Elaine head to toe. She was about an inch taller than he was. He wanted to say that he would love to be part of her life, but he knew she wouldn't share his point of view. He was about twenty-five years older than she. He said, "Let's examine the easy parts. The two personalities must have fine characters. There are no good marriages when one party or the other, or both, are selfish, ignorant, thoughtless, untrusting, inconsiderate, boorish -- I'm running out of adjectives. Decent people, that's what you need. People who want to make a go of it, who respect each other, who understand the needs of the other, all the business that's so obvious. The rest is magic. I can tell you a few things. We had those interests in common, the traveling and the trips to New York and the cultural events. Then the physical part. It was emotional and specific, never casual, nothing offhand. My wife did not have a beautiful body but she loved intimacy and affection and liked a prolonged session with chatter thrown in. And she did plenty of thinking about our life together, particularly the kids, on getting them civilized and educated. I wouldn't say that I found her endlessly fascinating but she was a great companion. I always loved being with her."

"That's a great tribute, Trevor. I don't suppose another woman will measure up to her."

"On the contrary, Elaine. I know what it is, experienced it for thirty-seven years. I'd start up with you if you weren't so damned young. We wouldn't have the same relationship that I had with my wife, but we'd work out something very satisfactory."

Elaine reached out and took Trevor's hand. It was an impulsive move. She had no idea where Trevor's words came from. He continued, "Between you and me there's plenty of good raw material. When it's in place and you want to make it work, it works."

They walked slowly to her apartment without saying much. They had uncoupled their hands when they left the water's edge and were walking on the soft sand.

When they reached her place, she asked him in for tea. As she was preparing it he went out on the terrace and surveyed the approaches to the beaches. He examined the flowers and herbs that she was tending in a series of pots. When they had finished tea, they moved toward the door. Unselfconsciously he placed his hands at her waist. He kissed her on the lips and brought his arms up around her body. He was gentle and thorough. Elaine thought he was making the kiss last for a day or two. He said, "Goodnight, lovely Elaine. I wouldn't wish it on you that you were sixty-four, but I sure wish I were forty."

The Community College made it a practice to hire native speakers for their language classes. While all teachers were conversant with the languages they taught, the quality of teaching varied from class to class. Methods differed.

The teacher in Elaine's class was named Arturo Valdez. He was born in Cuba and came to the United States in 1961 at the age of fourteen. His father had been an established physician in Havana and had decided to leave the island two years after Fidel Castro came to power. The father, Fernando Valdez, had planned for this eventuality during the last years of the Batista regime by moving some of his assets to a bank in Miami. When the family of four left the Havana airport by commercial flight, each member was allowed to take but twenty dollars out of the country. Fernando told the police officer who was dealing with their documents that he had brought one hundred dollars to the airport by mistake. The extra twenty dollars would have to be a gift. Both parties were satisfied with the arrangement.

Fernando had been to medical school in the United States. He was fluent in English and was able to associate himself with a hospital in Miami. He was required to pass examinations and in short order was treating patients, some from the Cuban colony, a few of whom had been his patients in and around Havana.

The son, Arturo, upon finishing at university, had been under slight pressure from his father to enter medical school. Arturo turned down his father and was surprised that the reaction was mild. "What would you like doing?" father asked son.

"I would like to be in the medical equipment business, supplying hospitals and doctors' offices. I was thinking of radiological and magnetic resonance imaging equipment. I think I could make a good living at it."

"There is a great deal of competition here in Miami. I know of several firms in that business," Fernando said.

"Dad, I'll move up the coast until I locate a city that needs me."

"Will you stay on the Atlantic Coast?"

"Yes. I want to be able to see Cuba out of my second floor window."

They both laughed and both knew that the son was expressing an urge to see Cuba again, not permanently, but for a good look.

"Both sides appear to be dug in," the father said. "Speaking of Cuba, it's a shame that we can't exchange freely: people, ideas, and cultures."

"I may have to move as far north as Daytona Beach. I hope it's not too far," the son said.

"Daytona Beach. That's nothing. Your sister's married and living in Madrid. Thank heavens for airplanes. We do get our annual visit."

Arturo carried out his plan. His father financed the venture. Arturo married an Anglo woman who produced two children, lighter in skin color than their father. They lived in a two-story house not far from the beach

Arturo told his students that he taught because of his love for the language. He was pleased, flattered even, that North Americans wanted to learn Spanish. He said he wished to teach beginners especially because he wanted them to begin correctly. He reminded them that they had learned English in the crib and had no memory of how they learned it. In his view, those starting out later needed to learn vocabulary, verbs, the present, past and future tenses, pronouns, the concept of masculine and feminine in nouns, and simple, frequently-used phrases. He maintained to his students that he benefited more than they did in the process, a notion his students had difficulty understanding. His wife dissuaded him from teaching a class more than one semester per year.

The favorite exercise had students take dictation of simple sentences he had assembled using words the students had learned previously and adding to these sentences words on that day's vocabulary list. The students would do their best to write down what he said. At the end of the dictation he would write what he had said on the blackboard so that the students could correct their errors. He had run across this method when learning French in high school. That teacher called the method *dictée*. Arturo had enjoyed the exercise when in the French class and his students enjoyed it now.

When the fifteen weeks were coming to a close and it was mid-December, the number of students had declined from twenty-one to thirteen. Arturo issued an invitation to his remaining students to come to his house and enjoy dinner accompanied by Spanish music. "You will meet my father. He is alone. His wife, my mother, died last year. And you will meet my wife, and the two children, and the husband of my daughter. He is from Madrid and you can practice your Spanish with him. He has a beautiful accent."

It was a festive party. The Christmas tree was up and the mantle piece decorated. There seemed to be candles instead of lamps in many places. Subdued Spanish music was playing in the background. Arturo's wife, elegantly dressed for the occasion, held in her hand the list bearing the names of the thirteen students. She greeted the students as they arrived and introduced them to the members of her family. Her father-in-law, Fernando, was distinguished looking. She called him Daddy.

On being introduced to Elaine, Fernando said, "I know a Roy Brewster. He was a student of mine for three years, learning Internal Medicine. Brilliant student. He now has a good practice of his own."

"It must be the Roy Brewster that I was married to for five years before he moved to Miami," Elaine said.

"Are you in contact with him?" Fernando asked.

"No. Not since the divorce. It's been ten years."

"He's changed in these ten years. Still very handsome but a few gray hairs. He has matured. I think the responsibility of keeping people healthy and alive has brought out the sympathetic side of his nature. When he first came to me he was in a hurry to learn everything. I told him to learn what there was to learn but also to look around the world. I think he did that."

Elaine said nothing. She was immersed in memories of Roy.

Fernando continued. "You might want to renew acquaintances. He has an attractive personality. We all hold him in high regard."

As others came to be introduced to Fernando, Elaine went off to talk to the young couple from Spain, and to ask them about their life there. As they talked, she thought about a flight from Miami to Madrid and a one-week stay in that city before touring the country. She had never left the United States and did not have a passport.

Elaine knew that Fernando would tell Roy that he had met her. She decided to do nothing about it. If Roy wanted to write or telephone, he was free to do so. Elaine wondered what Fernando meant when he said that Roy had matured. In her mind he was still the eager doctor intent of finding his way to the top.

Ten days had gone by. It was between Christmas and New Year. Elaine was washing dishes when the phone rang. She knew it would be Roy.

"Nice to hear your voice. How did you track me down?"

"Dr. Valdez, my maximum leader, ordered me to telephone you. He said that you didn't know how much I had changed, mostly for the better."

"The old match-maker. How would he know about the Roy that I knew?"

"I guess he read that into the divorce. I know that he had a long and successful marriage. I knew his wife quite well. I also know that they were devoted to one another."

"I think that I see the same thing in the son Arturo and his wife. Must run in the family," Elaine said.

"I'm coming to Daytona Beach in a couple of weeks for a medical conference. Would you have dinner with me?"

"Well, I could examine the new Roy, couldn't I? Of course that would wake up the past, which is sound asleep and lying there undisturbed."

"I understand the danger. I'll limit myself to finding out how you are."

"Don't harm me in any way."

"I'll be very conscious of your well being."

PART 8

Elaine suggested that they meet at Roy's hotel, in the lobby. He might kiss her on the cheek, but no more. She would drive herself home eliminating the possibility of a scene at the door. There would be no question of his coming in for a nightcap. It was the second week of January. Roy was staying at one of the better hotels in town.

She got out of her car in the well-lighted parking lot and felt herself tremble. She didn't think it was easy for any divorced couple to see one another again. The uneasiness for her centered on whether either or both of them would have any emotional reaction. At the time, ten years ago, Elaine had not felt anything over their parting. She had told herself all along that their love, what there was of it, was superficial.

Elaine knew that she had no clothes that Roy might remember and she had changed her perfume about four years ago. For this evening she wore a light wool dress of plain green. She thought is resembled split pea soup in color. The sales person had told her that it was a near-copy of a Paris fashion. The sleeves came to her wrists and the skirt to her knees. There was a ruffle – she didn't know any other term for it – that came down the right side from the waist to the hem. She liked the dark green buttons scattered around the front and at the wrists. She couldn't fix her hair the way Roy liked it because she had started wearing it short when she changed perfume. She no longer wore lipstick, but for him she applied a light layer from an old tube still in her dresser.

He was sitting in a chair that gave him a view of people coming in by the main entrance. He was distracted and looking away when she came in. She thought for a second of turning around but moved ahead in his direction. He saw her when she was halfway from the door to his chair. He came to his feet immediately, put a smile on his face and took a step in her direction. Both his hands went out and clasped hers. He leaned forward to kiss her on the cheek. First he said, "Elaine," and right after the kiss he said, "You've changed perfume."

It unnerved her that he noticed. She leaned forward and kissed him on the cheek, something she had not planned on. "Dr. Valdez is right. That little bit of gray goes well," she said.

"I've looked at the dining room and glanced at the menu. Could we stay here for dinner? It would keep us out of your car."

"That's perfectly fine. Ask for a dark corner. Who knows whether there will be a tear or a snivel?"

Roy took her arm at the elbow as they walked across the lobby. She looked at him and when he turned to look at her she said nothing but smiled at him. She knew she enjoyed being seen in public with a handsome, well-dressed man but she had never discussed this event with another woman so had no idea that she might be unusual. A man had told her once that he enjoyed the reflected glory of being seen in public with her. That could have been five years ago. Elaine could recall that moment easily and did so when dressing to go out and had done so earlier this evening.

After they ordered, Roy asked her if she minded if he blew out the candle. "Some things never change," she said. He always claimed that his eyes were sensitive and that there was ample light to see by. He didn't have to offer an explanation, as both knew it by heart.

Roy started by saying that Dr. Valdez had told him she was a nurse at the high school, no longer at the hospital. "Is it the high school you attended?" "Yes. But it's been remodeled. I see myself when I look at those seniors walking around the hall. I'm losing track of what it's like to be a kid or a young adult, as they say now. Is that a normal part of the aging process?"

"Perfectly normal. You and all of us are setting aside childish things and in the course of it we are becoming more responsible for ourselves and I guess for society at large."

"Said very seriously," Elaine reflected.

The conversation has been about her. He wanted to know the details of her work, the status of her parents and family, how she spent her vacations, and all about the new hobby, learning Spanish.

"It seems appropriate, living in Florida," she explained.

"I think it's more than that," he answered. "There's an urge to expand. I see it in nearly all my colleagues. The work at hand doesn't seem to suffice for the average mind."

They had been talking through the meal and beyond it. At least two hours had passed. They had finished the meal with coffee and brandy, a first for Elaine. She remarked on it and he said that he had had his first brandy in Mexico City and enjoyed it.

Elaine was well aware that the evening was about her. His explorations had been legitimate so she continued answering his questions and in the process talking about herself. In their life together he had not shown the interest to have this style of conversation. They had been about him.

When she thought it was time to hear from him she said so, but he answered, "I like talking about myself, but let's leave it for the next time, if you will permit a next time."

"More medical conferences here?"

"Not necessarily. I would drive up, stay here and if you have the time we could swim, walk, eat and talk. Would that be all right?"

"Yes. When would you want to do that?"

"Toward the end of the month. I'll get on the telephone and we'll firm it up."

He walked her to her car. She didn't know how it would play out. They were holding hands and when they reached the car she took her hand away and went to her purse for the keys. She turned toward him and he used the same motion he had in the past, of placing his hands under her arms, letting them slide down to her waist, and then pulling her toward him as he wrapped his arms around her back. It was so familiar. She had her purse in one hand and her other hand against a lapel. She placed her face against his neck to avoid being kissed.

"It's about two and a half weeks away," he said. Then he added, "I hope the Gulf Stream behaves itself so we can swim."

GORDON MCNAIR

PART 9

Roy had come and gone. They had been together one evening for dinner. That brief experience, Elaine knew, did not give her a complete view of Roy's personality as it might have changed over the years. A clear view of the new Roy, Elaine knew, could only come about by being together a fair number of times under differing circumstances.

Elaine had to admit that he had changed. His need to talk about himself had vanished, or at least diminished, to be replaced with an interest in her. She couldn't account for it. He would be back at the end of the month and the question of intimacy would come up even though he indicated that he would be staying again in the same hotel.

Dinner with Roy turned out to be more than an evening together. In the days that followed she thought about their five years together. He always drove too fast, particularly on the Interstate. She would remain silent as long as she could then let out a request that he slow down. He would answer that he was a safe driver. They would then fall into a prolonged silence as she thought about his lack of consideration. She remembered that he had stopped kissing her when he went to work and several times he hadn't bothered to say goodbye. She had to say that he was on his best behavior on the occasions when they arrived at his parents' house in North Carolina. He would put away his sarcasm, although he reserved a dose or two for his younger sister who was not gifted academically.

It was possible that he had advanced in many aspects, but in some, perhaps the majority, Elaine guessed that he would still be the old Roy.

Elaine had elected to attend Community College during alternate semesters rather than continuously. Trevor carried on, semester after semester. He claimed that he needed the routine to keep him engaged. He had retired the year before from the civil engineering company he had started thirty years previously. Retirement was not the correct term. He still held a consulting position with the firm. Elaine and Trevor had been out several times during this most recent semester. She found him easy company.

After Roy's visit, Trevor telephoned and asked her to go swimming with him. This particular winter the ocean was warm and not rough. He told her the water temperature was eighty-five degrees. For the occasion she wore a one-piece navy blue suit that was cut straight across the tops of her legs. At the store they referred to this type of suit as one having a modest cut. She did not like the suits that were cut to reveal the hip sockets. For the walk to the beach with Trevor she wore sneakers and a yellow robe. When they were near the water's edge, they removed the top layer and walked the few yards to the mildly breaking waves. She liked it that he didn't study her body as she removed her robe. It was obvious that he would have ample opportunity as they came out of the water and stood drying themselves. Trevor turned out to be lithe in the water. He dove through the small waves and swam all the strokes with ease. When she started swimming her freestyle in earnest, he had no difficulty keeping up with her. When they were on the beach he asked her if she had swum the stroke in high school or college. She told him that she had, but only in high school. He volunteered that he had as well but that in his day the stroke was still referred to on occasion as the Australian crawl.

They stayed in and around the water for an hour. When they walked to her place he asked her to come to his flat where he would prepare dinner. "Let me get out if this bathing suit," she said. Then she asked, "What's on the menu? I can always supplement."

"White wine, vegetarian lasagna, selection of fruit and strong coffee -- all very healthy."

As he prepared the meal, Elaine wandered about the living room and the dining room. He had already set the table for two. She asked Trevor if she could study the photographs on the walls. Trevor encouraged her. "Take it all in. It's my wife's doing. I wouldn't be able to hang pictures or arrange furniture."

There were photographs of his wife and himself and their four children at various ages. Indeed his wife was not a raving beauty but Trevor was clear in his claim that they had an affectionate, happy and interesting marriage. Elaine guessed that Trevor and his wife had bought this large apartment after their fourth child had moved out of the house.

There were additional photographs on the walls of the hallway. She explored this area and in the process looked into the two bedrooms, both large. In one, Trevor had added a long desk on which resided a computer and printer.

She returned to look into his bedroom. She imagined herself in the flat, not for an overnight tryst but permanently. She admitted to herself that she cared for Trevor and would not be thinking of living with him if she didn't. It was obvious to her that he had been building an attachment for her all along. Elaine found the collection of books on the Romans and

Greeks in a part of the living room. She examined the titles, recognized a few but had not read any.

At the end of supper, they had moved to the living room and were drinking coffee. Trevor cleared his throat, as though he were embarking on important matters, and started out. "I didn't get you over here for anything but the expressed purpose of feeding us, but I thought that I might let you know what's going on with me."

"We've known one another for over four months and continue seeing each other so I can imagine that something is stirring in you," Elaine said.

"How about romantic urges?"

"They're the best kind. Why don't you come sit next to me?" Elaine said, and she laughed a good-natured laugh.

"Let me tell you how I find you," Trevor said.

"Is that the same thing as telling me what you think of me?"

"Yes, a fine point. But either way I'd end up using the same words. I wish I'd made a list. I guess you never had any affectations or perhaps you went through the process of purging yourself. You represent a large expanse without clutter."

"You mean there's nothing there?"

"No. There's plenty of stuff but what you have doesn't keep me away from you. You don't put up any roadblocks. I don't have to change my personality to spend time with you. I don't want to fall in love with a student of Spanish; I want to fall in love with the chance of building something."

"Who said anything about love?" Elaine asked, smiling at him.

"The common expression is falling in love. It's a poor use of the verb 'to fall.' Most times when we fall in love we're happy over it. Great things can come of the condition, for both parties."

"Do you always talk this way, Trevor? Or are you having difficulty telling me that you are falling in love?"

"Well, I'm not at ease, if that's what you mean. About falling in love, it's too soon to tell. I'm moving in that direction. Is it a mistake?"

"It's too soon to tell, as you suggest. I saw my former husband the other evening. First time in ten years."

"Was it out of the blue?"

"No. The Spanish teacher's father, a well-respected doctor in Internal Medicine, has been Roy's principal educator in Miami. They've remained good friends and work at the same hospital. When he saw Roy he told him about meeting me at the Christmas party. Roy was on the way here to a medical conference so we ended up having dinner."

"When it doesn't work the first time usually it doesn't work the second time. People don't change that much. What went wrong the first time?"

"Roy was interested in a great career in medicine far more than he was in me."

"You think he's changed?"

"At dinner he forgot about himself and concentrated on me."

"Figure out a method of testing your thesis before you go back to him. There's some self-interest on my part, I'll admit, but there's observation over the years that backs me up."

Elaine sat comfortably sipping coffee. He had slipped his arm around her shoulders, the most demonstrative he had been. She thought about Trevor's words. Certainly they represented an opening salvo for her hand. She thought about her surroundings, how well Trevor's wife had put together the flat and how well Trevor had maintained it. They were both silent for a moment, then they looked at one another and smiled. It was a quiet, reassuring moment for Elaine. She was leaning against him and could feel the warmth of his body. In another moment she said, "Perhaps you should take me home."

Elaine and Trevor both put on sweaters. He asked, "Shall we take the long way?" Instead of the four-block walk they went to the ocean and turned north, walking between the beach and the first row of dwellings. It was a clear night and they were holding hands. Trevor stopped and looked up. He said, "If the Angel Gabriel were to come down with a marriage license and we both signed it, he could marry us on the spot. Just a thought."

"Is that a proposal?" Elaine asked.

"No. I'm warning you that one will be on the way soon."

"It's the twenty-four year gap that worries me," Elaine said.

"With good reason, but I'm in fine shape."

"Should we put one another through various tests?" Elaine asked.

"Nothing that a reasonable amount of time won't accomplish."

They continued walking to her apartment, holding hands. He sang a love song from the years of swing. She recognized the tune and the words were familiar. When he had finished, she said, "That's lovely. Do you have another?"

"Not at the moment. I'll find another and memorize the words. I used to be able to play the piano when I was young."

When they reached her place she said, "Trevor, I'm happy, confident, relaxed and all that business when I'm with you."

"That's because I accept you completely just the way you are. I think that's it."

"It's satisfying," she said

The plan had been settled upon and was not changed. Elaine and Roy had decided on the last weekend of January with Roy reserving a room in the same hotel that he had stayed in on his previous trip.

It was Elaine who selected a place to eat Friday night, a restaurant that featured sea food and lobster. The place was crowded and noisy and the effect was to make them sit close together. The atmosphere was not conducive to serious conversation. They talked about his life in Miami, his apartment, and the friends he had made. Elaine had driven to the hotel and they had gone to the restaurant in Roy's rented car. Upon returning, he parked next to her car and it was clear to Elaine that Roy was tired by the long day. He was ready for bed. They determined to meet at her place mid-morning, he being armed with a map, which she had drawn on the back of the paper place setting used by the restaurant. He kissed her lightly on the lips when she made no effort to turn her face.

The following morning they walked to the beach with the necessary equipment, which included an umbrella that Elaine used often. When they were seated on their towels, Elaine started applying sun lotion. As she tried rubbing it on her back he said, "Here." She handed him the tube. When he reached her shoulders she slipped off one strap then the other. It was an intimate act but Elaine could recall that he had done it many times. Perhaps he thought nothing of it but when he finished he leaned forward and kissed her where her hair met her neck, right in the middle.

Elaine was surprised by the kiss. "Part of the routine?"

"Unavoidable and certainly not routine," he answered.

Elaine was puzzled by Roy's interest. Could Dr. Valdez have been so persuasive? She had only talked to him for a few minutes at the son's party. Perhaps Roy was in search of a solution for his lonely life and Dr. Valdez' remarks had fallen on fertile ground. And she couldn't discount his sexual urges. He might have ended a relationship recently and his recollections of their times together had returned after ten years.

In Elaine's mind there was no substitute for being direct. The most straight-forward question she could think of was to ask, "Why me and why now?" But she thought there might be a more fruitful way to open the conversation. "We all change over time. Do you think you have?"

He reflected a moment, and then said, "I'm older."

"And who isn't?" she replied.

"With age has come more insight. I don't move as quickly, try as hard, and do as much as I used to. Believe it or not I'm more effective as a doctor and much easier to be with than in the old days."

"You used to pay a great deal of attention to yourself and not much attention to those around you, your wife included."

"I've had a decade to think about it. I realize now that I set it up so that love between us didn't stand much of a chance."

Elaine said nothing, being occupied with her reminiscences.

"There has been an outside influence," Roy continued. "A woman named Deborah came into my life. She had not married although she was attractive in so many ways. More than anything she made me appreciate the beauty that surrounds us and the miracle that life is. We would walk down a street and she would discuss the architecture. She had a passion for it. Sometimes it bordered on ecstasy. She appreciated what was in front of her more than I did. She said we were in an outdoor museum when on any city street."

"She sounds like a philosopher, Roy."

"Fair enough. She was a nature lover, too. She could identify the flowers and trees. She had studied biology and all of it meant a great deal to her. She was a specialist in sunrises, sunsets, shells you find on the beach, and the stars and constellations and the stories surrounding them."

Elaine interrupted him. "You've left out the important part, her personality. She must have been more than someone who came off as this encyclopedia."

Roy thought for a moment. "Of course you're right. She was so desirable. Made me want to hold her in my arms and rub her shoulders gently." He paused to decide on what to add. "She insisted on travel. Said you shouldn't go through life knowing only what you see every day. The first trip was to Florence and Rome. Almost two weeks in Italy. A repeat for her but she appeared not to mind. She avoided being the professor by having me read at night what we could see the next day."

"Does she speak Italian?"

"No, French. So, on the second trip, we toured France. She was at home there."

"Did the travel interfere with your medical practice?"

"In ways that I don't understand, these trips and the knowledge that came with them released me to absorb more medical information than I would have without them. Apparently you need to be rounded out."

"What happened to her?"

"Whisked away by another man. I was warming up to a proposal, made slow and over-confident because she is six years older than I. Someone from the Cuban community took her out of circulation. By now she's learned Spanish."

"Some set of circumstances made you telephone me when your Dr. Valdez reported that he had spent a portion of an evening with me. What was that all about?"

"Having had Deborah in my life and being made to learn how relationships are formed and developed, it occurred to me naturally that I should bring the new me to you. But before I leave Deborah let me say that she taught me the important lesson, which is that both parties are 100% responsible for what takes place. None of that 50% stuff. And of course she's right. When both parties accept 100% responsibility for the relationship things go well. I learned that."

"Is that what you're offering me?" Elaine asked.

"That's what I want to discuss with you, what is meant by 100%. The changes that both of us must make from our previous life together. Can we face up to the challenges and put a plan in place?"

"What's this 'we' business, as they say? I don't feel that I stood in the way of a successful marriage. I'd like to know what you plan to change. We could start there."

"I can't believe that the fault was entirely mine," Roy said.

They swam again, then stayed on their towels until they were dry. "Let's go up for lunch," Elaine said.

When they had eaten and she was at the sink, he came up behind her and slipped an arm around her waist. When she turned around he placed his other arm across her back. She could feel him against her the full length of their bodies. After they kissed she said, "This is the easy part, Roy. We've done this before. You know where I'm sensitive and it would be wonderful. But this time let's try to get the basics arranged properly then we can become lovers again. Could I talk you into that?"

"Sounds reasonable. I've started taking naps on a daily basis. That couch is magnetic."

Roy stretched out on the long couch and relaxed. Elaine went into her bedroom to fetch a light blanket. She draped it over him. He said something she did not understand. The nap sounded like a good idea. She went back to her bedroom and fell asleep.

About an hour later Elaine awakened Roy by placing a glass of orange juice on the coffee table. He looked at it and said, "Thoughtful." When he sat up, Elaine said, "I'd like to go back to the 100% business. I guess it's how you look at relationships now." Roy drank some orange juice, as though the act would make him think clearly.

He began with, "Taking from Deborah, her words as closely as I can remember them, is that each party is responsible for the well-being of the other and in order to do that one has to be thoughtful, considerate, caring, and honest. You can't adjust the amount of consideration you give on the basis of how much you get. That's a formula for disaster and therefore failure."

"I like it," Elaine said. "It eliminates the need to calibrate one's reaction based on the partner's behavior."

"Exactly. It's so simple. The natural instinct is to pay back, to return what you receive, or a little less. This way you and your partner only think of giving your best."

"Should we go over our five years together?" Elaine asked.

"It wouldn't be rewarding for me. Any examination would show that I gave less than you did. We can do it if you want, but there's nothing in it for me."

The unasked question, Elaine knew, was whether their living together, and perhaps remarriage, would take place in Miami or Daytona Beach. She would let the matter remain unexplored until Roy brought it up.

In the hour before he left Sunday afternoon, they were having lunch at his hotel. He asked her to spend a weekend in Miami. It was implied that she would stay at his apartment. Elaine thought that he needed to commit before she stayed over. She said, simply, "Thank you, Roy. I'll ponder the matter."

Her interpretation of his invitation was that she could see how he lived, and therefore how she would live. He would show her around Miami, a city she had seen only once. There was no discussion of his moving to Daytona Beach. It sounded to Elaine as though the continuity of his medical career trumped all other consideration.

GORDON MCNAIR

PART II

It had been an anxious weekend for Trevor. When he called Elaine and asked for either Saturday or Sunday she told him that Roy would be flying or driving up to see her. Elaine couldn't think of any reason why Trevor should not know what Roy was up to. Trevor had been told that the Valdez, father and son, had been responsible for the re-connection.

Trevor wondered whether to telephone Elaine Monday or Tuesday. If he telephoned Monday he might appear too worried. If he waited until Tuesday, Elaine might have slipped from his grasp. He would not know how, but she might have slipped away. He could not wait. He called her Monday evening when he guessed she was home and hadn't started preparing her dinner.

"I missed you, of course," Trevor said.

"As you know I was attending to important business," Elaine answered.

"We could have dinner then go for a walk along the beach and talk about things," Trevor said.

"I'll need to change clothes after dinner if we go to the beach," Elaine answered.

"We can do that at your place. I'll bring a canvas bag with a change of my own."

"Give me date and time," Elaine said.

"Tomorrow at six-thirty. I wish it were this instant."

"Well, why not this instant? We don't have to wait until tomorrow. Have supper and come over. We'll go for that walk on the beach. Can you be here in an hour?"

"Yes. So I get to see you tonight and tomorrow. What more could I ask?"

They both wore a sweater and windbreaker against the breeze. It was natural to hold hands. When they reached the water's edge they sat on the sand and took off their sneakers, stashing them in a knapsack he had brought. He helped her up and put his arms around her, kissing her several times. "I ought to thank you, because you're good for me, somehow," Elaine said.

They headed north. Elaine asked, "Want to walk on my left, away from the water? That would make us the same height." "It doesn't make any difference," he said. "Do I bore you with sighting the constellations?" he asked. He had shown her about finding the North Star after locating the Big Dipper and pointing out Orion, Cassiopeia, and the Pleiades. "I wish there were a constellation that led you into discussing love. I want to talk about love," he added.

"Do you suppose there's one in the Southern Hemisphere?" Elaine asked.

"Maybe one shaped like a heart."

"What did you want to say about love, Trevor?"

"That important feelings come at first sighting. In your case, it was when I looked up and saw you holding a tray with coffee, pie and a catalog, in the cafeteria."

"Was it the catalog?"

"No, silly. You have an inquisitive gaze. It's beguiling and tells me a lot."

"I'm mostly empty," Elaine said. "My gaze must be acquisitive rather than inquisitive."

"That's typical of you. Such self-deprecation. You have the most simple, unadorned, direct personality of anyone I've known."

"I try not to be complicated, if that's what you're getting at."

"Well, those first few minutes can be so informative. I wanted you right then and there."

"That was five months ago, now. What's been going on in your mind recently?"

"I've thought about whether the first impression was correct. The more I find out about you, the more the case keeps building, and I feel myself becoming more and more enamored."

"Trevor, you're making it too complicated. You started telling me about love. Do you want to tell me how and why you love me?"

"Yes, but I don't want to seem too abrupt. I also want to tell you the form it takes," Trevor said.

There was the least amount of annoyance in Elaine's voice when she said, "I know it's not easy but there's nothing more important in this world and I know you want to get it right." They were both quiet. Then Elaine added, "We were scheduled to do this tomorrow evening after dinner, isn't that right?"

"Yes, in fact."

"You would have had a chance to think it through and make a list. It wasn't fair of me to ask you over this evening. On the other hand, it may be better to hear it unrehearsed."

"I'll have to do the best I can," Trevor said.

"Why don't you push ahead and we can edit the material later on."

"Well, I've mentioned that you have this clear outlook. Your character is practically without blemish. You have as many fine traits as one could wish for: honesty, thoughtfulness, consideration, and generosity. I may have left out a couple."

"It's so good of you to say that I have these traits but can you specify the degree to which I have them?" Elaine asked.

"Over time, I suppose, I'll know more exactly. You make me want to support you, encourage you, guard you, provide you company, listen to you, and hear you. Does that make sense?"

"Yes, it does. There's a theory making the rounds that each party should be 100% responsible for the relationship. What do you think of that?"

"It's a well-known phenomenon. It's called love. When you're bats about somebody, that's exactly what you want to do -- make that person's life the centerpiece of your own."

"That's so reassuring, Trevor," Elaine said.

As they walked along holding hands, Trevor began to think of Roy. Roy had just spent a weekend with his former wife and who knows what he promised her? A fabulous new life in Miami, a life based on far more money than he had. It could have been Roy who planted the notion of 100% responsibility in Elaine's head. From what she had told him, Trevor calculated that Roy hovered around the 10% mark. No doubt Elaine did not yet grasp that with him, Trevor, she would get 100% on the first day and every day after. Did Elaine come up with a test that Roy could pass or fail? Trevor felt they had covered ample ground for one evening. He had hinted at marriage, at least he brought up the matter, and she had not turned him down.

They had come back to the spot where they had started their

walk. They put their sneakers back on and made their way to Elaine's apartment.

"Elaine, I had hoped this would be far more romantic and compelling than I've made it. It comes down to this. I'm crazy in love with you. I want to marry you. I want to be your partner in life. That should say it all."

"I heard statements but no question, Trevor."

"Will you marry me, Elaine?"

"That's a question a girl understands."

"Will you?"

"I'll give you an answer the next time we meet and if it's yes I might add what I feel for you, although a 'yes' ought to say it all."

"Are you going to ponder, mull over, or think about it, Elaine?"

"I like ponder."

"When shall I see you?"

"Tomorrow evening at 6:30, as planned. This is bound to be too emotional to go through in a restaurant. We'll take care of it right here at my place."

When Trevor came to her house the following evening, Tuesday at 6:30, and when she let him in, he could not detect which way she was leaning. "I think we should start with a drink," she said. He was pleasantly surprised that she had overdressed. She wore a simple black dress cut modestly in the front and black shoes with low heels. Her jewelry was simply a string of pearls and matching earrings. When he kissed her he breathed in the smell of her skin and hair and whispered, "You're lovely."

After they had taken their first sip, Trevor asked what he knew could be the wrong question. "Were you able to put your former husband to the test?"

"No, not really. We were limited to talking about our past and the future. There was no single thing he could say that would determine everything. I tried to listen to all he said and average it out. In the end I'm alone. Nobody can tell me what course to follow. I'm the responsible party. So no, there was no test."

Having asked one question that he ought not to have, Trevor went to the next one. "Was it Roy who introduced the notion of 100% responsibility?"

"Yes, but it came to him from a woman he was thinking of marrying."

Trevor did not answer. He waited for Elaine to carry on.

"On the beach last night you told me all those things you plan to do for me -- encourage me, guard me -- you remember the list."

"Yes," Trevor answered.

"If you give all that to me, do you expect to get the same thing back?"

"I think it's pretty certain, Elaine. It would be inevitable"

"How so?"

"Because a person of your nature couldn't fail to return what you received."

Trevor thought he might as well carry on and explore the biggest issue, the age difference. He was certain that she had spent many hours worrying over it. "Have you reconciled my age compared to yours, Elaine?"

She said nothing. She looked at him then took a sip of her drink.

Trevor filled the void. "Let me say that one year of a brilliant marriage is far more satisfying than five years of a mediocre one and that I'm prepared to offer you sixteen years in a row of an excellent marriage, right here in Daytona Beach."

"What happens after the sixteenth year? Elaine asked.

"By then I'll be eighty and I can't guarantee much after that. Just check the actuarial tables."

"So you think I should take the gamble?"

"Yes, and I'll take the gamble out of it. You'll have a better life from the first day."

They were seated on the sofa and Trevor had turned to face Elaine. He thought he would embark on a new tack. "Tell me, Elaine, have you had a dream all along about the man in your life?"

"Yes, before Roy even. It was never complicated. I wanted what Roy promised to be: as tall as me, handsome, professional, successful, what you call a good catch. More than anything else I was surprised that it didn't work out. I was caught off guard after the first couple of years when I was unable to add a little more fire to the mixture."

"When it didn't work out, what was the next step?"

"I'm from the good-looking social group of people, body and face. It was important to me that the man in my life matched me along those lines. When we didn't pan out I looked around at marriages that worked and found that they were not based on appearance but something else, perhaps spirit. And I know nothing about spirit -- but I must be learning. You're quite a bit older and not a creature of beauty, although you've kept yourself fit."

"Don't forget magic," Trevor said. "It's not magic, really," he corrected himself. "It's what exists in another person that we don't understand and we find it compelling. We only call it magic."

They sat still for a moment then Trevor asked, "Having given up on looks, have you put together a new dream for selecting men?"

"No, not yet. It's so simple to be with you. I wish that I could say more but I can't. I just look forward to being with you and when we're together I feel complete."

"My guess is that you've never been loved by a man and loved him in return, but you're feeling the start of it and if we are together the love will mature and you'll be as happy as you have ever been."

"How long will it take?" Elaine asked.

"I'm predicting three weeks. So will you marry me?"

"Yes, but."

"The 'but' means what?"

"I'll keep this apartment for the time being but we'll live together at your place and on the Fourth of July we'll make a final decision."

"What does the Fourth have to do with it?"

"All those fireworks."

Elaine was suspicious, as most women would be, that Trevor wanted more than anything else to have access to her body. It wouldn't surprise her, and only disturb her slightly, if this turned out to be the case as so many men had chased her on that basis. But she longed for more: a meeting of the minds, the start of an intellectual relationship, and an understanding and appreciation of each other's character and personality. It was for these reasons that Elaine asked for a six-month delay ending on the Fourth of July.

He shared the work in his apartment and that included preparing dinner. In fact he did more than half the work about the place. He would pull her chair from the table to seat her then lean over and kiss her on top of the head. He would open the door for her when they approached the car. She was too anxious to wait for him to come to her side to open the door on arrival. She realized that he was polite in all matters and had been raised that way. She brought it up to him one day and he told her that his father had educated him in many aspects of life down to the acceptable way of folding a letter and placing it in its envelope.

Although Elaine was a nurse she found Trevor concerning himself with her health, both medical and dental. This activity took the form of gentle questioning, not persistent and hard inquiries, but reminders and discussions of results. He concerned himself with the rest of her as well. There was a three-day trip to Puerto Rico so that she might be immersed in Spanish. He recognized that her time was more limited than his but introduced the Iliad and the Odyssey into her reading schedule. This opened a bond between them and led to discussions of ancient times in the days of Rome and Athens. She noted that Trevor did not play professor. He allowed her to conclude on her own.

Over the months Elaine decided that Trevor cared for and about her to an extent she had never felt before. He seemed to be pouring himself into her. She came to realize that affection flowed between them easily because nothing got in the way. He was kind and gentle, yet firm, in his kissing of her and placing his hands on her body. She felt safe in reciprocating.

As May rolled into June and the Fourth of July came into sight, apprehensions left her. Being loved by the right man in the right way made her secure. No other man in her past had been up to it.

EMILY EVANS

PART I

Andrew looked far down the beach and saw a woman in white coming his way. She would stop occasionally and pick up an object, a shell or a pebble. She made him think of a young woman in church two Sundays previously. He had taken his customary place in the third pew from the front when the young woman came in and installed herself next to him, but one place over. Had it been Easter Sunday one medium sized person would have separated them. He paid no attention to her at first, but when they had sung the entrance hymn, he turned toward her in the act of sitting down. She was remarkably beautiful. He guessed her age to be twenty-six and by multiplying this number by three he arrived at seventy-eight, his age exactly. He could have been her grandfather. At the end of the service she moved into the aisle and started speaking to a man about a fifty. Andrew thought the man might be her father, or a lucky suitor who had managed to corral somebody from the next generation. As he made his way out of church Andrew wondered if that affair would be worth it, how it would end up if the man were not her father. Who would suffer more as the affair wound down? He had just about put her out of his mind, but not quite, when the woman in white on the beach came up to him.

He took off his dark glasses and said good morning and gave a slight bow, just a nod really. She stopped and said, "Good morning. How are you?" It was the first time on this trip that anyone had gone beyond "Good morning" for an answer. He stopped too, removed his hat and asked, "Very well, thank you. How far are you going?"

She took off her glasses and hat and shook her head to make her hair fall in place. It was prematurely snow white. Andrew put her at fifty-two. That would be twice twenty-six, twice the age of the beauty in church and two-thirds his age. He had concluded some time ago that he was destined to avoid serious contact with any woman not in her seventies. Because there were so few to choose from he could stay at home as much as he wanted and avoid the social scene.

To his question, how far are you going, she said, "A way farther, then I turn around." "Mind if I accompany you?" he asked. "That's what I had hoped," she said.

They put on their hats and dark glasses and chatted through the preliminaries as they walked. She was here from Chicago, driven out by a terrible storm. Fortunately, she told him, the plans for the vacation had been made several months previously and the storm was coincidental. Her name was Emily Evans. She was in advertising, had not married, and owned her apartment downtown.

He reciprocated, discussing his deceased wife, their three children, his career and his house, which was far too big for him alone but he had grown accustomed to it. He liked particularly his library upstairs. He had fashioned it out of the largest of the children's bedrooms. He thought Emily had steered the conversation away from the topic at hand when she asked whether his children were married and how many children each had.

Andrew Wilson had tried many of the resorts on Mexico's West Coast. He liked them all, some more than others. He enjoyed walking on the beach at the water's edge, where the sand was hard. He would take off his sneakers, tie their laces together and carry them draped over his neck. He took all the precautions against the sun, which included a floppy straw hat, sun cream, dark glasses, a white shirt with long sleeves and khaki trousers. The sun would get to his skin on his two swims per day with the result that he was tanned lightly except for the center of his body, shielded as it was by his bathing suit.

This was his tenth winter of travel. He refused to think of the word *vacation* because a retired person doesn't take vacations. Vacations from what, he would ask himself. He lived in Southern California and his excuse for the trips was not to get away from the cold, because there was so little cold to get away from, but to have time to read without distraction. On trips to Mexico, he could read five to six hours per day. At home it might be half that due to interruptions, many originating with him. Andrew had determined a while before, in his early sixties, before he retired, that he would spend the declining years, as he categorized them for himself, by reading new material while not forgetting the classics that he had not got around to. On this trip, for instance, he had brought Chaucer, Steinbeck, Voltaire's biography of Louis XIV, the New Testament, two Saul Bellows and one William Styron. He did not bring any knee-breakers this time. Knee-breaker was the term he used for any book over 800 pages in length. In his own mind he always threatened to cut them into 200-page slices for portability or reading in bed, but could never bring himself to do it.

This was the third day on which he took a mid-morning walk on the beach, it being Thursday following his arrival at the resort mid-day

Monday. He was still very aware of women although he had reached the age at which he did not wish to establish a new family and devote the time required to tend to details and adapt to the antagonistic personality traits of a new woman, if indeed there were any such traits. He had lost his wife Maggie eleven years ago to one of those dreadful diseases that takes hold and never lets go.

Maggie and he had fought and raged at one another during their years of marriage, but not disastrously. It was never a matter of making up; they tired of arguing and went on to something new. He looked back and wondered what was so important about her taking half an hour longer to get ready than he thought necessary. He did not care to clean the garage and to do gardening and therefore would get infuriated when his wife brought up these matters on a Saturday morning. He couldn't understand why Maggie dug in her heels over the issue of taking his shirts, and occasionally his suits, to the cleaners. He suspected all along that there were deeper matters over which they could argue, but they never explored these possibilities. Andrew thought they enjoyed a certain amount of sparring – it was in their characters. Their children were accustomed to the frequent shouting and paid not the slightest attention.

They were nearing his hotel. Andrew said, "It's a pity you don't have a bathing suit on. We could go for a swim in front of my hotel."

"I'm wearing one under these clothes," she said.

"Is it white?"

"Yes. Bring down a bath towel. I'll wait for you out front and we'll take a swim."

He went up, changed, and came down wearing a terry cloth robe and carrying two towels. She had slipped out of her shirt and pants and was sitting on the sand. The bathing suit was cut modestly. It had a short skirt and hid a fair amount of her body.

"Give me a hand, please," she said. When she was standing, she said, "I have big hips."

"Very well, Madam," Andrew said. "I'll walk in front of you."

They said nothing as they walked to the water. It was warm enough that they could go in without gasps and commentary. When waist deep, she dove in and came up smiling. What a pretty face, he thought. It was his turn and he dove in. They swam for twenty minutes close to the shore, swimming back and forth in front of the place where they had left the towels.

When they were back on the beach, they sat on the sand and talked. When their suits were dry, Andrew said, "Let's move to the verandah and have a sandwich and a glass of wine, or whatever pleases you."

"Delightful," she answered.

She had put on her white shirt and pants, and he his terry cloth robe. As they ate, he did his best to understand her. Her hair was cut straight across the front and evenly around the sides and back. It reminded him of Joan of Arc in a sculpture of her he had seen. Her hands were of medium size with nail polish applied. The color matched the polish on the toenails. He had noticed while on the beach that she had pretty feet and that the big toe was not broken at the joint. His wife's feet were like that. His wife had not worn pointy shoes or high heels and Andrew guessed that the same applied to his new friend Emily.

She wore a smile or a pleasant expression and did not frown or grimace during the meal. They talked about Chicago and national politics and while she expressed her views and he his, Andrew was aware that she made no attempt to change his opinions. Once in a while she would ask a question so that Andrew had a second opportunity to make his point. He summed her up as an excellent conversationalist.

After lunch Emily said, "We have a problem in logistics. I would like to invite you to dinner at my place but you don't know where it is and I can't tell you how to get there. The buildings facing the beach look alike."

"I'll walk back with you and take notes and make sketches. I should be able to find it this evening. Shouldn't be difficult. What time do you want me?"

"Before dark," she answered. "Start out when the sun hits the ocean. We'll sit on the porch so bring a sweater."

He walked up the beach with her and located her building. "It's the one after those three trees and it's pinkish," he said after studying the area.

"I have hurricane lanterns and candles. I'll light three and place them on the table, up there, on the second floor. We can both watch the sunset for however long it lasts. Judging from our walk just now, it takes thirty minutes to get here from your hotel," she said.

"Yes," he reflected. "This is navigation the old fashioned way."

He followed the plan and arrived at her door. It was a simple apartment but it did have a well-equipped kitchen. She asked him to select the wine from the two reds on the counter and two whites in the refrigerator. She told him about what she had prepared for dinner. After he had opened a bottle of white wine they went out on the porch and sat in a comfortable sofa side by side.

"What did you do this afternoon after cooking?" he asked.

"I took a one hour nap under the supervision of my alarm clock."

"I'm surprised you brought one."

"It was a Christmas present advertised as a traveling clock. How could I leave home without it?"

He found her conversation straightforward and witty. It was as though she told you half, knowing that you could grasp the rest. He wondered if that trait came from the advertising world, whether working there induced one to talk in shorthand.

They ate slowly, she telling him about writing copy, handling an account, and organizing a campaign. He knew nothing about this field, having been a professor of physics, involving himself with research and teaching. He tried to reciprocate but acknowledged to himself what had been the case so many times before, that his specialty in physics, quantum electrodynamics, was too complicated to be explained to just anybody. The person you were talking to had to have the background.

He kissed her lightly on the cheek at the door. "Will I see you tomorrow?" he asked. "Mid-morning swim here if you want," she answered.

He thought about how much reading he could get in after breakfast. They agreed on 10:30. As he walked on the beach toward his hotel he wondered about her being alone in life. If she were playing her cards correctly she should be looking for men her age. She might be having a better time if she had taken a room in his hotel, or another, and surveyed the field for single men in their fifties. He knew it was impossible for her to think that he was under seventy-five. He had dropped too many hints.

They had spent part of each day together during their holiday. Andrew thought they had a good start on getting to know one another. He determined that he had read a good deal more than she had but recognized that he had a couple decades and some on her. She always held her own by understanding and interpreting correctly what he was saying. She knew a great deal about Chicago, its history and politics, and why she felt that it was the hub of commercial activity in Middle America. Andrew wanted to bring up St. Louis, Kansas City and Cincinnati but he knew better than to unsettle a cherished opinion. What would be the purpose, he asked himself.

They got around to a long conversation on marriage in which Emily searched for an explanation of why it had passed her by. Andrew guessed that she had had the same conversation many times with several people, most of them women.

She put the discussion in the form of a question: why had she gone through her twenties and not met the right man? Andrew felt it was his job to set Emily at ease. One of her early remarks was to the effect that she felt pretty enough, particularly when younger. She made reference to her hips once again. Andrew assured her that the shape of the body had little to do with it. "Here's what happens. A pretty face and a desirable body do indeed turn the head of a man, but I doubt that there is one man over thirty in the United States who has married a woman on the basis of irresistible breasts. And your hips, by the way, are not out of proportion with your height. I like them, in fact."

"You've been studying them?"

"Yes. How can I help it, even at my age? And you do have lovely legs. In Chicago, when the weather permits, I guess you wear short skirts."

"You have to be mindful of the wind," Emily said.

Then Andrew launched forth on his statistical analysis of the mating game. He claimed no expertise but knew a fair amount about statistics. He started in. "It's not you, Emily. It's the system. When you graduated from Northwestern at the age of twenty-two, I'm guessing, there might have been 50,000 young males within a forty mile radius with whom you might have connected. How many did you intercept?"

Emily reflected for a moment. "Let's say ten."

"The others, which large group contained a mate for you, went unexplored."

Emily said nothing.

"The system should work more like an auction," Andrew continued. "Stacks of résumés, statements of preferences, tastes, religious and social background and so on. Then some face-to-face meetings. You need much more interface. Believe me, it's nothing you did or did not do."

"I had some beaux," Emily said. "I've taken a few to bed and let a few others take me to bed but nothing happened. Never made the correct contact."

"Damned shame," Andrew said. "I suppose you wanted a family?"

"I thought three would be about right. I did want some time for a career."

"Was it always in advertising?"

"Yes, I really like it."

They fell silent. Dinner was over. They moved to the porch. The sun had set some time ago and they only had light from the kitchen. Emily had put out the candles in the hurricane lanterns. Andrew and Emily were on the sofa. Andrew said, "You're a lovely woman, Emily. Mind if I kiss you?"

"I'd like it," she said.

"How old are you?" he asked.

"Fifty-three. How old are you?"

"Seventy-eight."

Andrew thought that the exchange would bring an awkward pause but Emily said, "You've done lots of things correctly over the years, handsome." She leaned over, put an arm around his neck and they kissed. "You have to go. It's past my bed time."

EMILY EVANS

PART 2

Andrew became attached to Emily their last night together. They had dinner at a hotel not his own and when they returned to her place there was a farewell glass of wine followed by kissing at her door. She did not discuss the future and limited herself to saying something about her vacation having been filled by his companionship and she hoped for other adventures like this one. She did not single him out – he understood that. She kept it general by saying that vacations were meant to encompass the act of two people finding one another and growing close.

They had not touched the notion of bed. Andrew thought that the exposure of their bodies to one another over the course of the week might trigger something related to sex, if not the act itself, but nothing came of it.

Andrew stayed two days after Emily left, a time he did not enjoy. Emily, with her easy charm and simplicity, had moved into his thoughts. In the short interlude they had been together he had known companionship, amusement, distraction and the beginning of desire. Andrew thought it must be the same for Emily. They did exchange telephone numbers and addresses and he wondered who would contact the other first and what might be said.

Andrew chose to write a short, flattering letter in which he discussed the engaging traits he found in her. He wrote it in Mexico and mailed it on his first day home. It appeared to Andrew that Emily had written her letter to him two days after her arrival in Chicago. While there were pleasant parts to the letter, the middle two paragraphs disturbed him. It read in part, "I am tired. My morale is low. I'm thinking of resorting to medications. I am tired and sad and I don't say that so that you will console me. Just that you will understand my state of mind."

Andrew was disturbed by the repetition of the admission that she was tired. It appeared to be a case of clinical depression. He admitted to himself that he knew very little about mental health but he felt a strong desire to fly to Chicago to set things right. He recognized in his next thought that one doesn't burst in upon someone's life, utter platitudes and wave one's arms, and expect to make lasting changes. There had to be commitment. He called James, the rector at the Episcopal church he attended.

Andrew and James, or Jim, had hit it off right away. Andrew was on the vestry when the previous rector had been called away to become the dean of a cathedral. He joined the search committee to select the new rector. It had taken two months to interview the candidates. Jim got the nod because the committee found him to be straightforward, and because he had stabilized the parish where he had been for six years. Finally, they liked his wife. Jim had suggested to Andrew that he consider marrying again on the basis that unmarried men fall apart sooner than the married ones. He had never known Andrew's wife but he knew their children, spouses and the grandchildren. During the conversation that followed Andrew claimed that he was aware of the statistics on old people surviving, and that he liked the company of women and was on the lookout.

When Andrew telephoned Jim at the parish office it was as though two old friends were planning an outing. Andrew described Emily's letter to which Jim answered with an invitation for dinner. "Sally can add one. That will make three. You may get scrambled eggs. If I don't call back, the coast is clear and be at the rectory at 6:30."

It would not be accurate to describe these two men as drinkers, but when they were together in the early evening they did lead off with a cocktail, followed by what they called a "splash," really a second cocktail. They gave up wine at dinner as part of the bargain.

"I hope Sally will join us. I want her to read the letter," Andrew said when he arrived at the rectory. Jim assured him that his wife was home. He then fixed drinks, scotch for Andrew and himself. Sally's drink was sherry on ice, an odd concoction, Andrew thought. They seated themselves in a corner of the living room where they were close together.

"Tell us about the trip," Jim started out. Andrew went into detail, how he had met Emily, what took place between them, and about her life in Chicago. Sally asked about her family.

"Her mother and father have died. She's an only child. Never married. Her closest relative is a first cousin who is married but they have no children," Andrew said.

"Those of us with families are so lucky to be part of something. The poor dear, she goes home to a television set," Sally said. Andrew passed around Emily's letter. Sally read it and said, "You see why I'm a rector's wife. I get to read all this interesting stuff." She turned to Andrew and asked, "What's your next step?"

"I'm tempted to fly to Chicago and do what I can," Andrew answered.

Jim said, "If the diagnosis is correct, that she is clinically depressed, as you put it, then we have to recognize that the condition has been building for years. The aloneness has been wearing on her for thirty years. She can't stand it any longer." Jim was quiet for a moment then went on. "I see it among some of our older parishioners. They've lost a mate and the children live some distance away. They control it but only because it hasn't been building for years. Your Emily could be a different case."

"What do you feel, Andrew?" Sally asked.

"I feel I should go and do what I can, probably not very much, but as my wife used to say, when in doubt, show up."

"She was right," Sally said. "Do you see all the perils -- that you could be getting set up in some fashion?"

"Yes, but I'm all grown up. So what if some attractive woman takes me for a fool?"

"My concern," Sally said, "is that Emily has gone fishing and you are one among quite a few. The age difference tells me that. She feels that the cure for her is to have someone, almost anyone, in her life."

"But might you consider it rational behavior on my part to fly to Chicago and talk it over? I should be able to get it out of her why she tells me she's tired and says it twice in one letter."

Jim said, "You may be stepping into a minefield but as you say you are all grown up and anyway, what's wrong with a little excitement?"

"OK, then it's settled, at least in my mind. Emily might not see it that way. As you suggest, Sally, she could be working on her plan with a few other bachelors around town." Andrew seemed to have closed the discussion with his last paragraph. They gathered their glasses and napkins and moved into the dining room.

Sally wasn't finished. When she had put out the first course and they were seated, she said, "It's most disturbing to me that our Emily wouldn't be after someone her own age. As you describe her, she's not unattractive and should be able to land someone younger."

"Particularly when you think that she's in advertising," Jim added.

"I'll call her, sound her out. It's too mysterious to let go," Andrew said. With the two-hour time difference between the West Coast and Chicago, Andrew felt it was too late to telephone when he got home. The following afternoon at four o'clock, the earliest Andrew thought that Emily might be home, he telephoned. She picked up on the first ring. "Just got in," she said. "What a pleasant surprise!"

"Your letter arrived, of course. I've read it forty-three times," Andrew said. "I want to be with you, which I would feel even if there had been no letter, but I feel it more so now."

"I don't write that well," Emily said.

"Well, you described your condition and as a friend I want to spend some time face to face. I don't pretend that I can solve a crisis, if indeed there is a crisis, but I should be able to get you to tell me what's going on."

"What's going on? Not enough, perhaps."

"If I come for a weekend can we carry on where we left it and add frank discussion?"

"We should be able to do that. When you come, will you stay here with me?"

Andrew was startled. He said, "If I stay with you, I may try to have my way with you. I know myself that well."

"I'd like that," Emily said. "I hope that you would like it too," she added.

They arranged that he would arrive Friday afternoon and leave Monday about the time she went to work. They did not make any plans but she was worried about the weather. "Do you have a wool suit?" she asked. "I doubt it." "Well, bring a heavy sweater and jacket and don't forget a wool hat, scarf and gloves."

Andrew had talked over the phone to each of his children on

returning from Mexico, but he felt that he had to see them together to explain this new circumstance. He would use Emily's letter as his means of conveying the seriousness of the matter and he would not hide the fact that he would be staying with her.

Andrew's three children lived near one another, speaking in Los Angeles distances. He telephoned them and suggested they come to his house for dinner. He asked for a Wednesday evening meeting. They all knew that their father would prepare one of his two menus for seven adults, himself included, and the four grandchildren. Andrew's two standard dinners were salmon, broccoli and rice, and the other a beef stew with a side dish of vegetables. His son, after the greetings, always asked what was being served, in hopes that his father would come up with a something new. Andrew never gave him a straight answer. The adults assembled in the living room, with the four grandchildren going immediately to the study where they argued over which old movie of the 1940s in Andrew's collection they would watch.

The son was called Andy, Andrew being reserved for the father. The middle child, Betsy, had always assumed the role of peacemaker. His youngest child, a daughter named Karen, aged thirty-nine, had been married fourteen years but had no children. Her brother and sister used to make sympathetic remarks from time to time but had stopped about ten years ago and the family had accepted that Karen would not have children.

Andrew uncorked two bottles of white wine, there being seven adults. They settled down to hear more about the lady on the beach. Andrew opened the discussion by describing meeting Emily and their time together. He went on to the letter, handing it to Betsy, who read it aloud. Andrew was hoping for observations that had not occurred to him, but he was disappointed. Betsy and Karen wondered what Emily might be looking for. Andy was pleased that there could be romance after seventy-five. Andy's wife got to the point. "You should go. Her letter reads as though she's desperate and needs you, and that she's on the up and up. There's also a slim chance that you may get to the bottom of matters and resolve the issues between you two and between her and the world." Andy said, "Dad, do what's best for you. Take all the time you need before making any commitments."

"Do you like her, Dad?" Karen asked.

"Yes. She's warm, intelligent and good company. Another way of saying it is that she's tempting."

Betsy asked, "Will we know the results of the weekend?"

"Yes, full strength, no filters."

PART 3

Andrew had been thinking about his previous trips to Chicago. There had been conferences held at the University over the years on his area of physics. When he had retired six years previously, the relationships then in place had started to dry up. He thought he could renew contacts if there was a need. This train of thought came up because he was speculating that the important result of this weekend might be that he would move to Chicago as part of his arrangement with Emily. When the plane settled on the runway at O'Hare he realized that he knew nothing of the city itself, and had not even been to their great museum.

The blue van took him to the front door of Emily's apartment building. He was helped with his bag by the doorman who announced him. It was 6:15 on Friday and Emily was home. "Fourth floor. Turn to your right, 408," the doorman said.

Emily was at the door. "You still have your tan," were her first words. Then she added, "I see you dressed appropriately." When he was in the apartment, she placed her hands on his shoulders and kissed him on the lips. "This is a two-bedroom, two-bath place. The guest facilities are on that side. Why don't you unpack and make yourself at home?"

Andrew felt that Emily was treating him with great familiarity but then she had invited him for a weekend together and it wouldn't do to hold him at a distance. When he rejoined her in the living room she motioned him to sit on the sofa with her. "Here's a plan for the weekend," she said. "Object to anything you want to. Tonight an evening at home. You might have a favorite news program. After that I'll serve dinner. Tomorrow I'm taking you shopping. You hate shopping, don't you?" "Yes, I've always hated it. Had to wait for my wife endlessly." "Well, tomorrow we'll shop for you and I'll find out what it's like to wait for a man. And tomorrow afternoon we'll talk about my letter and everything in it. Not a word on that subject until then. Tomorrow night, we'll go out to dinner, and on Sunday, whatever you wish. Cultural events and dinner here again. Does that please you?"

They found his favorite news program from seven until eight, the one he always watched on Friday evenings. He asked her whether he was taking her away from a program she liked. She answered that she preferred reading about current events. "It's a bit stale that way, but less repetitious," she explained. But she watched the program with him. They sat together on a small sofa and started holding hands halfway through.

For dinner there was a stew that she had reheated, two vegetables and warm corn bread. It ended with a salad. He wondered how she would introduce the sleeping arrangement as he was installed in the guest bedroom. They had not said much one to the other while they cleared the table and washed the dishes but as activity drew to a close she turned to him and said, "Your dress code is pajamas, I should remind you."

"Do you favor pajamas over a nightgown?"

"I'm a nightgown person."

"White?"

"Yes, white. Has some lace and fluffy stuff. I think you'll like it. I forgot that it has ribbons."

He guessed she had bought it for the occasion.

After breakfast she declared that her favorite shirt on a man was made of alternate blue and white stripes, between five or six to the inch, and that she wanted to buy him one such, then a yellow sweater.

"I've always thought yellow a bit garish on a man," Andrew said. "Could I swing you over to something that has the colors found on a moor or a heath?"

"I've not walked in either, Andrew."

"I think the term heather describes what I'm looking for. I'll know it when I see it. My sweater at home has a hole at each elbow. I wear it in the house when reading a classic."

"It's a mood-setting piece, then. The flowers on a heath are purple and pink, I've read. I'm glad you'll recognize it when you see it."

They made it to the men's store of her choice and found both articles. The sweater that he liked, it turned out, was a mixture of green, brown and blue. They walked to the lakefront and studied the waves, the winds and the cloud formations. "I like cities on the edge of water. It sets one of the boundaries. Without it, the city would run out through the prairie right to the start of the next city."

"You're describing Los Angeles County," Andrew said.

"I've always thought they should draw a line around cities so that you had buildings up to the line then moved abruptly to farm land or forest."

They gave their views on city planning, he going on at length into the slow destruction of Southern California. He said the argument centered on this point, one side being concerned about accommodating the people who were moving in and the other side maintaining that if available housing were held to a minimum then the bulk of the people intending to move into Southern California would have no place to come to.

"It's time for late morning coffee," she said. They came into a coffee shop that had a fireplace with several plastic leather chairs around it. Andrew remarked that the fire consisted of ceramic logs fed by natural gas. They drank their coffee and warmed up from their time at the lakefront. Andrew said, "You were wonderful to me last night." She answered, "It comes from a long drought. A very long drought. I should say that it comes in part from that. The rest is you."

She explained that her office building was not far away and that if she were to take him there and show him where she worked, they could then go to her apartment and start the delayed conversation. "I feel the pressure building in me. I want to get it out," she said.

They were back in her apartment. It was mid-afternoon. Andrew had gone to his bedroom to fetch the letter. Emily brought out a half-full bottle of wine and two glasses and set them on the coffee table. They sat near one another and Emily said, "I don't drink this early in the day but on this occasion we might need it." Andrew pointed to the letter and said, "That's for your use in the event you want to remember exactly what you wrote."

She picked up the letter and read it through quickly. She placed it in her lap and turned toward Andrew. She would look at him and then turn away, speaking steadily. "I'll start at the beginning. When I was sixteen I imagined the man that I would meet, whom I would marry and we would have children. He had brown hair and brown eyes. He'd be bigger than me, but not much. He'd have light brown skin that carried a tan year round. He would be strong." She looked at him and asked, "Sound like anybody you know?"

"At the fringes," he answered.

"Then I wanted him to be intelligent and entertaining, and successful of course, and think the world of me. At sixteen I didn't go much beyond that."

"That's well organized at any age," Andrew said. Before she could start to speak, Andrew added, "The difference is that most men and women move into the marketplace to see what's there while you decided on the model you wanted and went looking for it."

"Exactly. It dawned on me in my late twenties that I should not reject men on the basis that they did not match my model. By then I had looked seriously at ten men or so and let plenty of passable material go by. But I wasn't worried. That came later."

"The passable ones found mates, I suppose," Andrew said.

"Yes, the eligible ones married and I can't tell you how the number of eligible men drops off when you hit thirty. The good ones are gone and those that are left seem to be the ones who can't make up their minds to commit, perhaps to anything."

"Was there a great day of awakening?"

"When I hit thirty I realized that the chance of finding him and having babies was diminishing precipitously. Yes, I would say that it was a major awakening." As Emily continued, Andrew recalled that when he started thinking about a woman for himself – he too was about sixteen – he hoped to find someone tall rather than short, on the basis that short people tended to be busy and aggressive while tall people were calm and less likely to argue and make difficulties. Andrew knew nothing of this on his own. It was information a boy two years older than he had given him. He also preferred a slim face to a round one and indeed his wife was tall and had a thin face. He realized that Emily had those two features. It turned out that his wife was argumentative and Emily not.

"I don't have to go year by year, Andrew. I should be able to shorten it. From thirty on I started to feel more and more alone. The opportunities to go out lessened. I began spending more time at home. There came the chance to socialize with women who were in my situation but I rejected that because the women in that group were already telling themselves that a part of life had passed them by. I didn't want to identify with them. First, my father died, then five years later my mother. I really felt alone and that feeling has not gone away. It grinds you down, this need to plan every weekend by yourself."

Andrew interrupted her. "There are twenty-three years between thirty and fifty-three. Did any Casanovas show up?"

"Yes. Five or six that I could say had possibilities. I've thought about them time and again. Should I have compromised? At the time I thought that I would be unhappy from the first day of marriage." Emily paused. Andrew guessed that she was evaluating once again the best of this group, wondering whether she had made a mistake. He said, "You make decisions as you go along in life based on the information available. I would guess that you did the right thing in each case."

She turned toward him, put on a smile and said, "That's easy for you to say." Then Andrew came around to a sentence in the letter. "When you write that you're tired and your morale is low and you're thinking about taking medications for depression, tell me what that's all about."

"I would say that I've been suffering from depression over the years. It's getting worse, or I think it's getting worse. As for medications, I understand that there are prescription drugs that do release tensions. I've not looked into it."

"Do you still function at work?" he asked.

"Yes, I'm at my best at work. Drives away all my problems. Let me bring you up to date. There we were coming toward one another on the beach and when we stopped and talked I realized that you resembled the man I'd always hoped for. First, your easy conversation, not particularly personal, but interesting. Then your ability to explain most anything, staying with the framework and leaving out the ornamentation. And you give your opinion and don't argue with me to adopt it. You have the correct amount of humor, being able to see the serious and the amusing aspects of people and situations."

"I hope you're exhausting the topic," he said.

"I'm back in Chicago and I think, or know, that you are someone I want and need in my life. You've told me the ages of your children and more recently your age. I don't want you to be seventy-eight. How about fifty-eight? Makes me sad to wait this long and be cheated at the last moment." She waited a little bit then asked, "Do you remember our first swim? When we came out of the water you shook the sand out of your towel and I asked you for it and went behind you and started drying your back. Do you remember that?"

"Of course. I hope you recall that I did the same to you."

"I put my hand on your shoulder. I wanted to feel your skin. I hope you didn't mind."

"No. Loved it, in fact."

"You have the most beautiful shoulders and chest."

"You may be overstating the case, dear one," he said.

He poured half a glass of wine in each glass then said, "I take a free-fall nap every afternoon. Free-fall means no alarm clock. Usually takes an hour. Can we take these glasses into your room and konk out for a while?"

"I've tired you out?" Emily asked.

He smiled at her but didn't say anything. He picked up the glasses and stood up. They moved toward the bedroom. She went into her bathroom and came out a moment later clad in a white bathrobe. He was still dressed and sitting on the side of the bed. She stretched out on the bed and he brought the comforter up around her. He leaned over and kissed her then he said, "I don't think you're depressed. I say that because you still function at work. You've been dealt some bad cards and been through plenty of lonely, sad times, but depressed you're not."

She took one of his hands in hers. "That's reassuring. I hope it's true. How do you know?"

"I've read all of two articles on the subject. There are several causes for depression and your experience of being alone is one of them. On the other hand, I read that women with everything – husband, children, career, house – become depressed. I read that hobbies and friends are repellents. But you still are productive at work, you make plans, you act, you appear to be optimistic, and you're great fun to be with."

They exchanged a few more ideas, finished the wine, and napped. When he came to he glanced at his watch and noted that he had slept for over an hour. Emily had moved close to him and was awake. He caressed her face and hair. "Do you see how exhausting all that talking is?" he asked.

She got up on one elbow, put her hand on his face and kissed him. "I've been watching you sleep. You really go at it."

He put his arms around her and pulled her close. "I'm catching a case of love," Andrew said. "Believe me, it's contagious," she said.

They had dinner at the restaurant she had selected and when they returned to her home, before any other plans could be put in place, he said, "It's only 9:30, but I can't think of anything more engaging than to be warm and comfortable and sexy with you in your bed."

"You're uncanny," she said.

As he changed into his pajamas, Andrew became more certain than before that Emily had managed her life properly and by some fluke had not met the correct man. He didn't know whether to believe her assertion that he was the chosen one. It seemed far-fetched. But he acknowledged that he had felt the first pangs of love. In a moment he would be in the presence of that lovely long face encased in white hair. "It's exactly the right combination," he thought. There was nothing inconsistent in her story. She was moving at a torrid pace and he sensed that they would derail, but in the meantime he let it go that she wanted her man in her life and was willing to take the steps necessary to make it happen. Then it occurred to him that he wanted a woman in his life. The problem with Emily was air miles separating Chicago and Los Angeles. He looked into the mirror and combed his hair and realized that there were no other problems to solve. If he wanted this woman he could have her. She was ready. Everything that she had told him so far could be, and probably was, the truth.

Sunday started with the papers. His habit was to get up early and watch a particular show. This Sunday they slept late and placed themselves in her living room so that they would be bathed in sunlight. He wondered if anyone would miss him in church at home. "The sun is feeble in the winter but it reminds me of the beach in Mexico anyway," she said. In the afternoon they went to the museum. He was impressed by the collection. They had a bite and went to a movie they had selected. They returned to her place where she prepared a simple supper. They were on the couch once again and she asked, "What time is your flight tomorrow?" He thought it was at ten with one stop to get him to Burbank. She took his hand and said, "We can talk and write and figure out the next visit. I don't want to wait too long." She paused. "I'm really pushing myself on you. That ought to be obvious. And by the way, you know how to take my sexual appetite from maximum to zero in two nights. So when we're in bed tonight, don't expect too much. I'm a woman and I'll be thinking about what to wear tomorrow and how to get back into what I'm working on at the office. Is that what marriage is like?"

"Marriage is anything you can imagine, two people attached emotionally, if they are lucky. There seems to be something to work on every other day. You and I like one another. That goes a long way." When she came to bed she said, "I figured out what to wear tomorrow while I was in the shower." He laughed and reached over to turn out the light.

It was early Monday morning at breakfast and Andrew knew it was up to him to bring up the matter of the next visit, either back here or in California. When he spoke of it, it was obvious that she had given it thought. "The difficulty with my going to California is that it will be understood by your circle that you're importing women. That could be costly. A favorite of yours could pull up the drawbridge. And then you would have to pass me by your children. They may not approve."

"I don't socialize a great deal and if I miss an invitation or two it's worth it. You are welcome anytime. The children will be curious but I guarantee that they will be accepting and polite. My daughter Karen, without children, will probably move in close to take a few soundings."

Andrew had been invited to dinner by his son and daughter-in-law. The meal had been cleared and they were having coffee at the table. Their two children were upstairs doing homework. Andy carried on with the subject at hand and said to his father, "No question that you should bring Emily to your house. You can do anything you wish. You don't need anyone's permission. When you talked to her about it, what did she say?"

"She was hesitant. She knew she would pass in review in front of you six and that my social circle would have been breached by an outsider, a mid-westerner no less."

"We're curious, Dad. For myself, I'm delighted there's love after seventy-five." Andy's wife said, in a stage whisper, "And don't you forget it."

"They've done studies on that, Andy. Attraction and love are not connected to age. Should she meet you individually or should I plan a party at my place and have us together?"

"Have it at your place. Have it catered. We may as well bring the kids," Andy said.

"Do you think Emily will feel overwhelmed?" Andrew asked.

Andy's wife, who had been silent, said, "Doesn't make any difference what formula you use. She knows that meeting the family is unavoidable. If she's the woman you say she is, we'll like her and she'll like us back." With that they set a date.

Andrew drove up Interstate 5, as he had done so many times over the years for himself or to pick up relatives and friends. He drove into the parking structure and went to the third floor right away, not wasting time hunting for a space on the lower floors. He walked across the road into the terminal, looked at his wristwatch, and sat down to read before moving into the baggage claim area where she had to appear.

He had not stood long when Emily came into view. She spotted him right away. She was wearing Navy blue trousers, a cream-colored blouse and a blue sweater with buttons down the front. They didn't say anything before they kissed. Anyone aware of them would think they were one of many married couples. It seemed to Andrew that she had brushed her teeth and applied perfume over Nevada.

He took her overcoat and made the motion of weighing it. She said, "You forget. I had to get to the airport." They moved to the end of the baggage carrier, which came in a straight line down one side of the hall. Andrew always used that spot because he could find access to the moving belt. They stood close together. She had her arm around his waist. She said, "Imagine, coming down from the airplane on a ladder. How quaint. I know I've never done that before."

"Lets you know you are in Southern California."

"And when it rains?" she asked.

"They pass out umbrellas. All very modern." He leaned toward her to kiss her and said, "I'm so glad to see you."

They drove the fifteen miles to his house. He pulled into the garage and was relieved that his neighbors were not outside working on a lawn or a flowerbed. Emily carried one of her two bags into the house through the kitchen. She put it down and started inspecting. She moved slowly through the rooms and stopped at the French doors at the end of the living room. "Mind if I open them?" she asked.

"No, of course not." Then Andrew said, "I spend a fair amount of time out there reading and drinking coffee, and doing a minimum of gardening." She moved about slowly, looking at the plantings. She came back to where the garden furniture was arranged around a table. "Did you put up the parasol before you came to fetch me?"

"Yes. I was out here for a while. Why don't you choose a chair and settle in? I'll get you the drink you ask for, if I have it."

She selected the garden chair still catching the sun's rays. The sun would set soon. He was standing near her chair. She reached out for his hand and rubbed the back of it against her cheek and kissed it. "Scotch and soda, and don't ask any questions."

She stretched her legs and let the perfect late winter day move in on her. What would it be like to marry Andrew and live here? She was certain that he was thinking of the same thing while he was in the kitchen. When he reappeared with two scotches, she said, "Since I saw you last I've been drinking water, milk, a little tea and plenty of coffee. I need a stiff one."

When they finished he said, "Let's go upstairs and get you unpacked." He showed her to one of the children's rooms. They left her bags there and went into his bedroom. She looked around and said, "Thoughtful of you to remove your wife's pictures."

"Open the top drawer of the bureau," he said. She did as he suggested and pulled out the first photograph. She studied it for a moment and turned to Andrew. "Is this why we are together?"

"We are together because we want to be. You and my wife may resemble one another, but you are quite different people. When I clear everything else away, what's left is that you are a joy to be with."

She put away the photograph and they sat on the edge of the bed. "I want to go back again to that first swim. I dove in and when I came up and looked your way, something came over your face. Do you recall that?"

"Yes, I recall the moment. I met my wife in the surf at Santa Monica. Turns out we were at the University together, at UCLA. We were diving through the waves. My first words to her were, 'Are you all right?' Not exactly a great line."

"It worked, of course," Emily said.

They lay on the bed and he told her he loved her. "That's a first for me," she said. And then she went on, "It has such a wonderful sound to it. It can't help to make me more affectionate towards you. I'll tell you my feeling tonight."

"Under cover of darkness?"

"Should loosen my tongue. What have you planned for us?"

"Nothing, really. Caterers are arriving at three o'clock tomorrow. The family arrives at six. Dinner at seven. Nothing the rest of the time you're here. I'm taking us to a good restaurant a few miles from here, on Sunset. You might see a celebrity if they're feeding tonight."

"I'm nervous over meeting your family. Is that OK?"

"Just means you care. They'll love you."

Under cover of darkness, as Andrew had remarked, Emily had told him that he brought stability and purpose into her life. It was his intense interest in her that she found appealing. "We don't know each other that well and not for very long, but I see for the first time how two people intertwining their lives can create something of enormous value to both."

"It's so simple, really," Andrew had said.

"If it's so simple, why is it so rare?"

"It's so rare because in most cases the ingredients don't match. The wrong people end up together and that wonderful affection can't develop between the two people. It doesn't stand a chance."

Moments later she had said, "I love you, darling." It was the first time she had uttered those words to a man and the first time she had used the word *darling.* "I don't understand it. It's so soon, so quick."

The following evening she was ready at five-thirty. She wore a black dress made of wool. The sleeves came to the elbow and the dress just to the knees. The dress was cut so that her pearls rested on her skin, yet nothing showed. She applied very little makeup and did not use earrings. She had set out deliberately to be more formal than the three women who were coming, although she was not much older than they were. She was being presented as a possible wife and stepmother, so it made sense to be more formal than they.

Andrew was aware that in the hour or so before dinner Emily made certain that she talked to the six adults and met their children. The children ranged in age from five to eleven and appeared to her to get along well together. The oldest of them, Andy's son, took charge of the other three. Emily wondered how he would develop.

She looked at Andrew across the room a few times during the hour and smiled. She hoped that he understood that it was going well. Andrew seated Emily to his right at dinner, not at the other end of the table. There were toasts, conversations and plenty of laughter.

The end of the evening came. The caterers restored order. Emily felt slightly on edge saying her goodbyes at the front door. Here she was new to the family, new to Andrew, and yet there she was acting as lady of the house saying goodnight to the three who had grown up there. Andy tried to make it easy for her. He put his arms around her lightly, kissed her on the cheek, and said only for her to hear, "Emily, you're terrific."

Andrew and Emily stayed downstairs for a while, holding hands on the large sofa. Emily acknowledged his family. "A monumental task creating those three children. Each a wonder. See what happens? They find appropriate mates and then fabricate the next generation. Aren't you proud?"

"Yes, but more than that I'm happy for them that they lead productive lives. I'd say that I'm blessed."

She got up from the couch, turned around and sat down again, facing him. She touched his hair and said, "Still more than half brown. I'd call it wiry. Gray at the temples. Distinguished professor of physics."

Before she could go on, he interjected, "Retired professor." She looked into his eyes and said, "No gray there, all good chocolate." She kissed his face. "I'm taking a hot shower and modeling some white silky pajamas for you. Hope you like them."

He thought he might remind her that she claimed to be a nightgown person in Chicago, but then he decided it didn't make any difference.

He smiled and cocked his head to one side. "I don't want to take anything away from your pajamas but I suppose you've noticed that it's what inside the pajamas that I gravitate to." She kissed him again and said, "Meeting the family had some stress attached to it. I'm going up. I'll track you down."

There were air trips in both directions. Andrew had been thinking about the effects on his life if he transferred it to Chicago. He couldn't imagine living there but on one trip he could no longer resist bringing up the move. He went right to the point and said to Emily, "How does one rebuild a life in a new city, after pulling out by the roots a lifetime spent elsewhere?"

She tried to sound casual but it was clear to Andrew that she had been analyzing the problem. She started out. "I think you break it down into its component parts. Isn't that one of the activities of problem solving?"

"Something you learned in college?" Andrew asked.

"In business school, in fact, also at Northwestern. They used to make us think about solving problems. I suppose they still do."

"Doesn't it come down to food, clothing and shelter?" he asked.

"You're oversimplifying and pulling my leg. Let's start with exercise. Have to find out what you are accustomed to. Then you need a place to do the exercises. You've mentioned church. The Episcopalians are waiting for you. That's easy. Then friends. Do you have acquaintances left over from your days in physics? And the last thing that comes to mind is some productive aspect to your life. There are tons of organizations that would eat you up."

Andrew wanted to ask her if she were reading from a list. "You forgot doctors and dentists."

"You could use mine," she volunteered.

These three-day contacts were reassuring to both. Andrew warmed to the embrace. She enveloped him in attention, discussion, and ample affection. She was a naturally warm, sensual creature and with that sustaining them, they floated along with the greatest ease. She kept him on her mind; that much was clear. There were those thoughtful conversations and small gifts, almost off hand, that told him so.

For her part, she lost all sense of loneliness and the despair that she had known so long. There was that sense of optimism, new to her, that love brings. He filled her life in the ways it needed it. So simple, as he had told her, because just by being in love they could produce alternately excitement and serenity for the present and inevitably they arrived at hope for the future.

While packing on a Sunday afternoon, he had asked, "Could the

Bard possibly know anything about parting that we do not know?" She answered right away. "No, but he knew it four centuries ago."

He had been back from Chicago for two days and was standing in the kitchen making a cup of tea. It was a Wednesday and four- thirty in Los Angeles, therefore six-thirty in Chicago. His phone rang and it was Emily on the other end as he expected.

"Dearest, I'm just going to say it. I believe that I'm pregnant."

Andrew was determined not to go blank. He would concentrate on the issue. "This is what you've wanted all your adult life, isn't it?" "Yes, of course." "How do you know you're pregnant?" "I started to feel different so I went to the drugstore and bought two pregnancy kits – different brands – and they both tested positive." "You haven't seen a doctor yet?" "No." "Good idea if you did that soon."

As they had been talking he wondered how a fifty-three year old woman became pregnant. He asked, "Have you been taking fertility pills?" "I should have thought of it, but no. You must be my fertility pill." "How so?" "I think that when a woman is madly in love and she wants a child, a minor medical miracle can take place. I had one final egg that passed through the various tubes and met one spermatozoa of yours." She trailed off and Andrew said, "I think we ought to get married, baby or no baby, come to think of it." "Well, I'd love that, of course."

"My minister could marry us. He's suggested that I should marry, if only for my health." "You can't get any healthier," she said. "He means mental health," Andrew answered. Andrew told her that the advantage of marrying in Los Angeles rather than in Chicago was that she might not be required to move so many people to the ceremony as he would if they were to marry in Chicago." She interjected, "I'm providing my own matron of honor."

It was her week for Emily to fly to Los Angeles. Before she left her doctor confirmed the pregnancy. She met the rector of Andrew's church and his wife, Jim and Sally. They both knew the in-and-outs of the marriage license and where to obtain it. Andrew and she went to a fine jeweler and bought the rings. The solitaire weighed one and a quarter carats to which Emily objected. "Too much money," she said. He maintained that it was in scale with her height and that she would get used to its size. They studied the calendar and selected a Saturday five weeks in the future. "I can't be showing at the ceremony," she said.

Before they married, Andrew worked on the problem of the move to Chicago. He had already determined that he would change little in his current life, that is, he wouldn't sell his house until his new life was far along, if then.

The transition to their new lives seemed easy for both. It was the season of warm months and Andrew adapted quickly to seeking air-conditioned places. Emily's apartment became too tempting and Andrew had to put pressure on himself to move out onto the city streets. Emily continued to work. Andrew insisted on doing half the housework, most of the shopping and some cooking. He told Emily that his decade as a bachelor had served some purpose and now he was ready to branch out and experiment with French cooking. He bought a book of recipes and a large frying pan for heating vegetables. He would cut peppers, a green one, also a red one and a yellow one, add to that onions and garlic, tomatoes and eggplant and fry them in olive oil before placing all of it in a stew pot. It was his first experiment. He had not got the knack of cooking rice and left it to Emily.

They were conscious of harmony. There never seemed to be a need to disagree and there were no flashes of temper that needed reconciliation. Andrew had to adjust to his having lived alone for a decade and it was all new to Emily. Andrew worked on making every day pleasurable and interesting for Emily. He thought she deserved the best he had to offer. He knew that he had found the easiest person in the world to be with. She was more quiet than talkative, but entertaining in the way she spoke.

On the matter of affection, Andrew thought she was outrageous. She might come to him while he was on the sofa and start by sitting on his lap and slowly pushing him over and lying on top of him. She would tell him that she couldn't help it. In bed she was playful and more than available. She said to Andrew once, "It's like having the same thing for breakfast every morning and enjoying it. I don't need variety. I just need you." At the start of the seventh month her doctor put an end to such pleasures.

For his principal hobby, Andrew went back to Latin. He had taken four years of it in boarding school and had enjoyed the grounding it gave him in grammar and vocabulary. He had always been aware of words and their uses, how to spell them and where they originated. He found a class at the University and enrolled. He was by far the oldest student. Some of the Latin came back to him. Most was new, which forced him to memorize. It came as a pleasant surprise to him that at the university level Latin was taught along with Roman civilization. This had not been the practice at his boarding school.

Andrew recalled a conversation he had with a medical doctor he did not know very well. Andrew had asked him if his career had been satisfying inasmuch as it appeared to have had many threads such as pathology, family medicine, and research into the prevention of cancer, and therefore no concentration. The doctor answered that each stage fed the next and he was satisfied that the number of his accomplishments and their importance would increase. Andrew concluded that his reading during the last decade would feed his interest in continuing the study of the Roman civilization. It gave him impetus in carrying on when his appetite slacked off, as it did from time to time.

Emily complained of headaches occasionally. They went away quickly and Emily blamed them on her pregnancy. The obstetrician in charge of Emily felt all along that she was proceeding normally through the stages and at the time of birth he told her that the labor and delivery were normal in all aspects. They had agreed to name the child Catherine and filled out the birth certificate Catherine Evans Wilson. Emily had said, "There's no use spending any time going over boy's names. I know this is a girl."

Betsy, Andrew's second child, mother of two, came to keep Emily company and tend to the baby. Emily took great delight in breast-feeding Catherine. Mother at last, she was indicating. Betsy returned home after ten days. Little Catherine was prospering.

PART 5

Andrew became head of household and took on most of his wife's duties. Six weeks after Catherine was born Emily admitted that her headaches were more frequent and severe. "Let's face it, could be a tumor tucked away in there somewhere," she said. Andrew ran his hand through her hair and waited for Emily to continue. "If it is that, they'll shave off my hair." "You could try wigs of different color," he said. "No one would recognize me." She waited a moment then said, "At fifty-three, almost fifty-four, I finally got it right. Went from nothing to everything in one year. Now they may be conspiring to take it away from me." "Who is they, sweetheart?" "A few evil cells," she answered. "We'll send the medicine men to do them in."

The conversation was taking place in the kitchen. Emily still had on her housecoat. She got up to get more coffee for both of them and remarked that some day soon her clothes would fit again. "Let's do more walking," she said. In a little while she unburdened. "If I die, what will you do with Catherine?" "As the politicians say, I don't deal in hypothetical questions. The statistics are getting better each year on these operations." Then he looked at her and said, "As you know, Catherine is in the best hands possible now. All I can say is that the care and concern for that child will go on unabated." Andrew didn't know whether Emily had been put at ease. She brought her chair next to his and asked, "Any important stories in the paper this morning?"

The neurosurgeon, in obtaining their permission to operate, had talked separately with Andrew and Emily. Perhaps Emily wanted it that way. In any event she stayed home with the baby when Andrew went to the doctor's office.

The neurosurgeon outlined a chronology for Andrew. There would be a CT scan, MRI scan, and X-rays, which he called stereotaxic X-ray measurements that would determine the exact location of the tumor in three dimensions. These procedures would be done prior to Emily's admission to the hospital. If an operation was called for, the neurosurgeon went on, Emily would be admitted, some of the earlier tests would be repeated, taking two or three days, and during the operation he would drill through the skull and extract a sample of the tumor for analysis by a pathologist. The analysis would take about two hours.

"Is that what you call a biopsy?" Andrew asked.

"Yes, the examination of tissue taken from a live body."

"What could be the results of this biopsy?"

"The worst outcome would be that the tumor was tucked away in a part of the brain difficult or impossible to reach and that the pathologist performing the biopsy determined that the tumor was an aggressive type, by that I mean an invasive tumor, called an astrocytoma grade III. If we find those conditions the best we can do is to send your wife home."

"How long would you keep her in the hospital?"

"If it is operable and we are successful, say two weeks. If it's the enemy

I just mentioned and the tumor is inoperable, she can go home the next day. She would only have been here three days."

"I was wondering about her milk. You know Emily has been breast-feeding her baby."

"No, I didn't know. What we tend to do with women who are nursing is to administer medication to slow down the production of milk. Once home, your wife could go back to nursing and her original capacity should return."

"I'd imagined that one could pump out the milk from her breasts and I'd get it to the baby."

"You'd have to move heaven and earth to get a hospital staff to agree to that. People on the surgical floor are too busy."

Andrew signed the paper giving the neurosurgeon permission to operate. Andrew assumed that the conversation between the neurosurgeon and Emily would be about the same as his. They did not compare notes but Emily did say, "Let's get this over with. Would you schedule the start of the tests?"

The results of the tests dampened any optimism that the neurosurgeon might have had. He reported to Andrew that the tumor, while in the frontal lobe, was recessed and difficult to reach. The tumor indeed was imbedded.

The afternoon after the examinations were finished, Emily sat in the living room nursing Catherine. "Tell me it's nothing I've done," she said.

"No, of course not. You've a victim of statistics."

"The same ones that made me wait thirty years for you?"

Andrew said nothing.

"I sense a morality play coming on," Emily said. "That too-long dry spell without my man to produce a family. Your late arrival on the scene to save me from spinsterhood. The miracle of the baby. I'm not barren. And now I'm being whisked away."

"You don't know that, darling."

"I suppose I feel it. How soon can we schedule the operation?" Emily asked.

Andrew made the arrangements. They did not discuss what would happen to Catherine if Emily should die. In fact, they discussed nothing of importance. Andrew sensed that Emily wanted the days to be normal and to achieve that state she discouraged any discussion of the eventualities. The days went by slowly but that could be accounted for by their avoidance of what was to come.

Andrew sat alone in a waiting room near the operating room. He came with two books and the day's paper. There was a television set against the wall, which he turned off. He would look at his wristwatch from time to time. He had seen Emily last when she was prepared for surgery. She had said, "Kiss me." Then she said, "Again, one last time." Andrew came back with, "It's not one last time. It's again."

He had been in the waiting room four and one-half hours when the neurosurgeon came in. He had removed his hat and gloves but still wore his green scrub suit.

"I have only bad news," the neurosurgeon said. "The biopsy showed that your wife's tumor is of the astrocytoma type that we talked about. It's an aggressive tumor and in this case there's no way of removing it without destroying the cognitive functions."

"What did you do?"

"We closed up the surgical site. She's now back in the recovery room."

"May I see her?"

"Yes, any time, but she's out of it right now. The anesthesia should wear off in an hour or two."

"I'm the one to tell her, then?"

"Yes, unless you would rather that I did."

"No, I'll tell her. When can she come home?"

"Tomorrow morning."

"How long does she have?"

"It varies, of course. The average is four months, but it can be longer." Then the neurosurgeon added, "I'm truly sorry. She is a lovely woman. When she came to discuss the operation, about the permission, I found her courageous, and easy to deal with. I could see that she has a beautiful mind."

Andrew commented, "I'm at a loss for words to tell you about her. She has that all too rare gift of expecting the best from herself and yet accepting what comes her way from others. Let me tell you, she's put me on my best behavior."

Andrew went to recovery and found Emily's room. She had a large bandage covering the area where the skull had been drilled. Andrew passed his hand lightly over her skull. He wondered how long it would take her hair to grow back. He moved a chair close to her bed and listened to the sound of her breathing. He would read a page or two from his novel now and again.

Emily did not awake at once. There were those faint nocturnal sounds that Andrew knew so well. Twenty minutes after the first murmur she opened her eyes, took her hand from his, and felt the bandage. "They didn't go in," she said. She lay still without saying anything. She stared at the ceiling and searched for Andrew's hand.

He said softly, "Hello, angel."

"I suppose I could become one soon." Andrew felt tears well up in his eyes. He stood up, leaned over, and kissed her.

"Maybe you'd like a coffee. Dinner will be in a little while. I'd like to stay."

"How long do I have?"

"The neurosurgeon was unsure. Let's wait until tomorrow to talk about that."

"What's left to talk about?"

"Whether you want coffee now and other important matters."

Andrew fetched Emily the following morning. They took a taxi home and Emily started nursing Catherine immediately. There was more milk available than she had hoped. When the baby fell asleep in her arms she looked up at Andrew and said, "Now is the moment, you promised. How long do I have?"

"The average is four months, but it could be a few years."

"I suppose at the end I'll be running on morphine so it could be less than four months."

"Emily, words escape me. There are no words, really. I can't express my sense of loss, my personal loss. I don't have any words. I can't be cheerful and entertaining as you go through this."

"I'll try to be cheerful, then. Wear lipstick, get dressed up, be your wife."

They tried to lead a normal life but it proved impossible. Emily might cry and when she did, Andrew comforted her. She enjoyed being held and kissed. She always perked up when she tended to Catherine, whether by giving her a bath, playing with her, or nursing her.

A week had gone by since she had returned from the hospital. Emily, out of the blue, asked whether they could ask Karen to come for a weekend.

"Yes, of course. What did you have in mind?"

"I want Karen to have Catherine, if you approve. Among our relatives, she's made to order. Your daughter-in-law and your other daughter are wonderful parents but Karen hasn't had a child. Should we ask her?"

"She'd be thrilled, I'm certain," Andrew said.

PART 6

When news came from Chicago that Emily had a brain tumor and would be operated upon, speculation arose among Andrew's three children and their spouses on the disposition of Catherine. It would not be likely that Andrew would attempt to raise the child in the event Emily died.

David, Karen's husband, worked in the business his father had started. Father and son managed the assets of upper middle-income families, many having inherited from their parents. David was interested particularly in increasing the value of a family's assets until the time of retirement when he would switch investments to producing income. There were two assistants who helped him with portfolios. David understood the federal tax code, concentrating on the portions dealing with capital gains and the estate tax. He liked his work and when discussions started between Karen and him that they might bring up Catherine, he denied to her that such an event would interfere with his life. Privately he wondered where the extra time would come from.

Karen had started in retail after college, taking a position in the personnel department of a large store. The work had merit but in the end she decided on having her own retail outlet. She purchased a store that specialized in clothes for working women and poured her energies into that small enterprise. David and Karen thought they would devote the following twenty-five years to their businesses and to their projects in the community. When Emily arrived on the scene, David was forty and Karen thirty-nine.

Each of Andrew's three children and their spouses affirmed that they would raise Catherine if Andrew asked them to. It would mean a return to diapers, night feedings, and the terrible twos, but they told themselves that a child was a blessing and between them they would turn Catherine into a fine adult.

Speculation had increased after Andrew telephoned his son with the outcome of the operation. Andrew had been brief. He asked Andy to relay the news to the others. The children telephoned Chicago, each in turn, and talked to Emily and their father.

A week passed before Emily telephoned Karen. As was her practice, she went right to the point. "Your father and I have been discussing the future, particularly Catherine's. We hoped that you and David could provide her an upbringing."

Karen had rehearsed her answer. She felt that expressing pleasure was uncalled for yet it would be inappropriate not to indicate that Catherine was a gift. Karen answered, "Emily, it's beyond my comprehension how life works. David and I have tried everything, and no child. Now my father meets you and because you are mad about one another a baby arrives. As a reward, a disaster strikes you and your baby falls into our lives, David's and mine. Who wrote this play?"

"I don't know who wrote the play. We can let your father ponder that question. Could you and David come to Chicago so that we can discuss this macabre business?"

"Yes, of course."

Emily went on. "I know we could do all this over the telephone, so this is a favor to me, your coming to Chicago. I want to hear myself discussing my child's future. It doesn't make any sense because you'll do what you think best anyway, but I want to have a hand in it."

"We'll come, be certain of that," Karen said.

Karen and David reasoned that it should be a short visit. They left Burbank for Chicago Saturday morning and planned to return on Sunday. Sleeping arrangements were not disturbed. The guest room had been turned into the nursery. Karen and David slept with Catherine. "You may as well learn the sounds," Emily told them.

There was a service attended by over 100 people. Karen and David flew in from California. The entire crew of the office came. The first cousin and his wife arrived. Many of Emily's friends were in attendance.

Andrew spoke about the miracle that Emily was and the pity that they could not have shared additional years. He spoke about Catherine, who was at the service in Karen's arms. He limited his remarks to the fact that Catherine was indistinguishable from Karen in her baby pictures. He thanked all of them, a few now new friends, for their acceptance of him and their generosity over the past year. He ended by telling them that it made sense for him to return to Los Angeles as his family was centered there. The rector of his new church conducted the service, even though Jim at his church in Los Angeles had offered to come.

The distasteful part began. As Andrew started to pack he felt as though he was disassembling Emily. Her apartment had been put together with care, piece by piece. Andrew had always admired the furniture and artwork. There was a sparseness that matched her personality. The effect had always pleased him. He determined that he would keep her furniture and exchange her pieces for those of his that he thought were second rate. "I can't build a museum to her," he thought, yet he wanted Catherine to inherit this furniture and art and photographs. He didn't envy Karen the job of telling Catherine how she had come about. Her grandfather was really her father. Her mother was her half-sister. She was a love child, surprising and treasured, accidental but none the less miraculous. He regretted that he wouldn't be around for another twenty years to help bring her up.

MOVING NORTH

MOVING NORTH

PART I

It is a town northwest of Mexico City. A stream courses through it during the entire year. The mountains to the north receive snow in the winter and the spring runoff permits the cultivation of the surrounding plain. The Indian population must have grown corn. When the Spaniards came and took title to the land they brought the crops and farm animals they were accustomed to at home.

The population of this town had increased slowly after its founding in the 1650s. By 1970 it was home for about 5,000 souls. There is no precise date for the founding of the town but carved in the cornerstone of the church was the date 1652. In the year 2008 the population had shrunk to under 3,000. Those missing from the census count had migrated to Mexico City or to the United States in search of living wages and opportunity.

The façade of the church faces the town square. The City Hall is on one side and the post office on the other. Straight ahead, away from the church, down a four-step flight of stairs, lies a park with trees and benches. Beyond the square is an open market where farmers sell produce on Saturdays. The center of the park is graced by a fountain that may never have operated, having been turned off earlier than the recollection of the oldest residents. They relate that the issue had been the waste of water.

As you face the church, on the left, are the remains of a square where young men and women met. In the middle of the square stands a statue of Benito Juarez, a president of Mexico in the 1860s. He was the first person with Indian blood to rise to this position. Around the statue is a rectangle the length and width of the church in which, in earlier times, young women accompanied by an older woman would circulate slowly in one direction while young men, unaccompanied, would circulate in the opposite direction.

The young people, for the most part, had known one another all their lives, being together in school and again in church. They exchanged glances and a few words. Intensions were made known. From the middle of the twentieth century, behavior among the young became less formal in Mexico as well as in the United States – perhaps all over the world. The young people no longer circled the statue, women in one direction and men in the other. Weeds were now growing on the square. The benches were still functional but the old people no longer sat on them in the early evenings. The two outdoor cafés that bordered the small rectangle were closed. One owner had moved to another part of town and the second had retired.

Women's clothes were tighter and revealed more than they had in the past. Young men and women developed a code of conduct in which they made their own decisions. The roles of parents were reduced in importance as their children reached maturity.

The postman for the town was Francisco Suarez. A few of his friends called him Pancho because Pancho Villa's first name was Francisco, and the postman had the same round face and mustache that General Villa had. There is a postmaster and there are two clerks to run the post office, and Francisco Suarez delivered the mail. He made the rounds on foot, covering the businesses and homes around the center of town. To deliver the occasional letter on the outskirts he rode his bicycle. He lived on the border of town in a house built by his father that he had enlarged. It is built of cinder block and Francisco has plans to enlarge it or build a small second house on the property for his son and oldest child, Enrico. There is enough land for fruit trees and a vegetable garden.

The property adjoining Francisco's is vacant. The couple who lived there has made a new home in Los Angeles. Their four children are grown up and have moved to Mexico City. They took this step when it became obvious that they would not find work in their town. The couple living in Los Angeles still holds title to the land and house; no one has come along interested in buying it. The postman was instructed by his departed neighbors to harvest the fruit from the trees and fence in a yard for chickens if he wished. The postman does indeed pick the fruit in season. His wife sells the crop at the market on Saturdays; the postman decided against raising chickens as many people already sell chickens and eggs at the market at a reasonable price.

Francisco is married to Maria Dora. They have three sons. It is 2008, and even twenty years previously it was obvious to many adults that the babies were coming faster than the jobs. Why have six children if they must move away? Some will go to a big city to find employment. Others will join the millions making their way north in the hope of finding opportunity.

Francisco and Maria Dora's oldest son is named Enrico. He is twenty years old. The next son is over eighteen and is named Cristobal. There is a third son, Hernando, who is sixteen

Enrico works for Francisco's best friend, Juan Aparicio. Juan is the owner of a large tract of land that has been in his family for generations. Enrico is learning agriculture. Juan and Louisa, his wife, have four daughters. The oldest is Maria Theresa, who goes by Theresa. Many girls are given the name of the Virgin as their first name and to avoid confusion go by their second names. There are no sons. The man who marries Maria Theresa, in time, will be the new master of the land and house along with Maria Theresa.

Enrico and Theresa have known one another since they were small children. As it is with children, they did not pair off until their last years in school. Enrico became acutely aware of women when he passed through puberty. Of course he had seen photographs of partially clothed women in magazines but these did not have the effect on him of seeing Theresa in a bathing suit. Juan built a small swimming pool on his property, fed by a stream. It was shallow enough to be warmed by the sun. Juan's style of swimming did not include any of the formal strokes. Swimming to him meant staying afloat. He was only interested in having his children conquer their fear of water. The depth of the pool was four feet. Only the children who could stand comfortably in four feet of water were allowed in unsupervised.

In the summer of their twelfth year Enrico and Theresa learned to swim. Juan taught them to float on their backs and also to put their heads under water. In her twelfth year Teresa wore a one-piece bathing suit. She had started her development and Enrico, fantasizing about what they might do if there were no others around, felt an erection come on more than once. In their thirteenth year, she had filled out and was allowed by her mother to wear a bikini. Enrico thought a great deal about her, particularly at night as he tried to fall asleep.

It was in this thirteenth year that Theresa turned sweet on Enrico. Although he had no inkling of it, it was he whom Theresa dreamed of marrying. He would work on the farm first and then when her father moved into late middle age he would be thrust to the position of importance in order to inherit the property along with Theresa. To Theresa it seemed an ideal life, removed safely from poverty. The land provided food and shelter. The water from the hills made cultivation possible. There would always be food to eat and extra food and animals to sell. Theresa imagined that Enrico would be pleased to be the chosen one. He would be surrounded by everything required to sustain an agreeable life and in addition they would have one another. Those driving impulses that he must feel in his loins could be translated into satisfaction. She would give herself to him without reservation. Many times she had looked at that strong body, perfectly formed, as they sunned themselves at the pool. At fourteen she had wanted him inside her in the worst way but she was reconciled to the long wait. First, she must make him focus on her and after that he had to recognize that a life in which he was married to her was superior to any other solution he might imagine for himself.

At the end of the schooling of Enrico and Maria Theresa, her father, Juan Aparicio, through his friend Francisco Suarez, arranged for Enrico to come to work for him. The offer had been preceded by conversations first between Theresa and her mother, and soon after between Theresa and both her mother and father. Theresa expressed her desire of spending her life on the family property and raising a family. She had no ambition to move to a big city or to migrate north.

The mayor of their town had mentioned to Juan that Theresa could come to work for him. He had been widowed recently and his youngest child was only six years old. Juan conveyed this offer to Theresa who turned it down immediately. While she would still live in the town where she was born if she worked for the widowed mayor, her plan of living her life on the land where her ancestors had lived would not be satisfied. She also guessed that the mayor, only in his thirty-ninth year, would focus on her if she were living in his home. She understood the power of her beauty.

Enrico saw Theresa most days. She was busy around the place and helped her mother run the house. Her three younger sisters were still in school. When Enrico started working at Juan's farm, it came to him that if he married Theresa his status in the town could change. He and Theresa would be heirs to the farm. It had become clear to him that Theresa wanted marriage and a family and that he was the logical man for her. He could sense her sweetness toward him on all occasions, and that included the times when he and the other workers on the farm came in for lunch, which was served at a long table in the kitchen. She would never pass up the opportunity to exchange pleasantries with him.

It seemed natural to Theresa to demonstrate her attractiveness to other men and this she did particularly to Cristobal, Enrico's younger brother. He was a year younger than she was and he had grown to resemble his older brother in appearance. His personality, however, was different. He was less serious and more light-hearted and amusing than his older brother. She had watched him grow up and noticed closely as he filled out and reached his full stature. He was a larger than Enrico and because of this he established himself easily among those his age. Theresa paid enough attention to Cristobal so that his brother would notice, but not enough to stir up a rivalry. In spite of mild flirtations it was clear to both brothers that Theresa wanted Enrico.

Theresa's work clothes were jeans and a tight shirt that showed off her body. She was almost as tall as Enrico and he could imagine that if they were in bed he could kiss her as the same time as their toes touched. When he came to her house on Sundays after church she would dress in the traditional fashion with her hair up and held in place with two large combs. The dress was white and went to the floor. She had several wide belts, red, blue, or green, which she wore alternately. The front of the dress was sufficiently open to show the top of her breasts. He had touched her there once. The occasion was leaving her house after a Sunday evening dinner as he was kissing her. She allowed his hand to rest on one breast for a moment before pulling it away. She said, "Enrico, you are a special man," and kissed him tenderly. It was clear to Enrico that he had to declare his intentions soon because the intensity between them was building.

Enrico and Theresa had been in the same year in school. He could look back and recreate her appearance to the time when they were ten years old. Beyond that she was just a child. He could recall when she developed, in her twelfth and thirteenth years. All the girls in the class went through the same changes. When Theresa singled him out, she did not tease him or make fun of him for a mistake he had made during recitation. She offered to help him with mathematics. He would wonder at the use he would find for algebra. She would tell him that the more he understood of mathematics the more he would grasp of the workings of the Universe. This was the most revealing comment he had heard from any source. As a result, he set Theresa aside as the first person to turn to for an explanation of most anything.

Their first kiss came in the final year of school. Both had experienced kisses with others. On this occasion he had borrowed the family pick-up and taken Theresa to a dance. When he brought her home they kissed at the front door and rather than break away she kept her arms around him and placed her head on his shoulder. Enrico thought it was natural yet exciting to hold Theresa in his arms. She said, "I like being with you. You dance so well and you always treat me with respect. He answered, "You are a lovely woman, Theresa." They kissed again.

When Enrico came to work for Theresa's father he knew nothing about farming. He started with the operation and maintenance of the machinery and then learned about planting, irrigation, harvesting and preparing produce for market. Other young men concerned themselves with farm animals. Juan Aparicio kept a horse so that he could ride over the ranch. Tractors had replaced draft horses some fifty years previously. He kept two cows for butter, cream and milk.

Enrico came frequently on Sundays after church. The invitation was always issued by either Juan or his wife. On occasion Theresa would go to the Suarez home. In either place Theresa assumed the role of a mature young woman, as though she were married, yet there was no husband for the moment.

Rather than bringing up the matter of their relationship, Enrico would mention to Theresa that he was interested in crossing the border and starting a new life. Theresa found all the difficulties with such a plan to which Enrico could only answer that ten million people had done it and managed to stay. The figure of ten million was in the press regularly and was discussed on the television news. She listed the language barrier, lack of job prospects and the fact that he had no contacts to turn to. "Here," she would say, "you have everything." Once she added, "Even me." Enrico was surprised by the remark but recognized in it a suggestion that needed to be addressed soon. For the moment he was quiet, but one day he declared that there was so much more to the world besides working on a farm in the town where he had been born. Theresa countered, "You know that I have hoped that our lives here can be made complete together, and in time we can take the places of my mother and father." Enrico answered, "Yes, I understand that. Perhaps their places are to be taken by one of your sisters and another man."

Theresa saw at once that the plan she had made for her life was not shared by Enrico. Nothing could be served by delay. "Enrico, if you make the move to the North, what will happen to you and me?"

"I will come for you," he answered.

"How long will it take?"

"In less than a year I will have a good job and know the language."

"I will wait a year, Enrico."

"Other men will want you. Will you wait?"

"Yes, I promise."

There were other conversations prior to his leaving for the border, but these few words summed up their feelings for each other.

Enrico had discussed his interest in migrating north with both his parents. On occasion, his brother Cristobal would take part. Enrico's father, Francisco, did not take his son's ambitions seriously. Enrico had steady work with regular wages and he also had Theresa. It was clear to Enrico's parents that Enrico and Theresa would marry. It seemed to them that Enrico's position was enviable and that his prospects would overcome Enrico's will to migrate. It would be impossible, Francisco felt, for Enrico to improve on his situation. How else could he become part owner of a productive farm and the sole owner of a woman with the qualities of Theresa?

When Enrico talked with his parents on the subject, his views of the country to the north seemed to be those that one would gather from films and TV. "The streets are clean and everything seems to work." "The toilets are always inside the house." "You can drink the water anywhere so you don't need to buy bottles of it." These were some observations that Enrico made, which Francisco could not refute. Francisco could point out that Enrico was talking about life in general in Mexico, and not about his own situation.

Enrico emphasized to his father that there was no corruption in the United States. Enrico had been told that the money siphoned out of the Mexican economy by corruption could be used to make many improvements in his country. His father asked him, "If we ended the corruption in our country, how would it affect us?" Enrico had no answer except to remark that it would be better if all citizens could keep their money rather than be forced to give a portion away.

Francisco dealt with the matter by saying that corruption was in the hearts of most men and many women in all countries. The difference between the United States and Mexico was only a matter of degree. Enrico had asked his father once, "Did you have to buy your job at the Post Office when you started?"

His father answered, "No, not buy it."

"Do you pay someone now?" Enrico asked.

"Yes, from my pay I give to the union. It represents us in negotiations. We pay the salary of the union worker. I believe they do that in the United States."

"Do you know where all the money goes?"

"Not exactly."

That conversation took place only once and Francisco drew from it that Enrico supposed that his father was a small part of a corrupt system and that there was no equivalent to it in the United States. Enrico would also point out to his father that Mexico's population was growing too fast to supply jobs to young people as they came out of school and entered the work force. Francisco was quick to remind his son that he and Enrico's mother had recognized the trend before he was born and had limited their family to three children, rather than have six as many parents did.

Enrico would speak of his dreams; who knows what he might

accomplish in life if he could work in a large organization with opportunities? Working on the farm meant to him that he could be a successful farmer as he and Theresa replaced her parents. But that was a small life and he could see the entirety of it, from beginning to end, after working for Juan and Louisa less than two years. With unlimited opportunity in the United States he might accomplish a great deal. His father caught the excitement in Enrico's voice.

Francisco would from time to time invoke the historical prospective. He had been born in 1955 while his father was born thirty years previously, in 1925.

Francisco said, "The great revolution of 1910 was over. People, mostly Indians, were liberated. The country became richer, though slowly. My father went barefoot but he did have sandals made from old automobile tires. He worked in the fields. He was a peon. He worked most of his life on a large ranch and he only sometimes had enough pesos. The owner of the ranch was good to him and his wife, my mother, and to us, the children. We lived in a small house and always had food. Toward the end of his life my father bought a radio and would listen to the music in the evenings. It was through his wife that he inherited this property. They started this house and spent their final years here."

"Why are you telling me these things when you have told them to me before?" Enrico asked.

"Because Mexico is changing. My father had a radio. I have a TV. I have a regular job at the post office so I can support my wife and my three children. I have shoes and clothes. We have a small truck. The next generation will have more. You will go to the doctor and the dentist, maybe even when there is nothing wrong. You and Theresa might go somewhere as tourists, not as illegal immigrants."

"But if I go up there where they have made all these changes years ago and I don't have to wait, why shouldn't I advance myself if I am able?"

"Because it is up to the young to make something of their country. If too many go to the North, many of our small cities and towns will dry up and die." Whenever Francisco expressed this opinion, he got little reaction from his son.

They had gone back and forth about going north several times. Francisco and his wife wanted very much for their oldest son to stay in his town of birth and have their first grandchildren. They loved Theresa as much as Enrico did, but they would not express these sentiments. It seemed fair to concentrate only on the practical reasons for Enrico to stay.

When the time came for Enrico to leave, the difficult moments were with his parents and his brothers, not with Theresa. She was understanding and made every effort to avoid tears. It wouldn't do to let Enrico know that he was breaking her heart. "Your father, our postman, will deliver your letters to me. I need to know where you are and what you are doing. Can you write me once a month?"

"Yes, and you will answer? I need news of you and my town."

"When I have received the twelfth letter I will know to expect you very soon."

Enrico's father drove him to the large town less than an hour away where Enrico took the bus to Monterrey.

Within a week of Enrico's departure, Theresa, through her mother and father, and from them to Francisco, extended an invitation to Cristobal to work on the farm and fill the vacancy created by his brother's departure.

Cristobal accepted immediately. Since finishing his schooling he had been using the family truck to operate his moving business, occupying two or three days a week on average. He would accept any odd job presented to him. The idea of working regular hours for a known salary, with lunch served in the kitchen of the big house on the farm, had great appeal. There was Theresa herself, followed by three sisters. He would be able to find the correct woman for himself from among these four. It appeared to Cristobal that Theresa was taken, but then his brother might come for a visit lasting a few weeks only to re-cross the border to the north.

In his third month on the job, Cristobal was invited by Theresa's parents to return to the farm for lunch after church. The long dress that he had heard about appeared. Theresa looked beautiful to Cristobal, with the hair piled up on her head, held in place with two large combs. After lunch they walked out of the house and sat on a bench in the shade of tall trees.

Theresa announced that there had been three letters from Enrico, a fact already circulated in the Suarez family. Francisco Suarez kept track of these matters and complained to his family if his son wrote more frequently to Theresa than he did to them. Theresa told Cristobal that Enrico liked the town he had found and that he was learning a great deal about carpentry and a surprising amount of English.

"You resemble your brother in the face, but your body is larger, perhaps stronger," Theresa said.

"Yes, I can lift him easily," Cristobal answered.

"You are more sweet and gentle than Enrico is. I think you are playful. It comes naturally to you."

"That is very kind, Theresa."

"There is a dance next week. If you took me I would not have to stay home and wait for Enrico's letter."

"Yes, I am honored to take you to the dance, Theresa, but people will talk."

"I promised Enrico that I would wait for him for a year. I did not promise to wait for him in a convent."

They attended the dance together. Tongues wagged all over town. Young men who would have kept their distance now recognized Theresa as provisionally available. Her social life started ever so slowly to occupy more of her evenings.

When they returned from the dance and Cristobal was walking Theresa to her front door, she said, "I hope you would like to kiss me. I know I would enjoy it."

In the fashion that Theresa arranged matters, it would be to her benefit to have Cristobal spend more time thinking about her than about her closest younger sister. Her name was Lela and she was as much younger than Cristobal as Cristobal was younger than Theresa, the difference in both cases being eleven months. Theresa knew Lela to be as pretty as she but then she had a more voluptuous body than Lela. Theresa knew as well that after giving birth to three children, which she hoped to do, that Lela would surpass her with the more desirable body, but she recognized also that men do not think deeply into the future. Theresa's task, she felt, was to locate the correct young man for her sister and have him move into the family circle.

MOVING NORTH
PART 3

A fine looking man in his mid-thirties walked into the restaurant and nodded to the lady at the cash register. She took a menu off the top of a stack and said, "Right over here, please." She led the man to a table near the window. When he was seated she asked him whether he might start with something to drink. Without hesitation he looked at her and said, "Yes, a *Dos Equis*, please."

The restaurant was in a medium to poor section of Monterrey, the capital of the state of Nuevo Leon. The city is situated about one hundred miles south and west of the closest point on the Mexican border with the United States. At that point the border is the Rio Grande. The fine-looking man came to this restaurant as part of his routine of making the trip north, from Monterrey to the state of Arkansas, where he lived. This would be his eleventh trip north in as many years. He was one of the early illegal migrants, having made his first crossing north before the tidal wave.

His roots were farther south, in the state of Coahuila. He was from a farm family and while he had thought about remaining on the farm he concluded that as an adventurer he should move away and try his luck in the United States, where there was reported to be opportunity for a hard working, law abiding person. His name was Antonio Martinez. He had thought of changing it to Tony Martin to give it an Anglo sound, but ended by simply shortening his first name to Tony. That would be among friends and co-workers. On his documents he kept the original name.

On that first trip north he had come into this restaurant for no particular reason except that there was a sign in the window advertising the beer he drank. He had fallen into conversation with an older man at the next table and they discussed how he planned to cross the border. It came out soon enough that Antonio was on his way to Nuevo Laredo where he would cross the bridge and make his way to the bus station and buy a ticket for a city to the north.

His new acquaintance at the next table said, "Fifty-fifty chance you'll get picked up by the Border Patrol." Antonio asked the man how he had crossed, if indeed he had, and how successful he had been. The man announced that he always flew. "You need to go over the heads of the Border Patrol," he said.

"Much money?" Antonio had asked.

"No, not bad when you consider that you don't have to try a second time," his neighbor answered.

Eleven years had gone by since Antonio's first trip as an illegal immigrant. Over the years on about half his trips, Antonio had discussed crossing the border with a young Mexican who he guessed was on his first try. Each time he had suggested the airplane trip. The young man to the right of Antonio on this occasion was finishing his meal. He still had on his hat, as most of the men in the restaurant did.

"Going north?" Antonio asked.

"Yes, tomorrow."

"How?"

"Bus to Nuevo Laredo."

"And then?"

"I have the name and address of a coyote. They take you across the border."

"You walk, run out of water, get picked up by the Border Patrol," Antonio said.

"You think all the time?" the young man asked.

"Often enough. The coyote has your money. You're in the bus back to Laredo."

"You have a better way?"

"Yes, of course. You have the worst way. Even if they don't catch you it's a long way to a job and a place to live. You run out of money and you think about going back to Mexico. The best way to go is by plane."

The young man introduced himself. "I'm Enrico Suarez."

"Antonio Martinez," the older man said. "How much money do you have," he asked.

The young man frowned and paused for a moment. "Two hundred seventy-five dollars," he answered. The older man scanned the face of the younger. "You have to shave off that mustache," he said. The young man said nothing. The older one added, "The hat goes too."

The older man asked, "Do you speak any English?" The answer came back, "Next to nothing."

"Can you be here this time tomorrow night?" the older man asked. "We fly the day after tomorrow in the morning."

"Where do we go?"

"In the direction of Houston then by car to Arkansas."

"Arkansas. I don't know any Arkansas."

"It's too complicated. I'll show you on the map tomorrow," Antonio said.

They were about to get up and pay their bills when Antonio asked, "Do you have someone waiting for you at home?"

"Yes, Maria Theresa."

"You will save up money and send for her?"

"Perhaps. I could save up money and go back to her."

"Is she beautiful?"

"Yes, very."

"Will other men come around?"

"Yes, I suppose so, but she promised."

"We have women in Arkansas from Mexico, from Nicaragua, and from Guatemala. Beautiful young women waiting to marry a young, handsome Mexican."

"Why are you telling me all this?" Enrico asked.

"Because you send money home. You have a little left over. You go to a dance and meet a lovely woman. Something starts between you two. The next time you send less money home. The memories of Theresa become faint. It's always like that with men."

"Impossible. Theresa and I are very in love."

"But it's the same way with Theresa. If you say she is beautiful she will meet a handsome man who will make her forget you. He could have a good job and be rich. He is right there in her town. You are up in Arkansas. That's the way it is when you leave home."

The young man lowered his head and said nothing. Antonio went on. "Tell me what you prefer, an Anglo woman who speaks Spanish, an Anglo woman who does not speak Spanish, or a Mexican woman?"

"Why would I want an Anglo woman who didn't speak Spanish?" Enrico asked.

"Because you learn English faster that way," Antonio answered.

"Are they pretty and slim, these three women?"

"Yes, all pretty and slim. What do you like best?"

"Theresa first, of course. After that I like the Anglo woman who speaks Spanish. I learn English slowly that way."

Antonio nodded. He stood up and said to Enrico, "OK, be here tomorrow this time and we fly the day after."

Antonio was in the habit of padding his schedule with an extra day. The pilot was not certain of the day he would make the roundtrip to Houston. Antonio never asked the reason but he assumed that the pilot waited for six passengers to materialize. On this trip there would be six passengers: four businessmen, himself and Enrico. Antonio would not approach a new migrant in the restaurant he frequented unless there was an empty seat in the plane. From the bar in his hotel, Antonio telephoned the pilot to tell him that he had a sixth passenger who could pay one hundred and fifty dollars. Then he asked the pilot about the stop for coffee and gas on the way to Houston. The pilot told him they would use strip number four. Antonio telephoned his wife in Arkansas and told her he would see her the day after tomorrow, gave her the name of the small airport, and in the following moment he mentioned that he had a friend traveling with him who preferred Anglo women who spoke Spanish. They only chatted for a few minutes. He asked her how their kids were.

Antonio didn't think that the pilot carried drugs on the plane. He knew that if the authorities found drugs in a plane they confiscate it and the pilot never sees it again. The businessmen in the plane could be visiting important people in Houston and it might be to arrange various transactions, legal or not. These men always carried briefcases. Antonio thought they might be lawyers. From year to year they would be different people. He never started a conversation with them beyond saying hello.

The landing strips they would drop into when they were half-an-hour out of Houston had a few light planes each. Antonio assumed that they belonged to local ranchers who used them to fly to San Antonio or Dallas. The pilot could buy gas and two out of the four airports had a café and a restroom. Number four was one of these. Antonio was aware that the pilot rotated between them. Antonio knew not to drink coffee when they were on their way to a strip that didn't have a café and restroom.

Enrico appeared that evening on time as he did the following morning at 7:30. Gone were the mustache and the white straw hat. Per instructions he had limited himself to a small case containing one shirt, a change of underwear, one pair of socks and toilet articles. Antonio carried a smaller case, which Enrico guessed carried only toilet articles.

"You still have one hundred and fifty dollars?" Antonio asked.

"Yes."

"And you have some papers?"

"Yes, I have a Social Security card."

"Made new for you here?"

"No. Made new for me in Los Angeles and sent to me by mail."

"Of good quality?"

"Yes. I compared it to others. Looks OK."

"How much?"

"Thirty dollars it cost me."

With that they walked to a taxi stand and rode to the airport. In the cab Enrico turned to Antonio and asked, "You are taking me to this Arkansas after we land?"

"Yes. My wife will meet us and we will drive across a piece of Texas, go north, then to my town. It's over three hundred miles. We will be in the car six or seven hours." Antonio went on. "You will stay with us for a few days then move to a new place. Start working right away where I work. You know about construction?"

"I can pound nails. Why do you do this for me?"

"When I came eleven years ago the Mexicans did so much for me. Money, clothes, food, a place to stay, a job and a very good woman. We married and have two children. You will do the same for the next ones."

"Maybe Theresa," Enrico said.

"Maybe," Antonio answered

They sat in the rear of the plane, as the pilot suggested. The other four passengers were businessmen wearing suits. All were Mexican. Antonio guessed that they were going to Houston for the day and returning to Monterrey by nightfall. They were silent in the plane, perhaps because it would take effort to talk over the sound of the engine.

Antonio pointed down when they flew over the Rio Grande. It was a thin strip of blue-grey. He said, "Border Patrol." Enrico nodded and smiled.

In another hour they started their descent and landed on a short strip. There was one building and around it were parked eight single-engine planes. Their wings were tied to weights on the ground against the winds that came up. The pilot taxied to the building and Antonio could see his car in the parking lot and his wife and another woman standing next to it. The passengers walked to the building. Antonio met his wife inside. They kissed briefly. She said to her husband, "You remember Anita?"

"Yes, of course, Anita. Nice to see you. I'd like you to meet Enrico Suarez."

Enrico reached out to take Anita's hand. He was conscious that his skin was rough from the work he had been doing. He could feel the softness of Anita's hand in his. He smiled when they exchanged the simple greetings in Spanish. Anita was as tall as Enrico and she had fair skin and light colored hair. There was a breeze outside and it had blown her hair around. She wore a dress and a sweater not buttoned up. Enrico noticed that Anita had the body he liked so much. It was rounded in the right places and perhaps soft and warm to the touch. He thought again about the roughness of his hands. He thought about Theresa.

They moved into the simple café and ordered drinks and sandwiches.

Enrico offered to pay but Antonio would not let him. He knew that Enrico was down to less than a hundred dollars.

Antonio's wife, Dolores, told them that they had left the house at one o'clock in the morning and that her sister was spending the night with the kids and would stay until they returned, perhaps around six in the evening.

Enrico asked Anita whether she was Anglo. He knew she must be but he wanted to talk to her. She said, "Almost. I'm one-eighth Cherokee, the rest Anglo." Antonio had to explain what Cherokee meant. "Then you are a citizen?" Enrico asked.

"Yes. Many generations," Anita answered.

Dolores took over the conversation, telling her husband that the kids wanted to go to Mexico to meet their relatives on Antonio's next trip to visit his family. "No more excuses," she said. "By next year I'll have my passport," Antonio answered.

They filed out of the building and into the car. Enrico was seated in the back with Anita. This was a four-door sedan and they had ample room.

After a little while on the road Enrico realized that he had fantasized all he could about Anita's body. He had moved to her face and studied it and remarked to himself that her upper lip was full to match her lower one and he wondered how her lips would feel against his mouth and how he would kiss her. More miles passed and Enrico found himself listening to the lovely, warm tones of Anita's voice. Her voice had a way of caressing him. She spoke Spanish in a slow, distinctive way that indicated she had learned it in an Arkansas school. He asked her about it. She said that it was her favorite course in high school and now on her job, running a cash register in a large store, she used the language everyday with her customers.

To speak, they turned their bodies to face one another so that their knees touched, her right to his left. Neither made any effort to withdraw. In the early afternoon they stopped for lunch and when they arrived at Dolores and Antonio's town they drove first to Anita's house. Both she and Antonio got out of the car. He thanked her for her company and bowed his head slightly and watched her as she went into her house. She turned to wave at him.

Antonio drove next to his house. Enrico noticed that the houses were ten minutes apart. Enrico met the two children and Dolores' sister, Sylvia. She was eager to return to her own family. Enrico was given the empty room and lent clothes from Antonio's closet. "We will go to the eleven o'clock mass tomorrow and you will need these," Antonio said.

At supper, Antonio explained to Enrico that they would drive to work together on Monday where Enrico would start to learn carpentry. He went on to tell Enrico not to expect any trouble.

"The North Americans want us here," he said.

"How so?" Enrico asked.

"They need the manpower, that's obvious. And the secret they never talk about is that they need the money they take out of our wages. People in the United States reach sixty-five and retire. The government sends them a check every month. To get the money, they take it out of everybody's wages, ours included. The more people retire, the more Mexicans they need. The border stays open."

"That's interesting," Enrico said. He waited a minute then added, "Last year the government in Washington spent many months talking about closing the border and about what to do with the thirteen million illegals. I watched it on the television every night. Then one day they stopped talking about it. Must have gone home. What's happening now?"

"They don't want to close the border so they talk for a few months then take a siesta. This last summer they talked about closing the border and about what to do with the illegals. If they talked about one subject at a time instead of both these subjects at once, they might agree but they don't want to agree." After Antonio had finished, Enrico had a puzzled look on his face. Finally Enrico looked at Antonio and asked, "Why?"

"Because the legal immigrants will vote some of them out of office."

"Why do they bother talking in Washington, then?"

"Because the old-timers, the people born here, expect them to."

"Funny system," Enrico said.

"Not more funny than other countries, like Mexico. We can make babies faster than we can make jobs."

Enrico was hoping to find rice and beans and two enchiladas on his plate but in their place he found an assortment of vegetables and a piece of chicken. As a guest, and after all that Antonio had done for him, he knew he had to clean his plate. Dolores and Antonio and their kids did not seem to mind eating vegetables. This is North America, he said to himself. Spanish was spoken at the table and he assumed that the kids were bilingual -- Spanish in the house and English elsewhere. He hoped that he would be bilingual himself someday soon.

Antonio had a few more items on his mind. "Did you know that if you are born here you are a citizen?"

"Automatic?"

"Yes. It's in the constitution."

"With all the illegals making babies here you might think they would change the constitution," Enrico said.

"Too much work," Antonio answered. Then he said, "You marry an Anglo and have one baby then you are husband of one citizen and father of another. Your troubles are over."

The table was quiet except for an exchange between the children. Then Enrico spoke up. "When will I see Anita again?"

Dolores answered, "Her family comes to the eleven o'clock mass. They always sit right in front of us."

Enrico could not repress a smile. He looked at Dolores and asked her, "If they are citizens why do women like Anita bother with us?"

"The Anglo men want to play around for a few years while they are young. They are not serious right away. The Mexican men, on the other hand, want to marry and have a family and play around later, after they have married. Some Anglo women such as Anita have finished school and are working. Marriage, that's their next step."

"Anita is very nice," Enrico said.

Dolores said, "Yes and she wants to travel to Mexico. She says that she likes the culture."

PART 4

Enrico could not account for his good fortune. Antonio and Dolores had been so kind. He felt that he had been adopted. He stayed with them two weeks and then moved to a small apartment. With his first paycheck Enrico purchased used furniture and kitchen utensils. His apartment had a combination living room and dining room next to a small kitchen. There was an opening between the kitchen and the dining area through which he could pass food. The telephone company assigned him a number. He purchased a used telephone at the Salvation Army and placed it in this opening between the kitchen and the dining area. He realized right away that he could telephone Theresa whenever he wished but he preferred to keep his distance. He found everything he needed at the Salvation Army and that included used clothes and a television set that worked. He would have to keep Antonio and Dolores' generosity up front in his mind and find gifts for them.

Antonio picked him up every morning and brought him home at night. Someday he would be able to buy a small truck similar to his father's. In the middle of the week Antonio and Dolores would invite him to dinner. He enjoyed the Mexican feel of those evenings. The conversation was held in Spanish and Dolores prepared enchiladas or burritos. She did not fix beans and rice but instead piled his plate with vegetables. "They are good for everybody," she would say. Enrico understood her to mean that just because he was up from Mexico didn't mean he had to stay on the Mexican diet. Dolores did make guacamole occasionally and she always had beer in the refrigerator for Antonio and him.

Enrico had started writing Theresa. His first letter to her was the first letter he had ever written. He drew a map of Arkansas and placed his town on it. He told her about his job and how happy he was to have been selected by Antonio and Dolores to receive their generosity. In the beginning he would devote a paragraph to the degree he missed her but as time went on he wrote less and less on the matter sensing that it no longer was the truth.

In his more than two weeks north of the border he had seen Anita on three Sundays. She always wore a different dress. He guessed that soon she would have to wear the first one again. After the church service, many members of the parish would move to the basement where they drank coffee and ate cake and cookies. On the fourth Sunday Enrico asked Anita for her telephone number, which she wrote down on the back of an announcement. He telephoned her that evening. It made him feel mature to have his own place complete with telephone. He asked her if he could see the store where she worked. Understanding that he did not have a car, she said that she would borrow her family's. Could he walk over to her house? Would next Saturday afternoon be alright? She would not be working that particular Saturday.

She dressed the way Theresa would, in jeans and a tight, pale red shirt without buttons, one that you pulled down over your head. She had on a cotton jacket of light yellow. While Theresa's hair was dark and her eyes brown, Anita's hair was light and her eyes were blue-grey-green. Her hair would lift in the lightest breeze. She wore it short. He was taken by her body, the perfect curves and the roundness. He was fascinated by her mouth and would glance at it now and again as they spoke. Both lips were full. Her voice was calm and quiet. He guessed she must be a tender and thoughtful person.

He now lived in his own apartment while Anita lived at home. She might never have experienced a man. His long and constant relationship with Theresa had kept him from sleeping with a woman. He had not calculated how he could find the opportunity to convince another woman to be intimate with him. The idea of spending time with a woman who accepted payment was out of the question. The risk of disease was unacceptable. It would be wonderful to lose his virginity but not at that cost. Theresa, he knew, would not yield up her virginity until the evening she was in her wedding bed. Such a night was still available to him but he knew the cost would be high. He would have to pledge the rest of his life to that farm. He had not known that a woman such as Theresa could become so attached to the land.

In their small town Enrico and Anita could find the usual recreation. In the mall where her store was situated there was a movie theater with several screens. At first Enrico understood little or none of the words exchanged between the actors but slowly his command of English grew. Enrico and Anita had starting speaking Spanish exclusively but as time went on she would intersperse more and more English.

Enrico's plan to get Anita to sleep with him required that she come to his apartment where he would cook dinner, always with her help. It appeared to Enrico that she allowed them to move ever so slowly to his goal. He thought it might be her goal too. He understood his situation well enough to know that he could not expect to get by scot-free. He would have to utter the warm sentimental words that let the woman know that he cares for her.

Anita's theme was gradualness. She allowed Enrico to kiss her and then to caress her. When they moved into his bedroom on early Saturday evenings she became more permissive. She would let Enrico take her clothes off to the waist. When he told her that he had purchased the means of prevention and was hopeful about the next step, she answered by wearing a skirt on their following evening together. He interpreted this as granting him permission.

When sex had become one of their habits, Enrico experienced an early lesson taught to a male. He started wondering about other young women in his town. He would see them and evaluate the possibilities. How different were they from Anita? Would they be more or less pleasurable in bed? How many women would it take and what span of years would be required for experimentation in order to succeed in his quest for the best possible mate? He made a connection between his interest in variety among female partners and his move away from Theresa and the life on the farm. Both indicated curiosity. As he thought about it, he assumed that he would have several jobs in his life, if not several careers. He wondered if several women and several jobs were connected.

Soon enough it would be a year that Enrico had been working in Arkansas. In her letters to him, Theresa kept track of time and looked forward to his return. In his letters to her, he acknowledged his intention to return but he would not indicate to her whether it was to stay for keeps, to return to Arkansas with her, if possible, or return without her. He would only admit that they had important decisions to make.

Concerning Anita, Enrico learned a second lesson of the maturing male. Now that he had achieved his goal, sex was no longer as important to him as it was while he was denied it and in the moments when it first appeared. He recognized a change in his relationship with Anita.

Previously he had been the initiator, but recently she had started to participate in getting them to bed. In his darkened bedroom she would take off all her clothes and then turn to him and start to unbutton his shirt. She had started caressing him while previously it had been his task to arouse her.

As he prepared himself for the return trip to Mexico, he thought about how Anita had replaced Theresa. While he longed to have Theresa to himself, all of her, he knew that little by little Anita, because it was she who was in front of him, had moved into the center of his life. He did not look forward to making the choice. Both women had been attentive and kind. Anita had given him what he wanted. She had made him feel manly.

He had left a letter from Theresa next to his telephone. Anita would see it and would read the return address on the upper left corner of the envelope. Enrico thought that the conversation the letter would stir up could help him through the difficult times he would confront soon. Anita might object to there being a woman waiting in his home town. She might address a series of questions. She might suggest to him what Theresa had on her mind as she was the woman he had left behind.

Anita glanced at the letter and made her assumptions. Enrico and she never discussed the matter. When he left after being in Arkansas eleven-and-a-half months he promised that he would return in three to four weeks. Those were the arrangements that he had made with his employer. At her request, he had given Anita his parents' address and telephone number and when he wrote them down and handed them to her, he asked her need for having the information. She answered that you can never tell; things come up. His employer might need him to return earlier than he had planned.

Enrico had his friend Antonio write down instructions for finding the pilot in Monterrey. If for some reason the man he had flown with was not available, Enrico felt confident enough to take a bus or taxi to the airport and look into available flights on private planes. Fly on Saturday, Antonio told him, and he would come to the airstrip to meet him. Enrico was doing well in carpentry – Antonio could see that on the job – and it was inconceivable to Antonio that Enrico would not return. Dolores had selected Anita as the young Anglo that he would find attractive and with whom he could start a family. Antonio thought that the trend in Congress was to allow illegal aliens to stay if they were employed, and particularly if they were employed and married to a citizen.

Enrico went by bus from Arkansas to the Texas-Mexico border at Laredo. He went across to the bus station in Nuevo Laredo and caught the first bus for Monterrey. The telephone call from Monterrey allowed Enrico's father to estimate when Enrico would arrive at the bus stop where they had separated eleven-and-a-half months ago. When Enrico came out of the bus they exchanged manly hugs and the father, Francisco Suarez, took his son's suitcase out of his hand and led them to the family truck that Enrico knew so well.

He asked first about his mother and brothers. His mother was well and waiting at home as was his younger brother. Cristobal, the middle son, would still be working at the farm on the job where he had replaced Enrico on his departure north. The arrangement between the two fathers was that Enrico would spend the remainder of the afternoon at home and then drive to the farm to spend the evening there, have dinner, and exchange with Theresa all that there was to exchange on their reunion.

When Enrico arrived at the farm the first person whom he saw was Cristobal who was backing a tractor into its shed. When they were face to face and shaking hands, Enrico knew that Cristobal was wearing on his face a look that Enrico had never seen before. Cristobal was normally jovial and Enrico expected him to start with a story or two, or to describe a funny experience that he had had. But he was withdrawn in some fashion, not meeting his brother eye to eye. Enrico concluded the obvious, that his brother and Theresa had reached an understanding. When Enrico had thought about his brother and one of Theresa's sisters over the months, and he had only thought a little about it, he surmised that Crisotbal and Lela, the daughter after Theresa, might find one another attractive.

The brothers talked about farm machinery for a few moments and then walked to the house. Theresa's mother and father, along with Theresa's three sisters, gave him a warm welcome. They referred to Enrico as the long-lost one who appeared to have changed to become less Mexican and more North American. Enrico did not press them for the changes they noticed because he knew there was none.

Theresa, he was told, was upstairs dressing. When the exuberance had died down she appeared wearing a dress of pale blue and carrying flowers from the garden in her hair. Enrico was stunned momentarily by her beauty. She came right to Enrico and said, "It's wonderful that you are back." She kissed him on both cheeks and thanked him for his letters.

Theresa asked her father if he would offer beers to the men. At that moment Cristobal stood and said goodnight and left by the kitchen door. Enrico assumed that his brother would ride the bicycle home, the one his father still used to deliver some of his mail. He guessed that the scene he had just witnessed had been organized by Theresa, her parents and Cristobal.

During dinner Enrico was encouraged to describe his life for the year gone by in as much detail as he wished. He spoke first about the miracle of Antonio and Dolores. He gave a fair amount of time to describing life on the job and his slow mastery of carpentry. He did not leave out mention of his wages and overtime pay. The family wanted to know his progress in English. He claimed that he was half-way to mastering the language. He said that he read the local newspaper most days and had learned from the material he found. He left out any mention of Anita although he alluded to having made a few friends at church.

When dinner was through, Theresa led Enrico to the bench under the trees where parts of their lives had played out. Enrico allowed Theresa to set the tone for the conversation. She started by telling him how glad she was to see him. She moved on to how well he looked. He could have changed the topic at any time but he had not made up his mind on what to say. He knew that during his stay he would be required to make the definitive statement that would tell Theresa exactly what he would do. She was not applying pressure and he felt no need to move in that direction on their first day reunited.

Theresa went on a new tack. "Cristobal has been sensitive to my needs. In your absence he has taken me to dances. It became important to me to spend evenings out of the house."

"This could develop into romance," Enrico said in a teasing manner.

"We are fond of one another and happy to be together. As you are, he is polite and respectful of me."

"There is probably more on his mind than that," Enrico said.

"I would not be surprised," Theresa said. "I allow him to give me the kiss that you would give me."

Enrico thought immediately that Theresa was making it simple for him. If he wanted to leave her he could do so knowing that his brother was next in line. He thought also that it would be normal for her to stimulate his interest with a suggestion of rivalry, if it was the case that she still wanted him.

The evening ended on this inconclusive note. Theresa suggested that she come to Enrico's house on the following evening and visit his family. Enrico supposed that they would not discuss important matters.

On his third day home, Enrico's mother and father questioned him. Was he staying, and if not, what could be his reasons for returning? It was natural that they suspected a woman had entered his life. If that was the case, would he provide details? Enrico could not evade. He spoke of this woman in his life who had been presented to him by Antonio and Dolores. He admitted she meant a great deal to him and that in her way she was as attractive as Theresa. With this comparison in place, the parents assumed that a romantic and sexual relationship had been established and that their son would return north.

On the fourth day Enrico received a telephone call from Anita. She went to the point. "I suspected as much over the past two weeks but I went to see the doctor who confirmed that I was pregnant."

Enrico's reaction was in the form of an additional lesson for males as they mature. Now that he was required to marry Anita he liked her a little less than the day before when he thought he was still free to choose. Enrico found no alternative to telling his parents and his brothers. He would not tell Theresa that he must marry as he was on his way to becoming a father but he would say that he had concluded that his future was up north and his trip south had been for verification and saying farewell to his previous life and the people in it. He knew that after he left, Cristobal would tell Theresa the remainder of the story.

Theresa waited for Enrico's departure. It was not long in coming. His stay in Mexico lasted two days less than two weeks. In the five days after Enrico left, Theresa discussed matters with her mother and father. It was decided that her father would suggest to Cristobal's father that Cristobal should feel free to announce to Theresa, to make known his interest in her.

The scene played out on the same bench where Theresa and Enrico had held their important discussions.

"I am of course overwhelmed by you, Theresa," Cristobal announced.

"I don't wish to overwhelm you or anyone else. I need the security, the happiness, the joy of having the correct man in my life. That's all I ask."

"I can provide that," Cristobal said.

Their kisses were less reserved than those exchanged between Theresa and Enrico. Cristobal was given more latitude in his explorations. Theresa reasoned that she might have been too stingy with Enrico and would not make that mistake again. They were married before Enrico and Anita's baby was born.

MOVING NORTH
PART 5

Enrico, now the seasoned traveler, telephoned Antonio as instructed. The landing strip would be number three, situated about ten miles from number four where they had landed the year previously.

Enrico felt that his Mexican life had ended once he was in the small plane. He looked out over South Texas at the farms and ranches. He had read enough history to know that Texas, once upon a time, was part of Mexico but had broken away in 1836 after the battle of the Alamo in San Antonio in which the Mexican general, Santa Ana, was victorious yet could not hold on to so vast a territory. He had heard many times that Mexicans were pouring back into the Southwest of the United States to reclaim what had once been theirs. When he thought of the Central Americans now living in all the states, far beyond the Southwest, he shook his head and smiled at the unpredictability of events.

His personal situation was never far from the front of his mind. He would think about Theresa and Anita alternately and together. No doubt he would tell all to Antonio in the six to seven hours that they would be together in the car. His principal concern was how he would react to being married and becoming a parent at his early age. He was twenty-one, as was Anita, and he recognized that they had traded their freedom for the pleasure of those early Saturday evenings in his bed. What was there about sex that made both of them risk this substantial change in their lives? All at once they would be fully grown up, hemmed in by the responsibilities of caring for this new life that Anita was producing. There would be other children, he guessed, it being normal to have a family of at least three. He would become part of Anita's family, part of his church, and part of the town where he worked and lived.

They started their descent into the airfield that Antonio and he called 'three'. There was one building and there were a few single-engine planes parked around it. Enrico could see cars parked next the building but could not pick out Antonio's. This was an airstrip where one could buy gas for the plane but not coffee and sandwiches.

He saw Antonio waving and guessed that he was waiving at the plane and not at him. In a moment the pilot had landed, taxied and turned off the engine. One passenger stepped out of the plane to let him out. He walked toward the building carrying his small suitcase. Antonio walked toward him. They exchanged a loose hug, each one placing an arm around the shoulders of the other. In no time they were on the road. Antonio said, "Our first stop in a few minutes will be at a restaurant. We'll have eggs and coffee and you can tell me everything."

They chatted about the flight and the ease with which Enrico had been able to return. Once settled in the roadside restaurant, and after they had ordered, Antonio moved the conversation to serious matters. "So you have given up the beautiful Theresa?"

"Yes, I have. On my way south I did not know what I would do. But I found out that my brother Cristobal is now in love with Theresa, as

I was. If they truly find one another I will not feel guilty about leaving her."

"You cannot have both Theresa and Anita," Antonio said. After a pause, he continued, "I should not say that. Very rich men have one wife and mistresses located here and there. But you have not become a rich man yet."

Enrico was adding cream and sugar to his coffee, as he had learned to drink it. He said, "I must tell you that I received a telephone call from Anita on my fourth day. She tells me she has seen the doctor."

"And?"

"And she is pregnant."

Antonio placed both his palms down on the table. "This is serious business, of course. We men like it better when we marry first and then talk it over with the wife and decide to make a baby. This way they build a trap for you. The door slams shut and you are no longer a free man."

"I have thought about it all the time since the moment Anita telephoned. I knew what I was doing. You sleep with me and if I get pregnant I will marry you. I think that's the deal." With that Enrico drank deeply of his coffee.

"The same thing happened to me, Enrico. The first child is always born early. But I am still married and Dolores is very good to me." They were both silent for a moment.

"You know," Antonio said, changing his tone of voice, "Anita is a prize. You are a lucky man. She speaks Spanish, wants to give love to you, wants to have a baby and she is so pretty."

"You think I should marry her, then?"

"Yes. I married Dolores. The smart thing to do is never look back. Just look ahead at what will happen and at what you will become. Your first life is over. I think this is what you wanted to happen."

Enrico let his head fall as though he was studying his empty plate. "I need to find courage, that's all. I'm getting what I wanted, as you say, and at the same time not wanting it."

Antonio, not wishing to prolong the conversation, rose to leave. Enrico paid for the meal and Antonio allowed him to. Enrico recalled his circumstances of the previous year. The ride to Arkansas was largely silent. Enrico, who had been gazing out the window, did say, "Well, I guess I will become a citizen of two countries."

It was well after sunset by time they made it to Enrico's apartment building. He called Anita right away. They knew they would see one another in church in the morning and they agreed to spend the remainder of the day together. Enrico was reconciled to proposing marriage when they were in his apartment.

When Enrico entered church and searched the pew where they always sat he saw Anita. She would be directly in front of him. She was wearing a dress with short sleeves made of material with a floral print. He knew the dress and it was his favorite. She had a fair collection, living at home and spending her money the way it suited her. She turned around as he slipped into his pew. He kissed her on the cheek and said in Spanish that he was glad to be home. It was the first time he had described the town that he lived in as home.

After the service both families went to the basement parish hall for coffee. Enrico could not tell whether her parents knew she was pregnant. He only glanced to notice that she was not showing yet. She would be soon. They repaired to Anita's house for lunch and only by mid-afternoon were they alone when Anita's family left the house. Enrico guessed that they had planned to absent themselves.

There were a few introductory remarks and then Enrico asked, "Do your parents know?"

"I told them right away. It's not something you hide for very long and when the family doctor knows, what's the sense?"

"You might have told me before you left," Enrico said.

"I could have but I wanted you to see the woman you left behind without knowing this."

Enrico was silent. Anita went on, "You left the envelope with Theresa's address on it. I think you wanted me to know."

"Yes, I did. I hoped that it would make us talk before I left."

"What did you want to tell me?" Anita asked.

"I don't know. Maybe it was better that we didn't talk."

"What took place between you two?"

"Not a great deal. She did not say that she wanted me. My brother is there waiting for me to disappear. I have the feeling that she is happier with him. So why did you telephone me on the fourth day?"

"I didn't want you staying there without knowing I was pregnant. If I told you before you went you might not have gone. This way you could decide when you knew everything with your Theresa right in front of you."

"Do you think we should get married?" Enrico asked.

"It's not necessary to get married. I can have the baby and live at home. My mother says it's a mistake to marry someone just because you're pregnant by him."

"What did your father say?"

"He doesn't say much. He usually agrees with Mom. He did say that most everybody does it before getting married."

"Do you want to marry me if I want to marry you?" Enrico asked.

"Is that what Antonio told you to say?"

"Something like that. He said that he got Dolores pregnant before they married and it turned out OK for them."

They both fell silent, sitting side by side on the couch. Enrico spoke first. "I never had a woman before you and would never go to a woman and pay for it because of the chances you get a disease. I can't take that chance. How did you take the chance with me when you knew you could get pregnant?"

"A part of me likes it. I did it a few times with a boy in high school. We were seniors. I wanted to do it with you. It's very exciting to have your hands all over me. I thought those things you put on always work. So I didn't think there was any risk." Anita paused for a moment. Enrico stayed silent.

"You know I want the baby. You're supposed to have kids when you're young. I know other girls who have a kid. It's different now. There's no shame to it. That's what my Mom says."

"If you are having the baby, I still think we should be married," Enrico said.

"The priest would marry us, but I guess we'd have to tell him," Anita said.

"Is what we did a sin?" Enrico asked.

"I think so but when you marry that makes things alright."

"My place is too small. We'll need another bedroom," Enrico said.

"You're supposed to get down on just one knee and ask me."

"Do you want a wedding dress?"

"I can use my Mom's. I tried it on." It had been her mother's idea to have her daughter try on the dress. The trying on of the dress had not occurred on Anita's return from the doctor's office. The suggestion had come from her mother several months previously when she and Enrico first started spending long evenings together in Enrico's apartment. Anita had always concluded that her mother was telling her that Enrico was a satisfactory man and that if she and Enrico wanted to marry, it was acceptable and a little more to Anita's parents.

"I can rent a tuxedo," Enrico said. Anita added, "We'll each have to buy a ring."

CARRIE RESTON

Edith Reston was in the sixth month of her pregnancy with her fourth child who, she hoped, would be her last. The two sons and a daughter born previously had been spaced out and it seemed to Mr. and Mrs. Reston that they would do what was required to stop at four. At about this time in her past pregnancies she and her husband Richard had selected possible names. Because they wanted a girl to keep the family in balance, the conversation was half as long as previous ones had been. Boy's names were not evaluated.

Their first child, a son, was named Walter so that he might aspire to be a medical doctor. Walter Reed was well-known and had departed this world a few years back after identifying the cause of yellow fever. The second son was named Benjamin so that he might become acquainted with the life of Franklin. The third child, their first daughter, was named Mary from the New Testament.

In selecting a name for this child, assuming that it would be a girl, Richard Reston led off by suggesting that an important name was needed so that the child would think of greatness when she thought of her place in the world. Edith said to her husband, "Do you mean something like Florence Nightingale?"

"Yes, exactly. I can think of three nicknames for Florence: Flo, Fanny and Florrie. They are not acceptable. I wouldn't want a daughter to be called Flo."

"Well, there are two great ladies in the women's movement, Elizabeth Cady Stanton and Susan B. Anthony. What do you think of them?" Mrs. Reston asked.

"Elizabeth is a lovely name," Richard answered, "but too popular for me and Susan doesn't sound distinctive enough."

"Do you want an Edith?" Richard asked.

"No. That's my name and I would find it too confusing to hear Little Edith and Big Edith around the house."

Richard advanced another idea. "I like Lucretia and Laetitia, both beautiful names." They looked at one another before Richard continued. "There was a Lucrezia Borgia, who poisoned a few people around Rome. And Leatitia, I think that's the original name for Paris. Lutèce, they wrote it."

Edith said, "In fairness, I think the evil one in the family was her brother, Cesare. I've read that there's no proof against the sister. And Laetitia has possibilities."

When Richard did not agree with his wife he either changed the subject or continued talking. He did not pause to offer a rational objection. Edith volunteered, "There is a Lucretia Mott in the women's movement. Suffragette, I think." When Richard appeared not to like any of her suggestions, Edith thought she might as well offer a name that he would object to. "There's Carry Nation," Edith said.

"Do you realize how much good whiskey she's caused to go down the drain, not to mention bars she's smashed up with that damned hatchet of hers?"

"All true," Edith said. "But she may have saved a few marriages, saved some children from going hungry, saved quite a few men from alcoholism."

"How do you spell her first name?" Richard asked.

"C-A-R-R-Y," Edith said.

"Doesn't surprise me a bit that she would spell it the masculine way. Can we make it C-A-R-R-I-E? Sounds more feminine," Richard said.

"I think it sounds the same spelled either way, dear," Edith said. "but when it's written out it does look more feminine." On that note they concluded their discussion. Should a third son arrive, they would reopen negotiations.

Carrie was descended from families with more daughters than sons. These daughters had married young men from various racial stocks with the result that she had in her background at least the following representation: Irish, German, English, Lithuanian, Jewish, and Italian. The parents thought that if they went back far enough they would find Dutch ancestors. Her father carried an English name, Reston, and her mother an Irish name, Collins. They felt that the mixture was typical of people living around New York, and that blending the races was healthy and rejuvenating. Carrie was born in the Borough of Brooklyn in August 1910. Her father worked at a bank and her mother had her hands full with her house and four children.

When Carrie was thirteen and starting to understand reproduction, she asked her mother why there were just four children in the family. Her mother told her that she would explain all she knew on the subject when the time came, perhaps in two years. Carrie went immediately to her sister who told her that she was sworn to secrecy. Her sister was two years older than she was, and Carrie supposed that their mother had told her sister recently. It made no sense to Carrie that some families had no children, some two, and a few nine.

Carrie's life had been on schedule. She entered first grade in her sixth year, seventh grade in her twelfth year, and passed the New York Regents' examinations in her eighteenth year. Some of her early experiences had to do with the war in Europe. She examined the map of the world and noted that the bulk of the fighting was taking place on the northeast corner of a medium-sized European country and it therefore must be a small war. Were it big, she reasoned, there would be fighting in all countries, or most of them. She heard about flying machines although she had never seen one, and understood that boats underwater could sink ships on the surface. She became aware in 1917 of the fever pitch in her own country when she started seeing men in uniform, then the following year when these men sailed across the Atlantic to kill and be killed by Germans. It ended in a palace in France where in a large room called the Hall of Mirrors men from many nations came to settle affairs and draw new lines on the map. When she was ten, her father would talk about hard times but they left soon enough. He continued at the bank.

In 1920, again when she was ten, she sensed that the whole world was changing. Women could not be denied the vote and men could no longer enter a bar for diversion. Her father had bottles of Canadian whiskey whose light brown contents he would pour into a glass on the weekend. "Perhaps you might not mention this to anyone?" He asked his children.

Dresses grew shorter. Hats that envelop the head came into style. Gone were brims and feathers. A few women smoked. Music changed and her mother bought a crank-up player and records. She had great difficulty in getting her husband to dance in the front hall where there were no rugs, but she made certain to teach her daughters a few steps. "You'll have to learn the Charleston from your friends," she said.

Carrie met the twenties with enthusiasm and loved the clothes and music. She knew early on that she could draw accurately and this interest brought her to the Brooklyn Museum and finally to the Pratt Institute. Her parents suggested that she take it upon herself to investigate admission. There was a choice, either a two or a four-year program. She and her parents chose the four-year course, which she pursued to completion even though by the end in 1932 hard times had returned.

Her father's bank stayed open while many others failed, taking with them deposits, savings, and jobs. The older of her two brothers returned home to live for a year when he lost his job and could not find work. In time, through a friend of the family, he started selling new cars at an agency. At once he found a room for rent and was back on his own.

It made sense to Carrie, upon graduation, to teach art inasmuch as she could not make a living by trying to sell her own artwork. The curriculum at Pratt had taken her through interior design and she enjoyed drawing rooms with furniture from several periods. The best she framed and kept on the walls of her room. The family was dutiful in praising her work. Some were watercolors and others were oils on canvas.

Carrie found a teacher's position at the high school she had attended. It was the fall of 1932 and she thought it wise to continue living at home in order to save money. Women's clothing style had changed again and she felt forced to put away her clothes from the previous decade. The new style for the thirties was more conservative and less costly than comparable items of dress for the twenties.

In teaching, her favorite class was drawing, in which she emphasized to her students the importance of bringing to life faces of men and women drawn on plain paper using pencils having leads of various thickness. She maintained to her classes that making two dimensions evolve into a third was the principal task of the artist. Perspective was the second, which technique she taught to advanced classes.

For her own paintings Carrie changed her subject matter from interiors to flowers. She thought she had met the challenges offered by interiors and was determined to move on. In her opinion, Fragonard was the most able among those who painted arrangements of flowers. She did not start with a bouquet, a complete arrangement in a vase, but rather with a single flower, or two or three, and the accompanying leaves. They were done in watercolor and with great attention to detail. She signed them, writing C. *Reston* alongside a stem, challenging the onlooker to locate her name. She framed them and found a gallery that would act as an outlet. She asked five dollars for herself, and was surprised that she sold a painting once every two weeks or so. The owner of the gallery told her that there was no single collector. Many of his clients were decorators and they selected her works to complete an arrangement on a wall.

Her older brother, Walter, showed no interest in medicine. He mastered the sale of new cars and made a sufficient amount of money to marry his sweetheart who was a telephone operator in an office building in New York City. She earned twenty-five dollars a week and he averaged twice that amount. The younger of her two brothers finished two years of college and won an appointment to the Naval Academy. He had settled on a military career and told his family that he might look into naval aviation. Her older sister married a man from the bank. Her father had brought him home and introduced them. He was attentive, intelligent, gauche socially, and relieved to find a pretty, attractive woman who was pleased to lead him at a comfortable pace to the altar. They married and started making babies.

Carrie took her time about men. She knew that it could be that men were taking their time about her. She couldn't bring herself to originating those signals which she knew were mating calls. If a man became interested in her, he was free to act accordingly. It was up to them, after all. She had not met a man she wanted and had no idea how she might react in the event a man came along who developed serious intentions. A few men came around, she had met them at Pratt, and there was an administrator from her high school. One of these men lived alone in an apartment where he expected he might start an affair with Carrie but she held to the notion she should have accepted a proposal for marriage before she found herself alone with a man. The idea intrigued her but being intimate with a man had to do with marriage and played no part in the relief of sexual desires, which she admitted were present.

It was her father who took an interest in her men. He had the upper hand in that his selection from the bank had suited Carrie's sister and their marriage appeared safe and sound. There were two children so far.

Carrie's father and mother met the men Carrie went out with. They came to pick her up. When a particular man stopped calling, her father wanted to know whether he was a leaky vessel or an empty one. Often he volunteered his opinion. His argument with Carrie was that she did not know the type of man that suited her and therefore could bounce off one after another before finding the right one, if ever. Carrie would argue that she would know him when he showed up. No amount of character analysis and planning on her part would describe the right man.

He mother, Edith, interjected herself once, when the three of them were in the kitchen. She asked her husband of his courting of her during the better part of 1901. Did he know exactly what he wanted? He answered that she was the obvious choice for him. Edith pressed on by asking her husband if he had made his list before meeting her. He answered that it was many years ago, thirty-two in fact, and he could not remember.

Carrie could not change her style. She never settled in her mind on an ideal man. She enjoyed some aspect of all of them and was aware that some abandoned her while she gave up on others.

By 1936, she felt pressure from both parents. It was time to live independently. A clean break became mandatory when she located a teaching position at an art school in New York City and an apartment in the mid-seventies one block west of the Park. Her father was considering retirement. Her parents were planning a trip to Europe and a two-week stay in the Caribbean. They were pleased with their four children and made it clear they felt they were making successes out of their lives.

CARRIE RESTON
PART 2

Suddenly there were more men in Carrie's life. A few fellow teachers at her new school became interested. She volunteered at the New York Historical Society where she met others. A new building was being planned. She resumed attending church services. She met people casually in her apartment building and in her neighborhood, which she defined as any place within five blocks. She even met a man on a Sunday afternoon in the Park. She was sitting on a bench reading two sections of the *Tribune* when he came by and sat down on the other end of the bench. Carrie noticed that he was not carrying any reading material and soon enough he asked her how she was. She answered directly and wondered what type of man this was who would come along and engage her in conversation. He continued talking, moving on to topics in her paper. He had a cultivated voice and she suspected he was educated. He didn't move toward her while sitting on the bench. After he had been there for a half-hour, he asked her whether she would join him for late afternoon tea at a place on Central Park West, which he patronized frequently. She accepted, thinking it safe but out of the ordinary. He gave her his name but she limited herself to her first name. He asked, "Carrie what?" She answered, "It's too soon for that."

While having tea, he told her that he had taken a trip to New England, driving his new car. He opened up to her and said that he had made the trip alone but wished all along that he had had company. He tried sports and volunteered that the Yankees were having a good year and the Series would likely be played against the Giants in New York. She admitted knowing nothing about sports so he dropped the subject. She did let him know that she taught art, although she didn't identify the school. When time came to go their separate ways he asked how he might contact her. She said, "Let me call you." With that he pulled a business card out of his wallet and handed it to her. She thanked him and put it in her purse without looking at it.

At home she took the card from her purse and read it. "Malcolm Savage," it said, along with an address downtown and two telephone numbers. It was clear that the address was for business. The two telephone numbers were identified appropriately. Because there was no firm indicated, Carrie concluded that he worked alone, perhaps at managing his affairs.

The card took its place on the mirror at her dressing table. Carrie was aware of it but did nothing about it for a month. On a Friday evening when there were no prospects for the weekend and Carrie had grown accustomed to social activity, she pulled the card from the mirror and dialed the telephone number at home. A woman answered and Carrie paused to consider hanging up. After a few seconds she asked, "Is Malcolm in?" The person at the other end said, "Yes. Who is calling?" "Could you tell him Carrie from the Park?"

Carrie heard the telephone being placed on a desktop and a voice calling for Malcolm. She could hear footsteps as he approached. "Carrie,

I'm so glad to hear from you," were his first words. Then he asked, "Where have you been? I'd given up on you." She explained that she had been too busy, which she knew was not true, and that she had free time in the coming weekend and wanted to know whether they could plan something on short notice.

"Well," he started out, "on short notice you say. My parents are having some friends in tomorrow evening and I'm expected. If you wish I can be in front of your door at 5:30. It's a blue Ford convertible. I just need your address. I'll ring your doorbell or you can be standing outside, as you wish."

They passed enough information between them, including her telephone number, so that there would be no difficulty in meeting one another. She asked him where his parents lived and he gave her an address off Riverside Drive, close to the river. It did not surprise her that he lived with his parents.

She chose to meet him on the street. He came by on time, pulled up, got out of his side and came around the car to let her in. She wore a white dress, which seemed appropriate for the summer months, and she carried a sweater and a small purse. She didn't notice Malcolm particularly except that he wore a jacket and tie. She didn't say anything for the moment. She looked at the inside of the car, and said almost to herself, "Very snappy." They made no effort to strike up a conversation as they drove north. He put the car in the garage and came around to let her out. She had her comb out of her purse and used it as they walked to the elevator. "Damage repaired," he said.

His mother greeted them in the fourth floor apartment. "Mother, this is Carrie Reston." "You're the girl Malcolm found in the Park." "Not exactly. We agreed to have tea." "I suppose it's the new way, but you're very pretty in fact." The two women looked at one another for a moment, and Mrs. Savage said, "You probably drink. Everyone drinks now. What will you have?" "May I have an old fashioned?" "Malcolm, find an old fashioned for Carrie. Not too strong. I must get back to my other guests."

They went into the next room where a waiter took their order. Malcolm led her to a sofa, but before they could sit down, Mr. Savage came into the room and walked over to them. He put out his hand and said, "Walter Savage." "I suppose you know I'm Carrie Reston." "They told me but I'd forgotten. Told me you teach art. Any men in your classes?" "Yes, just under half." "Seems like a strange thing for men to do," he replied. "I'll arrange to forward your sentiments to Leonardo and Michelangelo," she said. Mr. Savage snorted at that. "Malcolm's thought about doing art but it doesn't lead anywhere so he dabbles." With that he turned to his son and said, "Good to see you with a handsome woman."

Carrie turned to Malcolm and studied him for a minute. "What does your father mean when he says that you dabble?"

"It's the classic story," Malcolm answered. "Father's in charge of one of the three radio networks. He wanted me to join him, starting at the bottom when I finished college, but I couldn't do it."

"You're well educated. You sound like it."

"Yes, the best. I couldn't work my way up following in Father's footsteps."

"What's the address on your business card?"

"I manage some of the family's assets. Father rented two rooms for me downtown. He thought I would meet people in finance and land a regular job."

"You're on your father's personal payroll?"

"No, Carrie. My grandfather, in his will, look care of his college, his boarding school, a favorite charity, my mother, father, an uncle and me. There was plenty to go around."

"You're the only child?"

"Yes. But thank goodness Father and Mother are not, so there are first cousins."

Carrie felt that the cold father and the formal mother were profiled in any number of journals on psychology so that she was able to understand a portion of Malcolm's personality. It seemed odd to Carrie that she was starting out by meeting the family rather then ending there. The difficult part to understand of the recent past was meeting Malcolm in the Park. Shouldn't Malcolm have plenty of female friends to invite on a walk, to keep him company? Perhaps she shouldn't make too much of it.

····················· CARRIE RESTON ·····················
PART 3

Sonny Townsend never cared for his name. He changed it back to the original version when he enrolled in college in his freshman year. On all forms he wrote George Townsend, Jr., with no middle initial. He was the oldest of four children and was given his father's name. The family lived in the center of Pennsylvania. When it came time to select a college, he could have enrolled at an engineering school nearby or at the university in Philadelphia. He chose the latter. He was born in 1921 and started classes in the fall of 1939. In his first week, war broke out in Europe, and he sensed, as did many Americans of all ages, that they would play a part before the end.

The draft closed in on him early in 1942. Before it did, he volunteered for the Army Air Corps. Because he had finished two years of mechanical engineering and was partially through his third, he was assigned to maintenance and was taught the ins and outs of the B-24, a four-engine bomber called the Liberator. He went by ship to England in June 1943 and was assigned to a bombardment group. He became a crew chief, which position he held during the remainder of the war. Between eight and ten men took care of each plane, doing everything from changing engines to patching the skin where shrapnel had found its mark. In the course of the conflict his crew had had four bombers fail to return from a mission. Each time, ten aviators were killed in the air, or taken prisoner after parachuting to earth. A few managed to avoid capture and returned to England. Several ground crew personnel from his group and others volunteered for gunnery school to take their chances in the air over Germany.

Unless the weather was abominable, ground crews tended to wait for their planes to return from missions at their designated parking place. If a mission hadn't been too rough, the surviving planes returned as a group. The ground crews of those that failed to make it would usually wait for their planes, sometimes for hours. There were new planes with rookie air crews to fill the empty slots.

Inevitably George had come to know the air crews he served but after losing two planes he became less personal. At the end he knew he had survived the war by chance and the effect on him was to shut him down. He lost his enthusiasm and continued to do his job by rote. George left England in late summer of 1945. There was talk of moving many bombardment groups to the Pacific Theater, but before any plans were put into effect the war came to an end and he was discharged soon after.

George made it home after his twenty-fourth birthday. There was no celebration as he had been welcomed home during a one-week leave earlier. He contacted the University and found out that his junior year would not resume until the fall of the next year, there being too few students to organize a class of decent size any sooner. It was clear to George that he would complete his studies under the GI Bill but he had a good part of a year to wait. He wondered what he might do during the year. He came up with nothing but standard answers such as a trip, or a local job or getting re-installed in Philadelphia and finding work. It was his sister, the next younger child, who suggested that he do something entirely different so that he might get the war out of his system. "I hope to go to an art school when I graduate from high school," she said. She was eighteen by then. "Why don't you move to Philadelphia, look around, enroll in an art school and stay just one year, until next fall?"

"I know absolutely nothing about art, and besides I need to save my GI Bill. Can't waste any of it."

"I think Mom and Dad will pay for it. They've talked about doing something special for you while you were away." George thought his sister had invented his parents' intentions. Why wouldn't they have brought it up? But that's the way it turned out. He found space in a rooming house and shared the bath with two other men. He had no way of knowing about the quality of the art school. It was located downtown in a handsome building. He started classes in the fall of 1945, looking forward to a year of studies in art.

PART 4

Carrie and Malcolm were making steady progress. They met in August 1936. By the spring of 1937 she had found out about love, at least the first part when the man looms large and important and the woman feels amorous. She ascribed fine traits to him that were there but in smaller portions than she imagined. She overlooked his faults on the basis that they were parts of his personality and not really faults. She admitted that their relationship was not stressful so there were no reasons that he would not be easy to get along with, as he was entertaining and charming.

Malcolm felt the ground shifting under him. It was expected that he marry. His mother and father reinforced the position and they admired Carrie. "You'll never do any better," his mother had told him. And indeed Carrie brought a great deal into a marriage. She was intelligent, informed, humorous, and attentive. She was pretty and had a trim figure. Malcolm liked her thick brown hair, which she wore above the collar. She spent little time on it. It was not curly but had a wave. Malcolm was in the habit of placing his face against her hair and sometime kissing her on the back of her neck.

Carrie understood that Malcolm was in the process of selling his father's shares in the broadcasting company and reinvesting the proceeds in other firms. She understood the danger of concentrating the family wealth. She was relieved to find that Malcolm's work had value. Perhaps his importance in the family could continue to increase.

Malcolm proposed in late spring 1937. He came to pick her up to go to the movies. He brought flowers, which she had time to put into a vase before they left. He was slightly shy when he told her he loved her. After she acknowledged that she loved him as well, he said, "Well, in that case, why not marry me?" It was just as Carrie had imagined it would be coming from Malcolm, not dramatic and to the point.

After accepting the congratulations of both sets of parents, buying rings and setting the date, Malcolm introduced sex into their lives. Carrie reasoned that he was doing the appropriate thing. She could refuse him. They could wait until they were married, but it was certain that they would marry, so why not? Malcolm didn't hint. On a Sunday afternoon when they had returned from a walk in the Park and they were sitting on the sofa, he said, "It would be wonderful in bed with you." "I think so too," she said. Carrie knew it was the first time for her and sensed that it might be for Malcolm as well, but he seemed so sure of himself that she thought he must have had sex previously. On the third or fourth time her enjoyment grew and she felt more in love and more certain of herself than ever before in her life.

They were married after Labor Day and had known one another for over a year. She kept her teaching job and was proud of the raise she received and satisfied with the progress she was making as a teacher, this being the start of her sixth year. Malcolm continued in his work. He told Carrie that he felt certain that the terrible conditions the country had been suffering under during the Depression were improving. "It's not over, but it's easing," he would say. Carrie thought that part of the improvement could be caused by people becoming accustomed to the circumstances they found themselves in. That was her father's opinion and she respected him and his ability to have kept the bank open during difficult years.

The Savage and Reston families met and it surprised Carrie that Malcolm's parents took a liking to hers. She guessed that Mr. Savage did not meet bank managers often, if ever, and enjoyed hearing about business on a retail level. Of course he had intercourse with his bankers as part of running a large corporation, but that would be a different matter, the difference being the scale. The two mothers got along well. Mrs. Savage could not be brusque to Mrs. Reston; she was too decent, too devoid of deviousness to be a target for Mrs. Savage's blunt instruments.

Carrie was surprised that Malcolm could not reach out to a coterie of friends with whom they might socialize. He told her that people who go away to boarding school and college make friends but after graduation they go their own ways. Carrie selected from among the teachers at her school and a couple occupying an apartment in their building to create a circle of friends with whom they might go out occasionally.

An event occurred and then there were a series of them spaced apart by a month or so. A friend, or an acquaintance, or a person downtown would be a partner for dinner, never at their apartment. Malcolm would come home by ten or so and he would tell Carrie what had taken place, the topics of conversation and where they had had dinner, often at the same place. Malcolm's interest in her decreased and leveled off. Her reaction was to make certain that she would not become pregnant. Neither of them brought up the idea of starting a family. Carrie never confronted Malcolm on the matter.

Being married to Malcolm had definite advantages. She met a

different order of people through Malcolm's parents. Money does make a difference, she came to understand. The rich could be interesting. They had traveled. They would have been to museums and understood the collections. They talked about what they had read. They had been to parties and dances and knew the important places of amusement up and down the East Coast where they had gathered in season. Malcolm was a trifle uninterested in society, and while he discussed his point of view with Carrie, he made no effort to change her attitudes. He let Carrie have her fill. He suspected she would find much of society a waste of time. After a year or two, Carrie, pretty and articulate, and dressed fashionably, did sense that a little of this type of playing went a long way. She discussed it with Malcolm and told him she was coming around to his way of thinking but was thankful that he had been permissive in getting it out of her system. Carrie thought it had brought them closer together.

In late 1939, or thereabouts, Malcolm sold his 1936 Ford convertible and bought a car of the latest design – another Ford product, a convertible also, whose spare tire was bolted to the back in plain view. The grill resembled a fan. Carrie told Malcolm that it was very snappy, to use her expression. From the time of this purchase, however, life became more serious. In October 1940, a draft law was passed. The intention was to train men for one year in the event of war. Malcolm drew a low number in the draft and that, coupled with his having obtained a second lieutenant's commission in ROTC at college, made him join the service in April 1941. He wanted the infantry in the worst way, to earn captain's bars, to be a company commander and lead his troops into combat. The Army wouldn't hear of it. One of the pressing needs was for supply officers who could move vast amounts of materiel around the United States and around the world, if necessary. He went to supply school, became a first lieutenant in short order, and spent a fair amount of time in the evenings writing to his wife. They were both surprised that they could correspond.

They covered the obvious and then added observations that were original to them. Carrie grew tender over Malcolm and treated him with great care when he came home on leave. She would have quit teaching and moved close to his base and seen him frequently but they both agreed that it would be more appropriate if she stayed in New York, kept her job and maintained what they had come to think of as home. Carrie knew that their separation increased her husband's interest in her. He became more attentive than he had been in the last two years.

Late in 1942, Malcolm and his supply group were shipped to England. They went to a base in the south, near Portsmouth, the large naval base and home of the Royal Navy. It was clear that there would be an invasion of the continent. Carrie comforted herself that Malcolm wouldn't be storming beaches or leading his infantry company into combat. If he came into harms' way, it would be by accident. Carrie told her friends with pride that Malcolm was overseas. The questions she had about him remained but now there was a new appreciation that there was more to this man than she had expected.

The invasion came. Carrie learned a few months later that he had landed in Normandy on the third day. It was not censored in the mail that his group was on the continent. He wrote about seeing Paris again, ten years having passed. He wrote about how quickly cities and the countryside regained their peacetime appearances. He reported that the café life near his base was back to normal, or what he thought normal should be. A few locals gathered for cards, talk, and drink. The family that ran one of the cafés understood him. There was not a great deal to eat and he appreciated all the more the few dishes he was served. A bit of his school French had come back.

The telegram arrived from the War Department on the third day of January 1945. The Secretary of War reported that Major Malcolm Savage had been killed in action on the 17th of December. There were no details. Carrie had not counted on this eventuality. She left the telegram on the kitchen table, went into the bedroom, lay on the bed, pulled up the comforter and started crying. A few hours later, she got up, changed her clothes and took a taxi to Malcolm's parents. She could not handle the matter over the telephone. Carrie handed the telegram to Mrs. Savage who read the few lines and let out a scream, as though she were being stabbed. Her first action was to repair to a sideboard and pour two large glasses of sherry. Carrie didn't wait for her father-in-law to return home and she did nothing presently about her parents who were spending ten days in Florida. Her school gave her the rest of the week off.

Early in July she received a telephone call from a lieutenant of infantry who had been with Malcolm in his final hours. He wanted to know if she was interested in hearing what he knew. He had just returned from Europe and could manage the time off. He said that he had met Malcolm on a road in Belgium. He had come to the front in a supply truck filled with food and rifle ammunition. "There was no front. The Germans had come through, masses of tanks, just blowing us apart. Your husband started gathering the stragglers. They were mostly from our division but from different battalions. There was a ridge that came down to the road and he ordered the stragglers to form a line up there. I was towing a 105, that's a 105 millimeter howitzer, a field artillery piece, and he had me choose the emplacement that looked over the fields from the top of the ridge. The truck he came up in had gone back and by late afternoon four trucks showed up. There were two 50-caliber machine guns, four men for them, and probably 100 M-1s. The major must have pulled together more than four hundred men. He formed two companies and put a sergeant in charge of each. I was the only officer and my responsibility was the artillery piece and the two machine guns. When night closed in, maybe five in the afternoon, we had the two companies in place. You couldn't dig in. The ground was frozen, but the ridge had plenty of trees, some standing, others fallen. He walked along the ridge and talked to as many soldiers as he could. It was the best leadership we had seen in a week."

The lieutenant paused and asked Carrie if she wanted him to go on. He said the tough part was coming. She said she wanted to hear the entire story. He went on to say that as dawn came up he didn't permit any fires. They had to eat K-rations, which everyone had learned to hate long ago. They could smoke, but the men had to come off the ridge in turns.

"Early in the morning we heard tanks coming. We saw three on the road and we were ready to shoot, starting with the lead tank. They could have come down the road toward us but they turned and were going parallel in front of us, maybe three hundred yards away. My guess was that they would turn again and come across those frozen fields at us, possibly with some infantry behind them. The major was near me. He looked at me and said, 'The front one.' We blew him to pieces, got the second one, but the third one turned around. We fired again and missed. The major was on the ground. He stood up for a better look at what was going on, no doubt to see if there could be other tanks coming at us. I heard a machine gun fire a burst, maybe five or six rounds. The major fell to the ground. There were several clumps of trees out there and the Germans had a machine gun in one of them. I pulled the major in behind a tree and saw he had taken two rounds in the chest. Died immediately. I was in charge then. I sent word up and down the line that we were staying on the ridge. Nothing more took place. Late in the morning, about noon, we heard tanks coming up behind us. One of the sergeants had field glasses and he said they were Sherman's."

"Much needed help," Carrie interjected.

"It turned out to be an armored division. A colonel spent ten minutes with me, if that. We stood behind a clump of trees on the ridge, away from the Germans. I told him about the action earlier that morning.

He wanted to know who we were. When I told him your husband had picked up stragglers and placed them on the ridge he asked me for my name. Then he told me to contact the supply outfit, get him buried, write up the action and put him in for a Silver Star. I asked him what I should do with the men. He said to get them to the rear where they would be reassigned to another division. It didn't take ten minutes"

"I have the Silver Star and the commendation," Carrie said. "Did you write it?"

"Yes, I did, but other people write them over. I knew him for less than a day, Mrs. Savage, but you can learn a lot about a person in a hurry. Funny that he was in supply. I thought he was a very good infantryman and ready to fight."

"How did you track me down, lieutenant?"

"There were two letters from you in his pocket. I wrote down your name and address figuring that I would come here if I could. Those letters were added to his personal effects. Did you get them?"

"Yes, the last two letters I wrote him that he received. So you've read them. I wrote a couple after that, which he never got, I suppose."

PART 5

Malcolm had had a one-week leave in October 1942. He spent a year and a half between his arrival in England and the invasion. Seven months after landing in Normandy Malcolm had been killed in Belgium. It was now August 1945 and art school would start again soon. Carrie had been without her husband for three years. Memories of him started to fade. She would try to sum him up in her mind from time to time, to move from a series of disconnected recollections to a description of him that she might give to a friend, another widow preferably, who would ask, simply, "Tell me about your husband."

There was a framed photograph of Malcolm that Carrie kept on his dresser in the bedroom. She had started giving away the clothes in the dresser. The suits, coats, shoes and two hats went to a charitable organization that sold used clothes. On the three occasions that she went there she felt a terrible sadness as she guessed that the other suits on the racks had once been worn by young men who went off to war. Now, in all likelihood, they would be worn by other young men who were fortunate to come back. She started filling the four empty drawers of the dresser with her own clothes and let her dresses fill the space left vacant by his suits and jackets. Finally she took the framed photograph and placed it under the sweaters in the top drawer. She could not decide why she had hidden the photograph from her view. Perhaps she was ready to search for a new man. The most difficult aspect would be to adapt to the part played in the war by this new man and to accept his heroism and understand what it meant to him, if there had been heroic events.

The men would come. They always had. She would have to indicate that her widowhood had ended, not with joy but with acceptance. Hope and optimism and plans would mark the way. She had not thought about changing schools, but a telephone call from a school in Philadelphia she had heard about changed her mind. There would be an increase in pay, more responsibility, and for Carrie personally, the feeling of starting anew. And the school had at their disposal for a faculty member an apartment within walking distance of school.

Carrie had lived nine years at the New York address. When she tackled the move to Philadelphia, she realized that filling every closet over the years now had its cost. She had to transfer the contents of closets and dressers to the boxes that the movers brought. In two weeks they came and placed the boxes in a moving van along with her furniture. She had started teaching at the new school before unpacking the last box. The apartment was small but fancy. It had a front hall, kitchen and dining room. There was a living room, a spare room that she made into a study, a bedroom, the largest room in the place, and a bath that had been redone to modern standards.

Carrie's increased responsibility involved the curriculum and the authority to instruct three new teachers. She did not deviate from the importance of expressing the third dimension appropriately and mastering perspective. She had a good sense of what had happened and was continuing to happen in the visual arts. Paintings were no longer required to be realistic. Movements such as cubism had come along, and then faded, but left vestiges of experimentation.

The collectors and the viewing public were tolerating departures more than they did at the turn of the century. Carrie stuck to dogma, not entirely her own, that while it was acceptable to follow any path that an artist wished to follow, all artists must master the fundamentals so that the underpinning of any work was raw ability. She maintained, and it was religion with her, that an artist cannot become lost if there is a firm under-girding. She enjoyed showing Picasso's early works, those that he did up to the age of eighteen, and comparing them to the later ones. She wanted to demonstrate that he could paint in the classical manner as well as embark on his ventures. She thought Cezanne was the best of the recent painters, perfect in every line, master of composition and color.

For Botticelli she reserved the title *God.* "In no way do I wish to antagonize the believers among us, but in every field of human activity there are a few so competent that they deserve a special title and that is the only title that comes to mind for him." She went on to say that her students should study everything about this artist.

As she encouraged her students, Carrie acknowledged that they were at or near the bottom of the pyramid. She hoped that one or two would show flair and ingenuity and willingness to master the necessary techniques. But she recognized from her many years of teaching, thirteen so far, that while some artists could render a flower in an accurate and pleasing manner, these same artists might not be able to catch a person's appearance accurately. The resulting portrait would be fine, but it would not be of the person who posed for it.

Carrie looked for versatility. One of her heroes was Michelangelo. No person had ever done the equivalent of being the architect who finished St. Peter's Cathedral, painted the ceiling of the Sistine Chapel and sculpted a Pieta and a David. She thought that in mere mortals, and that would exclude Michelangelo, diversity came at the expense of accomplishment. An artist who tried to take on too many challenges risked being unproductive in all. It was appropriate for most people to find the work at which they might excel and avoid other temptations. Because she felt this way about art, she guessed it was true for all avenues. With this belief in mind, Carrie would encourage her students to concentrate until they had mastered one aspect of art, the one at which she and they thought they might do well.

The student body consisted equally of men and women. At Pratt there had been a few more women. Most of the men in her classes had been in the war and for some of them the war had been an extended interruption. These men had always wanted to be commercial artists or portrait painters or landscape artists. Others were interested in interior design and still others in how one decorates fabric. Only one of her students admitted to having no interest in making a career in art. He was waiting for his classes in engineering to continue at the University, which they would in the fall of 1946. Carrie was surprised that the administration had admitted him. The person in admissions to whom she spoke said that he had filled the last empty slot.

Carrie asked for his file and learned that George Townsend, Jr. came from a small city in central Pennsylvania and had completed two years of an engineering curriculum before spending three years in the Army Air Corps. His year of birth was 1921, and therefore he was eleven years younger than she was. He was handsome and well formed. One day in the fall he had come to class wearing a shirt with the sleeves rolled up. He had not buttoned the shirt to the top so that she could see some of his chest. His arms were covered with short blond hairs and the skin was tanned to a light bronze. He looked delicious to her.

They met as teacher and student. In drawing class he started poorly when he drew and shaded objects that she had selected. When the class moved to torsos, women's mostly, he showed his lack of ability and she found herself giving him more time than she gave the others.

When they were near one another, she became aware of his body. She could not deny that she would think about art for one minute then think about his chest and shoulders. She felt about him the way she had felt for no other man, her husband included. Had she made a list of traits that she found attractive, she would never have added the magnetism of a body. She needed to be with him in an intimate way, and talk to him about herself. It would be wonderful to have someone to confide in on all matters.

Carrie was thirty-five years old. The idea of having children had lost appeal. Her career appeared secure. She dismissed the notion that one man would appear who would be her companion to the end. There did not appear to be one model that would suit her needs. She thought that men would arrive as needed, each differing from the last as she changed over the decades. It was obvious to Carrie that George was aware of her. He flirted with his eyes and must have appreciated her appearance and her dedication to her work. He had made no advances but she thought that he could be tempted.

Men were not difficult to approach, she knew. There was a cafeteria in the neighborhood where teachers and students gathered for lunch, status forgotten. Carrie had written her telephone number on a small piece of paper, adding the initials CRS. She waited for a moment when others had gone back to school to hand the paper to George. "Could you telephone me tonight, say seven-thirty? This is a secret between you and me, of course."

He telephoned at the appropriate hour. Carrie suggested that he bring examples of his work. She wanted to show him the subtleties of shading so that the third dimension would be obvious to viewers. "If it's done well, you will have taken the first step toward being an artist," she said.

He came to her apartment the following evening carrying several of the sketches he had completed in class. They spent over an hour on the details and he told her at the end of the evening that he enjoyed the creation of art and if he were any better at it he might consider it as a career. But he went on to say that his heart was in engineering. She accepted that and asked him to telephone her again soon as they had more work to do.

He waited two days and telephoned. They decided on the evening following. George could not deny the tensions within him. She was so attractive. They were alone in her apartment. She might be interested in him, despite the age difference that he could see but could not determine exactly. The reason for her invitation didn't stand up very well. She must want him to show interest in her. After they had been working on the drawings for an hour or so, she prepared tea. She set the tray on the coffee table and as she sat down he placed an arm around her and pulled her toward him. There was no resistance. "Something's come over me. I haven't analyzed it yet," she said. He answered, "Whatever you feel, I feel as well, perhaps stronger."

They were in bed and had slept a while. She woke up and felt his face and put her hand in his hair. He woke up right away and asked, "Am I in heaven?" "We can't tell just yet," she said.

They were quiet for a long spell. Then Carrie said, "It goes back to a discussion that I would have with my father between the ages of fifteen and twenty, discussions on men. I was the fourth and final child and my father took great interest in finding the correct man for me, or rather in my finding the correct man. He thought I should be able to define the man that would appeal to me. My position was, and still is, that men come into your life with features you like to a greater or lesser extent, and then you sort it out over time."

"I don't understand how a lovely, intelligent woman such as you would not be married."

"I was, a little less than eight years. I lost him in the war. I'm a war widow."

"I'm awfully sorry. I had no way of knowing."

"You're beautiful, George. But you have to go back to the University in the fall. You'll need someone far younger than I so you can have those babies."

"Will you throw me out?"

"Yes, but not until the moment is right."

CARRIE RESTON

PART 6

The romance between Carrie and George proved satisfactory to both parties at the start. Carrie received George's undivided attention. He never glanced at another woman. He knew, however, that changes would come. In the fall, when he would return to the University, he admitted that there would need to be a new arrangement. They had constructed a life centered on art, which featured Carrie's teaching, happenings around her school, exhibits at the main museum of the city and new works in galleries about town.

Carrie understood nothing about mechanical engineering and could not take the time to learn what it consisted of. George explained Young's Modulus to her, which she was able to apply to human behavior. On that basis she absorbed it. Carrie was bending the top of a can of tomato paste to detach it from the can. George watched her apply eight bends before the top came off. He explained that if one applies less than a certain amount of bending, the top would never separate from the can. There is an amount of bending, Young's Modulus, which when exceeded guarantees that the top will separate. Carrie modified this law to people by classifying students into those whom she was bending sufficiently and those she was not. Those she was bending appropriately were learning, and those she could not bend, or were not allowing themselves to be bent, were not learning.

George had no objection to Carrie's interpretation. One day she asked him whether all the laws of physics had their equivalence in human behavior. "It's selective," he answered. "The speed of light does not apply, but old Newton, when he said that for every action there is an equal and opposite reaction, then certainly he was thinking of most of the humans he knew, including a few professors of physics at Cambridge."

They lived as a couple, George spending half his nights at Carrie's apartment. It became known around the school that they had paired off and those who were conscious of their ages speculated on the eventual disposition of the arrangement.

Carrie allowed the calendar to intrude in her life before George did. Early in the summer she had announced at breakfast, "Well, three more months."

"Three more months of what?" he had asked.

"This living together will come to an end, unfortunately, I think." She went on to say that the eleven years of difference in age had not disappeared. She added that when he returned to the University and finished his studies it would be natural for him to settle on a woman his age. She made the point that they had never planned to have children, and that was life's hard work, and he would want to undertake it with a young woman.

George fought it off but he recognized that he was missing conviction. He knew that Carrie was right. Before they separated, George found an apartment with a classmate. He was within walking distance of the campus. The parting was sudden and more dramatic than George guessed. After the matter of his apartment was settled, Carrie had said, "We can't let this move slowly to its death. It's the honorable thing to do to end it and force ourselves to start over in new directions." The words had been said when they were in bed and in each other's arms. He started to cry and continued to cry. He hadn't cried since childhood. He told her that he loved her and this for the first time. It ended there.

In the fall, Carrie was strolling through the rooms of the city's museum on the second floor, studying the art on display. This was not a traveling exhibition, but the permanent collection. She had seen these paintings before several times. As one does, she surveyed the other viewers studying the art. A man moving alone caught her attention. She felt that it was a shame to abide by society's rules, which did not allow them to meet now, perhaps ever. He looked to be taller than she and carried himself nicely. He wore gray trousers and a brown tweed jacket and had on a shirt and tie. Carrie guessed that he shaved in the morning and again in the evening in the event he was going out. He turned around and looked straight at her. They both smiled and in a moment she averted her gaze. She wondered if he turned around because he sensed that she was looking at him. She wondered also what he had felt in that moment they were looking at one another.

She moved through the galleries and eventually to the cafeteria downstairs. She did not turn around to see if he was following her, but when she passed the cash register and started looking for a table, she noticed that he was in line. When he had paid, he searched the tables, found hers, and moved in her direction. "May I join you?" he asked. It was not a particularly forward request as the cafeteria was crowded. He removed his tea and cake from the tray and said, "Do the same and I'll take your tray away."

When he returned and sat down, he said nothing. Carrie studied his face, and then asked, "Were you following me?"

"Yes," he said.

When he added nothing she wondered whether he was the most confident man she had met, or perhaps tongue-tied for the moment. "Were roles reversed in our society I would have followed you," she said.

With that, he said, "Remember, if you put yourself in that situation, you must find the courage to track down another person, to intrude yourself on them, without knowing anything about the other, not knowing how you will be received. Do you suppose you have that courage?"

"We'll never know, but I kept looking long enough to register something on you."

"Your gaze was very easy to read. It said, meet me in the cafeteria."

She smiled and said, "There's nothing worse than a missed opportunity."

He answered, "We don't know if there's any opportunity here, but if there is we aren't about to miss it."

They went on in that vein, she telling him soon enough that she had lost her husband in the war. He countered that his wife had sought a divorce. "I was away too long, perhaps. We were not the best match, I might add."

They volunteered from their résumés that she had started her second year at the art school and he was employed by the Pennsylvania Railroad in the legal department. He had gone off to Harvard from his native Tennessee and graduated in the class of 1931 and three years later from the law school. He had been in the N.R.O.T.C. and been commissioned an ensign at the time of graduation. He entered the service before the start of the war and ended as a commander, a skipper of a destroyer.

Carrie asked, "How many stripes on the sleeves? We've just had a war and I don't know the navy ranks and how they compare to the army's."

His answer was laconic. "I would be glad to tell you sometime, diagrams included. Remind me."

They continued talking for most of an hour. When it came time for the museum to close they were both in a mood to continue but Carrie begged off to prepare for her classes the following day. They had exchanged addresses and telephone numbers. He walked her to her trolley and started to shake her hand when suddenly he put his arms around her and kissed her on the cheek. She took a seat in the trolley and looked at him standing on the platform. He blew her a kiss and she smiled at him and kept looking at him. As the trolley moved away she waved.

His name was John Bell. When Carrie asked for his middle name, he said, "Cunningham, but I never use it." As he had graduated from college in 1931, he would be a year older than she; at least that was her estimate. His hair was black and he shaved down to the collar of his shirt. The backs of his hands were covered with black hair. Her husband, Malcolm, and George had nearly hairless bodies. John Bell, she guessed, had a great mass of hair on his chest and she wondered how he would feel against her when they were naked in bed. Carrie berated herself for not wondering about his character and soul. He had said that he would telephone the evening following, Monday evening.

The arrival of John Bell in her life killed the final emotions about George. She would think of him as recent history, but not with longing. To Carrie, it was obvious that John Bell wanted to marry again and have children. "We've been short changed, you and I. The war wasn't kind, you losing your husband, me having my wife grow tired of me." He said these words early on, before the closeness came. Carrie interpreted the words as meaning that if they were to marry, it would be with the understanding that they would try to have children.

They agreed to marry at Easter in 1947, less that half a year after they met. John declared that they should live in a house in West Philadelphia, close to both their jobs. There were desirable communities on the Main Line, but the train ride into town would be time consuming for both. He wondered why so many men subjected themselves to the daily round trip. They looked at the houses available in West Philadelphia and when they agreed on a property, John bought it. There was no question of taking out a mortgage. He paid the full amount. Carrie determined that after the wedding she would unravel the mystery of this vast purchasing power.

Carrie was unsettled by his style of love, at first. It was as though before a man married he fell in love with his wife-to-be and after the marriage ceremony he did not allow his love to diminish but added a layer of concern as the self-appointed head of family. Carrie thought at first that he was responding to a formula of his making that called for a certain behavior toward his wife, whoever she might be and whatever the relationship. She thought he might be reacting to the failure of his first marriage.

Carrie was pleased by his moments of impulsive sweetness. She was relieved that he took on more responsibilities than Malcolm or George had. Their sexual life was ample and satisfactory but she missed George's demonstrative ways. He had awakened a great deal in her. John, nevertheless, was more appealing. He placed her wishes ahead of his own, most of the time, and in her mind she categorized John as her thoughtful lover. Malcolm had been tentative, George impulsive. She would think about her history in bed with these three men and knew she and been fortunate in experiencing their variety.

Slowly, in the time required to bring about the first child, Carrie succeeded in understanding her husband's behavior toward her. The affection and politeness were obvious, but hidden from view and more difficult to grasp was that he thought about her, considered what she was doing with her life and career, evaluated her opinions and points of view, and organized their lives for what he thought would be the greatest prosperity. She knew that he never wanted said of him that he was not a very good husband. They did not talk about any of this, Carrie for her part fearing that discussing these matters might change his behavior.

From time to time, Carrie would reflect on her father's suggestion of years ago that she learn to describe the man she wanted for a husband. She had always avoided making that list because, as she insisted, each person was different and you never knew what might appeal to you strongly about this one or that one. And she reflected now, that if she had made a list, it could not have been a description of John. She did not know enough about men and marriage in her twenties to make such a list. She doubted that she could have made a list the day before she met John.

There was another child. John and Carrie moved into their forties. He became general counsel and she principal administrator at the art school. For Carrie there were several years of working half time in order to launch their two children in the proper direction.

WOMAN FROM PERU

WOMAN FROM PERU

PART I

Arthur Brooks was getting along in years, having hit seventy-five. Most of his systems functioned properly save his eyes. He could read with glasses but did not trust himself on the road and had given up driving. His son Alexander was at the wheel and Alexander's wife Ellen was in the back seat when they drove up to a fancy restaurant.

"Why are you saluting, Dad?" Alexander asked.

"I thought it was an honor guard greeting us,"

"No, Dad, those are the men who will park the car. This place is so fancy there's only valet parking."

"Had me fooled," Arthur said. His vision suffered from various causes and on this summer evening the sun still shone as they drove to this restaurant to celebrate Arthur's brother Bradford's seventieth birthday. When he walked into the darkened restaurant, Arthur could see very little. Sudden changes in light level threw him for a loop.

Alexander and his wife Ellen guided Arthur to the private room where the party would take place. In Arthur's generation there were nine brothers and sisters and between them they had produced 37 offspring. When Arthur spotted a tall woman nearby he assumed she was a niece. He walked up to her, placed an arm around her loosely and kissed her on the cheek. It wouldn't do that he failed to recognize someone in the family.

Ellen intervened and asked the woman, "Will you be helping tonight?"

"Yes. I'm one of two waitresses who will be serving you."

Arthur heard the faint accent, which he did not recognize. He had always been interested in people he met who were not born in the United States. He approached an extra foot and asked, "And where were you born?"

"I'm from Peru."

"And how did you get to the United States?"

"I came to Florida to study."

"How about Florida to California, how did you manage that?"

"I needed a change."

Arthur knew that he had met a dead end and altered his line of questioning.

"Is there a good man in your life?" he asked.

"A man. I don't know how good he is." Arthur then took a leap. "Do you want to marry him?"

"Yes."

"He hasn't proposed yet?"

"That's right."

"Why don't you propose to him?"

"I can't. I'm a woman."

Here it was again, a societal block standing in the way of progress. In this case, a lovely Latina was refusing to nail the man she wanted for the questionable reason that women do not propose to men. Arthur didn't have to talk to this woman about her position. He understood it thoroughly. It went like this. About fifty years ago a do-gooder discovered a chemical compound that interfered with a woman's reproductive cycle. If taken in the correct dosage at the proper intervals, the likelihood of pregnancy was reduced nearly to zero. The advent of this pill was regarded as a liberating force in women's lives. The truth, however, was quite the contrary. The pill enslaved women more completely than ever.

Men looked at the pill and saw it as a release from responsibility. After singling out a body that pleased, men would suggest that the woman move in with them. A few women understood the maneuver for what it was and turned down the offer. Most women, however, regarded this development as a road to marriage. Men, ever cavalier about the lives of women they involved themselves with, looked at the development as an opportunity for unfettered sex -- marriage and commitment be damned.

Arthur surmised that this striking Latina standing in front of him had been victimized by another crude male who was taking advantage of her dream of marriage and having a family. Arthur could almost hear her clock ticking.

"What is your name, dear?"

"Angelina."

"Well, Angelina, here's what you do. Chose a date in the near future, ask a friend if you can spend the night if you are forced to leave your apartment, then place two suitcases on your bed. Do you sleep together?"

"Yes. One very comfortable double bed."

"Place two suitcases on the bed and start filling them with clothes. When your man comes home --- what's his name?"

"Enrico."

"When Enrico gets home, he'll find you in the bedroom and ask right away what you are doing. You say you're leaving. He'll ask why. You tell him there's no future for you with him."

Angelina looked at Arthur and asked, "This friend whose house I will go to with two suitcases. Will that be you?"

Arthur, who had lost his wife six years previously, knew the answer would be no, but he injected a lengthy pause into the proceedings to make Angelina think he was evaluating her proposal. "Let me think it over during dinner," he said.

WOMAN FROM PERU

PART 2

Arthur did think about it at dinner. Angelina paid attention to her half of the table, making certain that her guests were well attended to. Arthur wondered whether her presence in his house wouldn't bring excitement. His neighbors would be on the telephone immediately but he was beyond caring about their reactions. Let them be jealous. As the dinner wore on, he felt himself moving from "absolutely not" to "possibly yes." He was retired and no longer carried business cards but did have calling cards, including his e-mail address, which he considered a modern touch. Only a few of his friends had purchased a computer and gone on line for the express purpose of communicating across state lines and oceans, mostly the Atlantic.

When the party was over, Arthur took a calling card from his wallet. As he moved out of the room he went past Angelina, handed her the card, and said, "Call me if you need me."

In the car, Arthur's son asked him if he had had a good time. Arthur reflected for a moment and said, "Picking up the check for a dozen people is a bit brutal, but I was able to order the wines and I made certain to have my favorites."

"I'm glad you're not driving, Dad," Alexander remarked.

Arthur fell silent. He started thinking about Angelina, the graceful way she moved about the room, the lovely young woman she was, and finally whether his son and daughter-in-law could be reading his mind.

Arthur did not know whether he had handled his life correctly since the departure of his wife. He was only sixty-nine at the time and seventy-five presently. There had been a few flings since his wife's death. The most memorable for him had been with a widow his age whom he met on a cruise ship. The ambiance out at sea and perhaps the gentle rolling motion had the expected results on both. They continued the affair with Arthur flying half-way across the continent. The arrangement came to an end when a local swain made an offer for the widow's hand. Proximity had won out. Great events can take place in one's life, Arthur came to realize, even if they did not finish properly. Arthur was uplifted by this relationship and learned the obvious lesson that pursuing the ladies out of town left his neighbors, those busy-bodies, filled with curiosity but out of the action: Arthur never told them anything.

Arthur now found himself contemplating a dalliance with a woman in her late twenties. She hadn't telephoned. Enrico could have been forced to propose by the sight of two half-filled suitcases on their bed. Only a week had gone by since they had met at the party and he would give it another week before attempting to push the thoughts of Angelina from his mind.

In that week of waiting, Arthur Brooks organized a thorough review of his life as he was leading it and examined the prospects for the remainder of it. He did not know how to proceed, never having taken such an inventory, so he fell to groping around. He had heard that one can't buy happiness, and he knew as well the snappy rejoinder to the effect that anyone who believes the notion doesn't understand happiness and knows nothing about money. In any event, he had plenty of money. He lived in the house he and his wife had bought ten years ago. It was absurdly too large but when you sell your business and have all this cash, what better investment is there? His children, son Alexander and three daughters, were educated and married. Arthur and his wife had told one another they needed guest rooms to accommodate visits from children and grandchildren.

In this examination of his life, Arthur went to happiness. What should he be doing to make himself happy? He guessed that answering the calls of duty were important – giving time to civic enterprises and continuing his association at church. If he did not continue his attendance at church, Arthur wondered who would come to his service, or would there even be one. Then staying in good shape, of course. No use planning anything without staying in robust good health. He had bought a 21-speed bicycle and rode it around his neighborhood, avoiding the hills. He continued his membership at the club, staying with tennis and swimming. He did what his doctor told him to do. He tried to lead a normal and sensible life, but finding the appropriate woman had escaped him to date.

The lovely lady from Dallas whom he had met on the cruise and pursued subsequently had been snatched away from him. Perhaps he was not intended to live in Dallas, although she had made him happy. Her presence in his life had contributed greatly to his level of happiness. Perhaps the young Peruvian could turn into an attractive alternative, although he recognized, as well, that she could represent disaster for him. No doubt she arrived in Florida with a student visa. On moving to California she went underground. Her visa had expired and she bought forged documents, a Social Security card and another student visa. These permitted her to work. That's how Arthur figured it. He did know that harboring an illegal alien was not a crime. He did know that paying an undocumented worker was against the law. If she moved in, there couldn't be any transfer of cash for services rendered. There might be a gift, of course. That was the sum of Arthur's opinions when the second Saturday came around. He couldn't get it out of his mind that Angelina would require two weeks to pass before she found sufficient courage to confront Enrico.

On Sunday afternoon the telephone rang. "This is Angelina," the warm voice said. "Tomorrow is Monday and the restaurant is closed. I'll start packing and if Enrico doesn't propose when he comes home from work I should be at your place between six and seven."

Arthur Brooks was pleased but surprised. "Of all your friends, why did you decide to call me?"

"They all live in apartments. I drove around to your address and you have a big house. Such a nice neighborhood."

That Monday evening Angelina did telephone. She had driven a short distance from her apartment, pulled into a parking place and dialed Arthur's number on her cell phone.

"Mr. Brooks, Enrico was very abusive. He let me finish filling the two suitcases and told me to leave. There are plenty of women, he told me."

"Well, drive on over. I'll open the garage door and you can come right into the empty slot. I sold my wife's car several years ago."

"This is very nice of you. I thank you."

"You're welcome. How long will it take you?"

"About twenty minutes."

Arthur was pleased that she had stopped the car to use her cell phone. He went upstairs to survey the guest room and bath, the one where he would install Angelina. He had conducted this examination several times previously. As he made his tour he told himself that there was no fool like an old fool, particularly as he had come to grips with that notion several years ago. It was the year he had stopped thinking of himself as middle-aged and admitted to being old.

When he returned downstairs he pushed the button to open the garage door, found his book, and settled in the breakfast area. He read but rehearsed initial conversations with Angelina at the same time, not doing justice to either activity. In a little while he heard a car pull in. He knew not to close the garage door. Angelina might feel trapped.

He opened the door from the kitchen. She was still in the car. She waived and smiled. She got out of the car and came around to shake hands. "Hello, Mr. Brooks. You have saved me. Enrico has a bad temper. I didn't realize he was so against marriage and having children."

"I'm surprised too," Arthur said. "Doesn't he think he was a baby once?"

Angelina reflected for a while. She said, "I don't know." She opened the doors on the passenger side so that she could take out the two suitcases. Arthur picked up one. They were medium sized. He asked, "What about the rest of your stuff?"

"I have a few books and the rest clothes. I'll arrange to go there when Enrico's at work."

Arthur headed upstairs to the guest room. "You should be able to unpack. The closets and bureaus are empty. Have you had supper?"

"No, not yet," Angelina answered.

"Come down when you are finished and we'll organize a meal."

"It's a lovely room," Angelina said when she came down to the kitchen. "How can I help?"

Arthur led her to the refrigerator. They looked at his supplies and selected salmon and broccoli. Angelina asked if he had rice, wild or white. She frowned when he said that he had only white rice. "I am very good in the kitchen," she announced. "Please let me fix dinner."

This was an offer that Arthur could not refuse. He opened a bottle of white wine and poured two glasses, placing one where Angelina was working. "It's for you, not the salmon," he said.

Arthur returned to his book but again couldn't concentrate. He was distracted by observing Angelina as she looked into each drawer and closet. Not only did she get dinner underway but also she set the table in the dining room. She was quiet except for occasional humming. Arthur didn't recognize the tune, no doubt a favorite from Latin America. She served dinner on two plates and notified Arthur that the meal was ready by asking him if he wanted mayonnaise with broccoli.

Arthur thought they might get down to business once seated at the table. He was interested principally in how long she planned to stay. Would it be about a week? Would she start searching for a place of her own? It occurred to Arthur to go over her financial situation, but did it only in his mind. He couldn't bring himself to utter the words. It might have been a lack of money that drove her to the abusive Enrico. She had her wages and tips but there must be a car payment and perhaps she was sending money to her family in Peru. All in all she might be living on a tight budget. Arthur determined to leave the subject alone. Angelina would bring up the subject of money soon enough. Most people do.

At the end of the meal Arthur went to the topic on his mind, and perhaps on hers. He asked, "Are you afraid of me in any way?"

She answered without hesitation. "No. You are not a man alone in the world. I met parts of your family at the dinner. They are fine people. I was impressed by your son Alexander and his wife Ellen. It's the people living alone who frighten me. That Enrico has no family in North America. He can act out when it suits him."

"What is he doing in the United States?"

"He has his green card and knows computers and he works with them. I don't understand any of it."

Arthur wanted to move to a short history of Angelina but thought it might be intrusive. She cleared the table, rinsed the dishes and put them in the dishwasher. She excused herself and went up to her room. He heard her speak briefly, no doubt on her cell phone. Then there was silence.

At the hour when he went to bed, he turned out the lights and locked various doors. When he reached the second floor, she was standing at her door, fully dressed. She said, "Thank you again. I'll see you tomorrow." She closed the door and Arthur waited for the sound of the dead bolt. He heard nothing.

The following morning, past seven, he heard a shower running. A few minutes later Angelina appeared, dressed in her bathrobe. Two pajama legs stuck out below the bathrobe, and two bare feet below that. She had washed and combed her hair. It was black and tight around her face. There was no makeup. Arthur thought she had a plain face that looked simply beautiful to him.

Arthur had followed his regular schedule, making coffee and starting on the paper. They exchanged pleasantries. He pointed to the coffee pot. When she was seated she asked for a section of the paper and he could see that she was studying the movie reviews. Perhaps she wished to be an actress. All he knew about her was that she worked in a fancy restaurant, wanted to marry and have children, and had not found the right man, or the right man had not found her.

Arthur knew he had to face the matter of access to his house. At the end of breakfast he went to a drawer, pulled out a garage door opener and a set of keys and handed them to her. "The front door and the door from the garage into this area," he said.

"This is so considerate," she said. "I must drive to my old place and bring over the rest of my clothes." Arthur calculated that these might be the second and final load. There were five trips in all, mostly clothes that ended up in her room. Four cardboard boxes stayed in the garage. Angelina explained that that they were books dear to her.

Angelina's days consisted of making a trip to her former apartment, working around her room, which Arthur always found to be immaculate, and reading outdoors on the patio in the early afternoons. She tended to head to work at 3:30, work the dinner shift and return by midnight. That's how she spent the first week with him.

She had obtained Arthur's permission to sit on the patio on garden furniture, protected from the sun by a parasol, which Arthur put up in May and took down in October. She did not volunteer so Arthur had to ask her what she read. The books turned out to be important fiction written in Spanish and translated into English. She had the Spanish versions as well. Arthur wanted to go on and find out more about her interest, but again when she didn't volunteer, he did not intrude. He suggested she could use the pool at any time and as he made the offer he knew that part of his reason was generosity and the rest of it his desire to see her in a bathing suit. He could anticipate the pretty sight it would be. She had thanked him. He guessed she would wait until they had become familiar one with the other before she exposed that much of herself.

WOMAN FROM PERU

PART 4

They settled into their routines. Arthur kept up his social activities, although he felt less pressure to seek out the company of women now that the lovely Angelina lived in his house. He did not ignore his exercises, peddling his bike and going to the club three times a week. He read, but it was mostly about investments. He had dreamed about collecting and reading the important books of Western culture but never set aside enough time for the task. He knew he was not an intellectual being and had known it all along as he built a successful business and poured most of his life into that activity.

Angelina kept steadily at her work. She drove to mass every Sunday morning. Arthur admitted that his attendance record was no match for hers. He accounted for her perfect record by her never hesitating, while on Saturday evening he would examine the prospects for Sunday morning. After finishing the transfer of her possessions from Enrico's apartment to his home, she took over from Arthur the management of part of his house. She would be at work five nights a week. On her two free evenings she prepared dinner. The spaces for which she assumed responsibility were the kitchen, breakfast area, dining room, stairway and her room and bath. There was plenty left over for Maria Dora, the maid from Guatemala who had been working for him and his wife since before they had purchased the house. Arthur told himself that Maria Dora was part of the family. When the two women met, they sized up one another after chatting in Spanish. The upshot was that their new names were Segnora Angelina and Segnora Dora. Arthur was certain that Maria Dora assumed that Angelina was the sleeping partner but Arthur could not detect any change in attitude toward him on Maria Dora's part.

Angelina enjoyed writing out menus and making lists of food. She would drive Arthur's car, with him in the passenger seat, to the supermarket. She guessed correctly that he selected a distant store to avoid neighbors and people from his social circle.

On a fine morning Angelina appeared in the kitchen at the usual hour. Arthur noticed right away that in place of pajamas sticking out under the bathrobe there were two bare legs. He guessed that she was naked, or had on underwear or was sporting a bathing suit. After breakfast, when the dishes were done, Angelina said, "Mr. Brooks, I would like to accept your offer to use the pool. By any chance would you like to swim with me and show me the strokes?"

So that's how it would be. He would not be required to sneak surreptitious glances from the kitchen window. She was about to allow him the pleasure of being around her for an hour or so, minimally dressed.

He reappeared with two large towels wearing a blue bathing suit and carrying a terrycloth robe. They went out to the pool and Angelina removed her robe. She wore a one-piece suit that provided Arthur with a complete description of how she was built. She stood near him and explained that she had learned to swim as a child but had never been taught the strokes. Arthur had always surmised that any woman with an attractive body knew the effect the female form had on a man. Arthur knew also that any initial sensation wore off over time – the half-life effect of stimulus – and it was certain that Angelina understood the phenomenon. She let him look at her angles and curves at close range. After five minutes of discussion they slid into the pool. Arthur did show her how to swim freestyle and promised that there was more that he could teach her.

When out of the pool she took her time drying off then stretched out the towel Arthur had provided and took the prone and supine positions alternately. Certainly Angelina wanted Arthur to see how she was constructed. It was not obvious to what end. If she decided that there would be physical contact between them, then Angelina would have to make the first move. Arthur couldn't force himself on her, even in the least amount, while she was a guest in his house and in a sense captive.

Three weeks had passed and still no conversation about when Angelina would depart. Arthur had grown to enjoy Angelina's presence and had no interest in forcing the issue. Alexander and Ellen knew of this new departure in Arthur's life. Alexander had only said that it was wonderful that his father had company. Ellen asked how permanent the arrangement might be. Arthur answered that a well-known feature of life consists of constant rearrangements and he would keep her apprised of developments.

Toward the end of the fourth week Angelina issued two declarations, both indicating to Arthur what had been on her mind. In the first, she said that she should be making new arrangements and added that she was in negotiations with another waitress about finding an apartment together. Arthur said that there was no need to hurry. The second declaration came in the form of a question. She asked Arthur whether there was a man for her in his family. He made the connection between this request and the viewing of her body poolside. "Is there a there a man for me in that large family of yours?" was the way she put it. Arthur liked the bluntness. "Those that I have met are attractive and have fine manners," she added. Arthur answered by saying that he would think about the remaining unmarried men in the Brooks family. Angelina went on. "Enrico and those other dogs take everything from a woman and give nothing back. Not another man will touch me below the neck until he is my husband."

Arthur thought that to be an unrealistic position. He said, "Angelina, most men want to know a fair amount about a woman before proposing marriage." Angelina thought a minute and answered, "I have waited eight years for a proposal while I serviced three men. No more."

It was obvious to Arthur that Angelina could not be dissuaded. He didn't know how much time he had to produce one of his relatives for her. "Describe the type of man you want," Arthur said.

Again, no hesitation. Angelina had him outlined in her mind. "A nice looking man, an Anglo to mix with my Latina. A successful person who will have a good career so that I can make a family. Someone who is intelligent and has the pleasing personality that you and your family have."

There was little in unmarried material to choose from in the family, Arthur knew, as most men had married in their late twenties. There was one wild bronco remaining, however. He was the oldest child of his brother Bradford, whose seventieth birthday was being celebrated on the evening that Arthur met Angelina. This son of Bradford, a certain Daniel, aged 31 to Angelina's 28, was different from the other Brooks. Essential to his personality was the belief that interesting aspects of life should be undertaken and explored as soon as possible, leaving no gratification delayed for future enjoyment. "I want everything now," Arthur summarized his nephew's attitude. Needless to say women were tops on his list of pleasures. That's what women are for: to be seduced, taken to bed and enjoyed. It was certain that this summed up his view. The family had tired of discussing Daniel's escapades. They had written him off as a partial person although they knew in their hearts that they longed to claim some of his personality as their own, and to taste the parts of life they forbade themselves.

Because Daniel could not combine his practice of eccentricity with holding down a regular job, he chose the life of photography, travel and writing. His performance was first rate but his income erratic. He lived in the guest house on yet another uncle's estate. Arthur did not know if there was rent to pay but he doubted it, at least not on a regular basis.

If Arthur was to bring Angelina up to Daniel, he had to know something about her past and to that end the following morning after breakfast was devoted to the topic. Angelina had not been forthcoming and he had not been inquisitive.

Arthur gave Angelina the reason for his need to know, and then launched into his list of questions. He started with her family. Her father was a professor of mathematics at the university in Lima. Her two brothers were in commerce. Her mother had managed the family since her marriage. They lived in a detached house about a mile from the university. Angelina's leaving for study in Florida was objected to by her family for no other reason than it was expected of her that she follow her mother's life. She had studied Spanish literature at the university and had read most of the output of the well-known authors from Spain and Latin America. Her dream was to master English, learn the Spanish classics translated into English, complete her education, and teach undergraduates at the university level in the United States. The lack of money derailed her. She was forced to wait on tables and reduce the amount of time spent in class at her school in Florida. She was thrown off track by the men she met, two of them from the Cuban community in Miami. They offered partial subsistence in exchange for favors and soon enough she realized that she was playing the mistress. Enrico came into view and suggested that she migrate to California with him and continue her studies in the vicinity of the corporation that was offering him a substantial position in his specialty. While Enrico represented a way out, he was from the same civilization as her two other men and his behavior resembled theirs. These men were attractive in some respects, Angelina admitted to Arthur, but they proved to be incapable of providing her what she longed for. Enrico was not a bad person, she said, but he could not face marriage. She thought it was a matter of fear. She represented everything that a normal man could hope for. That was her view of herself.

WOMAN FROM PERU

PART 5

Arthur had told Angelina that there was a bachelor about her age remaining unmarried in the family inventory. His name was Daniel. He traveled a fair amount and wrote photo-essays which he sold to magazines. He had returned recently from Afghanistan, after Bradford's birthday celebration. Arthur had not been face-to-face with Daniel since he came back but he was relieved that Daniel had visited a safe corner of that country. Family members tended to keep abreast of developments.

When Arthur telephoned Daniel to tell him about Angelina, Daniel remarked that a family member had told him that his Uncle Arthur was starting a harem of Latin American beauties. Arthur answered, "On the contrary, I'm saving this beauty for you and I want you to come over and meet her."

"Is she enthusiastic about me?" Daniel asked.

"Not visibly so, but certainly in her heart. It was she who asked me about bachelors in our family," Arthur answered.

They talked on for a few minutes. Arthur knew that Daniel would welcome a physical description. Arthur recounted the several swimming episodes and the existence of a conservative bathing suit and a bikini. "You'll have to see for yourself," Arthur said. He knew that Daniel would be hooked. Arthur guessed that the results of these conversations initiated by Angelina would be just as she had planned. Arthur was impressed at Angelina's ability to play her chess game four or five moves in advance.

The following Monday, when Angelina's restaurant was closed, Daniel came for a glass of wine, preparatory to taking Angelina to dinner. A new side of Angelina emerged, Arthur thought. The smile flashed frequently and she probed Daniel for other explorations prior to Afghanistan. Angelina's skin was dark, to the extent that people who originate on the Iberian Peninsula have dark brown skin. Arthur could not detect an Andean influence. She wore a blouse of heavy white material that contrasted with her black hair, red lips, and white teeth that gleamed when she laughed. Her laugh was quiet and had a seductive tone that Arthur found beguiling. He knew it was having its effects on Daniel. When the wine was finished, Angelina and Daniel went to his car and drove off to dinner. Arthur stayed at one of the living room windows long enough to see Daniel open the car door for Angelina. He suspected that the other men in her life had ignored this nicety. Arthur knew himself well enough that he would telephone Daniel should he fail in this courtesy. The Brooks family may not have produced intellectuals but the members had manners.

Arthur was perhaps too eager in his questioning of Angelina the following morning over coffee. Did she like him, was he chivalrous, what had they talked about, and did it come out that Daniel had traveled extensively in South America? Angelina appeared pleased at the experience, as well she might be, Arthur knew. It would be on their third encounter or so that Daniel would do his best to drag Angelina to his bed. Arthur knew Daniel's reputation on these matters.

Because of Angelina's work schedule Daniel started coming to Arthur's house in the morning. It was summer and his visits were occasions for a swim. The bikini appeared on the third such morning. Daniel's reproductive instincts had been raised to a high pitch by Angelina in her sedate bathing suit. He was nearly finished off by Angelina in the bikini. The white bikini contrasted against the dark skin and little if anything was left to Daniel's imagination. Arthur guessed that Daniel undressed her twenty-five times in his mind on each morning they spent around the pool.

It interested Arthur that Daniel would bring a draft of his article on Afghanistan, along with photographs, so that Angelina could read and comment. Arthur supposed that her study of literature made it possible for her to suggest changes and improvements in his presentation. Arthur was aware that they sat around the table with the parasol quite a few times discussing his writing. It was serious business. Daniel had said that his article would run 5,000 words.

One warm day toward the end of the summer, when Angelina and Daniel had had their swim, they sat at the table to have coffee. Daniel sat down first. Angelina came up behind him, smoothed his hair, and kissed him on top of the head. Daniel didn't turn around when he said to her, "Nothing below the neck, Angelina." She laughed, as did Arthur who overheard the remark as he was going inside.

The relationship was moving along and Arthur wondered if Daniel wouldn't break down soon under the regimen of abstinence. He telephoned Daniel and came right to the point. "How are you establishing yourself with Angelina? You are seeing a fair amount of one another."

"You've done me a favor, Uncle Arthur, but at a high price."

"How so?"

"Just between us men," Daniel said, "I don't know how long I can hold out. She is serious about nothing below the neck. It's that body, the tantalizing aspects of it. I may have to stop seeing her."

"What's the alternative?"

"You're a matchmaker at heart, I see. I suppose I could marry her, but that goes against my fundamental beliefs."

"And what might they be?"

"That you don't marry a woman just so you can take her to bed."

"Daniel, my boy" – Arthur knew he was being condescending – "some day you will marry and there will be at least three purposes: to take your bride to bed, to enjoy her companionship, and to have a family." Arthur stopped there and left a blank space, knowing that Daniel would be required to fill it.

"Are you suggesting that I will never be more fortunate than to have Angelina in my life?"

"That's what I'm suggesting. She's a catch. That's my opinion."

"I suppose you are right," Daniel said. Arthur heard a trace of resignation in his nephew's voice. There was a pause, and then Daniel said, "She would win."

Arthur said right away, "That doesn't mean you would lose." Arthur pointed out to Daniel that the relationship could stall. Angelina was ready while he was not. Daniel acknowledged the truth of what his Uncle Arthur had said. They ended the conversation at that point.

Angelina reflected that her blunt challenge to Enrico had yielded results. She had extricated herself from the grasp of that parasite. That was her phrase. And now she was close to having Daniel commit to her on a permanent basis. Allowing Arthur to suggest strategy had worked in the case of Enrico and it might work again with Daniel. The correct time to discuss matters was at breakfast. "Mr. Brooks," Angelina offered, "your nephew is perfect. He is the Anglo who could be my husband. I could have his babies. Nothing has happened yet. It has been three months and not a word about his intentions. What should I do?"

"All strategies involve risk but you cannot just wait for him. You have done that with three men and nothing developed. May I suggest something?"

"Of course."

"Discuss the fact that you have not been to Lima for three years and you want to see your parents so you might take a trip in the fall."

"What will he say? You seem to be able to predict."

"If he cares for you, the first words out of his mouth will be to ask you how long the trip will be and when you might return. If he doesn't care he'll ask you how often you write your family, or some such imbecility. My guess is that he cares a great deal for you so when he asks you when you will come back, you say in a couple of weeks unless something interesting develops. He will ask what you mean by that and you will tell him about a job offer or a valuable man. This, by the way, is the oldest trick played by women, the threatening-to-disappear act."

"It would be risking everything."

"Yes, but right now because you are ready, and he does nothing, the relationship could turn empty. You will find yourself starting to dislike him. So you might as well challenge him."

"Right here, at the side of the pool, tomorrow morning?"

"Yes. I'll go to the club so that you can be alone to discuss matters. Why don't you buy a new bikini this afternoon?"

"More daring?"

"That's not possible. Just new and different so that you start talking about your body and his desire increases."

The following morning, the conversation developed as Arthur has predicted. The new bikini brought on a longer than necessary conversation during which Daniel examined all aspects. "It's like the other one," he said, "but I like this one more and I don't know why."

Angelina approached the matter of her trip gingerly. "I envy you your trips. I haven't been to Lima for three years."

"Pretty city, Lima. I've been there several times. One of the oldest in South America."

"I'm starting to long for it and of course to be with my parents and brothers and the families they have created."

"Yes. You told me your brothers have married."

"There are beautiful and intelligent wives. Have I told you that each has two children?"

"Yes, you mentioned it. You gave me all the names but I've forgotten them."

"I could write them out for you and you could refer to them from time to time."

"Why don't you do that? Are you thinking about taking a trip?"

"Yes. It comes in and out of my mind."

"When might you do that?"

"This fall sometime."

"Would you stay for a little while then come back?"

"It depends. I might find interesting work or my father might arrange something for me at the university. Or, an old acquaintance could show up and we might find a liking for one another. An old flame reignited."

"My guess is that it would be a new flame because flames cannot burn at a low level for eight years," Daniel said.

They fell silent. Daniel was contemplating his life without Angelina. He tried imagining a trip to a part of South America that he had not visited where he could organize a photo-essay. "Have you been to the south of Chile?"

"No, not even to Chile," Angelina answered.

"They tell me that it is very beautiful and simple. Resembles California in the 1940s."

"That would be beautiful. Could you do a photo-essay?"

"Yes, that's what I was thinking. Do you suppose that we could to that together?"

"I could not introduce you to my family. They would think right away that I was your mistress. It would be unacceptable."

"But of course you are not my mistress."

"True. But that's what they would think. Maybe we could work on a project together some other time," Angelina said.

They swam for the better part of a half-hour. Angelina had opened this chasm between them. A coolness descended. Daniel realized that he no longer could be amusing and good company. Angelina might be off to another continent. He had to think. He kissed her lightly and left for home, saying that he had pressing work.

WOMAN FROM PERU

PART 6

Their relationship was young, a little over three months old. Daniel, at 31, knew that Arthur was right. He should marry and start a family. It could be that he would be forced to give up his itinerant life and find work that allowed him to stay put.

Angelina, at 28, had been living in hopes of marrying for eight years. She couldn't get that baby out of her mind. Her first lover, the Cuban in Miami, suited her but he was made of fragile material. He never said as much, but he treated Angelina as though there was no hurry, neither for him nor for her. His unwillingness to discuss marriage ended the affair. In general terms the same could be said for the second Cuban and for Enrico.

Angelina had come north to Florida bearing her family's view on social arrangements. Men did not string women along. Men did not make a practice of calculating how they would sleep with this one and that one. It was in their disposition, certainly, but the practice was to have two young people pair off, not living together, both sets of parents approving, and after a year or so to marry. On occasion the young people had known one another from birth. Once in a while they were found by family members who would bring them together. This is not to say that the arranged marriage was all the rage. This is to say that the particular segment of Lima society that Angelina came from took marriage seriously and frowned on young people maturing before they were mated. The newlyweds were young and fresh and understood that they would continue learning about life after their marriage. Angelina wondered if her moving out of her circle and away from her country had not been a colossal blunder. It preyed on her that she was no longer young and fresh. Indeed she was ripe and starting to mature.

In her view of Daniel, she perceived him as perhaps her last chance to attract a good man to be her husband, although a North American. She thought Daniel could be willing to settle for an incomplete life that did not provide him with the love of a woman, her companionship and the opportunity to construct a family whose members would grow up and in their turn produce a new generation. Angelina knew that she could provide these aspects of life to any man she chose. Her problem had been that those she had been attracted to viewed marriage as a trap. Daniel was yet to express himself on the matter.

It came out of Angelina one day. She had not forgotten the moment and Daniel was still thinking it over. They had gone to a mall in search of a jeweler where Daniel might find a replacement battery for his wrist watch. For this mid-morning trip Angelina had worn a blouse that fitted tightly and a straight skirt that hugged her body. Daniel noticed several men glancing at Angelina. He had felt the impact of her costume earlier that morning. Daniel turned to Angelina and said, "You have a great deal on display this morning."

"In some ways I'm proud of my body and I find it natural to wear these clothes," Angelina responded. When Daniel didn't say anything, Angelina added, "Does it upset you that I show too much?"

Daniel was honest. "Yes. When we are together it reflects on me that you want other men to look at you."

Angelina wanted to tell Daniel that society had developed a technique for a man to lay claim to a woman, including her appearance in public, but she refrained. She said, "Someday you might find yourself in a position to have a good deal to say on these matters."

Daniel knew precisely what Angelina meant and he also knew he wasn't prepared to lay claims to her so he let the moment pass. While still in the mall they entered a lady's wear store that Angelina could not resist. Inside Daniel caught their reflection in a mirror and noted how lovely she looked standing next to him. It was another moment of possession for him. When they left the stores and walked across the parking lot he took her hand.

Angelina's interest in Daniel's output of magazine articles seemed genuine to him. It was also the first time that a woman he was squiring about displayed the ability to analyze his output and give praise as well as make suggestions. One of her interests was the fit of his work with the whole of the writing industry. Were there subjects he might write about other than travel? Was he interested in writing at length rather than in 5,000 word segments? Might he try fiction? Did he prefer writing to photography? Daniel was flattered by the attention and wondered whether Angelina was casting herself as the life companion. In return, for the first time he inquired about the aims of a woman in his life. What might she do if she were to finish her education? Was teaching the natural goal? How did she feel about adopting a new country? He understood that this interest in Angelina was a form of ownership. He was starting to care.

Her domesticity frightened him at first. She was comfortable around the house. Arthur was treated as the father and he the husband, or at least the man even though he had no official position. She was at her best on an evening when Alexander and Ellen came to dinner. Now that Daniel was in the picture Ellen could be at ease over any relationship developing between Angelina and Arthur; and maybe, just maybe, Angelina would bring Daniel to heel. Of all the members of the Brooks family, it was Ellen who most disapproved of Daniel's treatment of women. She wanted to warn the next one of his behavior toward the previous one.

When Alexander and Ellen arrived, Angelina did not join in greeting them. It was not her house and she did not have a position in it. She asked Daniel to serve drinks, finding out before hand from Arthur what should be available. She had prepared the hors d'oeuvres and gone over the menu with Arthur. She asked Daniel to bring flowers for the dining room table. It was a warm evening and coffee was served outside. Daniel wondered whether any of this display of culture was for him. He concluded that she was behaving as she would at home in Lima. This is how she was brought up. Daniel was never told that it was Angelina who suggested to Arthur that he invite his son and daughter-in-law for dinner.

Daniel was getting a new perspective on the matter of Angelina's adamant refusal of sexual activity. He had assumed that Angelina was tired of being taken to bed by men who would abandon her in the end. Daniel admitted that this seemed a normal reaction to the treatment she had received. Undoubtedly she had a desire to be valued on other assets than her body. Perhaps Angelina wanted Daniel to think of her as a friend, a wife and a mother of their children. Maybe he should be respecting her intellect and her pleasing personality.

This was not a topic he could discuss with Angelina. It was up to him to decide on the merits whether there were other reasons for her abstinence. Expectations were building for both. Angelina hoped that he might become her husband. Daniel allowed himself a quick glance at permanence now and then. It became less frightening to him.

WOMAN FROM PERU

PART 7

"Uncle Arthur," Daniel said on the telephone, "a dark cloud, a large one, appeared on the horizon recently."

"How so?" Arthur asked.

"Angelina brought up the matter of a visit to Lima. Has she ever mentioned it to you?"

"No, it's never come up, but I understand that a woman might want to see her family every few years."

"There's an under-current of her staying in Lima if certain conditions are met."

"And what might they be?"

"Interesting work and the right man."

"Does she have the plane ticket yet?"

"No. This is a couple of months from now."

"My guess," Arthur said, "is that it will be a one-way ticket. If that's her choice she may not come back and you will be off the hook. No more worries about being forced to marry and you can move on to the next conquest."

Arthur could hear Daniel clearing his throat. He suspected that Daniel was stalling for time, organizing his thoughts. "It's not quite fair, this nothing below the neck," Daniel said. "Her kisses are extraordinary, always delivered standing up. Her lips are soft and warm. She presses her body against mine. It's more than a man should be asked to endure."

"Daniel, she's telling you two things – that she likes you a great deal and that the kiss is good but there's plenty more besides that."

"This is a woman of ultimatums," Daniel said. "First, nothing below the neck, and now, hurry up, I'm leaving for Lima."

"Look at it this way, Daniel. Previous men in her life have taken advantage of her and therefore nothing below the neck for you, or anyone else, for that matter. Then none of them has married her so that she can't do what women do, which is to build a family."

"I'm being victimized, Uncle Arthur. I was not around to play a part in her past."

"That's true, Daniel, but if there were no laws laid down now by her you would carry on the tradition. She wants to break with the past. She wants to stop supplying the needs of oversexed men."

"What am I supposed to do, Uncle Arthur, marry her?"

"Yes, marry her."

"I didn't think of myself as a problem solver."

"We've identified her problem," Arthur said. "Why don't you think about your problem and how she can solve it?"

"I didn't think I had a problem."

"You travel, take pictures and come home to write about the experience. How long can that last?"

"It's a pretty good life, Uncle Arthur."

"Yes, but a little emptier every day."

"Do you want me to marry her, Uncle Arthur?"

"Do you?"

"It's better than losing her, I guess. What should I do?"

"Admit she's playing a stronger hand than you are. Propose to her. Tell her that you love her and you cannot afford to let her out of your life. That you can go to Lima after you are married."

"That should work, Uncle Arthur. I'll look into my inner resources and see if I have the courage."

"One final thought," Arthur said. "If you are fortunate enough to marry her, make certain that you treat her as your wife for the rest of your life and not as a piece of steak."

"That's a lot to think about, Uncle Arthur."

Once Daniel sold himself on the idea, he wanted to move at top speed. He admitted to himself that he had to get to the ceremony rapidly before he lost courage. Daniel called Arthur to tell him that he would come over the following morning to propose. Arthur said he would absent himself the usual way, by cycling to the club.

The following morning Arthur was certain to leave home before Daniel made his by-now regular morning stop for a swim and a visit with Angelina. When he finished breakfast, he went to the club. Angelina stayed outside, reading the paper. She tended to be in bathing suit and robe when Daniel arrived.

He was a bit late. He came with two dozen roses, up the driveway and said her name. As usual, she returned with his name. He came into view and Angelina stood up at the sight of the flowers. "What are these?" she asked.

"They are two dozen red roses for you. Do you have a vase or shall we put them in the swimming pool?"

"Come in the kitchen. I know where the vases are kept. This is very sweet, what is the occasion?"

Daniel didn't smile, or show any emotion. He was too busy keeping control of himself. Angelina accepted the flowers, gave Daniel a brief kiss and went into the kitchen. She brought a vase from a large closet, placed the flowers in it, arranged them a bit, and filled the vase half-way. The vase was now on the breakfast table and Angelina was admiring them.

"Traditionally they mean I love you," he said.

Angelina turned around and delivered one of her powerful kisses. In this act her robe became untied. Daniels' arms were around her body. She said nothing about below the neck. He went to the script he had rehearsed. "Will you marry me?" he asked.

He felt relieved that he had been able to ask the question. He was surprised that he had been able to tell Angelina that he loved her and asked her to marry him in less than a minute.

Angelina took his hand and led Daniel into the living room. They had not been there alone since Arthur had introduced them over a glass of wine. They sat together on the sofa. Angelina said, "Did you say marriage?"

Daniel felt wooden. He looked at her and said, "Yes, marriage." Angelina spun around and faced him on the sofa and delivered another kiss. Her robe was still open and Daniel had his hands on her body again. She seemed not to object. What a little proposal will accomplish, he reflected.

It was obvious to Daniel that Angelina was thinking at a rapid rate. Her eyes were darting about the room. "I love you too, my handsome Anglo soon-to-be husband. I accept your proposal." There was silence, and then she added, "We could marry in Lima."

There it was, the counter proposal. Angelina had lowered the barrier from the neck to the ankles but in exchange they were to marry in Lima. In what he thought was a brilliant counter stroke, he said, "I'm not a strong person. Marry here and now, or never."

Angelina moved away a foot or so. "How can you tell me you love me, propose marriage, and issue an ultimatum? I mean, now or never is not romantic."

"I know, Angelina, but I'm not a man of vast courage. The thought of marriage has turned many powerful men into cowards. The mere suggestion will change them."

"How can you be a strong husband in the future if you are so weak now?"

"I can't explain everything," Daniel said.

Angelina stood up and walked to a large window overlooking the garden. She tightened the belt on her robe and stood there for longer than a minute. Finally she turned around and started speaking, not directly at Daniel but at the room. "My family is in Lima and has been there since the earliest days, before records. My family would be mortified if I were to marry here. Perhaps only my mother and father would fly here. It's a tradition that women marry where they are born in the midst of their immediate family."

The effect on Daniel of this speech was to make him gather strength. He realized that he had a few cards to play. He said, "My family lives within fifty miles, all of it." He thought he would let Angelina deal with that fact. She tightened the belt around her robe even tighter. Daniel added, "I have put a proposal of the table." He didn't know whether this might infuriate Angelina.

Angelina moved slowly to the sofa. She sat facing Daniel. "Can we marry in the Catholic Church that I attend?"

"Of course I'm not Catholic, if anything. I don't know that your priest would perform the service."

"My priest would marry us in the chapel but not in front of the main altar. I've already discussed the matter with him. And he did say that he would want a commitment that the children would be brought up Catholic."

"You've gone over this matter with your priest?"

"Yes, in general terms, before I thought you were interested in me."

"It's important for a woman to be prepared, isn't it?" Daniel asked.

"Yes, you need to be a few steps ahead."

"How soon can we be married, Angelina?"

"In six days," was the answer.

Their first step was to obtain the license. The second was to buy the rings and the third was to submit to an interview with Angelina's priest. They were married in seven days. Arthur gave a way the bride. Many Brooks were in attendance. Angelina and Daniel spent their wedding night in Daniel's garden cottage and proceeded to drive to the beach and take lodgings in a hotel for thee days during which time, as Angelina reported to Alexander and Ellen, her new cousins-by-marriage, they planned the rest of their lives.

Two weeks after their wedding they flew to Lima, met the family, and went south to Chile to gather information for a photo-essay. They returned after three months. A boy was born to Angelina nine months and three days after the ceremony. They named him Arthur.

ALBANY

Theodore C. Warner had decided early on, before college, that his principal aim in life would be to amass a fortune. On a winter's day, in his senior year in high school, he was seated in his local library, researching a topic assigned by his English teacher. After an hour of reading and taking notes, he thought he needed a diversion and walked to the magazines on display. They were the current issues. He picked out a business magazine and opened it at random, alighting on that year's list of the richest American families. Theodore was a senior in high school at the time, thirty-five years prior to the present. He thought later that the moment was prophetic.

As he read along he was impressed that big money was made in real estate. He supposed that one could borrow at the bank the money required to put up commercial buildings. The rental income paid off the mortgage and over time the person who had borrowed the money became the owner of the properties. But in bad times, Theodore reasoned, there would be vacancies among a collection of commercial properties and when the rental income dipped below the sum of his expenses, the banks that owned the mortgages he was paying on could seize the buildings, sell them, and recoup unpaid balances, leaving him with nothing, or very little but broken dreams.

In the list he found families that had started oil companies three-quarters of a century previously. When they had taken the first step, oil might have been selling at a dollar per barrel. Theodore was aware that the price of oil fluctuated and surely these families had borrowed money for drilling, for pipelines, and for refineries when oil was a dollar or two per barrel. They had no trouble paying off their loans when oil went to five dollars. Theodore guessed that it was too late to get into the oil business and compete against the big boys.

The computer industry deserved analysis. Perhaps the use of these machines would become widespread, or better, used world-wide, and he might find an opportunity for himself. It made sense to get in on the ground floor of a new industry and ride the wave. He would go to college, earn a degree in business, and upon graduation associate himself with one of the mainstream companies. Once he plunged in he knew he would swim like hell.

Theodore's father had preached to him that he should take an inventory of his assets. Many classmates outscored him in the sciences and math, and many others were better than he in English, history and languages. His edge, and he knew it to be a thin one, was his ability to work hard. He recognized that he didn't reason at a blazing speed; but he knew for a fact that he could memorize, and memorize he did to graduate just under the top quarter of his class. Off he went to a private university, the one his father had attended. There was no shortage of money. His grandfather had owned a farm. His father inherited it and founded a business that sold farm machinery. He then started an automobile dealership.

The major corporations sent members of their personnel departments to recruit from the graduating classes of the important universities. Theodore had done well in his four years, using the same work ethic that had propelled him through high school. From among the corporations that contacted him, he accepted an offer from a manufacturer of computers and office equipment. They told him that he need not understand the technology; it would come to him. They did expect him to learn the functions of all products, where they fit into a business and the problems they solved.

Theodore continued on his path. He worked harder than the other new recruits and ended the training period by being assigned to a choice territory where customers, old and new, would need the products being introduced by his firm.

Theodore had never started drinking. He realized in his freshman year in college that alcohol was a mind-altering, habit-forming drug. He was more interested in the best grades possible than he was in long hours of meaningless conversations and childish games. Women posed a problem. He wanted to sleep with them as much as his classmates did, but he begrudged the time required to court and seduce willing coeds. He did fall in with studious women he met in the library who were of like mind. In his four years, he found but three partners.

In his first years at work he held on to habits learned previously. There was more reward in preparing for sales meetings than there was in dinners out and social activities with the other young people. Each month he was one of the top sales persons in his territory.

A new industry was forming for the creation and sale of software. Without examining any particular businesses -- there were so few -- Theodore reasoned that while software engineers were expensive and marketing products worldwide was not easy on the pocketbook, the manufacturing costs were minimal. The product delivered to the customer consisted of a fancy cardboard box, a set of instructions, and a disk containing the software. The manufacturing costs would be two dollars while the customer paid a hundred dollars. Once sales attained sufficient volume to meet payroll, rent, expenses and taxes, then additional sales sent money to the bottom line, perhaps gobs of it. If Theodore could structure a startup so that he retained a third of the shares, and if the company was successful enough to take it public, and if the company was based on several software products whose sales skyrocketed, then he could retain most of his stock while now and then selling a few shares to allow for a fancy life. He might be able to make it to that list of rich Americans.

Theodore selected four software products for development. He would form a company around them. His father made the initial investment. Theodore found four more millions and with this five-million dollar nest egg he went into business. Software indeed turned out to be a tidal wave. Theodore swam like hell with not-surprising results.

As a young man Theodore had overheard two remarks that lodged in his mind. The first was in response to a question asked of an executive, whether most men had one or more mistresses during their career. The answer this person gave was that his business was his mistress. The other remark concerned the compensation that a chief executive might consider appropriate. The person Theodore had overheard thought for a moment and said, "Well, the whole purpose of having a business is to take money out of it."

Theodore derived comfort from both ideas. His business would be his mistress. He did not marry. He worked inordinately long hours. Later on, in his headquarters, he had installed next to his office a suite where he could sleep, shower and change clothes without leaving for home. His home was larger than medium-sized and staffed by two people whom he would telephone whenever he was coming home for dinner and the night.

Theodore pursued the ladies but not in an exclusive fashion. His rule was to be close to three women, no more, no less, at any time. He needed company and intellectual stimulation beyond contacts with the business world. He needed favors from his ladies. The rewards for his three were extravagance and interesting times. One of his equals in commerce, another head of a company, might invite him for a cruise on his yacht, which lodged in and around the Caribbean. One of his ladies would accompany him. Or he might like to take in an exhibition at the gallery of art in Chicago. He did not own a plane -- had thought about it. He preferred flying by commercial aviation first class and being met by a limousine and staying in one of the old, comfortable hotels. Another lady would accompany him to Chicago.

Theodore enjoyed skiing. He had frequented all the exciting slopes in the United States. He found them in the Rockies and the Sierra Nevada. For variety he had tried the famous resorts of the Alps. The European operation of his corporation generated ample cash, and after taxes were paid this money could be returned to corporate headquarters or could stay in the bank in Europe. Theodore determined on purchasing an estate in Switzerland, which would be in the proximity of some of his favorite ski resorts. His principal attorney in Switzerland agreed that the estate could be carried on the company's books as it would be used three or four times per year for meetings of the executives of the European operation. There were over two hundred employees of whom thirty or so would meet for strategy sessions. The auditors stipulated that as long as Theodore repaid the corporation for personal use of the estate he was free to stay there. That was the deal. He would invite one of his ladies to come for a week. She would be asked to pack after-ski clothes and fancy gowns for the evening. It didn't mater that she might not ski on the difficult slopes. The benefits included a steam room, massages, the use of a hair dresser, cocktail parties, dinners with Theodore's friends, some old, some new, and even a little skiing on the bunny slope. The ladies in question would return home treasuring memories of being pampered in an atmosphere that only a few breathed.

Theodore had reached the age of fifty-three when the first bit of bad news reached him, and reached executives all across the land. Theodore had joined the exclusive club of billionaires. His software company continued to grow. He enjoyed his life as he had organized it, although he knew he had not picked out a charity or two, or a university, so that he might endow them with his largess. He was honest with himself about giving away his money. Were he to do so in a meaningful way he would slip on the list of the wealthiest Americans. He wanted to be high on that list before he gained fame as a donor. He was what you might expect, an intelligent, driven, nervous person who knew everything about his business but held in his mind only a smattering of facts and impressions about everything else in the world. He was just shy of six feet, trim, well enough dressed, hair cut short, graying, and surprisingly kind and polite. Long since, the "Theodore C." portion of his name had become "The Chief," a nickname he did not object to. On one occasion some of his employees had given him a gold pen and pencil set on which "The Chief" was engraved. He usually carried the set in his breast pocket.

The bit of bad news that started appearing in financial pages had to do with stock options. Theodore and plenty of other executives whom he knew used options for recruiting and holding on to talented people. The date that appeared on the option was rarely the date on which the option was granted. If the common stock of Theodore's company was selling at thirty-five dollars on the day the option was granted, then the date affixed could be a recent date when the price was lower, either in the past or the future.

Theodore's most trusted attorney in the law firm that the company used advised him against the practice. He said it was illegal. Theodore told him that he would not grant any options to himself. The attorney told him that his finger prints would be all over the various documents. Theodore assured the board of directors that the practice was so widespread that nothing would come of it, admitting that technically it violated an aspect of the regulations.

When the first company was indicted for exactly the practices that Theodore was engaging in, a telephone call came in from the attorney who had warned Theodore against involving his company in the practice. "I'm not about to say that I told you so, Chief."

"You just did, Mike. Why don't we have lunch tomorrow? Can you be here at eleven forty-five?"

There was silence on the line as Mike looked at his calendar. "I'll be there, Chief. Eleven forty-five."

Theodore was in the lobby of his building by eleven-forty the next day. There would be no conversation on this matter in his office, and there would be no records kept of any kind.

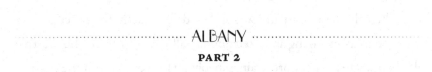

ALBANY

PART 2

Theodore watched Mike park his car, get out, and walk toward the main lobby. He waited until Mike had nearly reached the door when he stepped out to greet him. "Let's take my car," he said.

When they were seated with their seatbelts fastened, Mike said, "Most secretive of you, Chief. Usually we meet in your office and sandwiches appear."

"We're driving to neutral territory. I know a small restaurant that no one in our crowd uses. Frankly, I'm worried. This stock option business poses a threat, to me and to the corporation."

"What's the worst thing that could happen?" Theodore asked. He added, "You've had a day to mull it over. What have you concluded?"

Mike paused for a moment. He started by saying, "We are a New York corporation but this falsifying dates on stock options is a federal offense. We come under the jurisdiction of the New York branch of the Department of Justice." Theodore said nothing. Mike continued, "We could be looking at an indictment of the corporation, of your good self as the mastermind, and a few executives for going along with it."

"You're thinking of the chief operating officer and the chief financial officer?" Theodore suggested.

"Yes, among others. Guilt is easy to prove. Someone usually cops a plea and cooperates with the government. Fines for several and jail time for persons at the top."

"That would be me?" Theodore asked.

"There's no indictment yet, no trial, no verdict. You're getting way ahead of events," Mike said.

They pulled in to park. It was a small restaurant with a Thai menu. Theodore and Mike chose a booth in the back.

After they had been brought tea, Theodore said, "Because we're protected by attorney-client privilege I feel secure in suggesting some actions to you. Do the feds have plenty of lawyers in New York?"

"Yes, there are branches of the Justice Department in New York City and in Albany."

"So it's pretty local to us," Theodore said. "We should be able to monitor their activities."

"Will monitoring activities help you in any way?" Mike asked.

"Without it you're powerless. You need to know the direction they're taking and what they hope to gain, that is, the results they want to achieve."

"OK," Mike said. "You want to know whether they will indict the company, indict you, and how much punishment they want to deal out."

"Precisely, but at the same time we need to structure a response in order to minimize the amount of damage they can inflict."

"This is out of my range," Mike said. "I'm just Michael Devlin, corporate attorney. You're branching out to undercover business. Deal me out."

"I thought you would take that point of view so let me suggest you see Dieter and tell him what I've told you and ask him to come up with a plan that will have a good chance of lessening the impact. If there is to be an indictment, then we may not be able to stop it but if we can prevent my being named, and the other executives as well, then life will be made much simpler for all of us."

Dieter, as with most males born in Europe and North America, had first, middle and last names. Around Theodore's company this lawyer, living in Zürich, was known by his first name only. This would not be for reasons of secrecy. The exclusive use of his first name came about for two reasons: there was no Dieter with whom he could be confused and his last name contained eleven letters.

Theodore had found Dieter by asking an executive from a company in an allied business. The question asked was: "We'll need representation in Europe soon. Any ideas?" Theodore interviewed Dieter and senior partners in other law firms and selected Dieter because of his flexibility. He had said, among other things, "Yes, we have banking laws and I recommend that you have part of your money in a Swiss bank. And, yes, all of us try to run our lives within the law, but occasionally, inadvertently, the law jumps out at one of us in an unsuspected fashion and in those cases I might be of assistance to you." Theodore did not press for details but thought he might need to employ Dieter's services if unconventional circumstances arose.

"See Dieter, you say. Can't I just call him or write him a letter on plain stationery?"

"No, Mike. No telephone calls, no e-mails, no correspondence, no written records, not even much conversation. Make the trip to Geneva and cover the anti-trust situation in Europe with Dieter. I think five or six of our people are making the trip for the quarterly meeting. Don't fly with them. Take your wife if you want. You'll only need thirty minutes alone with Dieter, and you should be able to arrange that when you're there."

"You're moving this operation offshore? Is that it?" Mike asked.

"Yes, Dieter and I understand one another. He isn't a member of any syndicate but I have the feeling that he can arrange matters. I don't want any rough stuff. You can accomplish the same things with money."

"Whose money, Chief?"

"Well, mine, unfortunately. Had I heeded your advice none of this would be coming up. But I failed in that respect, so I'll pay. It's one of the rules we seem to live by -- you screw up, you pay."

"How much are you budgeting?" Mike asked.

"No idea. Let Dieter figure out how much he needs."

Except for a few unimportant details, this part of the conversation ended. They finished their meal while discussing the up-coming elections, state and federal. In the car, returning to corporate headquarters, Theodore gave a final instruction. "Call me for lunch when you return."

Mike's wife was eager to make the trip but she balked at spending four days at the corporate estate. She contacted the wife of the chief financial officer and they made plans to visit Bern, Luzern and Zürich. They would gossip, shop and learn all they could about the country. Her friend spoke some French and she a smattering of German. Neither was fluent but they assured one another that they would manage as most everyone in Switzerland spoke at least a bit of English.

Mike and Dieter did indeed discuss the views of the European regulators on price fixing and on monopolistic practices. They thought that their company was clean on these matters but they recognized that attention from the European regulators was the price you paid when you achieved dominance in any market. On the new matter, Mike asked Dieter to walk with him around the small lake on the estate.

"I'm not surprised, Mike. Perhaps it's the Chief's turn to suffer a little," Dieter remarked when Mike laid out the situation concerning the dating of options.

"It's not his style to suffer," Mike said. "He thought you might have ideas on saving him, or at least lessening the blow. He thought you might know where to apply pressure. Could you mount a campaign from here, that's what he's asking?"

"Yes, we could do detective work then apply pressure. I wouldn't do it myself but I would give the job to an international syndicate. Should I call them a crime syndicate? They're very good. How much does the Chief plan to spend?"

"We didn't discuss amounts," Mike said.

"These boys aren't interested for less than ten million. It's not worth it to them, and might I say, it should be the Chief's money, not the corporation's. He can always sell some stock and if he does we must handle the proceeds so that he pays his long term capital gains. It's one thing to bend the rules here and there but never run afoul of the IRS." Before Mike could respond, Dieter said, "Perhaps our law firm could buy the shares. We can find fifteen million. When this is all over we can sell off the shares and recover our investment."

"You jumped suddenly from ten to fifteen million," Mike said.

"Federal and state taxes should take a third, and by the way, do you involve yourself in listing the sale of these shares with the Securities and Exchange Commission?"

"No, not I. Another person in our firm takes care of that," Mike answered.

"We'll want access to the money. When the sale is complete I suggest we put the proceeds in a new numbered bank account that we may draw on. The Chief already has one. I don't know what's in there and I don't have a need to know. But I would want to be able to meet expenses without obtaining the Chief's permission at every turn."

"Do you suppose your legal bills can come out of the ten million?" Mike asked.

"I don't know, but you can't economize on matters such as these."

"It appears you have a plan in mind," Mike prompted.

"Yes, as we walk around this lake my mind is active. I see where we might go with this problem. I'll try to come to the States in two weeks and lay it out to the Chief. In the meantime, not a word to anyone, and that includes your wife."

"How do you stay current with what's happening on the other side of the Atlantic?" Mike asked.

"Every morning on rising I read a few stories in your three important papers. They're on the Internet. I've been following this story for a while. Have you been reading the reports of a certain Ann Newman? Her investigations seem to be quite accurate.

"In the New York paper? Yes, we all read her stuff. She's very good," Mike answered.

ALBANY

PART 3

Dieter telephoned Mike Devlin two weeks after the corporate meeting broke up, the meeting held at Theodore's estate in Switzerland.

"There are interesting developments coming out of Bruxelles that have to do with monopolistic practices. I'm coming over to discuss these matters in detail as they apply to us," Dieter said.

"And when might that be?" Mike answered.

"Did you know, my friend, that after a person makes a reservation and buys an airline ticket on a computer, the program asks whether another party has a need to know? Well, my computer, or my airline, has that feature and you should receive a copy of my reservation among your emails."

Mike was annoyed at Dieter's tone of voice, speaking as though he knew it all. He realized that at Dieter's age there was little hope of changing his personality. He decided against prolonging the conversation. He knew not to mention Theodore's name. After a few remarks on the weather they signed off. A day after Mike had received a copy of Dieter's travel plans he telephoned Theodore's personal secretary and suggested lunch between The Chief and himself a few days in the future to discuss the arrival of Deiter.

Mike picked up Dieter at JFK and as they were walking to Mike's car Dieter said, "Not a word about topic A in the car." Mike reasoned that Dieter suspected that his car could be bugged; that was reason one. Reason two could be that what Dieter had to say need only be told to The Chief. He, Mike, was being left out of the loop and except for an unsatisfied curiosity, he realized that it was best to remain ignorant. The sort of plans that Dieter and The Chief were cooking up could reverberate for several years to come. His contribution was to have carried a message from The Chief to Dieter, and although he could be accused of assisting in the formation of a plot, he doubted anyone would come after him.

It went off on schedule. Dieter rented a car from an agency near his hotel and drove to corporate headquarters where he picked up Theodore, who instructed him to drive to yet another small restaurant. When they were seated, Dieter said, "It's safe here. Very unpretentious." He passed his hand under the table, at which both he and Theodore chuckled. They changed the topic of conversation from the one in the car. "So, you found an organization, you said."

"Yes. When I approached them they told me they knew of this white collar crime here in the States and they had been wondering if they might profit from it," Dieter said.

"What did they say they might do?"

"They wanted a million up front and they bill against it just the way a law firm does. In fact, I was surprised how closely our operations resemble one another. They knew you by name and know the corporation and have a good idea of the size of your operation in Europe. Of course, that data is public knowledge."

"Were you able to describe the job to be done?" Theodore asked.

"Yes. The first request I made was no rough stuff. Let money talk."

Theodore interrupted. "Here we are trying to hide white collar crime and how do we go about it? By committing more white collar crime."

"Money is the root of all evil. People will do most anything for money, usually ridiculously small amounts of it," Dieter said. He went on. "Yes, it was so simple. The person I talked to agreed right away that their organization would infiltrate the prosecutors and do what they could to blunt their efforts."

"For them they are operating out of their country. Did that pose a problem?" Theodore asked.

"In the first place they don't have a country. In fact, they prefer operating elsewhere and that means removed from where they hang their hats for the moment. And in their view as the operation is in the States they are not breaking any European laws. Best of all worlds."

"How do they report any progress they make?" Theodore wanted to know.

"They report to me. If they make good progress you won't hear anything. You'll hear only if there are no results. Perhaps you will read items in your newspapers that you can decipher."

"And the money?"

"I meter it out. No one keeps any documentation. The money in your account moves slowly in their direction."

"And is there anything in this for you?" Theodore asked.

"That's the final discussion between you an me. The matter of money remaining for my firm gives me an incentive to conserve."

After the sale by Theodore of his shares to Dieter's law firm, the proceeds were split: five million dollars went to Theodore's account in New York to cover taxes and ten million dollars were converted into Swiss francs that were secured in a safe deposit box in the bank in Zürich that Dieter used.

An important man in the crime syndicate sat down with Dieter only once. Dieter had no idea how high up in the organization this man might be. He could be the head man. They met in a tavern, time and location being provided by the go-between who had put Dieter in contact with the syndicate. The headman and Dieter each had a beer and sandwich. They discussed sports, particularly the world cup matches coming up. When they had finished the head man said, "Let's walk for a little while and get some exercise." In the course of fifteen minutes Dieter was told that he would always talk to a new person and that any meeting might be organized differently. There would always be a code. For the next meeting the code would be "Adam and Eve." The head man verified that Dieter was fluent in German, French and English. "We are a diverse organization and conduct our affairs in various tongues." The head man said that he had studied the situation and thought it would be a simple enough matter to calculate where the pressure needed to be applied. He would assign one of his best people to manage the project and that at the next meeting, with another person, of course, he would be given a progress report and instructions on the first transfer of cash. "Don't expect details, old man. You'll only get enough information to keep up your spirits."

They ended by bargaining over money. "I think a million up front is a bit much," Dieter said.

"Perhaps you're right. Let's settle for half that amount," the head man agreed. "Have it with you in your car for the next meeting."

Dieter understood that the syndicate would get its money one way or another, just not when they wanted it. "How do you bill us?" Dieter asked.

"Around the office it's four hundred dollars per hour. On special assignments of course it's more. But remember, we're not using force. We have to use cash to persuade and to keep them persuaded. That can be expensive."

A week went by before Dieter received a telephone call at work. The voice, not the head man's, said that his contact, a woman about forty years old, would be outside a certain store with a few parking places in front of it. She would be wearing a beige coat but no hat. She knew Dieter's car and the number of the license plate and had studied several photographs of him. "How about five-thirty tomorrow afternoon?" the voice said. Dieter agreed and the voice asked, "Do you remember the code for the occasion and will you have the money?" Dieter said yes to both questions.

At the appointed hour Dieter drove up. A pleasant looking woman was in front of the store and when she spotted Dieter's car he watched her as she read his license plate. Dieter leaned over to open the passenger door and she slid in. "Good to see you, Adam," she said. "You might be Eve," he said. "That's so romantic," he added.

"If you have the money I have a brief message."

"Yes, it's right here. Go ahead."

"It's so brief. We start in New York very soon. There will be a report, but not from me, of course," the woman said

"Is that all?" Dieter asked.

"Yes, that's it. Let me have the money."

Dieter handed her a briefcase containing the half million. The woman told him where to let her out. It was about ten more blocks. She said, "The next password is Gustav Mahler."

"Yes, I like his music," Dieter said.

"As you notice there are two words. One person uses one and the other person uses the second. The sequence isn't important." All the reports Dieter received were delivered by different people, some men, and some women. The messages that they delivered were always transmitted orally and therefore were short.

There were a few more blocks to go. Dieter asked, "Is this your field of expertness, acting as a courier?"

"Yes. They trust me, but there is no pattern. Different places, different people, different jobs."

"I'll miss you, Eve," Dieter said as they reached her destination. She slid out of the car, holding the briefcase that Dieter had given her. It could have contained legal matters or a business plan.

ALBANY

PART 4

A middle-aged man stood up as Ann Newman came into the lobby of her apartment building. "Miss Newman?" he asked when she was a few paces from him. "Yes, and who are you?" she asked. "Craig Burton," the man answered.

"If you have a moment we could sit here in the lobby and I could tell you what I'm after."

"How do you know me?" Ann asked.

"I've been reading your columns and the paper was kind enough to print your photograph recently."

"And how did you know where I lived?" Ann frowned and turned her head slightly as a way of telling the man she was suspicious.

"I followed you from the office to here yesterday and my courage failed me at the last moment. Today I was determined to speak to you."

"Very well, we can sit on the sofa over there."

"As I said, my name is Craig Burton. I retired recently from a career in banking, in Chicago, the outskirts, and moved here. This is the most exciting city in the world, particularly if you want to write. I want to write on white collar crime and what you discuss in your columns is just down my alley."

"How do I fit into this?" Ann asked.

"I'm interested in fiction, changing and expanding your work into a novel on the subject of white collar crime. It would help me enormously if you could outline for me the law enforcement people, the Department of Justice people, those whom you know are working on the stock option business, the dating them backwards and forwards. Just write it up as you know it. Trust me; I'll change the names when I move to fiction. I just need the framework."

Craig Burton placed an envelope between himself and Ann. He said, "I've written out what I've just said and provided a telephone number. Could I have your draft in about a week?"

"I suppose so," Ann said. She took the envelope and felt it. It contained more than instructions. She opened the envelope after closing the door to her apartment. There was a simple sheet of paper accompanied by fifty twenty dollar bills. She counted them twice.

The note was written by hand. It said,

"Dear Ms. Newman: You need not do anything. If that is your choice keep the money. Should you decide to write up some of the goings on you know about, please do it in your hand. Computers seem to save everything. Here's a slip of paper with my phone number on it. Rest assured there is a great deal more money to reward you for helping me if you decide to. Yours, C.B."

Ann's next few moments were devoted to deciding how she would spend this one thousand dollar windfall. Then she tried to put the matter into perspective. It was almost certain that criminal intent was present. Why would a writer just getting started need to spend a thousand dollars for a moment's conversation in the lobby? If this Craig Burton was writing fiction he should be able to piece things together in his imagination. The most likely business was that Craig Burton and his cohorts had been hired to protect a firm that was implicated in the scandal.

What of it, though? All the information she had was public. She would not be breaking any laws by writing out a few notes. He wanted them written by hand, not in a medium that could be traced. And when he said that there was plenty more money where this had come from, did he mean five thousand, or even ten thousand? How do you handle that much cash? You can't deposit it in your bank account. They come around and ask questions. But you can keep it in your closet and put a few twenties in your purse as you need them. The effect is to be earning a higher salary than you really are, until the pile runs out. But it's all legal except you don't declare it for tax purposes. What do you write as the source of the cash on your 1040? A man I met in the lobby?

She started writing. Her objective was to supply plenty of good material, but to whet his appetite at the same time. In her columns for the paper she saved a nugget to lead into the next piece. She wanted to give Craig Burton what he asked for while leaving out details, which would make him ask for more. On the other hand, if she were too coy he might go elsewhere. She did not have any secrets at her finger tips. Other people knew what she knew.

At around nine o'clock on the third evening Ann dialed the number that Craig Burton had given her on a slip of paper. She noted that the paper used for the phone number was a bit stiff, as though cut from a five by eight index card. The paper used for his note was ordinary stock. The handwritings were different. Ann guessed that good old Craig did not want to allow her to demonstrate to anyone that the phone number and the note were linked by being on the same type of paper, written by the same hand with the same ball point pen.

Craig flipped open his cell phone and wrote down the number

appearing on the screen. Then he answered, "Yes?" She said, "Craig Burton, this is Ann Newman."

"I would guess you decided to write out something for me. It's most appreciated."

"How do I get it to you?" Ann asked.

"Why don't you leave it at the desk, downstairs? I'll pick it up tomorrow afternoon. The doorman can ask for photo ID if he wishes."

"How will I know if you like it?" Ann asked.

"If it's what I need, I'll be back right away and we can make arrangements. Do you usually write at the office, or do you do it at home?"

Ann realized that Craig wanted to verify that the number displayed on his screen was her home phone. "It depends. I write the bulk of my columns at work but this I've written at home."

"That's comfortable, at the breakfast table, with coffee."

"How did you guess?" Ann said.

The syndicate had on hand a dozen or so individuals, male and female, who could play bit parts on an as-needed basis. Some indeed were under-employed actors, others were waiters who worked at night and others were firemen who had those schedules of twenty-four hours on followed by thirty-six hours off, or thereabouts. These individuals did not know one another. They acted only as messengers. No rough stuff, just in and out. Most of them had posed for their photographs so that a driver's license or passport could be made in a jiffy. A driver's license was used only for photo identification so no need for a magnetic stripe or bar code on the back. The passports were more delicate than the drivers' licenses, as the name and the serial number had to match a real person who already had a passport and the age portrayed in the photograph had to match the date of birth. Without a valid number on the passport the person traveling wouldn't be able to return to the U.S.

At precisely three o'clock an actor in need of work walked into the lobby of Ann's apartment building. He said to the doorman, "I'm Craig Burton. Do you have an envelope for me from Ann Newman?" "Yes, let me see your driver's license, please."

At two minutes past three the alternate Craig Burton, who had come out of Ann's building and turned right, was walking slowly down the street. A cab pulled up and a woman leaned out the rear window and said, "Craig, what are you doing in this part of town? Hop in." This new Craig, who had never seen this woman, got into the cab. They exchanged envelopes. The new Craig knew that he had earned a thousand dollars in cash. It would tide him over.

The original Craig had rented an apartment in Queens and used the address to register a new cell phone. He lived in an apartment several blocks away where he took Ann's calls and wrote to her as he was instructed by his supervisor. He was paid on a higher scale than the messengers on the bottom rung. He checked the mail at the other apartment on a weekly basis. Nothing but bills and promotion pieces. When the business with Ann's account ended he would pay off the unpaid balance on the six months lease. Same with the cell phone account. The cell phone would go to the bottom of the East River.

The new Craig Burton got out of the cab after five minutes. The woman stayed in until she reached her subway entrance. She delivered the envelope to a man who would take it to the local director of this operation. This was Emil. He had come over from Austria for the express purpose. On being handed the envelope he said, "Thank you. Tell the woman that I might need her again."

The six pages in Ann's handwriting contained most of what she knew, which included the names of companies being investigated, indictments under preparation, names of prosecutors, names of directors of operations and locations of offices. Emil concluded that the top person was a lawyer at the Justice Department in Albany named Camille Conrad. Certainly she reported to yet another person, and it appeared that they made decisions that were subject to approval by the top rank. "That's where you apply pressure, where the operating decisions are made," Emil said to himself. To lessen the law's impact on Theodore Warner's company, he, Emil, would have to find a way of applying pressure on Camille Conrad.

Ann had left out the name of Eric Olson in her report. He was a lawyer well known for his defense of white collar criminals. His newest client was a victim of the dragnet to catch executives involved with dating stock options with the most rewarding date, and not necessarily the date on which the option was granted. He had been a great help to Ann in writing her columns. If the cash for what she had written was appetizing, that is, if the payment for the six pages of closely spaced script was generous, and if they asked for more, then she would give them Eric Olson's name as an independent source. After all, they would stumble across his name sooner or later. She may as well cash in on telling them first.

A different man than the one who had brought Ann's report to Emil showed up at Emil's the following morning at nine. He was given a description of a middle-aged man, a location, a password and an assignment. The description more or less matched Craig Burton. The location was a coffee shop that generally had more seats than customers. The password was Jeremy with the answer Stewart. The assignment was simple: deliver an envelope and report back that contact had been made. The messenger located Craig Burton easily enough. They had coffee, gossiped a bit about life in New York and passed the envelope. Craig did not open it until he was home. The note read, "It is good material. Ask the source for more. We will arrange to pay her five thousand dollars."

Craig left an envelope with the doorman at Ann's apartment. The note said, "Much valuable information, thank you. Do you have more?

We want to arrange to pay you for what you have done so far. Please be in the dairy section of the market around the corner on 74th Street, tomorrow afternoon at five forty-five and carry a large purse and leave it open. Once in a while these arrangements don't work, but if we fail, we'll try again." It was signed C.B.

Ann noticed that the handwriting was the same as she had seen previously. She showed up on time and lingered in the dairy section but when no one came by to put an envelope in her open purse she paid for her purchases and left. When she entered her building the doorman handed her a box, the type used by florists. "A man came by a little while ago. He says he knows you at work and he thought it was your birthday."

"A few days too soon, but thank you," Ann said.

"He put his card in the box, he told me," the doorman added.

Once in her apartment, Ann ripped open the box. There were a dozen roses and a note from Craig -- same handwriting. "Make certain to look under the flowers. Thank you. Do you have more details?" This time she found five thousand dollars in twenty dollar bills.

In the market she had noticed a man looking at her. He smiled. It occurred to Ann that they were testing her. It would have been easy to tip off the police who would have stationed plain clothed detectives in the store. They could have nabbed anyone slipping an envelope into her purse.

ALBANY

PART 5

When Eric Olson thought about Ann, the black bras she wore came to mind right away. Their first meeting had taken place at his office. She had been sent across town by her newspaper in New York to interview him. He was an attorney who defended people caught up in white collar crime. His new client had been indicted for the injudicious postdating of stock options.

Eric gave the interviews -- there would be several of them -- on the basis that he would discuss stock options and the current rash of postdating while not a word would be exchanged concerning his client. It was a spring day. Ann Newman arrived wearing a light, short coat. Eric helped her off with the coat and could not resist glancing down her front. He suspected that he helped women off with their coats for just that purpose. A black bra was in evidence, covered incompletely by a dark blue blouse.

Eric considered himself a master at establishing connections between how a woman wore her clothes, what she wore, and her level of sexiness.

In the case of Ann, as with any other woman, the color black indicated at least a medium interest in sex. She left unbuttoned the top buttons of her blouse to the degree that any person, without trying, could analyze the style and color of her underwear. In successive meetings with Ann, Eric's assumption was corroborated. She featured longish skirts with a slit up the side, short skirts, and tight blouses and sweaters.

Eric thought that she was not particularly pretty but had a lovely figure. He would find out later that she had not married. He wondered how many important men had come through her life and why one of them had not stayed for a long time. During the course of these interviews he started considering her as a candidate for a relationship. He hadn't been married either, acknowledging to himself that his desire for women had never been matched by a corresponding sense of devotion.

Eric had heard about first impressions, that most of them were correct. In thirty seconds he was supposed to gather an impression of Ann. He had heard either that 90% of the impression was correct, or that 90% of the time first impressions were correct. Eric recognized the difference between these conclusions but did not know which was right.

When the first interview was over and Ann had left, Eric went over those first thirty seconds. The events were fresh in his mind. She had come through the door to his office and extended her hand. Her grip was complete, that is, she thrust her hand completely into his. He did not ask about the coat but assumed that she wanted it off. He breathed in while near her hair to catch the scent of femininity. When there was none he concluded that she may have applied perfume in the morning, but by now, after lunch, it had evaporated.

Of course Eric had Ann's telephone number at work. He would call her now and again to give his opinions on the articles she was writing. He complemented her on her writing style, which made it easy to suggest modifications of content. They chatted more than talked over the phone.

On one of these calls Eric asked Ann to dinner. With the invitation came an exchange of addresses and phone numbers. Eric hoped that they would not discuss any aspect of business. In fact, he said, "Let's act like two ordinary people." She remarked, "You know perfectly well we're not that, Eric."

The dinner took place at an Italian restaurant near her residence, within walking distance. She wore a red dress. The top of her maroon bra was in evidence. Eric was no longer surprised. He expected it. They kissed goodnight at her door, a warm, tender embrace, in which the fronts of their bodies were in close contact, if not cemented. Eric estimated that they would be in bed after two more evenings together. That would be on the fourth date. Eric was off by one evening. When the event appeared inevitable, Ann announced that she had a long-standing commitment to fly to South Carolina to visit her mother for the weekend. As compensation, at the door, Ann whispered, "I'll make it up to you, Sweetheart."

An important attorney working in the criminal division of the Department of Justice's office in Albany had been reading the articles that Ann had written. This attorney, a female, followed the case Eric was working on. She had read the indictment of Eric's client and through the New York office found out who would be the judge in the case and when the trial was scheduled to start. There was coverage in the press, not because Eric's client was well known, but because postdating stock options had become a hot topic and this case might establish guidelines on how to handle similar cases around the country. When Eric was able to get a not-guilty verdict his star rose among those who needed defense as well as among attorneys on the prosecutorial side, for different reasons, of course.

This important attorney working for the Department of Justice in Albany, named Camille Conrad, had the wild idea that Eric might switch sides and work in her department for a short time, say two years. The attorneys in her department could learn the inner workings of the stock option game and prepare themselves for successful prosecutions. Camille Conrad had her impulsive side. Her secretary found the telephone number for Eric's firm. Camille dialed it herself. Within minutes of hoping to get Eric working for her in Albany she had him on the phone.

Camille Conrad, having reverted to her maiden name after a marriage to an executive in the Midwest that lasted fourteen years, had the type of résumé that placed her at the top of the list in any job search. Four years at a highly respected university (summa cum laude) was followed by graduating near the top of the class from the country's best law school. It was not surprising that she landed a clerkship with a recently-appointed associate justice of the Supreme Court. After a year in Washington, a law firm in Chicago accepted her gladly with the understanding that she would be made partner in a few years.

Her husband was made to order. He was a rising executive in one of the large public utilities and a nephew of the managing partner of her law firm. It was an easy, rapid, joyful courtship. As Camille looked over the breakup in her forty-first year, she would admit that she had gained the upper hand by means of a better mind, a clear idea of what she wanted out of life and each day of it, and interests in the civic life of Chicago that did not necessarily involve her husband. He remarried, not as the ink dried, but not long after. Camille had men in her life after her divorce but the character traits that broke up her marriage were still in evidence, perhaps accentuated, and they served to shorten her relationships.

After sixteen years at her firm, Camille thought about working for a state government or for the Feds at the Department of Justice. It was an easy matter to follow the positions as they became available, advertised as they were in the various registers. When the job opened in Albany her application consisted of a telephone call, submission of a résumé, a four-page memorandum on her views of dealing with white collar crime, and an interview. Her plans, as outlined in the four-page memorandum, clinched the position for her.

In the first words they exchanged, Camille sensed softness in Eric's voice. She expected fast talk, technical in nature. Instead he was asking her about life in Albany. The conversation made sense to Camille, as she reviewed it. She was asking Eric how they might hire him for two years to work in her department. Little wonder that he would ask her opinion of life in Albany and its surroundings. When he asked her whether she had been to Tanglewood, in Lenox, for the music, she did not know whether the question was personal, suggesting that he, Eric was more interested in her than the work.

When Camille sensed that Eric could be induced to move, she asked for his résumé and any additional information he wished to send. Eric said that he didn't have a résumé but would be glad to come up someday soon on the train and return to Manhattan in the evening. At that point Camille offered to have the federal government reimburse him. Eric turned down the offer on the basis that the national debt was already high.

Since her divorce Camille had grown lonely for a relationship with a man. She longed for serious discussions, not arguments, but conversations on politics and legal matters in which each side defended with energy the points of view held. She got a taste of that when Eric came to Albany. After preliminaries, Camille advanced the obvious idea that the government should prosecute and find guilty as many white collar criminals as possible, thereby saving from abuse the members of the population who could be disadvantaged by this criminal activity.

Eric answered that he thought the state was too powerful and could easily overwhelm the ability of accused persons to defend themselves, and that lawyers capable of mounting an effective defense were few and far too expensive. And that few accused persons had at their disposal the financial resources to pay the required legal fees to mount a defense. And that many unjustly accused persons were left ruined by their experiences in court. He thought that the aim of prosecuting nonviolent criminals was to put on notice all violators and potential violators. He said that the government's purpose should be to let the populace know that it was aware of a particular criminal activity and was clearing its throat on the matter. Eric told Camille that he thought jail time for nonviolent crime was uncalled for. Use fines and community service, he told her.

Both could site circumstances to advance their beliefs. Camille noticed that Eric did not try to win arguments. It was sufficient for him to make his case and be certain that Camille understood it.

This activity of verbal sparring had been missing in Camille's marriage and she held a longing for it. Camille had been a debater since she had learned to talk and it was this lack with her husband that made the sport more attractive now that she was single again. She fell in love with Eric's mind in those few hours that they went back and forth in conversation, first in her office, then at lunch.

She extended the offer that afternoon and Eric was off on the late train. It would not take him long to decide, he said. His partners at the firm could not understand his willingness to change sides, as they put it.

After all the pros and cons were debated, the partners granted Eric a two-year leave of absence from the firm. To indicate to them that he had no idea of making this a permanent move he said that he would hold on to his apartment on the Upper West Side. He could not tell them that he was sleeping with Ann the reporter, Ann of the color-coordinated underwear, Ann with whom marriage might be worked out. He guessed that she would be the magnet to keep him around New York City.

Ann was perplexed and saddened by Eric's decision. She thought, as he did, that things were moving along swimmingly. The dry spell of her late twenties and early thirties had come to an end. They enjoyed playful, comfortable time together. It seemed to her that both of them wanted to live together and perhaps have a child. There was enough time. They had endless material to amuse and entertain them, drawing as they would on the vast amount of information her newspaper turned out each day.

Eric said when he made his announcement that anything that either wished to have happen could still happen while he lived and worked in Albany. Weekends were free. She could come north. He was keeping his apartment. "I don't like that the person that hired you is a woman," Ann said. "You make a good point, Ann, but we can't put the women back in the kitchen." Ann frowned but said nothing.

Part of Eric's exit strategy was to tell Ann that he loved her. He felt that she might be placated by this assurance. She answered by saying, "I like your love but I would be happier with both of us living on the same island." It was Eric's turn to have nothing to say.

Camille was pleased and flattered in a professional manner that Eric would leave his firm and work in her department. She did not conclude that her department would come up with a burst of convictions. Instead she hoped that Eric would add a missing ingredient that would convert the young prosecutors from attack dogs to thoughtful monitors of successful executives with the aim of keeping them as law abiding citizens. She had bought Eric's point of view. Until just before his arrival, Camille herself and the attorneys who worked for her held the cynical view that money and the chance to get more could and did subvert all people in the commercial world.

Camille did not hide from herself her romantic interest in Eric. He was about her age. He had not married, and whatever love affair was brewing around Manhattan appeared not to be strong enough to hold him. Camille thought that it would take two months for Eric to make the first move, although she had taken a couple of pre-first moves herself.

She sent Eric to the real estate office that managed an apartment house two blocks from hers and she sent Eric to the furniture rental business that had outfitted several apartments in that building. So those were pre-first moves but her asking Eric to dinner for long discussions on pending and ongoing prosecutions were not viewed by Camille as moves on her part. They were continuations of conversations started at work. A first move, as defined by Camille, would be a telephone call from Eric asking her to accompany him to a fine restaurant in Albany.

Eric beat by ten days the two-month deadline that Camille had invented. It was a movie he wanted to see followed by dinner at a restaurant she had never heard of. They ended up being served at the bar. Camille was amused. She thought his taste was a bit rustic.

On their second outing Eric discussed his life in New York City, not in detail, and he said that he went home on most weekends. Camille interpreted that to mean that he would be available for evening discussions only Monday through Thursday. She registered no objections and changed the subject. If she could pull him away from whatever attraction there was in Manhattan, so much the better. She need not know the details.

Eric found Camille attractive. As a tall woman she could add or subtract ten to fifteen pounds and hide the difference from everything but her wardrobe. Eric guessed that at five ten she might weigh 140 pounds. He liked the way she moved in a graceful yet forceful way. She was obviously of Nordic extraction with blond hair, blue-grey eyes and light skin. He wanted to ask her about her genealogy but never got around to it.

It surprised Eric one evening when for the first time ever he acted as would a person under no restraints. They had finished dinner in Camille's apartment. She brought two mugs of coffee and set them on the table in front of the sofa. When she turned to sit next to him he reached out and placed both arms around her waist. He started kissing her and when she kissed him back he began caressing her. When there were no objections he continued but after a minute or so he said, "This might work much better in your bed."

That was the start of it. In no time they were intimate twice a week or more often. Eric knew enough about life, romance and sex to admit to himself that he was on a slippery slope. He would have to give up Ann or Camille soon enough. This business of having a lover in each city could not be sustained. At least he thought he could not carry it off beyond a month or so. He would break under the pressure.

A twist came in their relationship when after three or four weeks of having a willing partner in both Albany and New York, Camille insisted that Eric carry a set of keys to her apartment. That would be one for the front door downstairs and a key for her third-floor apartment. Eric objected, saying that he had no need for a set of her keys. She said he might call and say he was coming over at the moment she was contemplating a shower or would be out for twenty minutes buying food. Eric gave in. When he pulled out his key ring, Camille noticed that he carried only four keys. One was obviously for the car he had bought on arrival and she presumed that one was for his front door downstairs and another for the apartment. His fourth key was small and intended for the mailbox. Camille wondered where the keys for his apartment in New York were. She guessed they were on a separate ring that he would take to Manhattan Friday evenings. He pried open the ring with his finger nail and slid the two keys in place. There were six now.

One Monday Eric failed to show up at work. Camille assumed that he was held up in Manhattan for any number of reasons. She was surprised that he had not telephoned her. Late that afternoon a person from the park police came to the office. This man reported that Eric's car had been in the parking lot Saturday at closing time, at a park located about twenty miles from Albany. The driver, Eric Olson, the man assumed, had to have come on Saturday as the parking lot is checked and chained every evening. Hikers and picnickers used the place. Camping was not allowed. It was a simple matter for the park police to determine the car's owner from the license plates. Prior to coming to the office, the park policeman had gone to Eric's apartment building where the manager let him in to see whether Eric was there, dead perhaps. They looked for obvious clues as to Eric's whereabouts but found nothing. The manager knew where Eric worked.

As a routine measure the park police searched the park on Tuesday. It consisted of 2,500 acres of trails and woods. It would accommodate three Central Parks. They found nothing. The search was repeated Thursday with the same results. Camille thought that Eric had left the park in another car. She could not come up with a better explanation.

It occurred to Camille that a love triangle was at work. She knew nothing about Eric's New York interest and she knew that she was not involved in any way except that Eric was her employee and lover. Camille's game had been to pry Eric loose from the woman in Manhattan. If she were able to accomplish that feat she could look forward to remarriage to a man she admired. The only clue that could tie Eric to her was her keys on his key ring. She knew that she had not been involved in anything that could be judged illegal, but she knew as well that the publicity produced by the stray keys could be disastrous to her career.

A staff member of Ann's newspaper who lived and worked in Albany knew only that Ann and Eric had collaborated a few months back on a series of articles. This staff person did not know about the love affair between Ann and Eric and was surprised when Ann started crying over the phone when she called to tell Ann that Eric had not shown up for work. "I suppose he's dead," she said. "Somebody wanted him dead," she repeated.

Two weeks after a final search for Eric, a young couple went purposely off a trail in the park in search of seclusion. They stumbled on a shoe, a set of keys, and a wallet. They touched nothing except the wallet, which they checked for cash. They found five dollars, which they decided to leave. After marking the place where they had turned off the trail they reported what they had found to the ranger in the parking lot. A thorough search of the area was conducted. The second shoe was found along with fragments of material. The forensic specialists determined what Eric was wearing. They could find no trace of a skull or any bone fragments. The determination was that Eric was done in by one or more mountain lions, a species seen on rare occasions in this area.

The key ring contained six keys. Four were obviously for Eric's car and apartment. The police could not account for the extra two keys. The staffer for Ann's paper, keeping abreast of the investigation, called Ann. It turned out that Ann's apartment building had a doorman and that Ann had a single key for her apartment door and a small key for her mail box. In any event she had never given a set to Eric or any one else.

Camille waited for the investigation to come near her but it never did. The county lost interest in the matter when blame was placed on the mountain lions. The case was referred to an understaffed department that dealt with the rising population of wild life, most of them migrants from Canada who were heading south for warmer climate and a more plentiful supply of food.

Camille suspected the explanation for Eric's death. Had he been eaten by mountain lions there would have been bone fragments strewn about the site. He was alive, she speculated, either off on his own, or more likely, captive of a group that had its reasons to have him out of circulation for a while. She could not imagine that he was a threat while employed for the government. He was not a prosecutor, merely an advisor.

He had come to occupy a place in her heart. She admitted that to herself even though their romance had not had a chance to flourish. She understood his attraction: the clear mind with its amusing overtones; the positive way he approached life (problems were meant to be solved), the masculine handling of her, from his no nonsense conduct of discussions to being a forceful lover. She had not known these features in her marriage. While her husband was most everything a woman wanted and needed, he lacked extreme masculinity, the quality that made Eric so attractive to her.

She let two weeks go by, hoping that Eric would surface. When there was no trace of him she contacted the officials of the county and arranged to examine the items found at the site. The pieces of cloth that constituted his shirt and pants could have been torn up by an animal but there was no blood on any swatch. There should have been a belt, she reasoned. The wallet was suspect. A lion on a full stomach would not remove a wallet from his victim's trousers. Of course Eric could have pulled the wallet from his pocket so that it would be found. More than likely, it was left there by his abductors. Camille had heard that in extreme fright a person can and does jump out of a pair of shoes, but in this case, both shoes were untied, as though Eric had been ordered to remove them before putting on another pair, or they were taken from his closet.

Camille found nothing conclusive among Eric's articles although the untied shoes were a mystery. If she could be permitted to examine the remains from the site, then the county authorities might let her go through the papers in his apartment. Permission was forthcoming. Camille and a young deputy entered Eric's apartment. Camille and the deputy walked through the rooms and examined the contents in various pieces of furniture. The three drawers in the small piece of furniture next to his bed yielded nothing. The medicine cabinet in the bathroom held only common articles. His clothes were arranged neatly in two chests of drawers and a long closet. Each pocket was examined and yielded two ticket stubs to a movie theater in New York City.

Finally Camille sat at Eric's desk and opened his two-drawer file cabinet. The file cabinet was a masterpiece of organization. The hanging folders held the paid bills associated with keeping two apartments going, this one and his place in New York City. Only one file interested Camille and it held letters from a woman who signed them Ann. Camille knew that this woman must be the reporter who had been writing articles on dating stock options. Camille had read the articles and remembered the byline. She and the young assistant sat on the same sofa and read the contents of eight letters. Camille found no clues to Eric's whereabouts but it was clear that Eric and Ann were sleeping together on his weekends in the City. It didn't surprise Camille that Eric was sleeping with two women alternately. She resented that he could be attentive to her and at the same time very affectionate to Ann. Ann wrote as though marriage to Eric was in the offing. In her letters she addressed Eric as "My Darling."

While the young assistant was finishing reading the eight letters, Camille examined the pros and cons of bringing Ann into the search. Neither had a prior claim should Eric surface, but if she, Camille, was instrumental in restoring Eric to his previous life, then he might chose her over Ann for just that reason.

The aspect of her feelings for Eric that were new to Camille was the delight and abandon that they felt one for the other as evenings wore on. There had been a normal physical component in her marriage. A year after the wedding they had let go of prevention in hopes of having a child, and later a second. When no child arrived they did not take the next step and consult a physician. They told one another that if a child was meant to be, he or she would materialize.

In the case of Eric, Camille experienced a phenomenon new to her. She expected that having sex with him would bring the same pleasure as it had with her husband. It turned out to be vastly more pleasurable. Camille concluded that if a physical side to a relationship develops after the emotional part is in place and if the emotional part is intense then so would be the physical. On the evening that Eric put his arm around her as she sat down after placing coffee on the table, and pulled her toward him, she knew right away that they would end up in her bed, without clothes, building to that most common sex act with its pleasurable sensations and releases. They would engage in the act frequently, always with the same result. If she could recover Eric and bring him permanently into her life, what reason would there be to include Ann in any investigation she was conducting?

The days passed and Eric continued not to be heard from. Camille thought that the state would do little if anything until a judge declared Eric dead, and that could take years. But the car had to be sold as there were payments to be made. The contents of the apartment would be placed in storage and the lease terminated. His apartment in New York City held the same fate as did his car. Eric had mentioned that he was paying on a mortgage. If that were the case the apartment would be sold, the mortgage paid off, and any excess money would be added to his estate. Eric had mentioned to Camille that his only relative was a second cousin who lived in Buffalo. They had met rarely over the years. As there was no will, at least none had been found, this cousin could well be the sole beneficiary.

When a month had passed since Eric's disappearance, Camille changed her mind. She determined that it might improve her chances of finding him if she approached Ann. She wrote her at work identifying herself as Eric's supervisor who was making a continuing effort at finding the cause of his disappearance.

As soon as the mails permitted, Camille received a call at home in the evening from Ann. Yes, they could meet. The following weekend would be acceptable. Camille was coming down to the City to see friends. They would meet at Ann's apartment. Would noon Saturday be too soon?

Camille had no idea what Ann knew about her affair with Eric. There would be no reason for Eric to mention it to anyone. Camille, having read eight letters, knew what Ann felt for Eric. The meeting might provoke tears. Camille pieced together Ann in the first moments they were together. Ann stood straight and looked both sad and serious. Camille could measure Ann's beautiful figure and guessed that Eric had been captivated by it. She was not glamorous and perhaps that accounted for her having been overlooked during the early years when most young people pair off for the first time. While her face was plain, she did have a widow's peak and deep brown hair. The overall effect would be convincing to a man, particularly to Eric, who admired intelligence, which seemed to characterize her writing and the way she spoke. Camille knew first hand that Eric responded to physical beauty. Camille could not measure Ann's intelligence by looking at her but judging from her articles and her letters there was no shortage of brain power.

In preparation for her first meeting with Camille, Ann had prepared sandwiches and coffee. After introductory comments they had a brief lunch during which Camille asked whether Ann had access to Eric's apartment. "No, I had thought of exchanging keys with him but never brought it up. We were very close and it might have made sense." For obvious reasons Camille did not bring up the fact that she had gone through Eric's apartment in Albany. She did, however, ask Ann whether there was a way she, Ann, might ask an authority to accompany her into the apartment so that a clue or two to his disappearance might be found.

In a telephone call during the week, Ann was assured that two detectives had examined every scrap of paper in Eric's New York apartment. There would be no reason for a person not connected directly to the case to be granted permission to go through his affairs. The person to whom Ann spoke identified her correctly as the reporter who had written articles based in part on interviews with Eric. Ann guessed that Eric had clipped and saved her articles. Ann asked the person, "Was there an address book with my name in it, perhaps?" "Yes, I noted that you were listed by your newspaper as well as by your last name, and he has a file with your articles." The person went on to tell Ann that his partners in the New York law office had been interviewed and that no evidence had turned up.

Ann and Camille met again two weeks later in a restaurant near Ann's apartment. When they had finished lunch, Camille volunteered that her department missed Eric a great deal and that she missed his insight into the topic of stock options and the granting of them. "He's a fine lawyer," Camille concluded.

"He was a fine lawyer," Ann said.

"Are you convinced he's gone?"

"Yes, someone wanted him dead," Ann said. "There's someone out there involved in illegal activities that could have been exposed by Eric. There's a great deal of money involved and Eric might have been in a position of putting this person away for a long time."

"So you don't believe the mountain lion explanation?" Camille asked.

"Not a word of it. He was already dead and buried when his killers drove his car into the park and threw evidence around. When they were finished, they left in another car with another driver."

"Were you in love, you two?" Camille asked.

"Yes, we had started talking about marriage and I expected that I would be moving to his apartment soon. It's really a crushing blow. I'm thirty-three and can have a couple of kids. Now, I don't know."

They were quiet for a moment then Camille said, "You were lovers, of course."

"Yes, of course," Ann said. "He did wonderful things for my mind, my spirit, my optimism, and frankly was wonderful with my body. He was strong and gentle at the same time."

There was another quiet moment then it was Ann's turn. She asked, "And you two were lovers?"

"Yes. Apparently I had him during the week and you on weekends."

"I guessed that the moment I saw you," Ann said. "I can see how he would have found you irresistible."

"It's not often that a man creates two widows at once," Camille said.

ALBANY

PART 7

Emil was more accustomed to speedy results than he was to the snail's pace that characterized the federal government's building a case against a corporation. The federal prosecutors needed several individuals within a corporation to come forward with their evidence: stock options that they swore carried fictitious dates. The individuals were only suspected of having been granted these options. When they were promised immunity from prosecution they produced their evidence and indicated that they would testify.

When a case was assembled in parts, the prosecutors were able to persuade a judge most times to issue a warrant that authorized the federal agents to carry out a surprise search of corporate headquarters of the firm. At the close of the day these law enforcement men could be seen bringing boxes of documents to the lobby of the building.

After preparing an inventory of the results of the search, they loaded documents into waiting vans. Months would pass before the documents were studied and more months while a case was made in front of a grand jury, asking that body to come forth with indictments against several individuals.

From the time Emil arrived from Austria until Ann Newman was contacted, a mere two weeks transpired. Three more weeks went by before Eric Olson accepted the job offer in Albany. Emil and his syndicate had picked up the scent of Eric through the kindness of Ann's revelations. With the aid of inside information, obtained in the same fashion as Ann was persuaded, Emil determined that Theodore Warner's company was on the list for prosecution. He monitored progress in Albany week by week. The attorneys were so slow that Emil had to leave the States as his ninety days were up. Immigration authorities watched the date stamped on a passport when a person had come into the country. They tracked these dates on their computers. Emil caught up with a few friends in Vienna and spent an hour with the woman in charge of the operation. He returned after five days bearing a new identification. He was now Walter in his passport but his few contacts around New York still called him Emil.

The obvious pressure point was Camille Conrad. Emil knew that she and Eric had discovered one another romantically. Why else would he walk the two blocks from his apartment building to hers after he arrived home from work? The walk in the opposite direction occurred most of the time at two in the morning. He must be setting an alarm clock.

Emil knew that three employees in Theodore's company had come forth in exchange for immunity. The judge's granting of a search warrant was imminent. Theodore was made privy to this information through Dieter. He was told by Dieter to go through his files and notes and destroy any documents that linked him more closely than he already was to the stock option affair. There was nothing on the matter in the computer that he used for ordinary business activity.

Emil waited nearly four months from the time Eric moved to Albany until the syndicate picked him up. Eric and Camille were in love. Eric and Ann might be in love. Eric was sleeping with both women, but he could not be in love with both simultaneously. At least that was Emil's evaluation of this situation. Both women had a powerful interest in Eric. Both would have a reaction to his disappearance but Camille's would be stronger. Ann, after all, had been paid handsomely by a certain Craig Burton in twenty dollar bills for a great deal of information including Eric's name. Emil had nothing but his memory to guide him to the sum of nine thousand dollars being distributed to Ann, but that seemed about right.

Collecting Eric was routine. It was scheduled for a weekend that he planned to go to New York for a visit with Ann. Emil thought that Camille was gaining ground over her competitor, as Eric was now spending a weekend in Albany for each one in New York. When on his way to New York City, Eric stopped by the cleaners Friday afternoon to pick up a suit and shirts. He would finish packing, call a cab and head for the train station. When staying in Albany he would wait to pick up his cleaning on Saturday. If he did not materialize in New York until Saturday evening, Ann would guess that he was at his apartment across town or at his old law firm. That gave Emil and company twenty-four hours. Of course Emil did not pick up Eric. Two men experienced in that line of work did the job.

They were both minor criminals with records, victims of bad luck while committing petty jobs. Nonetheless this low-level business of picking up someone and delivering that person to another group was almost beneath their dignity. The pay was good, though.

Eric parked his car in the basement garage of his apartment building, exactly as he always did, in his assigned slot. He opened the rear door of his sedan to remove his cleaning. Two men, each holding a gun, walked toward him. One said, "Do you have all your stuff, Eric?" Eric looked at them and couldn't speak. The man who had addressed him closed the door and took Eric's set of keys out of his hand. He pressed the lock button for the doors on the small apparatus attached to the key ring "We're going up to your apartment. Not a word out of you."

They walked to the elevator and when they were inside, the man who had not spoken pushed the button for the third floor. This man knew to turn left when they got out. The guns had disappeared. The same man knew which door to enter. His comrade with the keys opened it and the three entered. When the door was shut, the man who had spoken in the garage said, "Eric, you might like to fix yourself a drink. Then we can sit down and I'll explain what this is all about."

Eric had recovered his voice. "Will you join me?" he asked.

The man who had spoken said, "Yes, it's unprofessional but a drink at this time of the day is appreciated."

"What will you have?" Eric asked.

"Same as you, Eric, and thanks."

Eric got out three glasses, ice, club soda and a bottle of bourbon. "Jack on the rocks," the other man said, looking at the bottle of bourbon. Soon they were sitting down, each man in an easy chair and Eric on the sofa.

"So here's the plan," the talkative one said. "Pack a suitcase, one that you will check."

"Airplane ride?" Eric asked.

"I suppose so. Leave on your suit and tie. My guess is that they're making a new passport for you. Leave your American passport here and let me have your wallet. It should be obvious that when they want your American passport to stay here they don't want people guessing that you left the country."

Eric handed over his wallet and asked, "What's the weather where I'm going? I should pack the right weight stuff."

"I don't know that. We know we're putting you in a car here in

Albany. You're packing three days of clean clothes. Wear your suit and tie. I've already said that. Take a carry-on with your book or whatever you're reading. And I was told to tell you this, you're a free man, you can do whatever you want but if you do something stupid, this woman of yours, Camille, will be liquidated sure as hell."

The man who was speaking turned to the other, "Camille's one broad. What's the other?"

"Ann."

"Yea, Ann. Something really stupid and it's the same for her." The man paused. "I don't have to tell you what something stupid means, do I?" Eric shook his head to indicate that he understood.

The man who held the wallet had put on cotton gloves. He pulled out each card and examined it and put it back. He took out the cash and counted it. "One hundred eighty bucks," he said. "Here, Eric, it's your money. Take hundred seventy-five. You could need a drink on the plane." He put five dollars back in the wallet, put the wallet in his coat pocket and handed the money to Eric. He asked, "You know why we do this?"

"No, not really."

"Anyone who finds a wallet takes out the cash and throws the wallet away, or turns it in, or drops it in a mail box. The cash's the reward. And the five bucks, a guy like you doesn't walk around with no money."

When they finished the drink, the man said, "Let's start packing, Eric. We'll want the shoes you'd wear if you went for a hike in the woods. And the pants and shirt you'd wear too."

"I thought I was taking a plane trip," Eric said.

"Yea, that's what I figure too, with leaving on the suit and tie and with making you a new passport. It looks like they want you eaten by mountain lions in a place near here. I don't know which one."

"I would be wearing a belt. Don't you want a belt?" Eric asked.

"If they wanted a belt they would have said belt."

"Well, I think it's an oversight," Eric said.

One of the men unbuttoned his shirt and pulled out a plastic bag of the type one gets with merchandize in a department store. Eric noticed that it was turned inside out.

"Let me have the hiking stuff, Eric," the man said. "I'll put it in your car and tomorrow they'll tear it up the clothes like mountain lions would and leave it in a park somewhere. That's what I'm guessing."

"How about my car?" Eric asked.

"If it's in the parking lot of a park, it'll just sit there all day tomorrow and at the end of the day the ranger will look into it. You should be over the Atlantic or more than likely already there, wherever you're going."

They retraced their steps, the three taking the elevator to the basement. At Eric's car, the man holding the keys opened the trunk and put in the plastic bag with the hiking clothes and the wallet. They walked out of the garage and a half block to a waiting car. One of the men opened the rear door and said to the two occupants, "This here's Eric." He indicated to Eric that he should get in, which he did with his suitcase ending up on his lap. The man handed Eric his carry-on and asked the occupants, "Who gets the keys?" He handed them over and looked at Eric. "Remember, Eric, don't do anything stupid." With that Eric and his escorts drove off.

In a few blocks, Eric said, "Tell me about liquidating someone these days. How do they do it?" The man sitting in the back with him said, "It's not our line of work, you understand, but you hire a hit man, or a woman for that matter, and they do the job with a gun and a silencer. Very quick. You don't know what's happening until it's over. They usually get fifty grand for it." They fell silent.

"Where are we off to?" Eric asked.

"We're headed south to the photo lab where you'll get a new passport."

"And then where?" Eric asked.

"It makes sense you're leaving the country. Why else a passport?" The three men were silent then the driver said, "We've been told that you are a free man. No kidnapping, no guns. But if you cut and run they'll rub out the two broads."

"They're superior women," Eric said.

ALBANY

PART 8

The laboratory where they ended up was in a densely populated area. They had driven down along the Hudson River, crossed on the Tri Borough Bridge to Manhattan and made it to the tunnel for Long Island at 36th Street. Once out of the tunnel, the man sitting next to Eric handed him a hood. "Wear this. I'll tell you when to take it off." Eric thought they had driven fifteen minutes when they came to a stop and turned off the engine. The man said, "Sit still. The driver's coming around to get you." It was still dark as they walked up a short flight of stairs and into a building. "Take it off the hood, Eric," the man said.

They went down a hall and entered a room where Eric was told to sit down facing camera and lights. There was a man operating the equipment but Eric couldn't see him clearly. He took several photographs of Eric then the driver said, "Come with me." They entered the kitchen and the man said, "We're leaving for JFK at nine this morning. So let's eat something and you can sleep a while on the couch in the living room. In the morning, when Eric was led out of the building to the car, he was made to put on a large pair of dark glasses, the type that people wear over their reading glasses. He looked around but couldn't see details.

They arrived at JFK at 9:30. Eric noted that he was now Robert H. Barnes: date of birth the same year as his, place of birth, Chicago, Illinois. Eric wondered who Robert H. Barnes was. He put the new passport in his shirt pocket, where he always carried his. The driver found their terminal and pulled along the curb ahead of the crowd getting out of cars. Eric and the man sitting next to him stepped out. Eric had his check-in bag and the man held his carry-on. "Here's your electronic ticket, Eric. We'll wait in line, get to the counter, check your bag, and get you a boarding pass. They'll ask for your passport and I'll stay with you until we get to security. Your password for the flight is Mark Twain."

When Eric was checked in, he and the man walked toward security. When they reached the end of the line the man took Eric's hand. "Happy landings, Eric. You've got the password?"

"Yes, all set. Paris I'm going to. Not a bad deal."

Eric went through security then found his gate. He sat on one of the semi-soft, black plastic chairs. Soon enough a man about his age sat next to him, put out his hand and said, "It's Mark, isn't it?" "Yes, yes, of course. Fancy meeting you here. I thought never the twain should meet." Eric had been rehearsing how he would handle his end of the password. He understood that if he failed to pick up his escort, something terrible could happen, either to Camille or Ann. This new contact seemed higher up the social ladder than the previous ones because of his facile use of the English language and his appearance. Eric still wore the clothes he wore to work yesterday. This man also had on a coat and tie. He said, "Let me see your boarding pass, Mark, please." The man studied it, compared it to his own, and said, "We're both in business class and you're sitting five rows ahead of me. When we get off the plane you'll be in front of me. Let me catch up in the jet way."

Eric thought the man was very solicitous. He asked Eric whether he had plenty of reading material. "Yes, I'm starting a book on Michelangelo. I think there are six hundred pages to go, so I'm all set, thanks." Then he asked Eric if he could buy him a drink. It was late morning. Eric looked at his watch and said he'd have drinks with his lunch on the plane. The flight was uneventful. They were in the air seven or eight hours and because they had flown through several time zones -- Eric thought it was six -- it made sense that they landed just as dawn was breaking. After passport control and finding their bags, the two were met by a Frenchman. More passwords. They drove by limousine out of the Paris area.

Eric asked, "Have you any idea where we're going?" His contact said, "I get relieved at Metz, so it'll be a different car and a new escort from then on." They were mostly quiet on the trip. Eric dozed as much as he could.

The new car, with new driver and escort, both speaking English with a German accent, headed east into Germany with Eric, now awake, grumbling about breakfast. They followed road signs to Munich and when on the outskirts pulled in to an American style motel. The driver went in to register them into two rooms, Eric staying with his escort. He suggested that Eric shower and put on clean clothes and they would repair to the restaurant for a full meal. "Eric, I'll order for you. The waiters don't need to hear your English. Tell me what you want now and I'll order the same." Eric thought it was accommodating of his escort to let him select. Eric reasoned that by now officials in Albany were awake to the fact that he was missing and that there would be a search starting for him. Perhaps that wouldn't be underway until Monday when Camille started wondering where he was or the park people traced his car back to his place of work.

After a fine German breakfast the three went back to the room Eric and his escort were occupying. "We don't have far to go, Eric. We're on

our way to Linz, in Austria. You can sleep in the car if you get tired."
Indeed the ride was not too long. Eric fell asleep and did not wake up
until he heard the tires of the car making that distinctive sound as they
changed from pavement to gravel. They were approaching a country
house that must have at least a dozen rooms. It seemed to Eric that this
would be his jail for the next few months. He saw two cars off to one side
of the house.

"End of the line," the escort said. He got out of the car holding Eric's
suit. Eric had both his bags. The two walked to the front door, which
opened as they approached. A large man with short black hair and a heavy
beard greeted them. "Eric, how are you? Please come in and stay a while."
The escort turned away without saying anything. Eric watched him get
in the front seat of the car and drive away. There were no passwords. Eric
concluded the two men knew one another.

"Come in, come in, Eric," his new host said. "Bring your bags upstairs.
I'll show you your room." Eric noted that a bathroom was included in
the suite. There was a large desk and accompanying chair and a television
set on a low table with yet another chair. The view was to a wide river.
"Which one is that?" Eric asked, pointing. "The Danube, on its way to
the Black Sea. We'll walk to the banks one day soon, perhaps tomorrow.
Come down when you're ready."

Eric unpacked his few clothes and placed his book about Michelangelo
on the desk. He always carried writing paper and envelopes but knew he
would have no occasion to use them. They stayed in his carry-on for the
time being.

"What shall I call you?" Eric asked his host when they were both in
the large living room downstairs.

"One"

"One?"

"Yes, 'One'. My comrade is 'Three.'"

"And who is 'Two'?" Eric asked.

" 'Two' is the woman who prepares our meals. She's a very good cook. We suggest lamb curry, as an example, and in a few days it appears. I'm not aware of any cookbooks. And the curry in its tureen sits on the sideboard alongside a bowl of steaming rice and dishes of condiments such as peanuts, shredded coconut, chopped hard boiled egg, yogurt, thin slices of banana, and my favorite, mango chutney."

"Will you put it back in the rotation very soon?" Eric asked.

'One' did not respond to the question. He changed the subject. "Our bar is complete. We usually have drinks before dinner and wine with. In this line of work inactivity is the great activity and we, 'Three' and I, have learned to read long books, watch television, old movies mostly, take walks in the country and write to our wives. The mail is not postmarked in Linz, of course. Other cities, sometimes in Germany."

"How does 'Two' pass the time?"

"She drives a lot, rarely shopping in the same store. She has about the same hobbies we do and likes the old movies."

Eric picked up a book on the table and opened it at random. He turned to 'One' and asked, "What is the language?"

"Bulgarian. 'Three' and I are Bulgarian. We are veterans of the secret police under the former regime. 'Two', by the way, is Romanian."

Eric thought the three of them were probably from other countries but spoke enough of the languages 'One' had identified so that he, Eric, would not be able to catch him in his lie. They chatted for a little while before 'Three' came downstairs. He might have been 'One's' brother. After introductions he asked, "Have you had the conversation yet?"

"No, waiting for you," 'One' answered.

"Why don't we go ahead?" 'Three' said.

"Very well," 'One' said. "There's a large company in New York State." 'One' gave its name. "They have been changing dates on documents. I don't understand the crime involved but apparently it is a crime to do that."

Eric interrupted. He said, "I know the company and I'm familiar with what they have been doing and it is against the law."

'One' went on. "As you say, changing dates is against a law that you have and the president of the company has been changing them, and who knows, in a trial he could be found guilty and sent off to prison for a while. It is that person whose money is paying for everything. Be certain to think about that everyday, Eric. And if we are successful and we leave this place to go on about our business, be certain to forget the entire incident immediately and for as long as you live."

"And how do I fit in?" Eric asked.

"Logical question," 'One' said. "There is a woman, Camille Conrad, who will determine the power applied by the government against the company and the president. This Conrad lady will be told that she must be very gentle."

"When will you tell her?"

"We will wait until she fears for your life and when she is involved in this case. Right now she might know that you are missing. Right now she is not working on the case against this company. When both conditions are met she is told to be gentle and if she fails, if she advocates a trial with violent results, you will be sacrificed, and she will know that she is the reason. She will know that she chose her career over your life."

"Me? Why me?"

"Because you sleep with her and she is in love with you. In other words, you are leverage."

"How do you sacrifice a person?" Eric asked.

"We kill him and put him in the Danube with his American passport in his pocket."

"My American passport is in Albany."

"That way the police think you are in the States when you are really here in this living room in Austria. And as for the passport we make a new one. You will no longer be Barnes. You will be dead and Eric again. We have photographs in New York."

"Let's assume Camille does what you suggest. How long will I be here?"

"You Americans are very slow. In the old days we would execute somebody first and get permission later. I guess in a month or so she will be fearful of your life, and the case against the company will be in front of her. So we tell her you are alive. That gives her hope. She then has the choice of making a vigorous trial against the company and the president and sacrificing you, or the other way around."

"So, how long?" Eric asked.

"We are guessing three months. We will become good friends. I teach you Bulgarian and you teach me English."

"Your English is very good," Eric said.

"And you will be overtaken by the cooking of 'Two.'"

"Perhaps you meant overwhelmed. It's better to say overwhelmed than overtaken."

"Yes, you are teaching me English already."

Eric wondered about 'Two'. After all she was female and he would be under house arrest for a while. A few hours later he met her. 'Three' did the introductions, whether in Bulgarian or in Romanian, Eric did not know. She looked to Eric to be about his age and there was little doubt that she had been sampling her own cooking. She appeared pleased to meet him, Eric thought. She extended her hand, looked him in the eye, said "Eric," and gave him a slight bow. Eric wanted to ask, "What's for dinner?" but refrained.

Eric's captors, or keepers -- he alternated terms in his mind -- were enthusiastic about walking, no doubt under the correct impression that exercise would be good for them. In fact, Eric grew to look forward to these excursions. In mid-morning they, 'One', 'Three' and Eric, would drive off to a new spot and after the first month to a place where they might have been previously. Each had a knapsack containing a bottle of water, sandwich and fruit. They might be gone until three in the afternoon when they returned for a nap before showering and dressing for drinks before dinner. 'One' and 'Three' were not as careful as Eric thought circumstances called for. When Eric asked them about it they told him that his disappearance had been in the New York papers for two or three days before editors lost interest in him. Eric had access to the European papers written in English, and he did watch CNN and BBC and he had to agree with 'One' and 'Three' that no national search was underway to locate him. No one suspected that he had flown over the Atlantic.

"You are nobody," 'One' said. "If you had family they would wonder about you and go to the authorities. There is no one who seems to care."

"How about the two women in my life?" Eric asked.

"Camille worries about you. Our contact in her office tells us that. We are near telling her that you are alive, and that it will be in her and your best interest to be very easy on that company. And for the other one, Ann, we will tell her also and let her know that you have read her dispatches to Craig Burton. She gave us your name for nine thousand dollars total. One thousand for a meeting, five thousand for six pages of names and tables of organization, and finally three thousand for your name and a few others she knew. You have an expression in the States that she fingered you for three thousand dollars."

"I haven't read anything that Ann has written," Eric said,

"We have the papers in her handwriting upstairs. You can read them after dinner," 'One' said.

It was after dinner. Eric, "One' and 'Three' were in the living room. BBC news was on the television. 'Three' picked a folder off the table, opened it and handed the sheets to Eric. The handwriting was unmistakably Ann's. He read the hand-written pages quickly and came to three typewritten pages containing the same information verbatim. Eric looked up at 'Three' who said, "You may copy that but I want the pages in Ann's writing now and the typewritten pages tomorrow.

Eric did copy the portions of the typewritten pages of Ann's material that concerned him when he was back in his room. He had been thinking about her during dinner. Her love of him was no doubt genuine but either she was susceptible to the whiff of money or naïve about the consequences of her actions, perhaps both. Eric agreed that he was the obvious target for the crime syndicate, but Ann lacked the wit to be suspicious. All that cash can be seductive, Eric acknowledged. It would be difficult to reconnect with her, if indeed he was given the opportunity.

What about Camille? About now, give or take a few weeks, she would be told that to secure his release she would have to cooperate, to do her best to change the direction that the prosecutors would take, from indictments of individuals to a settlement in which Theodore's company paid a substantial fine.

Eric hoped that Camille would hold him in her highest esteem, would wish to get him back, and would not sacrifice him over her moral standards. He knew now how the syndicate operated. There would be one conversation between the contact and Camille. It would be brief. Eric could envision how the contact would act on an evening the moment Camille returned home from work. The mechanism would be a telephone call from the contact's cell phone to Camille. "Come to the lobby immediately. Use the stairs. Don't wait for the elevator. If you're not here in forty-five seconds I leave. It's a message from Eric."

And when Camille entered the lobby from her apartment the contact would be studying his wristwatch. The words spoken by him could be, "Eric's alive. If you want him to return don't indict Theodore Warner. Work toward a settlement with the company, fines obviously." With that the contact would turn away and walk out of the lobby. He would have spoken for ten seconds. Camille would not have had a chance to utter a word.

Eric thought that if it played out that way and he became free to return home then the questions would start. Finally it would come out that Camille had yielded to pressure in order to save him. Her career would be in shambles. And, come to think of it, no one would hire him. Too much baggage, as they say. He would have been the victim yet ended up paying the price that ought to have been paid by Theodore Warner.

Two months into his captivity, Eric, 'One', 'Two' and 'Three' were joined by a fifth person. She was not 'Five', but went by Marie. 'Three' introduced her by saying, "Eric, we thought you might be getting bored with our conversation." Marie occupied the last bedroom in the house.

Her door and Eric's gave on the same hallway. She spoke English with a German accent and proclaimed herself to be an Austrian national. She joined them on their walks, ate meals with them, and focused her attention on Eric. He wondered about the purpose of introducing this new element into their circle. If he was patient, it would come out.

Marie explained to Eric that she was unemployed and had been hired to live in the house for a month. Her job was to introduce a feminine point of view into their conversations. She would be at all meals and join them on walks. She had not come in her own car but rather appeared in 'Three's' car with two large suitcases. In some fashion, she was also captive. Eric didn't believe any part of her story and decided to wait for her role to define itself.

At meals and on walks she proved herself to be a valuable companion. She had been educated at a university and knew literature and European politics thoroughly. She admitted to being thirty-two, married and divorced, without children. She claimed to have lost her job in the public relations department of a firm in Vienna. She accepted the offer of being a companion and conversationalist for a month. She said that the pay was good. She told Eric that she was treating the experience as an unusual vacation in the countryside. Eric, who had developed a suspicious streak, wondered why she never spoke about the life she had left. Certainly there were friends and relatives, associations she belonged to, activities with others, and so on. She limited what she wanted to put on display to the books she had read, or was reading, and the thoughts these texts generated. Eric did not ask questions. He let matters move along at the pace that 'One' and 'Three' set. Marie and 'One', or Marie and 'Three', would fall behind on their walks, giving them ample opportunity to discuss matters out of earshot.

Eric liked Marie. He hoped that she felt that way about him. The syndicate would have reasons to bring Marie into their fold but they could have no control over the reactions she would have for Eric, and of course they couldn't dictate to Eric how to feel about this young woman.

Eric tried to imagine Marie at nineteen. She might have been an athlete, running cross country races, or playing volleyball, or tennis, or all of them. Surely she skied. She had a lovely figure and dressed to it. Toward the end of the month that she was scheduled to stay, 'Three' arranged for Marie, Eric and himself to swim in a heated indoor pool not a great distance away. 'Three' procured a bathing suit for Eric and off they went. Eric thought that the purpose of the outing was to put Marie's physique on display. She came out of the woman's dressing room wearing a black one-piece bathing suit. Eric, who was already in the water, stopped and stared. She had a perfect body. It could not have been more appealing at nineteen.

In mid-afternoon, after the swim, Eric was reading in his room. He had left the door ajar. He heard Marie's door open and close and then her voice. "May I come in?" She was dressed for the evening in pants, blouse and sweater, in three shades of green. She sat on the bed, threw off her shoes and took the lotus position.

"Refreshed after the swim?" Eric asked.

"Yes, nice change from the walks." They were silent for a moment then Marie continued. "I've been asked to tell you that success is near. The parties are agreeing on fines to be paid and no one goes to trial. You will be free to go soon."

"Captivity has been more than tolerable this last month," Eric said.

"I am enjoying the experience as well," Marie answered. "There are details for you and me to arrange, a final chapter. The man who is the president of the software company wants you to stay out of the States for a long time. Before you come back he wants most of your memories of these last few months to have flown away. The syndicate does what it does best, arranges everything with money."

Eric interrupted. "Do you work for them, Marie?"

"I'll answer that later. Let me finish this part."

"Let me start with the passport. You came to Europe as Mr. Barnes. Four days after you, the real Mr. Barnes made the same trip as you did. One chance in a million. The French immigration people caught it and contacted the Americans but no one seems to have connected you to Eric Olson. A difficulty is that you ought not to return to the States on that passport. They would pick you up on arrival and it would require a great deal of explaining on your part. Why would there be two people named Barnes carrying a passport with the same serial number? And lastly, it would be appreciated by the people at the software company if you did not reappear."

"I'm longing to see Camille again, of course."

"When I was nineteen, a young man my age and I were in bed together, the first time for both of us. After, when we were dressing, he pulled me into his arms, then sat on the bed and buried his face between my breasts and told me that he loved me. I realized that a man's love can be spread out to your mind, your personality, attitudes, points of view, conversations and finally body. A man can love your body along with the rest of you. I thought that you could spend tonight in my bed with me and find out if you could love my body. It might be a good place to start."

"That's wonderful for me," Eric said. "What do you get out of it?"

"I enjoy the sexual part of life and from the results of tonight we can see if the remainder of the syndicate's plan appeals to us."

"Syndicate's plan, you say. You do work for them, obviously. Why don't we find out what you and the syndicate have cooked up? I suspect that I will be bought off, and I don't care for that one bit."

"First you get a new identity. Tonight at dinner they will find a new name for you, one you like, and make a Canadian passport for you. May I suggest that you keep Eric as your middle name? I like it."

"I'd never thought of being a Canadian," Eric said. "I'll have to start disliking Americans."

"And then the reason I was selected is this: they thought I was a good partner for you, that we could live together and perhaps marry if you wanted."

"Do you?" Eric asked.

"Yes, I enjoyed it the last time."

"What happened?"

"He drank and suspected that there were other men in my life. He became violent."

"You do turn their heads, Marie."

"Here is their plan. Money at the base, as you say. You accept to become a Canadian. They arrange papers so that you have permanent status and the right to work in Austria and can move toward citizenship. You should learn to speak German. And the money part, it's very rich. As long as we are together for ten years we are paid every year. Beyond that I haven't heard yet."

"This is one time the syndicate is wrong. We must be together because we both want to be. How much are we paid, by the way?"

"I think fifty thousand dollars per year. That's for each one."

"That's an awful lot of money to walk away from, but when people give you money they own part of you, if not all of you." Eric paused for a moment then went on in the same direction. "Money ruined a perfectly good woman in New York. Money allowed individuals who did not abide by the law to go free."

"You are so moral, Eric."

"Let's go down to drinks. After this night together in your bed everything might come into focus for both of us," Eric said.

Eric spent half the cocktail hour enjoying his drink and the easy camaraderie with 'One', 'Three' and Marie. The other half he spent allowing his new circumstances to wash over him. He had a choice to make: should he return home and attempt to re-assemble his life, or should he accept their offer and become a Canadian citizen residing in Austria?

Eric understood that money had won. Those who had committed minor crimes on paper were not punished. Eric did not enjoy using those terms, crime and criminals, when they were associated with non-violent transgressions of the law, particularly in instances when there were no identifiable victims. As far as Eric was concerned neither the general public nor the public good had been a victim. He understood that driving a bullet into the body of an intended victim was a heinous crime, but did not understand that circumvention of the fine print in legislation was an act that warranted imprisonment, ruined reputations and ruined careers. Eric concluded that he held these views, these particular notions of justice and fairness. He did not know where they came from. Not many shared them with him. His view was reinforced when a powerful government and its able prosecutors crushed a not-so guilty person.

If money had won, then Theodore Warner was off the hook. The corporation had agreed to a fine as long as there were no indictments. No matter how Camille and he phrased their denials, there would always be suspicions that she had been lenient in order to save his life. Eric had nothing but warm feelings for Camille. Ann was a different matter. She had sold his name for a goodly sum. To be fair to her he had to ask himself if he would resist a windfall if roles were reversed. Ann must have seen the risk to herself of broadcasting his name. All that was ancient history by now and while he could return to her he might not be able to put life back into his practice of the law.

Marie was an unknown quantity. How do you evaluate a friendship of less than a month's duration, made the more charming with the promise of one night in bed? She was interesting on an intellectual level.

She could not have invented on the spur of the moment an agile mind, well-founded arguments and provocative conversations. On the matter of her past, he had no idea. He guessed that she was soiled merchandize but not damaged goods. She, as Ann, had responded to expediency. She had put a price on her companionship, including her body. Eric could believe the portions that he wished about her past. If they accepted the offer acting jointly, they might construct a fine life. Europe is an enjoyable place to live. Marie was a good place to start. It was high time he learned a second language.

Eric kept leading his double life, of being in the living room with the rest of them while reviewing his status as the small victory celebration progressed. 'One', 'Three' and Marie were chatting and laughing and why shouldn't they? As parts of the syndicate they had played their roles in accomplishing the wishes of Theodore Warner. His wallet had been lightened but he was a free man.

And what about the fifteen million dollars that Theodore raised by selling shares in his company? It had taken 300,000 shares at fifty dollars each to raise fifteen million. Dieter and his law partners knew that the value of these shares had been depressed by ten dollars each on the rumors that Theodore's company was involved in the practice. Dieter was betting that when Theodore's company was cleared, an eventuality he would have a hand in, the stock would bounce back. The shares would be sold immediately and the law firm might clear an easy few million dollars.

The final owners of the shares, European citizens, would be the ones who had financed the operation. They had subverted Ann, and changed Camille from a strict abider of the law to a woman who cut corners to save him, Eric knew. These new stockholders had financed the operation, paid for Emil, Craig Burton, various messengers, kidnappers, passport forgers, airplane tickets, drivers, rental cars and a rented country estate.

At the end of the trail these new stockholders, unwittingly, were dangling ten years of wages in front of Marie and him. Eric understood what he was gaining and losing. He had no idea about Marie. She was tempting, though. If the accused could be found innocent by spending money, then that is as it should be, Eric concluded. They weren't that guilty after all.

They had consumed their drinks and were moving toward the dining room. 'One' had come up to Eric and said quietly, "Let us have your preliminary reaction to the offer at breakfast." Eric was finished living in the shadows. He entered into the general spirit of the evening with reminiscences of their last three months together. He thought he had come up with his conclusions. Eric took Marie's hand as they went up the stairs to their bedrooms. "I liked the new name we agreed on," he said. "So did I, and the fact that I can still call you Eric," Marie added.

When they were at his door he placed his arms around her and kissed her hard, not in any tentative fashion. He said, "Marie, I think we should accept their offer. It has plenty of promise."

"When would we begin?" she asked.

"Immediately, this instant," he answered.

Fred Weekes lives in Lakewood, Washington, a city forty-five miles south of Seattle on the I-5 corridor. After a career in business and engineering he retired to writing on topics that interested him: World War II aviation, general reference, and love stories. Some of these titles are available through iUniverse. He enjoys writing romances. They may be his favorites. This book of short stories will be followed by a study of the history of Communism as understood by a young naval officer. Naturally there will be romantic interludes added to this examination.

The room that Weekes writes in has a fine view of a lake. Waterfowl are in abundance and an occasional heron and eagle come by.

Weekes holds degrees from the University of Pennsylvania and Catholic University of America. He prizes these as he sees no chance of earning additional degrees.